D1435965

ED McBAIN

Also by Ed McBain

The 87th Precinct Novels

Cop Hater * The Mugger * The Pusher (1956)
The Con Man * Killer's Choice (1957)
Killer's Payoff * Killer's Wedge * Lady Killer (1958)
'Til Death * King's Ransom (1959)
Give the Boys a Great Big Hand * The Heckler * See Them Die (1960)
Lady, Lady, I Did It! (1961)   The Empty Hours * Like Love (1962)
Ten Plus One (1963)   Ax (1964)   He Who Hesitates * Doll (1965)
Eighty Million Eyes (1966)   Fuzz (1968)   Shotgun (1969)
Jigsaw (1970)   Hail, Hail, the Gang's All Here! (1971)
Sadie When She Died * Let's Hear It for the Deaf Man (1972)
Hail to the Chief (1973)   Bread (1974)   Blood Relatives (1975)
So Long as You Both Shall Live (1976)   Long Time No See (1977)
Calypso (1979)   Ghosts (1980)   Heat (1981)   Ice (1983)
Lightning (1984)   Eight Black Horses (1985)
Poison * Tricks (1987)   Lullaby (1989)   Vespers (1990)
Widows (1991)   Kiss (1992)   Mischief (1993)

The Matthew Hope Novels

Goldilocks (1978)   Rumpelstiltskin (1981)
Beauty and the Beast (1982)   Jack and the Beanstalk (1984)
Snow White and Rose Red (1985)   Cinderella (1986)
Puss in Boots (1987)   The House That Jack Built (1988)
Three Blind Mice (1990)   Mary, Mary (1992)

Other Novels

The Sentries (1965)   Where There's Smoke * Doors (1975)
Guns (1976)   Another Part of the City (1986)   Downtown (1991)

THREE NOVELS OF THE 87th PRECINCT

HE WHO HESITATES

JIGSAW

HAIL, HAIL, THE GANG'S ALL HERE!

Ed McBain

BCA

LONDON NEW YORK SYDNEY TORONTO

CONTENTS

HE WHO HESITATES

This is for Elaine and Albert Aley

1

When he awoke, the windows were rimmed with frost and the air in the room was bitter cold. He could not remember where he was for a moment. His bedroom back home was always cold on a winter's morning, but this was not his bedroom, and for a moment he grappled with its alien look and then remembered he was in the city. He got out of bed in his underwear and walked swiftly across the wooden floor to where he had put his clothing on a chair the night before.

The room was sparsely furnished. A bed was against one wall, a dresser on the wall opposite. There were two chairs in the room: the wooden one over which his clothes were hanging, and a stuffed easy chair near the curtained window. There was a sink in the corner, but the bathroom was in the hallway. He sat on the wooden chair as he tied his shoes, and then walked quickly to the sink, where he began washing. He was a huge man, six feet five inches tall and weighing two hundred and ten pounds. His hands were immense, brown and calloused like a farmer's. He soaped his face, and then scooped up water from the sink, splashing it onto his massive nose and high, chiseled cheekbones, his full mouth and roughhewn chin. He rinsed the soap away from his eyes and then opened them and stared at himself in the mirror for just a moment. He reached for the towel and dried himself.

He supposed he should go to the police.

God it was cold in this room.

He wondered what time it was.

He walked swiftly to the chair and pulled on his shirt and buttoned it, and then slipped his tie under the frayed collar without tying it, just letting the ends hang loose on his shirt front, putting his heavy tweed jacket over it, and then crossing his long arms in front of him and slapping his sides to generate a little warmth in his body. He went to the window and pulled back the yellowed lace curtain and looked down past the FURNISHED ROOMS sign to the street two stories below, trying to determine the time by the number of people awake and moving around.

The street was empty.

He knew he should go to the police, but he didn't want to go barging in there at six o'clock in the morning – well, it was probably later than that. If it was only six, it'd be dark out there, wouldn't it? The street was empty only because it was so damn cold, that was all. He wouldn't be surprised if it was nine, maybe ten o'clock already. He let the curtain fall and then walked to the closet and opened it. A small and very old suitcase rested on the floor of the closet. The suitcase belonged to his mother and there was a single sticker on it, a yellow and green one with the words NIAGARA FALLS, NEW YORK in a semi-circle and a painting of the falls in white and blue in the middle of the sticker. She had gone there on her honeymoon. This was the only piece of luggage she had ever owned, and she gave it to him each time he came into the city to sell the woodenware. He usually came maybe three, four times a year. This was the first time he'd come in February.

He remembered all at once that tomorrow was Valentine's Day.

He would have to send his mother a card.

He took his heavy green overcoat out of the closet, the one he always wore to the city during the winter months, and carried it over to the bed, dropping it there. He went to the dresser and picked up his small change, which he put into the right-hand pocket of his trousers, and then picked up his wallet, looked into it, and then removed the money he had got yesterday for the woodenware. He counted the money again – it was exactly a hundred and twenty-two dollars – and then put it back into the wallet and went to the bed again, and picked up his coat, and put it on, his massive shoulders shrugging into the air as he performed the operation.

He buttoned the coat, then walked back to the sink and looked at himself in the mirror again. He looked all right. He didn't want the police to think no bum was walking in there.

He wondered where the police station was.

He would have to ask the landlady, what was her name?

If she was awake.

He was hungry too. He'd have to get him some breakfast before he went to the police.

He wondered if he should pack the few things he'd put in the dresser or wait until later. He supposed it would be all right to pack them later. Maybe he ought to mail the money to his mother, though. That represented a lot of work, that hundred and twenty-two dollars, a lot of work. And it had to last until maybe April or May when he'd be coming to the city again – well, when his brother would be coming, anyway. Yes, he'd pack later.

He went out of the room, locking the door behind him, and went down the steps to the first floor. The linoleum on the stair treads was old and worn; he had noticed that when he'd taken the room two nights ago. But the reason he'd come all the way uptown here for a room was because he knew it'd be a lot cheaper than a hotel. So he wasn't about to start complaining about the worn linoleum, hell with that. So long as the bed was all right and didn't have anything crawling in it, why that was good enough for him. He was only paying four dollars a night for the room, you couldn't do much better than that unless you wanted to go down to Skid Row, he wasn't about to go sleeping with a bunch of drunken bums.

The landlady's apartment was on the ground floor at the end of the hall. The hall smelled nice and clean, she'd been scrubbing it on her hands and knees the day he'd taken the room, that was Tuesday. He'd known right off it was going to be a clean place without any bugs in the bed, that was the important thing, the bugs. Don't take no bed with bugs in it, his mother had said. He didn't know how you could tell if a bed had bugs in it until you got into the bed with them, and then it was probably too late to do anything about it, they'd eat you alive. But he figured the smell of that disinfectant in the hallway was a sure sign this lady was clean. She probably used something on the coils of the bedspring too, that was where the bugs hid. His mother always washed out the bedspring coils back home with a toothbrush and ammonia, he didn't know why ammonia, but he supposed it killed anything that was in there. Sometimes she sprayed them, too, with some kind of bug killer. She was very clean.

He wished he knew what time it was because he didn't want to get the landlady out of bed if it was too early in the morning. Well, he had to tell her he was leaving today, anyway, settle up with her. He lifted his hand and tentatively knocked on the door.

"Who is it?" she said.

Good. She was awake.

"It's me," he answered. "Mr. Broome."

"Just a minute, Mr. Broome," the landlady answered. He waited while she came to the door. Somewhere in the building, upstairs, he heard a toilet flush. The door opened.

"Good morning," he said.

"Good morning, Mr. Broome," the landlady said. Dougherty, that was her name. Agnes Dougherty, he remembered now.

"I hope I didn't wake you up, Mrs. Dougherty," he said.

"Nope, I was just having my breakfast," she answered. She was a small, thin woman wearing a faded wrapper imprinted with primroses. Her hair was in curlers. She reminded him of his mother, small like that. Don't ask me how I ever give birth to a young horse like you, his mother always said. It *was* kind of funny, when you thought of it, her so small.

"What was it you wanted, Mr. Broome?"

"Well, I'll be leaving today, and I thought—"

"Oh, so soon?"

"Well, I finished what I had to do here, you know, so—"

"What was that, Mr. Broome? Come in, won't you, have some coffee with me."

"Well, ma'am—"

"Come in, come in," she said in a perky sort of bright cheerful voice; she was really a very nice little lady.

"Okay," he said, "but only 'cause I have to come in anyway to settle up with you."

He went into the apartment and she closed the door behind him. The apartment smelled as clean as the hallway did, with the same strong disinfectant smell. The kitchen linoleum had been scrubbed bare in spots, so that the wooden floor beneath it showed through, and even the wood in those spots had been scrubbed almost white. A clean oilcloth with a seashell pattern covered the kitchen table.

"Sit down," Mrs. Dougherty said. "How do you like your coffee?"

"Well, ma'am, I usually have it black with three sugars." He chuckled and said, "My mother says I get my sweet tooth from my father. He died in a train accident when I was only seven."

"Oh, I'm sorry to hear that," Mrs. Dougherty said, bringing a clean cup to the table and then pouring it full to the brim with coffee.

"Well, I hardly remember him."

"Here's the sugar," she said, and moved the bowl toward him. She sat at the table opposite him, picking up a piece of toast she had bitten into before answering the door. Remembering her guest, she said, "Would you like some toast?"

"No, thank you, ma'am."

"Are you sure?"

"Well . . ."

"I'll make you some," she said, and rose and went to the counter near the sink where she took a slice of bread from its waxed wrapper and put it into the toaster. "Or would you like *two* slices?" she said.

He shrugged and smiled and said, "I guess I *could* eat two, ma'am."

"A healthy appetite's nothing to be ashamed of," she said, and put another slice of bread into the toaster. "Now," she said, and came back to the table. "You were telling me why you were here in the city."

"Oh, to sell our wares, ma'am."

"What wares?"

"We've got a woodworking shop, just a small one, you know."

"Who's we?"

"Oh, me and my brother."

"Where's that?"

"Up in Carey, do you know it?"

"I don't think so."

"It's just a small town. Huddleston is the nearest *big* town, I suppose.

"Oh, yes, Huddleston," Mrs. Dougherty said.

"There's skiing up there, if you ski."

Mrs. Dougherty laughed. "No, no, I don't ski," she said, and sipped at her coffee and then put down the cup and jumped up when she heard the toaster click. She brought the two slices of bread to the table, and moved the butter dish and the marmalade pot toward him. She sat again. As he buttered his toast, she said, "What do you make in your shop, Mr. Broome?"

"All sorts of woodenware."

"Furniture?"

"Well, not really, We make benches and end tables, stuff like that, but nothing really big. Mostly, we do salad bowls and cutting boards and wooden utensils, you know, small things. Also, my brother does some carving."

"That sounds very nice," Mrs. Dougherty said. "And you bring it into the city to sell, is that it?"

"We sell it up there, too," he said, "but not really enough to keep us going, you know. During the summer, it's not so bad because there're a lot of people up that way looking for antiques, and we get some of them stop by the shop, you know. But in the winter, it's mostly skiers up that way, and only time they'll stop in is if it's a rainy day and they can't ski. So I try to get in the city three, four times a year, mostly during the winter months." He paused. "First time I ever been here in February."

"Is that right?" she said.

"That's a fact, ma'am," he said.

"How do you like it?"

"Well, it's sure cold enough," he said, and laughed. He bit into the toast, completely relaxed, and then lifted his coffee cup and said, "Say, what time is it anyway?"

"A little bit past eight," she said.

"I guess I overslept," he said, and laughed.

He wondered if he should ask her about the police station.

"What time do you usually get up?"

"Back home? In Carey, do you mean?"

"Yes."

"Well, my mother's up and bustling around the kitchen pretty early, you know. My father used to be a railroad man, and he had an early run, so she's used to getting up early, I guess she's puttering around out there at five, five-thirty every morning. My kid brother's a light sleeper and we share a bedroom, you know, we've just got this small little house there, not much more than a shack really, so when she starts puttering around and he starts stirring, well you just might as well get up yourself, that's all," he said, and began laughing again.

"You've got a good hearty laugh," Mrs. Dougherty said. "Most big men have that kind of laugh."

"That a fact?"

"That's been my observation," she said.

He thought this might be a good time to ask her about the police station, but he didn't want to get her upset or anything, so he lifted his coffee cup and sipped at it, and smacked his lips, and then bit into the second slice of toast.

"I want to pay you for last night." he said, "I only paid you for one night in advance, you know."

"That's right," Mrs. Dougherty said. He began reaching into his pocket for his wallet, and she quickly said, "Well, finish your coffee first, Mr. Broome. There's nobody chasing you for the money."

"Thank you, ma'am," he said, and smiled and took another bite of the toast.

"How old are you, Mr. Broome?" she said. "Do you mind my asking?"

"Not at all, ma'am. I'll be twenty-seven in May. May the twelfth."

"I figured about that. How old is your brother?"

"Twenty-two." He paused. "Tomorrow's Valentine's Day, you know," he said.

"Isn't anyone going to send me a valentine?"

"You never can tell, Mrs. Dougherty," he said. "I'm going out to buy my mother one right this minute, soon as I leave here."

"That's very nice," Mrs. Dougherty said. She paused, and then smiled weakly, and then said, "We never had any children."

"I'm sorry to hear that, ma'am."

She nodded. He finished his coffee and then reached into his wallet and handed her a five-dollar bill. "I'll get you your change," she said.

He stood alongside the table while she went into the other room for her handbag. He decided not to ask her where the police station was. He didn't want to upset her, especially now that she seemed to be upset already about not having any children who could send her a valentine the way he was going to send his mother one. He wondered if his mother would get it in time. He supposed she would. If he bought it first thing, even before he went to the police station, and mailed it right away, he was sure she'd get it by tomorrow morning.

"Here you are, Mr. Broome," she said, and came back into the kitchen. He took the dollar bill, tucked it into his wallet, and then put on his overcoat. "When you come to the city again, I hope you'll be back for a room," she said.

"Oh, yes, ma'am, I will," he said.

"You're a fine gentleman," she said.

"Thank you, ma'am," he said, embarrassed.

"In this neighborhood . . ." she started, and then closed her mouth and shook her head.

"I'll be back later to pack," he said.

"Take your time," she said.

"Well, I have a few errands to do, actually."

"Take your time," she said again, and walked him to the door.

The drugstore was on the corner of Ainsley Avenue and North Eleventh Street. A lunch counter ran along the left-hand side of the store. The remainder of the place was given over to drugs and sundries. A rack of paperback books, their titles and covers screaming for attention, stood before a row of hot-water bottles. Beyond that, and somewhat apart from the heap of combs and syringes behind it, was a rack of greeting cards. He walked past the books – something called HOW TO DO IT ON AIRPLANES caught his eye – and directly to the greeting cards. An assorted array of birthday cards was spread out on the rack – Birthday Son, Birthday Daughter, Mother, Father, Brother, Sister, Grandfather, Grandmother, and Miscellaneous Relatives. He scanned them quickly, glanced briefly at Condolences, Anniversary, and Birth and finally came to the section devoted exclusively to valentines. More and more of the cards each year were comical. He didn't care much for that kind of card. Most of them, matter of fact, he didn't get the humor of. He looked down the row of labels at the top of the rack, and saw that these cards were classified, too, almost the way the birthday cards had been. There were cards for Sweetheart, Wife, Husband, Mother, Father; he didn't bother going down the rest of the row because what he was interested in was a card for his mother. He looked at two or three of them, and then found a nice card with a real satin heart on the front of it, and pink ribbons trailing from the heart, and the word *Mother* in delicate gold script across the top of the card. He opened it and started to read the little poem inside. Sometimes, you found a nice-looking card but the words were all wrong. You had to be careful.

He read the verse over again, and then read it a third time, pleased with the sentiment, appreciative of the way the lines scanned. He wondered how much the card cost. He liked it, but he didn't want to go spending too much for a card. He walked over to the cash register. A colored girl was sitting behind it, reading a magazine.

"How much is this card?" he asked.

"Let's see it," she said. She took the card from him, turned it over, and looked at the price on the back. "It's seventy-five cents," she said. She saw his expression, and smiled. "There are cheaper ones there, if you look."

"Well, I like this one," he said.

"It *is* a nice one."

My Mother

The joy you bring to me each day
Cannot in mere words be expressed.
The million things you do and say
Confirm you are the very best.
And even when the day is done,
And weary walk I up the stair,
Who waits for me? The only one

To smile, to greet, to love, to care —
My mother.

"Yeah, I like the poem. Most of them have terrible poems."

"It's a nice poem," the girl said, glancing at it.

"Seventy-five, huh?"

"Yes, that's what it says on the back. See?" She turned the card over and held it out to him. She had very long nails. She pointed to some letters and numerals printed on the bottom of the card. "See where it says XM-75? that means seventy-five cents."

"Why don't they just mark it seventy-five cents?" he asked.

The girl giggled. "I don't know. They want to be mysterious, I guess."

"Yes, well, XM-75 is sure mysterious," he said, and smiled, and the girl smiled back. "Well, I guess I'll take it," he said.

"Your mother'll like it," the girl said.

"I think so. I need some stamps; do you sell stamps?"

"In the machine," the girl said.

"And, oh, wait a minute . . ."

"Yes?"

"I want to get another card."

"All right," she said.

"Don't ring that up yet."

"I won't."

He went back to the rack and bypassed the Mother and Wife and Sweetheart section, searching for a section labeled Friend or Acquaintance, and finding one marked General, and then looking over the cards there until he found one that said simply, To Someone Very Nice on Valentine's Day. There wasn't any poem inside the card. All it said was Have a Happy. He took the card back to the cash register and showed it to the colored girl.

"Do you like this one?" he asked.

"Who's it for? Your girl?"

"No, I don't have a girl," he answered.

"Oh, sure, come on," she said, "big handsome fellow like you."

"Really," he said, "I don't have a girl," and realized all at once she was flirting with him.

"Who's it for?" she asked archly.

"My landlady."

The girl laughed. "You must be the only man in this entire city who's sending a card to his landlady."

"Well, I am," he said, and laughed with her.

"She must be something, your landlady."

"She's very nice."

"A blonde, I'll bet."

"Well, no."

"What then? A redhead?"

"No, no, she's—"

"Or maybe you like darker girls," she said, and looked him square in the eye. He looked back at her and said nothing.

"*Do* you like dark girls?" she said.

"I like dark girls," he said.

"I'll just bet you do," she said, very softly.

They were both silent for a moment.

"How much do I owe you?" he asked.

"Well, let me take a look at the one for your landlady," she said, and turned the card over. "Seventy-five and . . . twenty-five is a dollar."

He reached into his wallet and handed her a bill.

"Didn't you say you wanted stamps?"

"Yes?"

"Do you have change for the machine?"

"Yes, I think so," he said.

"Machine's right over there," she said, gesturing toward it with her head. She rang up his dollar bill, and then reached for a paper bag below the counter. "Are you from the neighborhood?"

"No."

She watched him as he put his money in the machine and then pulled the lever for the stamps.

"Out of town?"

"Yes."

"Where?"

"Carey, do you know it?"

"I don't think so."

"It's near Huddleston. Do you ski?"

"Me?" the girl said, and laughed.

He licked the stamps and put one in the corner of each envelope. "Do you have a pen?" he asked.

"Sure," she said, and handed him one from alongside the cash register. "Did you ever see a colored person skiing?"

"Tell you the truth," he said, "I've never *been* skiing, so I wouldn't know."

"Oh, I'm sure there's one or two," she said. "There *must* be one or two in the whole United States, don't you think?"

"I guess there must be."

"Yeah, but I don't know any of them," she said.

"Neither do I."

She glanced at the envelope he was addressing. "Who's Dorothy Broome?" she asked.

"My mother."

"What's your name?"

"Roger Broome."

"I'm Amelia," she said.

"Hello, Amelia."

"Amelia Perez." She paused. "My father's Spanish."

"All right, Amelia," he said, and looked up at her and smiled, and then began addressing the other envelope.

"This is the one to your landlady, huh, Roger?"

"That's right."

"Mrs . . . Agnes . . . Dougherty." Amelia grinned. "Some landlady."

"She really is," Roger said.

"Mmm."

"Well," he said, and looked up and smiled. "That's that."

"Mailbox right outside," Amelia said.

"Thank you," he said. They stared at each other for a moment. "Well." He shrugged. "Well, so long."

"So long, Roger," she said behind him.

He stopped at the phone booth on the way out and opened the directory, first looking up POLICE, and then turning to the CITY OF section and finding a listing there for POLICE DEPT. His finger skipped over the various headings, Alcoholic Unit, Bomb Squad, Central Motors Repr Shop, Hrbr Precinct, Homicide Squads, Narcotic, Safety, Traffic, Youth – where were all the individual precincts? What did a man do if he simply wanted a cop? He closed the directory and walked back to the cash register. Amelia looked up.

"Hi," she said. "Did you forget something?"

"I'm supposed to meet a friend of mine outside the police station," he said, and shrugged. "Trouble is, I don't know where it is."

"Go across to the park," she said, "and start walking uptown on Grover Avenue. You can't miss it. It's got these big green globes out front."

2

The big green globes were each marked with the numerals "87." They flanked the closed brown entrance doors of the building, the building a soot-covered monotonous gray against the gray early-morning sky behind it. Roger stood across the street near the low stone wall marking the park's northern boundary on Grover Avenue, and looked at the building and wondered if anyone was inside; the doors were closed. Well, he thought, you can't expect them to leave the doors open in the middle of winter. Anyway, the police are always there, that's their job. They don't close on Saturdays, Sundays and holidays.

He looked at the building again.

It wasn't a very cheerful place sitting there across the street covered with the dirt of maybe half a century, its windows protected by wire-mesh grilles on the outside, the interior hidden by partially drawn and faded shades within. The only friendly thing about the place was the wisp of smoke that trailed up from a chimney hidden by the roof's parapets. He wondered how many policemen were inside there, and then he wondered if he should go in. Maybe it was too early to be bothering them. He walked up some fifty feet to where there was an entrance break in the low stone wall, and then walked into the park and onto the gravel path paralleling the stone wall. He looked across to the police station again, and then sat on a bench with his head partially turned so that he could watch the building.

As he watched, the front door opened, and a stream of uniformed policemen came down the steps chatting and laughing; it looked for a minute like all the cops in the city were pouring out of that door. They came down the low flat steps to the sidewalk and began walking off in different directions, some of them heading downtown and others heading uptown, some of them turning at the corner and heading north toward the river, and half a dozen of the rest crossing the street and coming directly to the wall entrance he himself had used not three, four minutes ago. Inside the park, two of them turned left and started heading up the gravel path in the opposite direction, and two of them cut across the grass and what looked like a bridle path and waved at the last two cops, who were coming right past the bench where Roger was sitting. He looked up at them as they went by, and he nodded at them briefly. One of the cops, as though he recognized Roger as somebody he greeted every morning (which was impossible since Roger had never been on this bench across from the police station in his life), sort of waved at him, and smiled, and said, "Hi, there," and then turned back to the other cop and picked up his conversation as both of them continued on the path heading downtown.

Roger watched them until they were out of sight.

He turned on the bench again and busied himself with looking at the police station across the street.

He supposed he would have to talk to a detective. That was probably the thing. You probably went in and said you wanted to talk to a detective, and they probably asked you what it was in reference to, something like a bank or a business office, he supposed.

He didn't like the idea of talking it over with somebody before they let him see a detective. That bothered him a little. He wanted to see a detective right out and clean, get it over with, instead of a lot of talk with a uniformed cop.

"That's what they are in there, all right," the voice said.

He turned, startled. He had been so absorbed with watching the building that he hadn't heard footsteps on the gravel path, and was surprised now to see a man sitting on the bench opposite him. It was still maybe quarter of nine in the morning, maybe a little earlier, and the temperature was, oh, he would guess somewhere in the twenties or even the upper teens, and the two of them were the only ones sitting in the park, facing each other on opposite benches.

"What?" he said.

"That's what they are in there, all right," the other man said.

"That's what who is in where?" he asked.

"Cops," the other man said. He was a small dapper man of about fifty, wearing a black overcoat with black velveteen collar and cuffs and wearing a gray fedora pulled rakishly over one eye. He had a small pencil-line black mustache and a black bow tie with yellow polka dots, the tie showing in the opening of his coat like the gaily painted propeller of an airplane. He gave a small meaningful contemptuous jerk of his head toward the police station across the street. "Cops," he repeated.

"That's right," Roger said.

"Yeah, *sure* that's right," the man said.

Roger looked at him, and nodded, and then dismissed him with a brief shrug and turned back to study the police station again.

"Have they got somebody in there?" the man asked.

"What?" Roger said, and turned again.

"In there."

"What do you mean?"

"Are they holding somebody?"

"I don't think I know what you mean."

"Of yours," the man said.

"Of mine?"

"In there."

"What?"

"Are they *holding some*body of *yours* in there?" the man said, impatiently.

"Oh. No. No, they're not."

"Then why are you watching the building?"

Roger shrugged.

"Look, you don't have to put on airs with me," the man said. "I've been in and out of that place more times than you can count on your fingers and toes."

"Mm?" Roger said, and was about to get up and move out of the park, when the man rose and crossed the gravel path and sat on the bench alongside him.

"They've had me in there on a lot of little things," the man said. "My name's Clyde."

"How do you do?" Roger said.

"Clyde Warren, what's yours?"

"Roger. Broome."

"Roger Broome, well, a new broom sweeps clean, eh?" Clyde said, and burst out laughing. His teeth were very white. His breath plumed vigorously from his mouth as he laughed. He lifted one hand to brush away a frozen laughter tear from the corner of his eye. His fingers were stained with nicotine. "Yessir," he said, still laughing, "a new broom sweeps clean, they've had me in there on a lot of little things, Roger, oh yes, a lot of little things."

"Well, I guess I'd better be getting along," Roger said, and again made a move to rise, but Clyde put his hand gently on his shoulder, and then removed it immediately, as though suddenly aware of Roger's size and potential power and not wishing to provoke him in any way. The sudden retreat was not wasted on Roger, who felt himself subtly flattered and hesitated on the bench a moment longer. After all, he thought, this man's been inside there, he knows what it's like inside there.

"What do they do?" he asked. "When you go in?"

"When you *go* in?" Clyde said. "When you *go* in? You mean when they *take* you in, don't you?"

"Well, I suppose so."

"They book you, if they've got anything to book you on, and then they take you back to the detention cells on the first floor there and keep you locked up until it's time to go downtown for lineup and arraignment, that's if your offense was a felony."

"What's a felony?" Roger asked.

"Death or a state prison," Clyde answered.

"What do you mean?"

"The punishment."

"Oh."

"Sure."

"Well, what sort of crimes would that be?"

"Burglary is a felony, murder is a felony, armed robbery is a felony, you get the idea?"

"Yes," Roger said, nodding.

"Indecent exposure," Clyde said, "is only a misdemeanor."

"I see."

"Yessir, only a misdemeanor," Clyde said, and grinned. His teeth were dazzlingly white. "They're false," he said, following Roger's gaze, and clicked the teeth in his mouth to prove it. Roger nodded. "Sodomy, on the other hand, is a felony," Clyde said. "You can get twenty years for sodomy."

"Is that right?" Roger said.

"Absolutely. They've never had me in there on sodomy," Clyde said.

"Well, that's good," Roger said, not knowing what sodomy was, and really not terribly interested in what they had had Clyde in there on, but only interested in what it was like once they got you inside there.

"For them to have a case of sodomy," Clyde said, "it's got to be against the other person's will, or by force, or under age, you know what I mean? They've never had me in there on that."

"Do they take your fingerprints?"

"I just told you I've never been in there on sodomy."

"I meant for anything."

"Well, sure they take your fingerprints, that's their job. Their job is to take your fingerprints and get your hands dirty and make life miserable for you whatever chance they can get. That's what being a cop means."

"Mm," Roger said, and both men fell silent. Roger glanced over his shoulder at the police station again.

"I've got a place near here," Clyde said.

"Mm," Roger said.

"Few blocks east."

"Mm."

"Nice apartment," Clyde said.

"Do they let you make a phone call?" Roger said.

"What?"

"The police."

"Oh, sure. Listen, would you like to come up?"

"Up where?" Roger said.

"My place."

"What for?"

Clyde shrugged. "I thought you might like to."

"Well, thanks a lot," Roger said, "but I've got some things to do."

"Maybe you could come up later."

"Thanks, but—"

"It's a nice place," Clyde said, and shrugged.

"Well, the thing is—"

"They've never had me in there on anything big, if that's what's bothering you."

"That's not—"

"I'd have told you if it was anything worse than a misdemeanor."

"I know, but—"

"They just think it's fun to pick me up every now and then, that's all." He made a contemptuous face, and then said, "Cops."

"Well, thank you very much," Roger said, standing, "but—"

"Will you come up later?"

"No, I don't think so."

"I have a poodle," Clyde said.

"That's—"

"His name is Shatzie, he's a nice dog, you'd like him."

"I'm sorry," Roger said.

"Please," Clyde said, and looked up at him.

Roger shook his head.

"No," he said.

He kept shaking his head.

"No," he said again, and then walked away from the bench and out of the park.

He found the post office on Culver Avenue and he went in and made out a postal money order for one hundred dollars, made payable to Dorothy Broome. The money order cost him thirty-five cents, and he spent another six cents for a stamped envelope, which he addressed to his mother on Terminal Street in

Carey. He put the money order in the envelope, sealed it and then took it directly to the window and handed it to the clerk.

"Will that get there by tomorrow?" he asked.

The clerk looked at the address. "Supposed to," he said. "If you bring it in before five, it's supposed to get there by tomorrow. I can't vouch for the post office up there, though. They may let it lay around two, three days."

"No, they're very good," Roger said.

"Then it should get there tomorrow."

"Thank you." he said.

He came out of the post office and looked up at the sky, and figured there was just one more thing he had to do before going to the police station, and that was call his mother in Carey to tell her not to worry, that he wouldn't be home tonight the way he'd promised. A clock in a jeweler's window told him it still wasn't nine o'clock, but that was all right, his mother would have been up a long time already, just like he'd told Mrs. Dougherty. He wondered what Mrs. Dougherty would think when she got his valentine, he wished he could be around to see the look on her face when she opened it. Smiling he continued down the side street, looking for a phone booth. A bunch of teen-age boys and girls were standing on one of the front stoops, talking and laughing and smoking, all of them carrying schoolbooks, the girls clutching the books to their small high perfect breasts, the boys carrying them at arm's length or on straps. They'll be going to school any minute now, Roger thought, and remembered when he'd been going to school in Carey, and put the memory out of his mind, and saw the candy store some fifteen feet beyond where the kids were laughing and talking. He went into the store, saw the phone booth at the rear, and stopped at the counter to get change for a dollar bill. He waited until a fat Spanish woman came out of the booth. She smiled up at him as she went by. He sat in the booth smelling of her perfume and her sweat, and dialed the area code for Carey and then the number, Carey 7-3341, and waited while the phone rang on the other end.

"Hello?" his mother's voice said.

"Mom?"

"Roger? Is that you?"

"Yes, Mom."

"Where are you?"

"The city."

"Did you sell the stuff?"

"Yes, Mom."

"How much did you get?"

"A hundred and twenty-two dollars."

"That's more'n we figured, ain't it?" his mother said.

"It's forty-seven dollars more, Mom."

"That's right, it is," his mother said. "That's very good, son."

"It's because I went to that new place I was telling you about. The one I noticed in December, when I was in just before Christmas, do you remember?"

"Downtown there? In the Quarter?"

"That's the place. You know what he gave me for the salad bowls, Mom?"

"Which ones? The big ones?"

"Well, both."

"How much did he give you, Rog?"

"I sold him a dozen of the big ones for a dollar and a half each, Mom. That's more'n we get for them in the shop."

"I know it is. Is the man in his right mind?"

"Sure, he's going to mark them up quite a bit, Mom. I wouldn't be surprised he gets three, maybe even four dollars for those big ones."

"What about the little ones? How much did he pay for those?"

"He only took half a dozen of them."

"How much?"

"A dollar each." Roger paused. "We sell them for seventy-five at the shop, Mom."

"I know," his mother said, and laughed. "Makes me wonder if we're not selling ourselves cheap."

"Well, we don't get the crowd, you know."

"That's right," his mother said. "When are you coming home, son?"

"I sent you a money order for a hundred dollars, Mom, you look for it tomorrow, okay?"

"Okay, when are you coming home?"

"I'm not sure yet."

"What do you mean?"

"Well, there's—"

"What do you mean, you're not sure yet?"

"When I'll be home," Roger said, and the line went silent. He waited. "Mom?" he said.

"I'm here."

"How's . . . uh . . . how's Buddy?"

"He's fine."

"Mom?"

"Yes?"

"About . . . uh . . . coming home."

"Yes?"

"I don't know when."

"Yes, I heard you say that the first time."

"Well, there's something I've got to do, you see."

"What is it you have to do?" his mother asked.

"Well . . ." he said, and allowed his voice to trail into silence.

"Yes?"

"Actually," he said, "Buddy's there."

"Buddy's only a boy."

"Mom, he's twenty-two."

"That's a boy."

"I'm not much older than that myself, Mom." He paused. "I'm only twenty-seven, Mom. Not even."

"That's a man," she said.

"So I don't see—"

"That's a man," she said again.

"Anyway, I'm not sure what'll be. That's why I sent you the money order."

"Thank you," she said coldly.

"Mom?"

"What?"

"Are you sore?"

"No."

"You sound like you are."

"I'm not. My oldest son wants to leave me alone up here in the dead of winter—"

"Mom, you've got Buddy up there."

"Buddy is just a boy! Who's going to run the shop while you're gone? You know I haven't been feeling well, you know I—"

"Mom, this just can't be helped, that's all."

"*What* can't be helped?"

"This . . . thing I have to do."

"Which is what?"

"Mom, I guess if I wanted to tell you about it, I'd have done that already."

"Don't get fresh with me," she said. "You're still not too big to take down your pants and give you a good whipping."

"I'm sorry," he said.

"Now, what is it that's happened?"

"Nothing."

"Roger—"

"Nothing!" he said sharply. "I'm sorry, Mom, but it's nothing."

The line was silent again.

"You'll hear from me," he said, and before she could answer, he hung up.

3

The man huddled in the doorway of the building next to the candy store seemed to be about Roger's age, a tall thin man with a slight reddish-brown beard stubble. He was wearing a gray overcoat, the collar of which was turned up against his neck and held closed around his throat with one hand. He wore no hat and no gloves. His hand holding the coat collar was a deadly white. The other hand was in his pocket. He was watching the high school girls going up the street when Roger came out of the candy store. As Roger went past the building, he shifted his attention to him and came out of the doorway and down the steps.

"Hey!" he said.

Roger stopped and waited for the man, who walked up to him leisurely and without threat, smiling pleasantly.

"You looking for something?" the man said.

"No," Roger answered.

"I mean, you're not from the neighborhood, are you?"

"No."

"I thought maybe somebody sent you up here."

"For what?" Roger said.

"Anything you want," the man answered, falling into step as Roger began walking again. "You name it, we got it."

"There's nothing I want."

"You want a woman?"

"No, I—"

"What color? White, black, brown? Tan? Yellow even, you name it. We've got a whole streetful of women up here."

"No, I don't want a woman," Roger said.

"You prefer little girls maybe? How old? Nine, ten, eleven? Name it."

"No," Roger said.

"What then? Junk?"

"Junk?"

"Heroin, cocaine, morphine, opium, codeine, demerol, benzedrine, marijuana, phenobarb, goofballs, speedballs, you name it."

"Thanks, no," Roger said.

"What do you need then? A gun? A pad? An alibi? A fence? Name it."

"I'd like a cup of coffee," Roger said, and smiled.

"That's easy," the man said, and shrugged. "Here you meet a genie ready to give you three wishes, and all you want's a cup of coffee." He shrugged again. "Right around the corner there on the avenue," he said. "Coffee and. Best in the neighborhood."

"Good," Roger said.

"I'll join you," the man offered.

"How come everybody's so eager to join me this morning?" Roger asked.

"Who knows?" the man said, and shrugged. "Maybe it's national brotherhood week, huh? Who knows? What's your name?"

"Roger Broome."

"Pleased to know you, Roger," he said and relaxed his grip on the coat collar just long enough to extend his hand, take Roger's, and shake it briefly. The hand returned immediately to the open collar, pulling it tight around the throat. "I'm Ralph Stafford, pleased to know you."

"How are you, Ralph?" Roger said.

They turned the corner now, and were walking toward a small luncheonette in the middle of the block. A vent blew condensing vapor out onto the sidewalk in an enormous white billow. There was the smell of frying food on the air, heavy and greasy. Roger hesitated outside the door, and Ralph said, "Come on, it's good."

"Well, all right," Roger said, and they went in.

The place was small and warm, with eight or nine stools covered in red leatherette and ranged before a plastic-topped counter. A fat man with hardly any hair was behind the counter, his sleeves rolled up over muscular forearms.

"Yeah?" he said as they sat down.

"Coffee for my friend," Ralph said. "Hot chocolate for me." He turned to Roger and lowered his voice confidentially. "Chocolate makes my back break out in pimples," he said, "but who gives a damn, huh? What is it you're up here for? You're not a bull, are you?"

"What's that?" Roger asked.

"A cop."

"No."

"What then? A T-man?"

"No."

"You sure?"

"I'm sure."

"We had a guy around here two, three months ago – wait a minute, it must've been just before Christmas, that's right – he was a T-man, trying to smell out some junk. He had some case." Ralph paused. "You don't look like a fed to me, I guess I can take a chance."

"What kind of chance?"

"I mean, man, suppose you're a fed, what then?"

"What then?"

"Suppose I'm holding?"

"Holding what?"

"Some junk."

"Oh."

"It could be bad for me, you know."

"Sure," Roger said.

"I'm taking a big chance just being nice to you."

"Yes, I know." Roger said, and smiled.

"You're not, are you?"

"No."

"The Law, I mean."

"That's right."

"Good."

There was a pause as the man behind the counter brought their beverages and put them down. Ralph picked up his hot chocolate, sipped at it, and then turned to Roger again.

"What *are* you?" he said. "If not The Law?"

"Just a person. Ordinary person, that's all."

"What are you doing around here?"

"I took a room up here a few nights ago."

"What for?"

"I came to the city to take care of some business."

"What kind of business?"

"Some stuff I had to sell."

"Hot bills?"

"No."

"You're not pushing, are you?"

"What do you mean?"

"No, I guess you're not." Ralph shrugged. "What *did* you come to sell?"

"Bowls. And spoons. And benches. Things like that."

"Yeah?" Ralph said skeptically.

"That's right. We've got a little woodworking shop upstate, my brother and me."

"Oh," Ralph said. He seemed disappointed.

"So I brought the stuff in to try to sell it."

"How'd you get here?"

"In the truck. We've got a little pickup truck, my brother and me."

"What kind of truck?"

"A '59 Chevy."

"Can you carry a lot in it?"

"I guess so. Why?"

"Well, I mean how *big* a load can it carry?"

"I don't know exactly. It's not *too* big, but I suppose—"

"Could a piano fit in it?"

"I guess so. Why? Do you want to move a piano?"

"No, I'm just trying to get an idea. There are times when guys I know could use a truck, you follow?"

"For what?"

"To move stuff."

"What kind of stuff?"

"Stolen," Ralph said conversationally, and took another sip at the chocolate.

"Oh," Roger said.

"What do you think?"

"I don't think I could let you have the truck to move stolen goods."

"Mmm," Ralph said, and studied him for a moment, and then sipped at the chocolate again.

The door to the luncheonette opened. A tall heavy man wearing a brown overcoat came into the room, closed the door noisily, took off his coat, hung it on a wall hook, rubbed his hands together briskly, and came over to the counter.

"Coffee and a French cruller," he said to the counterman, and then turned to glance at Roger, and noticed Ralph sitting at the end of the counter. "Well, well," the man said, "look what crawled out from under the rocks."

Ralph looked up from his chocolate, nodded briefly, and said, "Good morning."

"I thought you hibernated from Christmas to Easter, Ralphie."

"No, only bears hibernate," Ralph said.

"I thought what you did was hole up in that apartment of yours with enough heroin to last you through the whole winter, that's what I thought you did."

"I don't know what you mean by heroin," Ralph said.

"Who's your friend here?" the man asked. "One of your junkie playmates?"

"Neither one of us are junkies," Ralph said. "You know I kicked the habit, what are you making a big fuss about?"

"Yeah, sure," the man said. He turned to the counterman. "You see this guy, Chip?" he said. "This guy is the biggest junkie in the neighborhood. He'd steal his grandmother's glass eye to hock it for a fix. Am I right, Ralphie?"

"Wrong," Ralph said. "Wrong as usual."

"Sure. How many crooked deals do you get involved in every day, I mean besides the normal criminal act of possessing narcotics."

"I'm not involved in any criminal activity," Ralph said, with dignity. "And if you care to shake me down right now, I'd be happy to have you do so. Voluntarily. If you think I'm holding."

"You hear that, Chip?" the man said to the counterman. "He wants me to shake him down. I've got half a mind to do it. When they're so eager for a shakedown, it usually means they've got something to hide."

"Argh, leave him alone, Andy," the counterman said.

"Sure, leave him alone, Andy," Ralph said.

"To *you*, pal, it's Detective Parker. And don't forget it."

"Excuse *me*, Detective Parker. Pardon me for living."

"Yeah," Parker said. "Thanks," he said to the counterman as he put down the coffee and cruller. He took a huge bite of the cruller, almost demolishing it with the single bite, and then picked up his coffee cup and took a quick noisy gulp and put the cup down on the saucer again, sloshing coffee over the sides. He belched and then turned to look at Ralph briefly, and then said to Roger, "Is he a friend of yours?"

"We just met," Ralph answered.

"Who asked *you?*" Parker said.

"We're friends," Roger said.

"What's your name?" Parker asked. He picked up the coffee and sipped at it without looking at Roger. When Roger did not answer, he turned toward him and said again, "What's your name?"

"Why do you want to know?"

"You're consorting with a known criminal. I have a right to ask you questions."

"Are you a policeman?"

"I'm a detective, and I work out of the 87th Squad, and here's my identification," Parker said. He threw his shield, pinned to a leather tab, on to the counter. "Now what's your name?"

Roger looked at the shield. "Roger Broome," he said.

"Where do you live, Roger?"

"Upstate. In Carey."

"Where's that?"

"Near Huddleston."

"Where the hell is Huddleston? I never heard of it."

Roger shrugged. "About a hundred and eighty miles from here."

"You got an address in the city?"

"Yes, I'm staying in a place about four or five blocks from—"

"The address."

"I don't know the address offhand. A woman named—"

"What street is it on?"

"Twelfth."

"And where?"

"Off Culver."

"You staying in Mrs. Dougherty's place?"

"That's right," Roger said. "Agnes Dougherty."

"What are you doing here in the city?"

"I came in to sell the woodenware my brother and I make in our shop."

"And did you sell it?"

"Yes."

"When?"

"Yesterday."

"When are you leaving the city?"

"I'm not sure."

"What are you doing with this junkie here?"

"Come on, Parker," Ralph said. "I told you we just—"

"Detective Parker."

"All right, Detective Parker, Detective Parker, all right? We just met. Why don't you leave the guy alone?"

"What is it you think I've done?" Roger asked suddenly.

"Done?" Parker said. He picked up his shield and put it back into his coat pocket, turning on the stool and looking at Roger as though seeing him for the first time. "Who said you did anything?"

"I mean, all these questions."

"Your friend here has been in jail, how many times, Ralphie? Three, four? For possession once, I remember that, and weren't you in for burglary, and—"

"Twice is all," Ralph said.

"Twice is enough," Parker said. "That's why I'm asking you questions, Roger." Parker smiled. "Why? *Did* you do something?"

"No."

"You're sure now?"

"I'm sure."

"You didn't kill anybody with a hatchet, did you?" Parker said, and laughed. "We had a guy got killed with a hatchet only last month."

"An ax," the counterman said.

"What's the difference?" Parker asked.

"There's a difference," the counterman said, and shrugged.

"To who? To the guy who got hit with it? What does he care? He's already singing with the choir up there." He laughed again, rose, walked to where he had hung his coat, and put it on. He turned to the counterman. "What do I owe you, Chip?" he asked.

"Forget it," the counterman said. "Mark it on the ice."

"Uh-uh," Parker said, shaking his head. "You think I'm a coffee-and-cruller cop? You want to buy me, you got to come higher. What do I owe you?"

The counterman shrugged. "Twenty-five," he said.

"How *much* higher?" Ralph said. "I know guys who bought you for a fin, Parker."

"Ha ha, very funny," Parker said. He put a quarter on the counter and then turned to face Ralph. "Why don't *you* try to buy me sometime, pal? Sometime when I catch you red-handed with a pile of shit in your pockets, you try to buy your way out of it, okay?"

"You can't fix narcotics, Parker, you know that."

"Yeah, worse luck for you, pal." He waved at the counterman. "So long, Chip," he said. "I'll see you."

"Take it easy, Andy."

At the door, Parker turned. He looked at Roger without a trace of a smile and said, "If I see you hanging around *too* long with our friend here, I may have to ask you some more questions, Roger."

"All right," Roger said.

"I just thought you might like to know."

"Thanks for telling me."

"Not at all," Parker said, and smiled. "Part of the service, all part of the service." He opened the door, went out into the street, and closed the door noisily behind him.

"The son of a bitch," Ralph whispered.

4

It was just the idea of going in there that he didn't like. He stood across the street from the police station, looking at the cold gray front of the building and thinking he wouldn't mind telling them all about it if only it didn't mean going in there. He supposed he could have told that detective in the luncheonette, but he hadn't liked the fellow and he had the feeling that telling this could be easy or hard depending on whether he liked the fellow he was telling it to. It seemed to him that Ralph, who was a convicted burglar and a narcotics user (according to the detective, anyway), was a much nicer person than the detective had been. If he was sure he could find somebody like Ralph inside there, he'd have no qualms at all about just crossing the street and marching right in and saying he was Roger Broome, and then telling them about it.

He supposed he would have to begin it with the girl, and end it with the girl, that would be difficult, too. Telling them about how he had met the girl. He couldn't see himself sitting opposite a stranger at a desk someplace inside there and telling them how he had met the girl, Molly was her name. Suppose they gave him a detective like that fellow Parker in the luncheonette, how could he possibly tell him about the girl, or about how they'd met or what they'd done. The more he thought about it the harder it all seemed. Walking across the street there and climbing those steps seemed very hard, and telling a detective about the girl seemed even harder, although the *real* thing, the *important* thing didn't seem too hard at all, if only he could get past the other parts that were so very difficult.

He would have to tell them first, he supposed, that he hadn't been looking for a girl at all last night, although he didn't know why that would be important to them. Still, it seemed important and he thought he should explain that first. I wasn't looking for a girl, he could say. I had just finished my supper, it was around seven o'clock at night, and I had gone back to the room and was just sitting there watching the street and thinking how lucky I'd been to have sold the salad bowls so high and to have made a new contact here in the city, that store in the Quarter.

Yes, he supposed he could tell them. He supposed he could walk in there and tell them all about it.

Last night, he had thought he should call his mother back home in Carey and tell her the good news, but then it seemed to him the happiness he was feeling was a very private sort of thing that shouldn't be shared with anybody, even if it was someone as close as his own mother, that was the trouble with

Carey. That small house in Carey, and his mother's bedroom right next door, and Buddy sleeping in the same room with him, all sort of cramped together, there was hardly any time to be alone, to feel something special of your own, something private. And the room in Mrs. Dougherty's house, it was pretty much the same as being home, having to go down the hall for the toilet, and always meeting somebody or other in the hall, the room itself so small and full of noises from the street and noises from all the pipes. What Carey missed, and what the room here in the city missed, was a secret place where a person could be happy by himself, or cry by himself, or just *be* by himself.

He left the room feeling pretty good, this must have been about seven-thirty, maybe eight o'clock, but not looking for any company, instead really trying to get out of that small room and into the streets, into the larger city, so that the happiness he was feeling could have a little space to expand in, a little space to grow. He wasn't looking for a girl. He just came out of the room and down the steps and into the street – it was very cold last night, colder than today – and he pulled up his coat collar and stuck his hands in his pockets and just started walking south, not knowing where he was going, but just breathing the air into his lungs, cold and sharp and even hurting a little bit, it was that cold.

He must have gone six or seven blocks, maybe it was more, when he really began to feel the cold. It hit his feet all at once, and he felt his toes were going to fall right off if he didn't get inside someplace quick. He was not a drinking man, he didn't usually drink more than a beer or two, and he didn't much like bars, but he saw a bar up ahead and he knew if he didn't get inside someplace real quick he was going to have frostbite, well, he didn't know if he was *really* going to have frostbite, but it sure *felt* like it.

He couldn't remember the name of the bar, he supposed they would want to know its name and exactly what street it was on.

He must have come six or seven blocks, was all, walking straight south on Twelfth Street, from the rooming house. But he didn't know what avenue that would have been. He thought the bar had a green neon sign in the window. Anyway, he went in, and took a table near the radiator because his feet were so cold. That was how he happened to meet Molly. He wasn't really

No, he thought.

No, it doesn't sound right, that's the difficult part about telling it.

He could visualize it all in his head, just the way it had happened, but he knew that going into that police station and telling it to a detective it would come out all wrong, he just knew it. Sitting face to face with somebody he didn't know and telling him about how the girl had come to the table after he'd been sitting there a couple of minutes, no, he knew it wouldn't come out right, even though he could see it plain as day inside his head, just the way it had happened, her coming to the table and stopping there and looking down at him with a very peculiar annoyed look on her face, her hands on her hips.

"What's the matter?" he said.

"You've got a lot of nerve, mister," she said. "You know that, don't you?"

"What do you mean?"

"You see that pocketbook there in the corner, what do you think that pocketbook is doing there?"

"What pocket — Oh."

"Yeah, oh."

"I'm sorry. I didn't see it when I sat down."

"Yeah, well now you see it."

"And there wasn't a glass or anything on the table, so I—"

"That's 'cause I didn't order yet. I was in the powder room."

"Oh," Roger said.

She had red hair, and the red hair was the only attractive thing about her, and he suspected even that was fake. She was wearing fake eyelashes, and she had penciled fake eyebrows onto her forehead and had made her mouth more generous by running a fake line of lipstick up beyond its natural boundaries. She was wearing a white blouse and a black skirt, but her breasts under the silk blouse were very high and pointed, with that same fake look the eyelashes and the lipstick and the eyebrows had. Her hair was a bright red, almost an orange, straight from a bottle, he supposed. She was altogether a pretty sad specimen. Even her legs weren't too hot; he supposed there was nothing she could do to fake *them* up a little.

"Well, I'm sorry," he said, "I'll just take my beer and move to another booth."

"Thanks," she said, "I'd appreciate it."

She kept standing by the booth with her hands on her hips, waiting for him to pick up his bottle of beer, and his half-full glass of beer and move to another booth. The trouble was he had taken off his shoes in order to warm his feet against the radiator, which was on the wall under the table, and he had to put his shoes on now before he could move. He swung his stockinged feet out from under the table and then searched for his right shoe. He put that on while she watched him silently with her hands on her hips. Then he reached under the table for the second shoe and couldn't find it, and got down on his hands and knees and went searching for it that way. She just kept watching with her hands on her hips all the while, not saying a word until finally she said, "Oh, for Pete's sake, never *mind! I'll* move! Would you please hand me my bag?"

"I'm sorry, but—"

"Don't be so sorry, for Pete's sake, just give me my bag!"

"I took off my shoes because—"

"What *are* you, a farmer or something? What do you think this is, your own living room? Taking off your shoes? In a public place like this? Boy, you've really got some nerve, mister, I'm telling you!"

"It's just that my feet—"

"Never mind!"

"Here's your bag."

"Thank you. Thank you a *whole* hell of a lot," she said, and swiveled off angrily to a booth across the room and at an angle to the one he occupied. He watched her backside as she crossed the room, and thought some women just didn't have anything, some women were just the unlucky ones in this world, they didn't have pretty faces, nor good legs nor breasts, and even their backsides looked like a truckdriver's.

It seemed to him he always got the ugly girls.

As far back as he could remember, even when he was in the second grade at Carey Elementary, when his father was still alive, all he ever got was the ugly girls. There was Eunice McGregor, who was possibly the ugliest kid ever born to anyone in the United States, well, her mother was no prize either, that was for sure. But she had a crush on him, and she told everybody she loved him, and she warned him she would break his nose – she was a very big girl – if he didn't give her a kiss whenever she demanded one, God she was ugly. That was in the second grade. After his father died, it seemed he got the ugly girls more and more often. He couldn't understand why they were all so attracted to him. His mother had been pretty as a picture when she was younger, and she still had a fine handsome look about her, it was the bones, you couldn't rob a pretty woman of her facial bones, they were always there, fifty, sixty, even into the seventies. His mother was only forty-six, and she still had those fine bones; sometimes she would actually laugh at some of the girls who were attracted to him. She told him once that she thought he was purposely looking for all the ugly ducklings he could find. He sure as hell couldn't understand what she'd meant by that. He hadn't said anything to her, he didn't like to contradict her when she said something, she'd only think he was being sassy. But he'd thought about it a lot. It made him wonder, what she'd said.

Looking across to where the redheaded girl was adjusting herself in the booth opposite, doing so with all the fuss and annoyance of somebody who is just about fit to bust, he felt the same happiness he had felt before leaving the room at Mrs. Dougherty's. He watched the girl with an odd, rising feeling of tenderness toward her, pleased by the very fussy little annoyed female things she was doing in the booth opposite, pulling the skirt down over her knees, and smoothing the front of her blouse, and tucking back a stray wisp of hair, and then glancing around for the waiter and signaling to him in a prissy, annoyed, very dignified, feminine way, he almost burst out laughing. She made him feel real good. Now that his feet were warm again (his mother had told him never to take off his shoes when his feet were cold, just leave them on until the feet warmed up inside, and they wouldn't never get cold again that whole day, but he never listened to her about his feet, they were *his* feet and he by God knew how to make them warm) – now that his feet were warm, and now that he had a good glass of beer inside him and was in a nice warm place with a juke box going at the other end with a soft dreamy song, now he began thinking about how much money he had got for the stuff he'd brought to the city, and he began feeling very good about it again, and he thought somehow the redheaded girl, well, the *fake* redhead, had something to do with the way he was feeling.

He watched her as she ordered, and then he watched as she got up and walked to the juke box and made a selection, and then went back to the booth. Nobody in the place was paying the smallest bit of attention to her. There were maybe a dozen or so men in the bar, and only four girls besides the redhead, but nobody was making a rush to her booth, in spite of the shortage. He sat and watched her. She knew he was watching her, but she very carefully made sure she didn't look once in his direction, pretending she was still very angry because he had taken her booth.

He knew he would go to bed with her.

He wasn't at all excited by the idea because she wasn't pretty or even attractive. He just knew he would go to bed with her, that was all. He just knew that before the night ended, he would be in bed with her.

Sitting on the bench opposite the police station now, he wondered how he could explain to the police that he had known he would be going to bed with the redheaded girl. How could he explain to them that he had known he would go to bed with her but hadn't been excited by the idea, how could he explain that?

How could he go in there and tell them all about this? What would his mother think when she – well, it didn't matter, that part of it certainly didn't matter. It was just sitting across from somebody and talking about taking a girl to bed that would be very difficult. There wasn't anybody in the world he talked to about things like that, not even his mother, certainly not his mother, nor even his brother Buddy. How could he tell about Molly to a strange detective?

The idea came to him like a bolt of lightning, just like that, pow, out of the blue.

He would telephone.

He would go to a telephone booth, but wait, there were no separate listings for the precincts, how could he possibly

Parker, that was his name. The detective in the luncheonette. Parker, of the 87th Squad, and the globes across the street were each marked with an 87, which meant this was Parker's precinct. Okay, he would call police headquarters and say that he was supposed to call a detective named Parker of the 87th Squad, but he had lost the number Parker had given him, and would they please give him the number. Maybe they would connect him direct, maybe they had a big switchboard down there that connected to all the precincts in the city. Or maybe they would simply give him the number of the 87th Precinct and then he would call it himself and ask to talk to a detective – not Parker, absolutely *not* Parker – it would be as easy as that.

Pleased, he got off the bench.

He took a last look at the police station, smiled, and walked out of the park, looking for the drugstore he had been in earlier that morning.

5

The sergeant who answered the phone at police headquarters listened patiently while Roger told his invented story about Detective Parker, and then said, "Hold on, please." Roger waited. He assumed the sergeant was checking to see if there really was a Detective Parker in the 87th Squad. Or maybe the sergeant didn't give a damn one way or the other. Maybe he received similar calls a hundred times, a thousand times each day. Maybe he'd been bored stiff listening to Roger's story, and maybe he was bored stiff now as he looked up the number of the precinct.

"Hello," the sergeant said.

"Yes?"

"That number is Frederick 7-8024."

"Frederick 7-8024, thank you," Roger said.

"Welcome," the sergeant answered, and hung up. Roger felt in his pocket for another dime, found one, put it in the slot, waited for a dial tone, and began dialing.

FR 7

Quickly, he put the receiver back onto the hook.

What would he say when they answered? Hello, my name is Roger Broome, I want to tell you about this girl Molly, you see we met in a bar and

What? they would say.

Who? they would say.

What the hell is this all *about*, mister?

He sat motionless and silent for perhaps three minutes, staring at the face of the telephone. Then he felt in the return chute for his coin, leadenly lifted his hand, and deposited the dime once again. The dial tone erupted against his ear. Slowly, carefully, he began dialing.

FR 7,

8, 0,

2, 4.

He waited. The phone was ringing on the other end. He listened to it ring. The rings sounded very far away instead of just a few blocks from where he was. He began counting the rings, they must have been having a busy time over at that station house, seven, eight, nine

"87th Precinct, Sergeant Murchison."

"Uh . . . is this the police?" he asked.

"Yes, sir."

"I'd like to talk to a detective, please."

"What is this in reference to, sir?"

"I'd . . . uh . . . like to report . . . uh . . ."

"Are you reporting a crime, sir?"

He hesitated a moment, and then pulled the receiver from his ear and looked at it as though trying to make a decision. He was replacing it on the hook just as the sergeant's voice, sounding small and drowning in the black plastic, began saying again, "Are you reporting a—" click, he hung up.

No, he thought.

I am not reporting anything.

I am getting out of this city and away from all telephones because I don't want to talk to the police. Now how about that? I do not wish to discuss this matter with anyone, least of all the police, so how about that? Damn right, he thought, and opened the door of the phone booth and walked out of the booth and across the length of the drugstore. The colored girl, Amelia, was still behind the cash register. She smiled at him as he approached.

"You back again?" she asked. "I didn't see you come in."

"Yep," he said. "Bad penny."

"You mail your cards off?"

"Yep."

"Did you find your friend at the police station?"

"Nope."

"How come?"

"I figured there couldn't be no friends of mine at the police station."

"You can say that again," Amelia said, and laughed.

"What time do you quit?" he said.

"What?"

"I said what time do you quit?"

"Why?"

"I want to get out of the city."

"What do you mean, out of the city?"

"Out. Away."

"Home, you mean?"

"No, no. Not home. That's the same thing, ain't it? That's the same old box. The city's a great *big* box, and Carey's a tiny *small* box, but they're both the same thing, right?"

Amelia smiled and looked at him curiously. "I don't know," she said.

"Go take off your apron," he said slowly, "and hang it on that hook right there, you see that hook?"

"I see it."

"Hang it on that hook right there, and tell your boss you have an awful headache—"

"I don't have a headache—"

"Yes, you *do* have a headache, and you can't work any more today."

Amelia looked at him steadily. "Why?" she said.

"We're going to get out of the city."

"Where?"

"I don't know yet."

"And when we get out?"

"We'll see then. The big thing now is to do what we have to do, right? And what we have to do is get away from this city real quick."

"Are the cops after you?" she asked suddenly.

"No." Roger grinned. "Cross my heart and hope to die, the cops are definitely *not* after me. Now how about that? Are you going to get that headache and hang up that apron and come with me?"

Amelia shrugged. "I don't know."

"When *will* you know?"

"The minute you tell me what you want from me."

"*From* you? Who wants anything *from* you?"

"When you're colored, *everybody*."

"Not me," Roger said.

"No, huh?"

"No."

Amelia kept looking at him steadily. "I don't know what to make of you," she said.

"The apron," he whispered.

"Mmm."

"The hook," he said.

"Mmm."

"Headache."

"Mmm."

"Can't work."

"Mmm."

"I'll meet you outside. Five minutes. On the corner."

"Why?" she said again.

"We're gonna have fun," he said, and turned and walked away from the cash register.

She didn't come outside in five minutes, and she didn't come outside in ten minutes, and by the end of fifteen minutes he realized she wasn't going to come out at all. So he peeked over the stuff piled in the front window of the drugstore and saw Amelia at the cash register making no sign of taking off the apron or of telling the boss she had a headache, so that was that. He walked away from the drugstore, thinking it was a shame because she really was sort of pretty and also he'd never been out with a colored girl before and he thought it might be fun. Now that he had decided not to go to the police with his story, it never once entered his mind that he should go home to Carey. He had tried to explain to Amelia that Carey, and the city, and the police station sitting on the edge of the park were all one and the same thing, that it was just a matter of degree as to how you classed them one against the other. The police station was a small box, and Carey was a slightly larger box, and the city was the biggest box of all, but all of them were trying their hardest to keep a man all closed up, when all a man wanted to do every now and then was relax and enjoy himself. Which is what he thought he and Molly were going to talk about last night, when they were discussing loneliness and all. But then, of course, she had begun to talk about that man in Sacramento, instead.

He had never really had a pretty girl in his life, and Molly was plain as hell until about two o'clock in the morning, he supposed that was when it was, well, never mind that. This colored girl behind the counter was pretty to begin with, which was why she hadn't come out to meet him, he could have told her beforehand she wouldn't, none of the real pretty girls ever did. It was probably just as well. Anybody from back home spied him in the city with a colored girl on his arm, even though she was part Spanish, hell, he didn't want his mother getting wind of nothing like that. Not that he cared much about what his mother thought. If he cared about that, he'd be running right back home to Carey instead of staying here and planning to have a little fun with his time.

He wondered where he should go now that the colored girl had spoiled his plans. Actually, he hadn't had any plans even when he was hoping she'd come out to meet him. But she'd have been somebody to laugh with and talk to and show off for, and, well, he'd have come up with something, he just knew he would have. Maybe he'd have taken her to a movie with a stage show, he'd been to one the last time he'd come to the city, it was pretty good.

"Hey," the voice behind him said, "wait up!"

He recognized the voice with surprise and turned to see Amelia running to catch up with him. She was wearing a pale-blue coat with the collar pulled up high against her chin, her head covered with a vibrant-blue kerchief. She came up to him panting, vapor pluming from her mouth. Catching her breath, she said, "You sure are a fast walker."

"I didn't think you were coming."

"The boss had to arrange for relief. It took a few minutes."

"Well, I'm glad you're here," Roger said.

"I'm not sure *I* am," Amelia said, and laughed. Her complexion was smooth and unmarked, her color a warm brown, her eyes a shade darker, her hair beneath the electric-blue kerchief a black as deep as night. When she laughed, a crooked tooth showed in the front of her mouth, and sometimes she lifted her hand self-consciously to cover the tooth, but only when she remembered. She had good legs, and she was wearing dark-blue, low-heeled pumps. She was still out of breath, but she kept up with him as he began crossing the street, and them impulsively took his arm.

"There," she said, "what the hell! If we're doing this, we might as well *do* it, huh?"

"What?"

"I mean, if I'm *with* you, I'm *with* you. So I'm with you, so I'll take your arm the same way I'd take the arm of a colored fellow I was with, right?"

"Right," Roger said.

"I've never been out with a white man before."

"Neither have I," Roger said, and burst out laughing. "With a colored girl, I mean."

"That's good," Amelia said.

"Why?"

"I don't know. I wouldn't like to think you were one of those guys who just dug, you know, *all* colored girls. That would make it a drag."

"There isn't a single colored girl in all Carey," Roger said.

"They're all married?" Amelia asked seriously, and he burst out laughing again. "What's the matter?"

"I mean there *aren't* any," Roger said. "Not a one."

"That's too bad," Amelia said. "What do you do for race riots?"

"We pick on Jews," Roger said, and realized he had made a pretty good joke, and was pleased when Amelia laughed at what he'd said. He didn't really know why there was any humor in his comment, except that the people in Carey *didn't* pick on Jews. In fact there was one Jew in all of Carey, a man named Samuel Silverstein, who ran the hardware store and who had arthritis, poor man, why would anyone want to go picking on him? He knew he never would have said anything like that to his mother or to Buddy, but somehow being with Amelia made him seem witty and daring, which was why he had made the joke. He was suddenly very glad she'd come after him.

"You always go chasing strange men in the streets?" he asked.

"Sure. You always go telling strange girls to hang up their aprons and pretend to be sick and—"

"A headache isn't sick," Roger said.

" – and meet you on street corners, and then disappear?"

"Right into thin air!" he said. "Mandrake the Magician!"

"That's what you do, huh?"

"Yeah, I'm a magician," Roger said, beaming.

"You go into drugstores and work your charms on poor little colored girls."

"*Are* you poor?" he said.

"I'm very poor."

"Really?"

"Hey, mister, you think I'd joke about being poor?" Amelia said. "What the hell is that to joke about? I'm *very* poor. I mean it. I, am, very, poor."

"I am very rich," Roger said.

"Good. I knew one day I'd meet a white millionaire who'd take me away from it all," Amelia said.

"That's me."

"Mandrake."

"Yeah," he said. "Yesterday, I made one hundred and twenty-two dollars. How about that?"

"That's a lot of money."

"Today, I've only got, oh, maybe fifteen dollars of it left."

"Easy come, easy go," Amelia said, and shrugged.

"What I did was mail a hundred to my mother."

"Up in Gulchwater, right?"

"Up in Carey."

"Oh, I thought it was called Gulchwater Basin."

"No, it's called Carey."

"I thought you said it was Gulchwater Depot."

"No, Carey."

"Alongside Huddlesworth, right?"

"Huddleston."

"Where they toboggan."

"Where they ski."

"Right, I knew I had it," Amelia said.

"Anyway," Roger said, laughing, "I sent her – my mother – I sent her a hundred, and I paid four dollars for my room, and I bought the cards and some stamps and had some coffee and paid for Ralph's hot chocolate and—"

"Ralph?"

"A fellow I met." Roger paused. "He's a drug addict."

"You meet nice people," Amelia said.

"He was," Roger said. "A nice person, I mean."

"My mother has told each and every one of us in our house," Amelia said, "that if we ever touch any of that stuff, she will personally cripple us. She means it. My mother is a very skinny woman made of iron. She would rather see us dead than on junk."

"Is it that easy to get?" Roger asked.

"If you have the money, you can get it. In this city, if you have the money, you can get anything you want."

"That's what Ralph said."

"Ralph knows. Ralph is a very wise man."

"Anyway, here's what I've got left," Roger said, and reached into his pocket and pulled out a folded packet of bills and transferred those to his left hand, and then reached into his pocket again for his loose change. The change totaled seventy-two cents, and the bills were two fives and four singles. "Fourteen dollars and seventy-two cents," he said.

"A millionaire. Just like you said."

"Right."

"Right," she said.

"What would you like to do?"

"I don't know," she said. "Show me the city. Show me *your* city."

"My city? This ain't *my* city, Amelia."

"I mean the white man's city."

"I wouldn't know *his* city from *your* city. I'm a stranger here."

"Looking for a friend outside the police station," she said suddenly.

"Yes," he said, and watched her.

"Who you never found."

"Who I never bothered looking for."

"Bad place to look," Amelia said. "Where are you going to take me, mister? Uptown, downtown, crosstown? Where?"

"I know where," he said.

"Where?"

"There's a place I've always wanted to go. My mother brought me to the city for the first time when I was ten years old, and we were suppposed to go then, but it rained that day. Come on," he said, and took her hand.

"Where?" she said.

"Come on."

The Ferris wheels were motionless, the roller-coaster tracks hung on wooden stilts against a forbidding February sky, devoid of hurtling cars or screaming youngsters. The boardwalk stands were sealed tight, shuttered against the wind that howled in over the ocean and raised whirling eddies of sand on the beach, leaping the iron-pipe railing and hurling itself hopelessly against the weathered boards. Last summer's newspapers fluttered into the air, yellowed and torn, flapping wildly like alien birds and then soaring over the minarets of an amusement called The Arabian Nights. The rides huddled beneath their canvas covers in seemingly expectant watchfulness, waiting for a sparrow, silent, motionless, the wind ripping at the covers and making a faint whistling sound as it caught in metal studs and struts. There were no barkers touting games of chance or skill, no vendors selling hot dogs or slices of pizza, no sound but the sound of the wind and the ocean.

The boardwalk benches were a flaking green.

An old man stood at the far end of the boardwalk, looking out over the ocean, unmoving.

"You've never been here before?" Amelia asked.

"No," Roger said.

"You picked the right time to come."

"It's kind of spooky, isn't it?" he said, and thought of Molly the night before.

"It's like standing on the edge of the world," Amelia said, and he turned to look at her curiously. "What is it?" she asked.

"I don't know. What you said. I felt that a minute ago. As if there was just the two of us standing on the edge of the world."

"The three of us."

"What? Oh, yes, the old man down there."

"He's really my *dueña*," Amelia said.

"What's that?"

"A *dueña?* That's Spanish for chaperone. In Spain, when a young girl goes out with a boy, she has to take along a *dueña*, usually an aunt or some other relative. My father told me about that. He's Spanish, you know, did I tell you?"

"Yes."

"I mean, he's not Puerto Rican," Amelia said.

"What's the difference?"

"Oh, in this city, there's a *big* difference. In this city it's pretty bad to be colored, but the worst thing you can possibly be is Puerto Rican."

"Why's that?"

"I don't know," Amelia said, and shrugged. "I guess it's more fashionable to hate Puerto Ricans now." She laughed, and Roger laughed with her. "My father's name is Juan. Juan Perez. We always kid around with him, we ask him how his Colombian coffee beans are coming along. You know, have you ever seen that television commercial? It's Juan *Val*dez, actually, but it's close enough. My father loves when we kid around with him that way. He always says his coffee beans are doing fine because he's got them under the tree that is his Spanish sun hat. He really *is* from Spain, you know, from a little town outside Madrid. Brihuega. Did you ever hear of it?"

"Brihuega Basin, do you mean?"

"No, Brihuega."

"Oh yes, Brihuega Depot."

"No, Brihuega."

"Near Huddlesworth, right?"

"Near Madrid."

"Where they fight camels."

"No, bulls."

"I knew I had it," Roger said, and Amelia laughed. "Well, now that we're here," he said, "what are we supposed to do?"

Amelia shrugged. "We could neck, I suppose."

"Is that what you want to do?"

"No, not really. It's a little too early in the day. I got to admit, though . . ."

"Yes?"

"I'm very curious about what it's like to kiss a white man."

"Me, too."

"A colored girl, you mean."

"Yes."

"Yes."

They were both silent. The wind caught at their overcoats, flattening the material against their bodies as they looked out over the water. At the far end of the boardwalk, the old man was still motionless, like a salt-sodden statue frozen into position by a sudden winter.

"Do you think the old man would mind?" Amelia asked.

"I don't think so."

"Well . . ." she said.

"Well . . ."

"Well, let's."

She turned her face up to his, and he put his arms around her and then bent and kissed her mouth. He kissed her very gently. He thought of Molly the night before and then he moved away from her and stared down at her face and she caught her breath with a short sharp sigh and then smiled mysteriously and shrugged and said, "I like it."

"Yes."

"You think the old man would mind if we did it again?"

"I don't think so," Roger said.

They kissed again. Her lips were very wet. He moved slightly away from her and looked down at her. She was staring up at him with her dark brown eyes serious and questioning.

"This is sort of crazy," she whispered.

"Yes."

"Standing here on a boardwalk with that wind howling in."

"Yes."

"Kissing," she said. Her voice was very low.

"Yes."

"And that old man watching."

"He isn't watching," Roger said.

"On the edge of the world," Amelia said. And suddenly, "I don't even know who you are."

"My name is Roger Broome."

"Yes, but *who?*"

"What would you like to know?"

"How old are you?"

"Twenty-seven."

"I'm twenty-two." She paused. "How do I know . . ." She stopped, and shook her head.

"What?"

"How do I know you're not . . . a . . ." She shrugged. "A . . . Well, you wanted to know where the police station was."

"That's right."

"To meet a friend, you said. But then you came back to the drugstore and you hadn't met this friend of yours at all, so how do I know . . . Well, how do I know you're not in some kind of trouble?"

"Do I look like somebody who's in trouble?"

"I don't know what a white man in trouble looks like. I've seen lots of colored people in trouble. If you're colored, you're *always* in trouble, from the day you're born. But I don't know the look of a white man in trouble. I don't know what his eyes look like."

"Look at my eyes."

"Yes?"

"What do you see?"

"Green. No, amber. I don't know, what color are they? Hazel?"

"Yes, hazel, like my mother's. What else do you see?"

"Flecks. Yellow, I guess."

"What else?"

"Myself. I see myself reflected, like in tiny funhouse mirrors."

"Do you see trouble?"

"Not unless *I'm* trouble," Amelia said. She paused. "*Am* I trouble?"

He thought again of Molly and immediately said, "No."

"You said that too fast."

"Don't look at me that way," he said.

"What way?"

"As if . . . you're afraid of me all at once."

"Don't be silly. Why should I be afraid of you?"

"You have no reason to—"

"I'm five feet four inches tall, and I weigh a hundred and seventeen pounds. All you are is six feet nine—"

"Six-five," Roger corrected.

"Sure, and you weigh two hundred pounds and you could break me in half just by—"

"Two hundred and ten."

" – snapping your fingers, and here we are all alone on a godforsaken boardwalk—"

"There's an old man down there."

" – in the middle of nowhere, with nothing but the ocean in front of us, and those deserted buildings behind us, so why should I be afraid? Who's afraid?"

"Right," he said, and smiled.

"Right," she agreed. "You could strangle me or drown me or beat me to death, and nobody'd know about it for the next ten years."

"If ever," Roger said.

"Mmm."

"Of course, there's always the old man down there."

"Yeah, he's some protection," Amelia said. "He's probably half-blind. I'm beginning to wonder if he's *real*, as a matter of fact. He hasn't moved since we got here."

"Do you want to go?" he asked.

"Yes," she said. And then, quickly, "But not because I'm afraid of you. Only because I'm cold."

"Where would you like to go?"

"Back to the city."

"Where?"

"Do you have a room?" she asked.

"Yes."

Amelia shrugged. "We could go there, I guess. Get out of the cold."

"Maybe," Roger said.

They turned their backs to the ocean and began walking up the boardwalk, out of the amusement park. She looped her hand through his arm, and then rested her head on his shoulder, and he thought how pretty she was, and he felt the pressure of her fingers on his arm, and he remembered again the way he had never got any of the pretty girls in his life, and here was one now, very pretty, but of course she was colored. It bothered him that she was colored. He told himself that it was a shame she was colored because she was really the first pretty girl he had ever known in his life, well, Molly had been pretty last night, but only after a while. That was the funny part of it; she hadn't started out to be pretty. This girl, this colored girl holding his arm, her head on his shoulder, this girl was pretty. She had pretty eyes and a pretty smile and good breasts and clean legs, it was too bad she was colored. It was really too bad she was colored, though her color was a very pleasant warm brown. Listen, you can't go losing your head over a colored girl, he told himself.

"Listen," he said.

"Yes."

"I think we'd better get back and maybe . . . uh . . . maybe you ought to go back to the drugstore."

"What?" she said.

"I think you ought to go back to work. For the afternoon, anyway."

"What?" she said again.

"And then I can . . . uh . . . pick you up later, maybe, after work, and . . . uh . . . maybe we can have supper together, all right?"

She stopped dead on the boardwalk with the wind tearing at the blue kerchief wrapped around her head and tied tightly under her chin. Her eyes were serious and defiant. She kept both hands gripped over the brass clasp at the top of her handbag. Her hands were motionless. She stared up at him with her brown eyes flashing and the blue kerchief flapping in the wind, her body rigid and motionless.

"What are you talking about?" she said. "I told my boss I had a headache. I can't just walk back in now and tell him—"

"We could meet later," Roger said. "For supper."

"Are you—" She stopped the words and let out her breath in exasperation, and then stared at him solemnly and angrily for several moments, and then said, "What the hell is it?"

"Nothing."

"Two minutes ago, you were kissing me as if—"

"It's just that I promised somebody—"

"Well, what scared you off, that's all I want to know. Don't you like the way I kiss?"

"I like the way you kiss."

"Well, then what? I mean, if you're afraid of being seen with a colored girl, I mean taking a colored girl up to your room—"

"It's not that."

"I mean, we can always go back to my house, where we'll be *surrounded* by colored people and also by *rats* running out of the walls, and leaky pipes, and exposed wiring, and—"

"There are rats where I'm staying, too."

"Of course, my *mother* might not like the idea of my bringing home a white man. She might actually begin singing the same old tune she's been singing ever since I was a darling little pickaninny, 'Honeychile stay away from de white man, he is only out to get in yo sweet little pants and rob you of yo maiden.'"

"Look, Amelia—"

"The only thing my mother doesn't know, made of iron though she is, is that her darling little Amelia was robbed of her 'maiden' on a rooftop the summer she was twelve years old, and it wasn't a white man who did it, or even a white *boy*. It was six members of a street gang called the Persian Lords, the biggest blackest niggers you ever saw in your life." Amelia paused. Bitterly, she said, "My *dueña* was away on vacation that summer, I guess. At the beach, don't you know? Sand Harbor, where all the society ladies spend their time, naturally. What the hell is it, Roger?"

"Nothing."

"You're not a faggot, are you?"

"A what?"

"A fairy, a pansy."

"No."

"Then why—"

"I'll meet you later, that's all," Roger said. "It's just that my friend – the one I told you about?"

"Yes?"

"I have to see him, that's all."

"He's a very convenient friend."

"I have to see him," Roger said.

Amelia sighed.

"I have to."

Amelia sighed again.

"Come on, let's go back," he said.

"I'll give you my home number," she said. "I won't go back to the drugstore, not after I told him I had a headache."

"All right."

"Will you call me?"

"Yes. Yes, I think so."

"Why do you only think so?"

"Because I . . . Amelia, please don't . . . don't push me, huh? Just don't push me."

"I'm sorry."

"I'll try to call you. We'll have supper together."

"Sure."

They barely spoke on the subway ride back. They sat side by side, and occasionally Amelia would turn to look at him, but he was busy thinking about Molly and about what he had to do. It was foolish to even imagine any other way.

He had to go to the police, that was all there was to it.

He left her off on the corner of her block. It was almost twelve noon. The wind swept through the narrow street, and she clutched her collar to her throat and ducked her head.

"Call me," she said.

"I'll try."

"I'll be waiting." She paused. In a whisper, she said, "I like the way you kiss, white man," and then she turned and went up the street and into one of the tenements.

He watched her until she was out of sight, and then began walking toward Grover Avenue and the police station.

6

It was beginning to snow.

The flakes were large and wet and they melted the moment they touched the asphalt streets, melted on the tops of parked automobiles, and on the lids of garbage cans standing alongside shining wet tenement stoops. In the park, on the stone wall bordering the edge of the park, and on the rolling ground and jutting boulders of the park itself, the snow was beginning to stick, covering only lightly and in patches, but sticking nonetheless. He walked alongside the stone wall with its pale-white, almost transparent covering of snow, and looked across at the police station and then took a deep breath and sucked in his belly and crossed the street.

He went up the steps. There were seven of them.

There were two doors. He tried the knob of the one on the left, but the door did not open. He reached for the knob directly to the right of the first one. The door opened on a very large room with grilled windows running its entire length on the left-hand side and with a large raised wooden counter that looked something like a judge's bench in front of the windows. A hand-lettered sign on top of the counter, bold black on white, read ALL VISITORS MUST STOP AT DESK. There were two uniformed policemen behind the muster desk. One of them was wearing sergeant's stripes. The other was sitting behind a switchboard and was wearing earphones. A railing had been constructed some four feet in front of the desk, with lead-pipe stanchions bolted to the floor, and with a horizontal piece of pipe forming the crossbar. An electric clock was on the wall opposite the desk. The time was twelve-fifteen. Two wooden benches flanked a hissing radiator on that same wall, and a small white sign, smudged, and lettered in black with the words DETECTIVE DIVISION, pointed to an iron-runged staircase that led to the upper story. The walls were painted a pale green and looked dirty.

Two men were standing in front of the muster desk, both of them handcuffed to the pipe railing. A patrolman stood to the side of the two men as the desk sergeant asked them questions. Roger walked to one of the benches opposite the muster desk, and sat.

"When did you pick them up?" the sergeant asked the patrolman.

"As they were coming out, Sarge."

"Where was that?"

"1120 Ainsley."

"What's that? Near Twelfth? Thirteenth?"

"Thirteenth."

"What's the name of the place?"

"Abigail Frocks," the patrolman said.

"She does?" the sergeant asked, and all the men – including the two in handcuffs – burst out laughing. Roger didn't see what was so funny.

"It's a dress loft up there on Ainsley," the patrolman said. "I think they use it for storing stuff. Anyway, there's hardly ever anybody up there, except when they're making deliveries or pickups."

"Just a loft, huh?"

"Yeah."

"They got a store, too?"

"Yeah."

"In this precinct?"

"Yeah, it's just a little place on Culver."

"Abigail Frocks, huh?" the sergeant said, and all the men giggled again. "Okay, boys, what were you doing coming out of Abigail Frocks?" the sergeant said, and again everyone giggled.

"We was after the pigeons," one of the men said, suppressing his laughter and becoming serious all at once. He seemed to be about twenty-five years old, badly in need of a haircut, and wearing a gray suede jacket with gray ribbing at the cuffs and at the waist.

"What's your name, fella?" the sergeant asked.

"Mancuso. Edward Mancuso."

"All right, now what's this about the pigeons, Eddie?"

"We don't have to tell him nothing," the second man said. He was about the same age as Mancuso, with the same shaggy haircut, and wearing a dark-brown overcoat. His trousers seemed too long for him. "They got us in here for no reason at all. We can sue them for false arrest, in fact."

"What's *your* name?" the sergeant asked.

"Frank Di Paolo, you know what false arrest is?"

"Yeah, we know what false arrest is. What were you doing coming down the steps from that dress loft?"

"I want a lawyer," Di Paolo said.

"For what? We haven't even booked you yet."

"You got nothing to book us *on*."

"I found jimmy marks on the loft door," the patrolman said drily.

"That must've been from some other time it got knocked over," Di Paolo said. "You find any burglar's tools on us?"

"He knows all about burglar's tools," the sergeant said, and then turned to Di Paolo and said, "You know all about burglar's tools, don't you?"

"If you live in this crumby neighborhood, you learn all about *everything*," Di Paolo said.

"Also about how to break and enter a dress loft and steal some clothes? Do you learn all about that?"

"We was after the pigeons," Mancuso said.

"What pigeons?"

"*Our* pigeons."

"In the dress loft, huh?"

"No, on the roof."

"You keep pigeons on the roof of that building?"

"No, we keep pigeons on the roof of 2335 Twelfth Street, that's where."

"What's that got to do with the dress loft?"

"Nothing," Mancuso said.

"*We* ain't got nothing to do with the loft, either," Di Paolo said. "We were only in that building because our pigeons were on the roof."

"We only went up to get them," Mancuso said.

"What's the matter?" the sergeant asked. "Don't your pigeons know how to fly?"

The patrolman laughed.

"They've got pigeons that don't know how to fly," the sergeant said, encouraged, and the patrolman laughed again.

"They know how to fly, but sometimes they don't come back when you call them. So from where we were on *our* roof, we could see these two birds sitting on the roof of the building where the *dress* loft was in—"

"Oh, you *knew* there was a dress loft in that building, huh?"

"No, we didn't know until we got over there. When we was climbing to the roof, we saw the sign for the dress loft."

"And decided to jimmy open the door while you were at it."

"What jimmy? We were going up the roof for our pigeons."

"Where are they?"

"Where's what?"

"The birds."

"They flew away when we got up there."

"I thought they didn't know how to fly."

"Who said that? *You* said that, not us."

A man came down the iron-runged steps leading into the muster room, and the men at the desk turned momentarily to look at him. He was well-dressed, clean-shaven, with eyes that slanted to give his face an almost Oriental look. He wore no hat, and his hair was a sandy brown, cut close to his head, but not in a crew cut. He was reading something, some form or other, as he crossed the room, and then he folded the form and put it in his inside jacket pocket and stopped at the desk. The sergeant looked up.

"Dave, I'm going out to lunch," the man said. "Anybody calls for me, I'll be back around one-thirty, two o'clock."

"Right, Steve," the sergeant said. "You recognize these two?" he asked.

The man called Steve looked at Mancuso and Di Paolo and then shook his head. "No," he said. "Who are they?"

"A couple of pigeon fanciers." The sergeant looked at the patrolman, and the patrolman laughed. "You don't make them, huh?"

"No."

The sergeant looked at Di Paolo and said, "You see this fellow here? He's one of the meanest cops in this precinct. Am I right, Steve?"

The man, who was obviously a plainclothes detective, smiled and said, "Sure, sure."

"I'm only telling you this because if you're smart you'll give your story to *me*, and not wait until he gets you upstairs. He's got a rubber hose up there, right, Steve?"

"*Two* rubber hoses," the detective answered. "And a lead pipe."

"There ain't no story to give," Mancuso said.

"We was going up after the pigeons, and—"

"See you, Dave," the detective said.

"—that's the truth. We spotted them on the roof from where we was flying the pigeons—"

"So long, Steve. In February?"

"What do you mean?"

"Flying your pigeons on a day you could freeze your ass off?"

"What's that got to do with . . ."

Roger stood up suddenly. The detective had gone through the door, and was heading down the front steps of the building. The desk sergeant looked up as Roger reached the door, and then – as though noticing him for the first time – asked, "Did you want something, mister?"

"No, that's all right," Roger said. He opened the door quickly. Behind him, he could hear Di Paolo patiently explaining about the pigeons again. He closed the door. He came down the front steps and looked first to his left and then to his right, and then saw the detective walking down Grover Avenue, his hands in the pockets of his gray tweed overcoat, his head ducked against the wind. Swiftly, he began following.

He could not have said what it was that had forced him to rise suddenly from that bench. Perhaps it was the way they had those two fellows trapped, the way they were trying to make out those fellows had tried to rob the dress loft when it was plain to see that all they'd really been after was their pigeons up on the roof. Perhaps it was that, or perhaps it was the way the detective had smiled when the sergeant said he was one of the meanest cops in the precinct. He had smiled and said, "Sure, sure," as if he wasn't really a mean cop at all, but simply a guy who had a job to do and the job only accidentally happened to deal with men who maybe were or maybe weren't trying to break into dress lofts.

There was something good about that detective's face, Roger couldn't say what. He only knew that there were bums in this world and there were nice guys, and this detective struck him as being a nice guy, the same way Parker in the luncheonette had struck him immediately as being a bum.

He sure walks fast, though, Roger thought.

He quickened his pace, keeping sight of the gray overcoat. The detective was tall, not as tall as Roger himself, but at least six-one or six-two, and he had very broad shoulders and a narrow waist, and he walked with the quick surefootedness of a natural athlete, even on pavements that were getting very sloppy with fallen snow. The snow was still wet and heavy, large flakes filling the air like a Christmas card, everything gray and white and sharp, with the buildings standing out in rust-red warmth. Everyone always thought of the city as being black and white, but during a snowstorm you suddenly saw the colors of the buildings, the red bricks and the green window frames and the yellows and the blues of rooms only glimpsed behind partially drawn shades. There was color in the city.

Following the detective, he began to feel pretty good again. He had always liked snow, and it was beginning to snow pretty heavy now, with the streets and sidewalks turning white, and with the snow making a funny squeaking sound under his shoes as he walked into the large swirling flakes. In Dick Tracy, whenever it snowed, the guy who drew the cartoon always made these big round white circles, they filled the whole page almost, he sure knew how to make it snow. It snowed in Dick Tracy sometimes three, four times every winter.

The detective had turned the corner into a side street, and Roger quickened his step, slipping on the sidewalk, regaining his balance, and then turning the corner and seeing the detective stop in front of a restaurant just short of the middle of the block. The detective stood with his hands in his pockets, his head bent, hatless, his brown hair covered with snowflakes and looking white from a distance. He was probably waiting for someone, Roger thought, and then looked around for a place where he could stop without attracting attention. That man up there is a detective, he reminded himself. He knows all about following people and about being followed, so make up your mind quick, do something. Either walk past him, or turn back, or find a place where you can hide, or pretend to be waiting, no, I'll go right up to him, Roger thought. I'll just go right up to him and tell him what I have to tell him, what's the sense of kidding around?

He was walking toward the detective when the taxi-cab pulled up, and the woman got out.

The woman was beautiful.

Roger was perhaps eight or ten feet away from her when she got out of the cab, her skirt pulling back over her knees momentarily as she slid over on the seat, her hand moving swiftly to lower the skirt as she paid the driver. The detective extended his hand to her and she took it and raised her face and her eyes to his, a rare and lovely smile coming onto her face, God she was beautiful. Her hair was black, and her eyes were a very deep brown, and she smiled up at the detective with her eyes and her mouth and her entire face, and then stood beside him on the sidewalk and kissed him briefly on the mouth, not on the cheek or the jaw, but a swift sudden kiss on the mouth. She moved away from him and took his hand, her fingers lacing into his, and they began walking toward the door of the restaurant. The snow caught in her hair at once, and she shook her head and tilted her face, grinning, and he thought at first she was one of those girls who get the cutes whenever they're around a man. But no, it was something else, he couldn't quite place what it was at first. And then, as they opened the door and walked into the restaurant, he realized that the woman was simply very very happy to *be* with this man.

Roger had never been loved that way.

He opened the restaurant door, and followed them inside.

Abruptly, he thought of the girl Molly.

7

He had walked over to her table across the bar, and she had looked up at him briefly and then gone back to her drink. She was drinking something in a small stemmed glass, a whiskey sour or something, he figured. She looked up at him with disinterest, and then turned back to her drink with disinterest, as if she were equally bored with everything and everyone in the world.

"I'm sorry I stole your table," Roger said, and smiled.

"Forget it," she told him.

He stood by the table, waiting for her to ask him to have a seat, but the girl just kept looking at the open top of her glass, where some white foam was clinging to the inside, a kind of empty despair on her face, a sadness that made her look even more plain than she actually was.

"Well," he said, "I just wanted to apologize," and he started to move away from the table, thinking she wasn't interested after all, didn't want him to sit with her. And then, all at once he realized that the girl probably wasn't used to approaches from men, didn't know how to handle a man coming to her table and flirting with her. He stopped dead in his tracks and turned to the table again, and said, "Mind if I sit down?"

"Suit yourself," the girl said.

"Thanks."

He sat.

The table was silent again.

"I don't know why you bothered asking," the girl said, looking up briefly from her drink. "I thought you just sat wherever you pleased." She lowered her eyes. Her hand came out, her fingers began toying with the stem of the cherry in her glass.

"That was really a mistake," he said. "I really didn't know anyone was sitting there."

"Mmm, yeah, well," the girl said.

"Would you like another drink?"

"Are you having one?"

"Just a beer. I don't care much for hard liquor."

"I don't, either," the girl said. "Unless it's something sweet. Like this."

"What is that, anyway?" Roger asked.

"A whiskey sour."

"That's what I thought it was." He paused. "How come a whiskey sour is sweet?"

"I ask them to go easy on the lemon."

"Oh."

"Yeah," the girl said.

"Well, *would* you like another one?"

The girl shrugged. "Sure. Why not?"

Roger signaled the waiter. When he came to the table, Roger said, "I'll have a glass of beer, and the lady would like another whiskey sour."

"Easy on the lemon," the girl said to Roger, not the waiter.

"Easy on the lemon," Roger said to the waiter.

"Right," the waiter said, and walked away.

"My name's Roger Broome," Roger said to her. "What's yours?"

"Molly Nolan."

"Irish," he said, almost to himself.

"Yes. What's Broom?"

"English, I think. Or Scotch. Or maybe both mixed," Roger said.

"*B-R-O-O-M?*"

"No, with an *E*."

"Oh," she said, as though the *"E"* made a difference. The table was still again.

"You come here often?" Roger asked.

"First time," Molly said.

"Me, too."

"You live in the neighborhood?"

"No," Roger said. "I'm from upstate."

"I'm from Sacramento," Molly said. "California."

"No kidding?"

"That's right," she said, and smiled. She isn't even pretty when she smiles, Roger thought. Her teeth are too long for her mouth and her lower lip has marks on it from her bite.

"You're a long way from home," he said.

"Don't I know it," she answered.

The waiter came to the table with their drinks. They were silent while he put them down. When he walked away, Roger lifted his glass and extended it toward her.

"Well," he said, "here's to strangers in the city."

"Well, I'm not really a stranger," she said. "I've been here a week already." But she drank to his toast anyway.

"What brought you here?" he asked.

"I don't know." She shrugged. "Opportunity."

"Is there?"

"Not so far. I haven't been able to get a job yet."

"What kind of work are you looking for?"

"Secretarial. I went to a business school on the Coast. I take very good shorthand, and I type sixty words a minute."

"You ought to be able to get a job easy," Roger said.

"You think so?" she asked.

"Sure."

"I'm not very pretty," she said flatly.

"What?"

"I'm not very pretty," she said again. She was staring at the fresh whiskey sour, her fingers toying again with the cherry. "Men want their secretaries to be pretty." She shrugged. "That's what I've found, anyway."

"I don't see what difference it makes," Roger said.

"It makes a lot of difference."

"Well, I guess it depends on how you look at it. I don't have a secretary, but I certainly wouldn't mind hiring someone who looked like you. There's nothing wrong with your looks, Molly."

"Well, thanks," she said, and laughed in embarrassment, without really believing him.

"How'd your folks feel about you coming all the way East?" he asked.

"I don't have any folks."

"Oh, I'm sorry to hear that," he said.

"They both died when I was nineteen. My father died of cancer, and then my mother died six months afterwards. Everybody says it was of a broken heart. Do you think people can die of a broken heart?"

"I don't know," Roger said. "I suppose it's possible."

"Maybe," Molly said, and shrugged. "Anyway, I'm all alone in the world."

"You must have relatives," Roger said.

"I think my mother had a brother in Arizona, but he doesn't even know I exist."

"How come?"

"Oh, my father had an argument with him long before I was born, about a deed or something he said belonged to my mother, I don't know, something to do with land in Arizona. Anyway, my uncle hauled my father into court, and it was a big mess, and my father lost, and everybody stopped speaking to each other right then and there. I don't even know his name. My uncle's, I mean. He doesn't know mine, either."

"That's a shame," Roger said.

"Who cares? I mean, who needs relatives?"

"Well, it's nice to have a family."

"Mmm, yeah, well," Molly said.

They were silent. Roger sipped at his beer.

"Yep, I've been all alone since I was nineteen," Molly said.

"How old are you now?" he asked.

"Thirty-three," she answered unflinchingly. "Decided it was time for a change, figured I'd come East and look around for a better job. So far, I haven't found a goddamn thing."

"You'll find something," Roger assured her.

"I hope so. I'm running out of money. I was staying downtown when I got here last week, but it was costing me twenty dollars a day, so I moved a little further uptown last Friday, and even that was costing me twelve dollars a day. So yesterday I moved to a real dive, but at least I'll be able to hold out a little longer, you know? This city can kill you if you don't watch out. I mean, I left California with two hundred and fifty dollars and a suitcase full of clothes, and that was it. I figured I'd be able to land something pretty quick, but so far . . ." She shrugged. "Well, maybe tomorrow."

"Where'd you say you were staying?" Roger asked.

"The Orquidea, that's a hotel on Ainsley. There's a lot of Spanish people there, but who the hell cares, it's very inexpensive."

"How much are you paying?" Roger asked.

"Seven dollars a night. That's very inexpensive."

"It certainly is."

"It's a nice room, too. I always judge a hotel by how fast they are on room service, and whether or not they get your phone messages right. Not that I've gotten any phone messages since I checked in – after all, it was only yesterday – but I *did* order a sandwich and a glass of milk from room service last night, and they brought it right up. The service was really very good."

"That's important," Roger said. "Good service."

"Oh, sure it is," Molly said. She paused and then asked, "Where are *you* staying?"

"Oh, in a furnished room on . . . uh . . . South Twelfth, I guess it is."

"Is it nice?"

"No, no, it's pretty crumby. But it's only for a few nights. And I didn't want to spend too much money."

"When are you leaving?" she asked.

"Tomorrow, I guess. Tomorrow morning."

"Mmm," she said, and smiled weakly.

"Yep, tomorrow morning," he repeated.

"Mmm."

"How's your drink?" he asked.

"Fine, thank you."

"Not too sour, is it?"

"No, it's just right." She smiled again, lifted her glass, and sipped at it. A little foam clung to her lip, and she licked it away. "Do you like this city?" she asked.

"I don't know it too good," he said.

"Neither do I." She paused. "I don't know a soul here."

"Neither do I," he said.

"Neither do I," she said, and then realized she was repeating herself, and laughed. "I must sound like a poor little orphan child, huh? No parents, no relatives, no friends. Wow."

"Well, I'm sure you have friends back in . . . what was it . . . Sacramento?"

"Yeah, Sacramento. I had a very good friend there, Doris Pizer is her name, she's Jewish. A very nice girl, though. In fact, one of the reasons I came here was *because* of Doris. She went to Hawaii."

"Oh, yeah? Is that right?"

"Mmm," Molly said, nodding. She lifted her drink again, took a quick sip at it, put it down, and then said, "She left last month. She wanted me to go with her, but I'll tell you the truth, heat has never really appealed to me. I went down to Palm Springs once for a weekend, and I swear to God I almost dropped dead from the heat."

"Is it very hot in Hawaii?"

"Oh, sure it is." Molly nodded. "She got a job with one of the big pineapple companies. Dole, I think, who knows?" She shrugged. "I could have got a job there, too, but the heat, no thanks." She shook her head. "I figured I'd be better off here. It gets cold as hell here in the winter, I know, but anything's better than the heat. Besides, this is a pretty exciting city. Don't you think so?"

"Yes."

"It's a pretty exciting city," Molly said.

"Yes."

"You never know what's going to happen here, that's the feeling I get. I mean, who knew I was going to meet *you* tonight, for example? Did *you* know?"

"No, I didn't."

"Neither did I. That's what I mean. This is a very exciting city."

"Yes."

"So, you know," she said, picking up her drink and draining the glass this time, "when Doris left I really didn't have anything to keep me there any longer. In Sacramento, I mean. It's a nice place, and all that, but it takes me a while to make friends, and with Doris gone, I figured this was as good a time as any for me to pick up and explore the country a little myself, you know? What the hell, this is a big country. I was born in Tacoma, Washington, and then we moved to Sacramento when I was eighteen, my parents died when I was nineteen, and I was stuck in Sacramento from then on. So it was a good thing Doris went to Hawaii, if you know what I mean, because it goosed me into action." She giggled and said, "Well, I don't exactly mean goosed."

"I know what you mean," Roger said. "Would you like another drink?"

"I'll fall flat on my face."

"It's up to you," Roger said.

"No, I don't think so. Are you having another one?"

"I will, if you will."

"You're trying to get me drunk," Molly said, and winked.

"No, I don't believe in getting girls drunk," Roger said.

"I was only teasing."

"Well, I don't get girls drunk."

"No, I don't think you do," Molly said, seriously.

"I don't."

"I don't think you *have* to."

Roger ignored her meaning. "So if you want another drink," he said.

"Yes, thank you, I will have another drink," she said.

"Waiter," he called. The waiter came to the table. "Another beer, and another whiskey sour," Roger said.

"Light on the lemon," Molly said.

"Light on the lemon," Roger said to the waiter. He liked the way she told *him* what she wanted and not the waiter. Somehow, this was very flattering, and very pleasing, almost as if the waiter didn't exist at all. He watched as the waiter walked back to the bar and placed the order. He turned to Molly then and said, "How's she doing out there? Doris."

"Oh, fine. I heard from her only last week. I still haven't answered. She doesn't even know I'm here."

"What do you mean?"

"Well, I decided very suddenly, and her letter arrived the day before I left, so I didn't get a chance to answer it. I've been so busy running around trying to find a job since I got here . . ."

"She's probably wondering why you haven't written."

"It's only been a week," Molly said. "Since I'm here, is all."

"Still. If she's a good friend . . ."

"Yes, she is."

"You ought to let her know where you are."

"I will. I'll write to her when I get back to the hotel tonight." Molly smiled. "You make me feel guilty."

"I didn't mean to make you feel guilty," Roger said. "I just thought since Doris seemed to mean so much to you—"

"Yes, I understand, it's all right," Molly said, and smiled again.

The waiter brought their drinks, and left them alone once more. The crowd in the bar was thinning. No one paid them the slightest attention. They were strangers in a city as large as the universe.

"How much are you paying for *your* room?" Molly asked.

"What? Oh . . . uh . . . four dollars. A night."

"That's *really* inexpensive," Molly said.

"Yeah." He nodded. "Yeah, it is."

"Is it a nice room?"

"It's okay."

"Where's the loo? Down the hall?"

"The what?"

"The loo." She looked at his puzzled expression. "The toilet."

"Oh. Yes. Down the hall."

"That's not so bad. If it's a nice-sized room, I mean."

"It's pretty fair-sized. A nice lady runs it, I've got to tell you, though . . ."

"Yes?"

"I saw a rat there."

"Rats I can do without."

"You and me both."

"What'd you do?"

"I killed it," Roger said flatly.

"I'm even afraid of mice," Molly said. "I could never find the courage to kill a rat."

"Well, it *was* pretty horrible," Roger said. "This area's infested with them, though, you know. I wouldn't be surprised if there was more rats than people in this area."

"Please," she said, wincing. "I won't be able to sleep tonight."

"Oh, you very rarely *see* them," he said. "You might hear one of them, but you rarely see them. This one must have been an old guy, otherwise he wouldn't have been so slow. You should have been there. He got up on his hind legs when I backed him in the corner, and he—"

"Please," she said. "Don't." And shuddered.

"I'm sorry. I didn't realize—"

"That's all right." She picked up her drink and took a swallow. "I'll never be able to sleep tonight," she said, and very quickly added, "Alone."

Roger did not say anything.

"I'll be scared to death," she said, and shuddered again, and again took a swallow of her drink. "Aren't you ashamed of yourself, scaring a girl half to death?"

"I'm sorry," Roger said.

"That's all right," Molly answered, and finished her drink, and then giggled. "How large is your room?" she asked.

"Fair-sized."

"Well, how large is that?"

"I don't really know. I'm not too good on sizes."

"I'm *very* good on sizes." Molly paused and smiled tentatively, as though embarrassed by what she was about to say and do. She picked up her empty glass and tried to drain a few more drops from it, and then put it down on the table and said, very casually, "I'd like to see that room of yours. It sounds really inexpensive. If it's a good-sized room, I might move from where I am. That is, if it's really as inexpensive as you say it is."

"Yes, it's only four dollars."

"I'd like to see the room," she said, and raised her eyes from her glass for only a moment, and then lowered them again.

"I could take you there," Roger said.

"Would you?"

"Sure."

"Just for a minute. Just to see what it's like."

"Sure."

"I'd appreciate that," Molly said. Her eyes were still lowered. She was blushing furiously.

"I'll get your coat," Roger said, and stood up.

As he helped her into it, she glanced up over her shoulder and said, "How did you kill it? The rat, I mean."

"I squeezed it in my hands," Roger said.

The headwaiter was leading the detective and the woman to a table as Roger checked his coat. The woman was wearing a pale blue dress, a jumper he supposed you called it, over a long-sleeved white blouse. She smiled up at the headwaiter as he pulled out the chair for her, and then sat, and immediately put both hands across the table to cover the detective's hands as he sat opposite her. "Thank you," Roger said to the hatcheck girl, and put the ticket she handed him into his jacket pocket. The headwaiter was coming toward the front of the restaurant again. He looked French. Roger hoped this wasn't a French restaurant.

"*Bonjour, monsieur,*" the headwaiter said, and Roger thought Oh boy. "How many will you be, sir?"

"I'm alone," Roger said.

"*Oui, monsieur,* this way, please."

Roger followed the headwaiter into the restaurant. For a moment, he thought he was being led to the other end of the room, but the headwaiter was simply making a wide detour around a serving tray near one of the tables. He stopped at a table some five feet away from the detective and the woman.

"*Voilà, monsieur,*" the headwaiter said, and held out a chair.

"How about the table over there?" Roger said. "Near the wall."

"*Monsieur?*" the headwaiter said, turning, his eyebrows raised.

"That table," Roger said, and pointed to the table immediately adjacent to the detective's.

"*Oui, monsieur, certainement,*" the headwaiter said, and shoved the chair back under the table with an air of annoyed efficiency. He led Roger to the table against the wall, turned it out at an angle so that Roger could seat himself on the cushioned bench behind it, and then moved it back to its original position. "Would *monsieur* care for a cocktail?"

"No," Roger said. "Thank you."

"Would you like to see a menu now, sir?"

"Yes," Roger said. "Yes, I would."

The headwaiter snapped his fingers. "*La carte pour monsieur,*" he said to one of the table waiters and then made a brief bow and disappeared. The table waiter brought a menu to Roger and he thanked him and opened it.

"Well, what do you think?" the detective said.

The woman did not answer. Roger, his head buried in the menu, wondered why the woman did not answer.

"I suppose so," the detective said.

Again, the woman did not answer. Roger kept looking at the menu, not wanting to seem as if he were eavesdropping.

"Well, sure, you always do," the detective said.

The funny thing, Roger thought, without looking up from the menu, was that the detective was doing all the talking. But more than that, he seemed to be holding a conversation, saying things that sounded as if they were answers to something the woman had said each time, only the woman hadn't said a single word.

"Here are the drinks," the detective said, and Roger put down his menu and looked up as a waiter in a red jacket brought what looked like two whiskey-sodas to the table. The detective picked up his glass and held it in the air and the woman clinked her glass against his, but neither of the two said a word. The woman took a short sip of her drink and then put it down. Glancing briefly at their table, Roger saw that she was wearing a wedding band and an engagement ring. The woman, then, was the detective's wife.

The detective took a long swallow of his drink, and then put the glass down. "Good," he said.

His wife nodded and said nothing. Roger turned away and picked up the menu again.

"Did Fanny finally get there?" the detective asked.

Again, there was a long pause. Roger frowned behind his menu, waiting.

"Did she give you any reason?" the detective said.

Another pause.

"What kind of excuse is that?" the detective said.

Roger put down his menu and turned.

The woman's elbows were on the table, her hands were poised in front of and a trifle below her face. Her fingers were long and slender. The nails were manicured and polished a bright red. As she moved her hands in a fluid, swift series of gestures, the nails danced like tiny flames.

For a moment, Roger didn't know what she was doing. Was she kidding, was that it?

And then he saw her face behind the hands.

Her face was more lovely than he realized, the black hair combed sleekly back from the woman's forehead, the black eyebrows arched high over deep brown eyes, no, one eyebrow was dropping now, dipping low over her left eye in a sinister frown, the woman's mouth was curling into a sneer, her nostrils were dilating, her hands moved differently now, they moved in the exaggerated slick oiliness of a silent movie villain, the woman's fingers touched her upper lip, twirled an imaginary mustache, the detective laughed, the mask of villainy dropped from her face, her eyes sparkled with humor, the white teeth flashed behind her lips, the smile broke on her face like the sound of bells, and all the while her long slender fingers moved, the detective watching her hands, and then shifting his attention to her face again, the entire face in constant motion, her mouth and her eyes augmenting the music of her hands, the sound of her hands, her face open and honest and naive, the face of a little girl, mugging, exaggerating, acting, explaining. Why, she's talking with her face and her hands! Roger thought, and suddenly realized the woman was a deaf-mute.

He turned away because he didn't want her to think he was staring at her handicap.

But the detective was laughing. His wife had apparently finished her story about Fanny, whoever *that* was, and now the detective was laughing fit to bust, sputtering and choking and damn near slapping the table top, so that Roger himself was forced to smile and even the waiter, who had padded up the table to take Roger's order, smiled with him.

"I'd just like some eggs," Roger said.

"*Oui, monsieur,* how would you like your eggs?"

"Gee, I don't know," Roger said.

"Would *monsieur* care for an omelette, perhaps?"

"Oh, yes," Roger said. "Yes, that's good. What kind of omelettes do you have?"

"Cheese, mushroom, onion, jell—"

"Mushroom," Roger said. "That sounds good. A mushroom omelette. And some coffee. *With* it, please."

"*Oui, monsieur,*" the waiter said. "Any salad?"

"No. No, thanks."

"*Oui, monsieur,*" the waiter said, and moved away from the table.

". . . began talking to Meyer at first and Meyer listened for a few minutes and then asked the priest if he would mind telling this to me instead. I was pretty surprised when he came over to my desk, because we don't usually get priests up there, honey – not that it isn't a very religious place, and holy and all that."

He grinned at his wife, and she returned the grin. God she's beautiful, Roger thought.

"Anyway, I introduced myself, and it turns out the priest is Italian, too, so we went through the Are *you* Italian, too? routine for a couple of minutes, and we traced my ancestry back to the old country, it turned out the priest wasn't born anywhere near my parents, but anyway he sits down at the desk and he's got a slight dilemma, so I say, What's the dilemma, Father, meanwhile thinking my *own* dilemma is I haven't been inside a church since I was a kid, suppose he asks me to say five Hail Marys?

"The priest tells me that he had a woman in the confessional this morning, and the woman confessed to the usual number of minor sins and then, unexpectedly, said she had bought a gun which was in her purse at the moment, right there in the confession box, and she was going to take it to the shop where her husband worked and wait for him to come out on his lunch hour when she would shoot him dead. She was telling this to the priest because she expected to shoot *herself* immediately afterwards, and she wanted the priest's absolution in advance.

"Well, honey, the priest didn't know what to tell her. He could see she was very upset, and that she wouldn't sit still for a lecture on what a big sin murder was. She hadn't come there to ask the priest's *permission*, you understand, all she wanted was his forgiveness. She wanted to be blessed in advance for knocking off her husband, and then for taking her own life. Well, the priest took a chance and told the woman it would be nice if they prayed together a little, and then while they were praying he sneaked in a little subliminal commercial about how sinful it was to kill, Thou Shalt Not Kill, the fifth commandment, and then he explained how she was about to commit a *double* mortal sin by first putting her husband on ice and then doing a job on herself, didn't she have any children? No, the woman said.

"Well, the priest wasn't too happy to learn she was childless because children are usually a good thing to play on. So he very quickly said Haven't you got parents or brothers or sisters who'll be worrying about you, and the woman said Yes she had parents but she didn't give a damn what *they* thought and then said Forgive me, Father, because she'd just cursed in the confessional box, no less church. The priest forgave her and they continued to pray together for a little while, with the priest furiously wondering what he could do to stop this woman from polishing off hubby as he came out of his shop with his lunch box under his arm.

"That was why he'd come up to the office, hon. He told me that a priest, of course, is sworn to keep the sanctity of the confessional, which is exactly what was causing his dilemma. *Had* the woman confessed to anything, or *hadn't* she? How can a person confess to a sin that hasn't been committed yet? Was the thought the same thing as the act? If so, the world was full of thoughtful sinners. If not, then the woman hadn't done anything and her confession wasn't a confession at all. And if it *wasn't* a confession, then what sanctity was the priest protecting? If it *wasn't* a bona fide confession, then why wasn't it perfectly all right for him to go to the police and tell them all about the woman's plans?

"It's *perfectly* all right, Father, I said to him, Now what's the woman's name, and where does her husband work? Well, I couldn't get to him quite that fast. He wanted to discuss all the philosophical and metaphysical aspects of the difference between contemplated sin and committed sin, while all the while the clock on the wall was ticking away, and lunchtime was getting closer and closer, and that poor woman's husband was *also* getting closer and closer to a couple of holes in the head. I finally convinced him by saying I thought he had come to the police for the same reason the woman had gone to him, and when he said What reason was *that?* I told him I thought he wanted to be absolved. What do you mean *absolved?* he said. I told him he wanted to be absolved of possibly causing the death of two people by remaining silent when he wasn't even positive of the doctrine involved, the same way the woman wanted to be absolved. I told him I thought *both* of them wanted those deaths to be stopped and that was why the woman had gone to him, and that was why he had come to me, so what was the woman's name, and where did her husband work? This was a quarter to twelve. He finally told me, and I had a patrol car sent out to pick her up. We can't book her for anything since she hasn't committed a crime or even attempted one, and there's no such thing as suspicion of anything in this city. But we can hold her for a while until she cools off, and maybe scare her a little . . . Oh, *wait* a minute."

Roger, who was listening intently, almost turned to the detective and nodded in anticipation.

"We *have* got her on something, haven't we? Or maybe, anyway."

The woman raised her eyebrows inquisitively.

"The gun," the detective said. "If she hasn't got a permit for it, we can charge her with that. Or at least we can *scare* her with *threatening* to charge her. We'll see how it goes. Boy." He shook his head. "The thing about it, though, is I'm *still* not sure whether the priest copped out or not. Did she confess, or didn't she? It bothers me, hon. What do *you* think?"

The woman's hands began to speak again. Roger did not know what she was saying. Occasionally, he glanced at her as the wonderfully fluid fingers moved

in front of her face. He had never been loved by a beautiful woman in his life
– except, of course, his mother.

The waiter brought his omelette.

Silently, he ate.

Beside him, the detective and his wife finished their drinks, and then ordered
lunch.

8

He followed the detective and his wife to a subway kiosk, where they embraced and kissed briefly, and then the woman went down the steps and the detective stood on the sidewalk for a moment or two, watching her as she descended. The detective smiled then, secretly and privately, and began walking back toward the station house. The snow was very thick now, thick in the air, falling in great loose silent flakes, and thick underfoot where it clung to the pavement and made walking difficult.

Several times on the way back to the station house, he almost approached the detective and told him the whole story. He had overheard enough during lunch to know that this was the kind of man he could trust, and yet something still held him back. As he thought about it, as he walked behind the detective and wondered for perhaps the fifth time whether he should approach him now or wait until they were back at the station house, it seemed to him the reason he felt he could trust this man was simply because of the way he'd treated his wife. There had been something very good and gentle about the way those two looked at each other and talked to each other, something that led Roger to believe this man would understand what had happened. But at the same time – and curiously, considering it was the man's wife who had caused Roger to trust him – the wife was *also* responsible for his reluctance to approach the man. Sitting alongside them, Roger had shared their conversation, become almost a part of it. He had watched the woman's face and had seen the way she looked at her husband, had watched her hands covering his, had watched the score of gentle tender things she did, the secret winks, the glances of assurance, and had been suddenly and completely lonely.

Walking behind the detective now in a silent white world, he thought of Amelia and wanted to call her.

But wait, he thought, you have to tell the detective.

They were approaching the station house now. The detective stopped at a patrol car parked outside the building, and the patrolman sitting closest to the curb rolled down the window on his side. The detective bent down and looked into the car and exchanged a few words with the cops inside, and then he laughed, and the patrolman rolled up the window again, and the detective started walking up the seven flat steps to the front doors of the precinct.

Wait, Roger thought, I have to

He hesitated on the sidewalk.

The detective had opened the door and gone inside. The door eased shut behind him. Roger stood on the pavement with the snowflakes falling fat and wet and floppy all around him, and then he nodded once, sharply, and turned and began looking for a telephone booth. The first one he found was in a combination pool room and bowling alley on the Stem. He changed a dollar bill at the desk – the proprietor made it clear he didn't like making change for the telephone – and then went to the booth and closed the door and carefully took from his wallet the folded slip of paper with Amelia's number on it.

He dialed the number and waited.

A woman answered on the fourth ring. It was not Amelia.

"Hello?" the woman said.

"Hello, could I talk to Amelia, please?" Roger said.

"Who's this?" the woman said.

"Roger."

"Roger who?"

"Roger Broome."

"I don't know any Roger Broome," the woman said.

"Amelia knows me."

"Amelia isn't here. What do you want?"

"Where is she?"

"She went downstairs to the store. What do you want?"

"She asked me to call. When will she be back?"

"Five, ten minutes," the woman said.

"Will you tell her I called?"

"I'll tell her you called," the woman said, and hung up.

Roger stood with the silent receiver to his ear for a moment, and then replaced it on the hook and went out of the booth. The man behind the desk gave him a sour look. A clock on the wall told him it was almost two o'clock. He wondered if Amelia would really be back in five or ten minutes. The woman who'd answered the phone had sounded very colored, with the kind of speech that could sometimes be mistaken for white Southerner, but more often was identified immediately as coming from a Negro. It was just his luck, he thought. The first pretty girl he'd ever met who seemed to take a real liking to him, and she had to be colored. He wondered why he was bothering to call her at all, and then decided the hell with her, and headed back for the police station.

I mean, what's the sense of this, he thought. What am I putting this off for? It's got to be done, I've got to go in there sooner or later and tell them about it, so it might as well be now. What do I get by calling Amelia, she's probably up on the roof with one of those Persian Lords she was telling me about, getting her ass screwed off, the hell with her.

The thought of Amelia in embrace with one of the Persian Lords was infuriating to him, he didn't know why. He barely knew the girl, and yet the idea of her being laid by one of those gang members, no less *all* the members of the gang, filled him with a dark rage that twitched into his huge hands hanging at his sides. He had half a mind to tell the police about *that*, too, about young punks jumping on a nice girl like Amelia, she was probably a slut anyway, letting them do that to her.

He heard voices in the park.

Through the snow, he heard the voices of children, loud and strident, cutting through the falling snow, a sound of glee, a half-remembered sound, he and his father on the small hill behind the clapboard house they'd lived in near the tracks when Buddy was still a baby, "Off you go, Roger!" and a push down the hill, the rush of wind against his face, his lips pulled back over a wide joyous grin, "That's the boy!" his father shouted behind him and above him.

There were three boys with sleds.

He walked into the park and sat on a bench some fifteen feet from where they were sliding down a wide snow-covered slope, the snow packed hard by the runners of their sleds. The boys couldn't have been older than six or seven, probably kindergarten kids who'd been let out of school early, or maybe first-graders, no older than that. Two of them were wearing old ski parkas, and the third had on a green mackinaw. The one with the mackinaw had a woolen hat pulled down over his forehead and his ears and damn near over his eyes as well. Roger wondered how he could see where he was going. The other two were hatless, their hair covered with snow. They yelled and screamed and shouted, "Watch me! Hey, watch me!" and took running starts and then threw the sleds down and leaped onto them in belly-whops and went down the hill screaming happily all the way, one of them imitating a police siren with his mouth. Roger got up off the bench and walked to the crest of the hill and waited for them to climb up again. The boys ignored him. They were talking among themselves, reliving the excitement of the ride down the hill – "Did you see the way I almost hit that tree?" – pulling the sleds behind them on their ropes, glancing back over their shoulders down the hill every now and then, anticipating the next ride down. The one with the mackinaw walked past Roger, took a deep breath and then turned to face the downhill slope again, ready for another run.

"Hi," Roger said.

The kid looked up from under the woolen hat pulled almost clear down over his eyes. He wiped a gloved hand across his running nose, mumbled, "Hi," and turned away.

"The hill looks good," Roger said.

"Mmm," the kid mumbled.

"Can I take a ride?"

"What?"

"Can I take a ride?"

"No," the kid said. He looked up at Roger in brief contempt, took his running start, threw himself onto the sled, and went down the hill again. Roger watched the sled go. He was still angry at the thought of those Persian Lords jumping Amelia, and he was also beginning to get a little apprehensive about what might await him in the police station across the way, nice detective or not. Besides, this snotnosed little kid had no right to talk to him that way. His hands began to twitch again. He waited for the boy to climb back to the top of the hill.

"Didn't your mother teach you any manners?" he asked.

The boy looked up at him from under the hat. The other two boys had stopped some three feet away, and they were staring at Roger curiously, with that odd, belligerent, somewhat frightened look all kids wear when they're expecting crap from a grownup.

"Why don't you get lost, mister?" the kid said from under his hat.

"What's the matter, Tommy?" one of the other boys called.

"This guy's some kind of nut," Tommy said, and he turned away and looked down the hill again.

"All I did was ask you if I could have a ride," Roger said.

"And I told you no."

"What's that sled made of, gold or something?" Roger asked.

"Come on, mister, don't bug me," Tommy said.

"I want a ride!" Roger said suddenly and harshly, and he reached out for the sled, grasping it near the steering mechanism at the top, and pulling it away from Tommy, who clung to it for just a moment before releasing his grip. Tommy was the first to begin yelling, and the two other kids began yelling with him, but Roger was already running, propelled at first by anger and then by a rising exhilaration as he moved toward the brow of the hill and threw the sled down and then hurled two hundred and ten pounds of muscle and bone onto it. The sled made a sound beneath his weight as though it would splinter, but it began sliding immediately and the forward motion eased the strain of the load, gravity pulling the sled down the slope, gaining momentum, two hundred and ten pounds hurtling down the hill, faster, faster, he opened his mouth and yelled like a kid, "Wheeeeeeeeeeeeeeee!" as the sled raced through the falling snow. Behind him, Tommy and the other kids were shouting and ranting and running down the hill after him, he didn't give a damn about them. His eyes were tearing from the wind roaring over the front end of the sled, the big falling flakes made visibility almost impossible, the sled suddenly turned over and he rolled into the snow, the sled flying up into the air, he landing on his side and continuing to roll down the hill, laughing as his coat and his trousers and his face and his hair got covered with snow, and then finally sitting up at the base of the hill, still laughing, and looking up to where Tommy and the others were yelling as they retrieved the sled from a snowbank.

"Call a cop, Tommy," one of the boys said.

"Go on, do it," the other boy said.

Roger got to his feet. Laughing, he glanced over his shoulder once, quickly, and began running.

He wondered how much time had passed. Was it five or ten minutes already, would Amelia be back?

He laughed again. That ride had really been something, he'd left those little yelling bastards clear up at the top of the hill, boy that had really been something. He shook his head in bemused wonder and then suddenly stopped and threw back his head and shouted "Yahoooo!" to the falling snowflakes, and then began running again, out of the park. He stopped running when he reached the sidewalk. He put his hands into his coat pockets and began walking at a very gentlemanly dignified pace. He could remember him and his father and the fun they used to have together before Buddy was born, and even when Buddy was just a little baby. And then of course when Buddy was two, his father had got killed, and it was Roger who'd had to take care of the family, that was what his mother had told him at the time, even though he was only seven years old, *It's you who's the man in the family now, Roger.* Riding down the hill on that kid's sled had been just like it was before his father died, just a lot of fun, that was all. And now, walking like a gentleman on the sidewalk, this was the way it got *after* his father was killed in the train wreck, you couldn't kid around too much anymore, you had to be a man. *It's you who's the man in the family now, Roger.*

Seven years old, he thought.

How the hell can you be a man at seven?

Well, I was always big for my age.

Still.

He shrugged.

He was beginning to feel depressed, he didn't know why. His face was wet with snow, and he wiped one hand over it, and then reached into his pocket for a handkerchief, and wiped his face again. He guessed he should try Amelia. He guessed he should go talk to that detective.

He began making bargains with himself. If the next car that comes down the street is a black Chevrolet, then I'll go to the police station and talk to the detective. But if the next car that comes down is a taxicab, I'll call Amelia. If it's a truck, though, I'll go back to my room and pack my bag and just go home, probably be best anyway, people worrying about me back home. No cars were coming down the street for a while because the snow was so thick, and when one finally did pass, it was a blue Ford convertible, for which he had made no provisions. He said the hell with it and found a phone booth and dialed Amelia's number.

The same woman answered the phone.

"What do you want?" she said.

"This is Roger Broome again," he said. "I want to talk to Amelia."

"Just a minute," the woman said, and then she partially covered the mouthpiece and Roger heard her shout, "'Melia! It's your Mr. Charlie!"

Roger waited.

When Amelia came to the phone, he said immediately, "Who's Mr. Charlie?"

"I'll tell you later. Where are you?"

"I don't know, somewhere near the park."

"Did you want to see me?" Amelia asked.

"Yes."

"I can't come down for a while. I'm helping my mother with the curtains."

"Was that your mother who answered the phone?"

"Yes."

"She sounds very sweet."

"Yes, she's a charmer," Amelia said.

"What did you say you were helping her with?"

"The curtains. She made some new curtains, and we were putting them up."

"Can't she do that alone?"

"No." Amelia paused. "I'll meet you later, if you like."

"All right. When later?"

"An hour?"

"All right. Where?"

"Oh, gee, I don't know. How about the drugstore?"

"Okay, the drugstore," Roger said. "What time is it now?"

"It's about two-twenty, I guess. Let's say three-thirty, to be sure."

"Okay, the drugstore at three-thirty," Roger said.

"Yes. You know where it is, don't you?"

"Sure I do. Where is it?"

Amelia laughed. "On the corner of Ainsley and North Eleventh."

"Ainsley and North Eleventh, right," Roger said.

"Three-thirty."

"Three-thirty, right." Roger paused. "Who's Mr. Charlie?"

"*You're* Mr. Charlie."

"I am?"

Amelia laughed again. "I'll tell you all about it when I see you. I'll give you a course in black-white relations."

"Oh, boy," Roger said.

"And other things," Amelia whispered.

"Okay," Roger said. His heart was pounding. "Three-thirty at the drugstore. I'll go home and put on a clean shirt."

"Okay."

"So long," he said.

"So long," she said.

A squad car was parked at the curb when he got back to the rooming house.

The car was empty. The window near the curb was lowered, and he could hear the police radio going inside. He looked up the steps leading to the front door. Through the glass panels on the door he could see Mrs. Dougherty in conversation with two uniformed policemen.

He was about to turn and walk off in the opposite direction when one of the cops looked through the glass-paneled door directly at him. He couldn't turn and walk away now that he'd been seen, so he walked casually up the steps and kicked snow from his feet on the top step and then opened the door and walked into the vestibule. A radiator was hissing behind the fat cop, who stood with his hands behind his back, the fingers spread toward the heat. Mrs. Dougherty was explaining something to the cops as Roger stepped into the vestibule. ". . . only discovered it half an hour ago when I went down to the basement to put in some laundry, so that was when I called you, hello, Mr. Broome."

"Hello, Mrs. Dougherty," he said. "Is something wrong?"

"Oh, nothing important," she said, and turned back to the policemen as he went past. "It's not that it was new or anything," she said to the fat cop. Roger opened the inner vestibule door. "But I suppose it was worth maybe fifty or sixty dollars, I don't know. What annoys me is that somebody could get into the basement and . . ."

Roger closed the door and went up the steps to his room.

He had just taken off his coat when the knock sounded on his door.

"Who is it?" he said.

"Me. Fook."

"Who?"

"Fook. Fook Shanahan. Open up."

Roger went to the door and unlocked it. Fook was a small, bald, bright-eyed man of about forty-five, wearing a white shirt over which was an open brown cardigan sweater. He was grinning as Roger opened the door, and he stepped into the room with an air of conspiracy, and immediately closed and locked the door behind him.

"Did you see the cops downstairs?" he asked at once.

"Yes," Roger said.

"Something, huh?" Fook said, his eyes gleaming.

"What do they want?"

"Don't you know what happened?"

"No. What?"

"Somebody robbed the bloodsucker."

"Who do you mean?"

"Dougherty, Dougherty, our landlady, who do you think I mean?"

"She's a nice lady," Roger said.

"Oh boy oh boy oh boy oh boy," Fook said. "A nice lady, oh boy oh boy."

"She seems like a nice lady to me," Roger said.

"That's because you've only been here a few days," Fook said. "I've been living in this dump for six years now, *six* years, and I'm telling you she's a bloodsucker and a tightwad and the meanest old bitch who ever walked the earth, that's what I'm telling you."

"Well," Roger said, and shrugged.

"I'm glad they robbed the old bitch."

"What'd they take?"

"Not enough," Fook said. "You got a drink in here?"

"What? No, I'm sorry."

"I'll be right back."

"Where are you going?"

"My room. I've got a bottle in there. Have you got some glasses?"

"Just the one on the sink there."

"I'll bring my own," Fook said, and went out.

Well, Roger thought, I suppose she had to find out it was missing sooner or later. It was just that I didn't expect her to find out so soon. Or maybe I didn't expect her to call the police even if she *did* find out. But she did and she has, and they're downstairs now, so maybe this is as good a time as any to get drunk with Fook. No, I'm supposed to meet Amelia at three-thirty.

I should have been more careful.

Still, at the time, it seemed like the right thing to do.

Maybe it was.

A knock sounded on the door.

"Come in," he said.

It was Fook. He came in carrying a partially filled bottle of bourbon with a water glass turned upside down over the neck of the bottle. He put the bottle down on the dresser and then walked quickly to the sink, where he picked up Roger's glass. He went back to the dresser, put Roger's glass down, lifted the upturned glass from the neck of the bottle, put that one down beside the other and then lifted the bottle.

"Say when," he said.

"I'm not a drinker," Roger said.

"Neither am I," Fook said, and winked and poured half a tumblerful of whiskey.

"That's too much for me," Roger said.

"All right, I'll have this one," Fook said, and began pouring into the other glass.

"That's enough," Roger said.

"Have a little more. We're celebrating."

"What are we celebrating?"

Fook poured another finger of whiskey into Roger's glass and then carried it to him. He extended his own glass and said, "Here's to Mrs. Dougherty's loss, may the old bitch be uncovered."

"Uncovered?"

"By insurance." Fook winked, raised his glass to his lips, and took a healthy swallow of the bourbon. "Also, may this be only the first of a long line of losses to come. May some no-good thief sneak into the lady's basement *tomorrow* night and steal perhaps her washtub, and the *next* night her oil burner, and the *next* night her underwear hanging on a line down there. May all the crooks in this crumby city come to Mrs. Dougherty's basement night after night and pick it clean like a bunch of vultures going over her bones. May loss pile upon loss until the old bitch has nothing left but the clothes on her back, and then may some bold rapist climb through her window one night and do a job on the scrawny wretch, leaving her nary a nightgown to keep her warm. Amen," Fook said, and drained his glass. He poured it full again, almost to the brim. "You're not drinking, my friend," he said.

"I'm drinking," Roger answered, and sipped at the bourbon.

"An icebox," Fook said.

Roger said nothing.

"It strikes me as amusing that anybody would come into Mrs. Dougherty's basement and steal an icebox, I beg your pardon, a *refrig*erator, that has been sitting there for God knows how long gathering dust. It raises a great many questions which to me are both amusing *and* amazing," Fook said.

"Like what?"

"Like number one, how would anyone *know* the old bitch had an icebox, I beg your pardon a *refrig*erator, in the basement? How many times have you been in the basement of this building?"

"I've never been in the basement," Roger said.

"Exactly. I've lived in this crumby dump for six full years, and I've been down there only twice, once to put an old trunk of mine on a shelf and another time when Mother Dougherty fainted at the sight of a rat down there and screamed loud enough to wake the whole building, me included, who went down there to find the scrawny witch spreadeagled on the floor unconscious with her dress up round her skinny ass, a sight to make a man puke, have another drink."

"I haven't finished this one yet."

"So how would anyone know there was a refrigerator down there, that's number one. And if he *did* know about the refrigerator, then he also knew it was a vintage appliance, circa 1939 or '40, and worth perhaps ten dollars, if not less. Why would a man go to the trouble of stealing a decrepit wreck like that? Why, *lifting* the thing alone would be enough to give a man a hernia." Fook poured another drink and then said, "I'm talking about a normal man like myself. A man *your* size could lift it without batting an eyelash."

"Well, I don't know," Roger said, and shrugged.

"In any case," Fook said, "how would anyone *know* it was down there, number one – and number two, why would anyone *want* to steal a piece of garbage worth at most five or six dollars?"

"Maybe he had some need for it," Roger suggested.

"Like what?"

"I don't know," Roger said.

"What, why*ever* he did it, I'm glad he did it. I only wish he'd taken more while he was at it. Isn't it just like that old bitch, though, to go screaming to the cops immediately over a piece of junk like that old refrigerator? She's tying up the whole damn police force over a machine that was worth three or four bucks."

"Well, there were only two cops down there," Roger said.

"Those are the beat cops," Fook said. "In a burglary, they always precede the bulls. You wait and see. The bulls'll be here today asking questions and snooping around, wasting the taxpayers' time and money, and all for a lousy refrigerator that wouldn't bring two and a half bucks on the open market, have another drink."

"Thanks," Roger said, and extended his glass.

9

The knock on the door awakened him.

Fook had left at about a quarter to three, taking the remainder of the bourbon with him. Roger had drunk only the two drinks, but he wasn't used to hard whiskey, and he must have begun dozing shortly afterward. He wondered what time it was now. He couldn't have been asleep too long. He sat up in bed and looked around the room, dazed, and then blinked as the knock sounded again.

"Who is it?" he asked.

"Police," the voice answered.

Police, he thought.

"Just a moment," he said.

It was probably about the refrigerator. Fook had said detectives would come around asking about the refrigerator. He swung his legs over the side of the bed and went to the door. It was unlocked. He twisted the knob and opened the door wide.

Two men were standing in the hallway. One was very tall, and the other was short. The tall one had red hair with a jagged white streak across the right temple.

"Mr. Broome?" the short one said.

"Yes?" Roger answered.

"I'm Detective Willis," the short one said. "This is my partner, Detective Horse. We wonder if we could ask you a few questions."

"Sure, come in," Roger said.

He moved back and away from the door. Willis entered the room first and then Horse – had he said *Horse?* – came in after him and closed the door. Roger sat on the edge of the bed and then indicated the two chairs in the room and said, "Have a seat, won't you?"

Willis sat in the hard-backed chair near the dresser. Horse – his name *couldn't* be Horse – stood just behind the chair, one hand resting on the dresser. They were both wearing heavy overcoats. Willis kept his buttoned. The other one had opened his; he was wearing a plaid sports jacket. Roger could see a leather gun holster clipped to his waist in the opening of the coat and jacket.

"I'm sorry,"' he said, *"what* did you say your name was?"

"Me?"

"Yes. Um-huh."

"Hawes."

Roger nodded.

"H-A-W-E-S," the detective said.

"Oh." Roger smiled. "I thought you said Horse."

"No."

"That would be a funny name. Horse, I mean."

"No, it's Hawes."

"Sure," Roger said.

The room went silent.

"Mr. Broome," Willis said, "we got a list of all the tenants from your landlady, Mrs. Dougherty, and we're just making a routine check through the building. I guess you know a refrigerator was stolen from the basement sometime last night."

"Yes," he said.

"How did you hear about it, Mr. Broome?" Hawes asked.

"Fook told me. Fook Shanahan. He has a room down the hall."

"Fook?" Hawes said.

"I think his real name is Frank Hubert Shanahan, or something like that. Fook is a nickname."

"I see," Hawes said. "When did he tell you about it, Mr. Broome?"

"Oh, I don't know. What time is it now?"

Willis looked at his watch. "Three o'clock."

"About a half-hour ago, I guess. Or maybe fifteen minutes, I don't know. He stopped in to tell me about it, and we had a few drinks."

"But you hadn't known about the refrigerator until he told you, is that right?"

"That's right. Well, actually, I knew something was wrong when I got home a little while ago because I saw Mrs. Dougherty downstairs talking to two policemen."

"But you didn't know exactly *what* was wrong until Mr. Shanahan told you about the refrigerator."

"That's right."

The two detectives looked at him and said nothing. It almost seemed for a moment that they had no further questions. Willis cleared his throat.

"You understand, Mr. Broome," he said, "that this is all routine, and we're in no way implying—"

"Oh, sure," Roger said.

"The logical place to start an investigation, though, is with the tenants of a building, those who would have had access—"

"Oh, sure," Roger said.

"—to the item or items stolen."

"Sure."

The room went silent again.

"Mr. Broome, I wonder if you could tell us where you were last night."

"What time last night?"

"Well, let's start with dinner. Where did you have dinner?"

"Gee, I don't remember," Roger said. "Someplace around here, a little Italian restaurant." He paused. "I'm not too familiar with the city, you see. I don't get in too often. I've only been here a few days this trip."

"Doing what, Mr. Broome?"

"Selling woodenware."

"What's that, Mr. Broome? What kind of woodenware?"

"We've got a little shop up home, we make coffee tables and bowls, spoons, things like that. We sell the stuff to places in the city. That's why I'm here."

"When do you plan to go home?"

"I really should be getting back tonight." Roger shrugged. "I sold all the stuff yesterday. I've really got no reason to hang around."

"Where is that, Mr. Broome? Your home."

"Carey." He paused. "It's near Huddleston," he said automatically.

"Oh, yes," Hawes said.

"You know it?"

"I've skied Mount Torrance," Hawes said.

"You have?"

"Yes. Nice area up there."

"Well, our shop is on 190, just east of Huddleston. The turnoff just before the mountain road."

"Oh, yes," Hawes said.

"How about that?" Roger said, and he smiled. "Small world."

"It sure is," Hawes said, and returned the smile.

"What time would you say you had dinner, Mr. Broome?" Willis asked.

"Must've been about five."

"So early?"

"Well, we eat early back home, I guess I'm used to it." He shrugged.

"What'd you do after dinner?"

"Came back here."

"What time was that?"

"Six-thirty? Around then."

"Did you stay in after that?"

"No."

"Where'd you go?"

"To a bar."

"Where?"

"Right in the neighborhood, oh, no more'n six or seven blocks from here, walking south on Twelfth Street."

"Would you remember the name of the bar?"

"No, I'm sorry. I really went out for a walk. I only stopped in the bar because I was getting kind of chilly. I'm not usually a drinking man."

"But you did have a drink with Mr. Shanahan just a little while ago, didn't you?" Hawes asked.

"Oh, yeah, *that*," Roger said, and laughed. "We were celebrating."

"Celebrating what?"

"Well, I shouldn't even tell you this, you'll get the wrong idea."

"What's that?" Hawes said, smiling.

"Well, Fook doesn't care too much for Mrs. Dougherty, you know. He was glad somebody stole her old refrigerator." Roger laughed again. "So he wanted to have a few drinks to celebrate."

"You don't think *he* stole it, do you?" Willis said.

"Who? Fook? No." Roger shook his head. "Oh, no, he wouldn't do anything like that. He was just glad it happened, that's all. No. Listen, I don't mean to get Fook in trouble by what I said. He's a very nice person. He's not a thief, I can tell you that."

"Mm-huh," Willis said. "What time did you leave the bar, Mr. Broome?"

"Midnight? I don't know. About then."

"Do you have a watch?"

"No."

"Then you're not sure it was midnight."

"It must've been around then. I was pretty sleepy. I usually get pretty sleepy around that time."

"Were you alone?" Hawes asked.

"Yes," Roger said, and looked at the detectives squarely and wondered if they could tell he had just lied to them for the first time.

"What'd you do when you left the bar?"

"Came back here," Roger said. That was true, anyway. He *had* come back to the room.

"And then what?"

"I went to bed." That was true, too.

"Did you go right to sleep?"

"Well, not right off." He was still telling the truth. More or less.

"When *did* you fall asleep?" Hawes asked.

"Oh, I don't really remember. A half-hour, an hour. It's hard to tell just when you drop off, you know."

"Mmm," Willis said, "it is. Did you hear anything strange while you were in bed trying to fall asleep?"

"What do you mean, strange?"

"Any strange noises."

"Well, what kind of noises?"

"Anything out of the ordinary," Hawes said.

"No, I didn't hear anything."

"Anything wake you during the night?"

"No."

"You didn't hear any noises in the street outside, you know, maybe men's voices, or the sound of someone struggling with a heavy load, anything like that?"

"No, I didn't."

"Or something being dragged or pulled?"

"No. This is the third floor," Roger said. "Be pretty hard to hear anything like that, even if I wasn't asleep." He paused. "I'm a pretty sound sleeper." He paused again. "Excuse me, but would you know what time it is?"

Willis looked at his watch. "Three-ten," he said.

"Thank you."

"Do you have an appointment, Mr. Broome?"

"Yeah, I'm supposed to meet somebody."

"What do you suppose that refrigerator was worth?" Hawes asked suddenly.

"I don't know," Roger said. "I never saw it."

"Have you ever been down in the basement of this building?"

"No," Roger said.

"Mrs. Dougherty says it was worth about fifty dollars," Willis said. "Do you agree with her?"

"I never saw it," Roger said, "so I couldn't say. Fook says it wasn't worth more than a few dollars."

"The only reason we bring up the value," Willis said, "is that it would make a difference in the charge."

"The charge?"

"Yes, the criminal charge. If the value was under twenty-five dollars, it would be petit larceny. That's only a misdemeanor."

"I see," Roger said.

"If the crime's committed at night, and the property is taken from the *person* of another," Willis went on, "that's automatically grand larceny. But if it was taken from a dwelling place . . ." Willis paused. "Somebody's house, you know?"

"Yes?"

"Yes, and at *night* also, then the value has to be more than twenty-five dollars for it to be grand larceny."

"Oh," Roger said.

"Yeah. Grand larceny's a felony, you know. You can get up to ten years on a grand larceny conviction."

"Is that right?" Roger said. "For a measly twenty-five dollars? Boy!" He shook his head.

"Oh, sure," Willis said. He looked at Hawes. "You got any questions, Cotton?"

"Are those the only windows?" Hawes asked.

"Those?" Roger said. "Yes, they're the only ones."

"You don't have any facing on the back yard?"

"No."

"I just can't see anybody hauling that heavy refrigerator all the way out to the front of the building," Hawes said. "A car or a truck must have backed into the alley to the basement door. That's what I think." He shrugged. "Well, Mr. Broome wouldn't have heard it, anyway. His windows face the front."

"That's right," Roger said.

Willis sighed. "You've been very co-operative, Mr. Broome. Thank you very much."

"I hope we haven't kept you from your appointment," Hawes said.

"No, I'm supposed to meet her at three-thirty," Roger said.

"Thanks again," Willis said.

"Glad to help," Roger said. He walked them to the door. "Will you be needing anything else from me?"

"No, I don't think so," Hawes said. He turned to Willis. "Hal?"

"I don't think so, Mr. Broome. I hope you understand we *had* to make a routine check of all the—"

"Oh, sure," Roger said.

"Chances are this was a neighborhood junkie," Hawes said.

"Or a kid. Sometimes it's kids," Willis said.

"We get a lot of little thefts," Hawes said. "Not much we can do about them unless we're lucky enough to turn up a witness."

"Or sometimes we'll catch some guy, oh, maybe six months from now – on something else, you understand – and he'll tell us all about having swiped a refrigerator from a basement back in February. That's the way it goes." Willis smiled. "We try to keep up with it."

"Well, I wish you luck," Roger said. He opened the door.

"As far as you're concerned though," Hawes said, "you can forget all about it. Go home, stay a few days, entirely up to you. We won't be bothering you any further."

"Well, thank you," Roger said.

"Thank *you* for your time, sir," Hawes said.

"Thank you," Willis said.

They both went out. Roger closed the door behind them. He waited until he could no longer hear their footsteps, and then he locked the door.

Molly's scarf was in the bottom drawer of his dresser.

10
───

They had come back to the room at a little past midnight, coming quietly up the steps to the third floor, walking past Fook's apartment, and then pausing silently outside Roger's room as he searched for his key and unlocked the door. They stepped inside, and he closed the door behind them, shutting out the light from the hallway. They stood in darkness for several seconds while he groped for the light switch just inside the door. When the light went on, Molly seemed surprised that he hadn't tried to kiss her in the dark.

"This is very nice," she said, looking around the room. "Very nice."

"Thank you," he said. They were both whispering. No one had seen them come into the building, and no one knew she was here in the room with him, but they whispered nonetheless, as though the entire building knew they were alone together, as though each and every one of the tenants was eavesdropping.

"It's not too small at all," Molly said.

"No, it's all right. Plenty of room for just one person."

"That's right," Molly said. She took off her coat and scarf and put them over the arm of the easy chair. "Well," she said, "this is really nice. Maybe I'll move. Do you think there are any vacancies?"

"Gee, I wouldn't know," Roger said. "But actually, this room'll be empty tomorrow, you know. I'll be going back to Carey tomorrow."

"That's right," she said, "I almost forgot."

"Yeah," Roger said, and nodded.

She sat on the edge of the bed. "It's too bad you're going back so soon," she said.

"Well, there's really no reason for me to stay any longer, you know. My mother's expecting me, so really I have to—"

"Oh, sure," Molly said. "This is very comfortable. The bed."

"Yeah, it's not a bad bed," Roger said.

"It seems very comfortable. I hate lumpy mattresses, don't you?"

"Yes."

"Or ones that are too soft."

"This one is pretty good, actually," Roger said. "You get a good night's sleep on it."

Molly leaned back suddenly, swinging her legs up on to the bed and stretching her arms over her head. "Mmmm," she said, "this sure feels good." She smiled at Roger. "I'd better be careful or I'll fall asleep."

"Well," Roger said, and smiled.

"Do you know what gets me about looking for a job?" she asked.

"No what?"

"My feet. They're killing me. Would you mind if I took off my shoes?"

"No, not at all."

"I'll be leaving in a minute," she said, sitting up, and crossing her legs, and taking off first one high-heeled pump and then the other. "But while I'm here I might as well take advantage of the opportunity, huh?"

"Sure," Roger said.

"Ahhhhh," she said, and wiggled her toes. "Ahhhh, that feels good." She put her arms behind her, the elbows locked, and stared up at him. "Aren't you going to take off your coat?" she asked.

"What? Oh. Oh, I thought—"

"I've got a few minutes," she said. "We don't have to rush right out again. I mean, not unless you want to."

"No, no," Roger said.

"Besides, it feels so good with these shoes off," she said, and smiled.

"Just make yourself comfortable," he said. He took off his coat and went to the closet with it. "I'm sorry I can't offer you a drink or anything, but I haven't got any in the room."

"Oh, that's all right," she said. "I don't drink much anyway."

He hung his coat on a hanger, and then took Molly's from the chair and put it over his on the same hanger. He looped her scarf over the hanger hook, and put everything back in the closet. "If the liquor stores were open," he said, "I'd go down for some. But I think—"

"No, I don't mind. I hope I didn't give you the impression that I drink a lot."

"No, I didn't get that impression."

"Because I usually don't, except socially. It's been so depressing, though, marching around this city and not being able to find anything. It can get really depressing, I mean it."

"I can imagine," Roger said.

"Boy, it's good to get out of those shoes," she said, and she leaned back, propping herself on one elbow so she could watch him. She smiled. "Is that the only light in here?" she asked.

"What?"

"The light. It's kind of harsh."

"There's a lamp on the dresser," Roger said. "Would you like it better if I—"

"Please. It's just that lying back like this, I'm looking right up into the light there."

"I'll just put this one on," Roger said, and went to the dresser. He turned on the small lamp, and then flicked out the overhead light. "How's that?"

"Better," she said. "Much better."

She closed her eyes. The room was silent.

"Mmm," she said. She stretched and then leaned back and said, "I really better be careful or I *will* fall asleep."

"It's early yet," Roger said.

"The night is young, huh?" she said, and giggled. "Be funny if your landlady walked in here tomorrow morning and found a strange girl in your bed, wouldn't it?"

"Well, she never walks in," Roger said. "Nobody ever bothers you here."

"You mean you've had strange girls in here before?"

"No, I didn't mean *that*," Roger said.

The girl giggled. "I know. I'm teasing." She opened her eyes and looked at him solemnly. "I'm a big tease."

Roger said nothing.

"Though not that way," Molly said. She paused. "Do you know what I mean?"

"I'm not sure."

She smiled briefly, and then sat up suddenly, swung her legs over the side of the bed and said, "I'm getting your bedspread all wrinkled. Your landlady won't like that a bit. I mean, she may not object to girls in your room, but I'll bet she doesn't like a wrinkled bedspread or lipstick all over the pillow."

"Well, she's never found any lipstick on the pillow," Roger said, and smiled.

"No, and we're not going to *give* her any to find, either." She padded to the dresser in her stockinged feet, opened her bag, took out a Kleenex, and leaned close to the mirror. She wiped off her lipstick quickly, and then put the tissue back into her bag. "There," she said, and smiled at him. He was beginning to dislike the way she was making herself so comfortable, the way she was moving around the room so easily and naturally, as if she owned the place. He watched her as she went to the bed and pulled back the bedspread and fluffed up the pillows. "There," she said again, and sat on the edge of the bed.

She smiled at him.

"Well," she said, "here we are."

The room was silent again. She stared at him levelly.

"Do you want to make love to me?" she asked.

"That's not why I brought you up here," he said quickly.

The smile was still on her face, but it seemed to have weakened somewhat, as though his words had embarrassed her, or injured her. He didn't want to make her feel bad, and he certainly didn't want to hurt her. But at the same time, he didn't particularly feel like getting involved with her, not in that way, not with a girl as plain as she was.

"I mean, I didn't bring you up here to take advantage of you," he said gallantly. "I only wanted to show you the room because you said maybe you—"

"I know."

"—might want to move if it was a good-sized room."

"It's a good-sized room," she said.

"But, believe me, I wasn't planning—"

"And it's a very comfortable bed," she said.

"—on taking advantage of you, if that's what you thought."

"That's not what I thought."

"Good because—"

"I didn't think you'd take advantage of me."

"Good because—"

"It wouldn't be taking advantage of me," Molly said flatly.

He looked at her silently.

"I have a lot to give," she said.

He did not answer her.

She stood up suddenly and pulled the flaps of her blouse out of the black skirt. Slowly, she began unbuttoning the blouse. There was something ludicrous about her performance. She stood alongside the bed with her head erect, the flaming red hair burnished in the glow of the single lamp on the dresser, her hands slowly unbuttoning the blouse, staring at him, her eyes serious and solemn in the plain face, the fake eyelashes, the penciled eyebrows, the pointed fake breasts in the padded bra slowly revealed as her hands worked the buttons at the front of the blouse. She threw the blouse and the bra onto the bed behind her and then unzipped the skirt and stepped out of it. He felt nothing. He looked at her as she took off the rest of her clothing and moved toward him, an oddly shaped woman with tiny breasts, large bursting nipples, wide in the hips, far too wide in the behind, thick in the thigh and ankle, there was nothing exciting about her, nothing attractive about her, he felt no desire at all for her. She moved into his arms. She was very warm.

They whispered in the night.

"I sometimes feel all alone in the world," she said.

"I do, too."

"I don't mean alone just because I have no parents, or because Doris went off to Hawaii, not that way, not that kind of alone. I mean *really* alone."

"Yes."

"Alone inside," she said.

"Yes."

"Even when I'm surrounded by people. Even when there are people everywhere around me, like in that bar tonight, before I met you."

"I almost didn't come over to you."

"Because I'm not pretty," she said.

"You're beautiful," he said.

"No, please . . ."

"Yes."

"Please don't lie to me."

"You're the most beautiful girl I've ever known in my life."

"Ahhh," she said.

"Yes."

"Ahhh."

"Molly, you're beautiful," he whispered.

"I'm a good lay, is what you mean?"

"Yes, you're a good lay, but—"

"Mmmm, and that's it."

"No."

"Yes, that's all of it. Roger, please, I *know*."

"How do you know?"

She shrugged. "You're a man. I know what men want."

"That's not all I want," he said.

She moved closer to him. She buried her face in his shoulder. Her lips vibrated against his skin as she spoke. "You're the only man who ever told me I was beautiful," she whispered. She paused for a long time. "Roger?"

"Yes?"

"Tell me."

"What?"

"Tell me again."

"What?"

"Don't make me beg."

"You're beautiful," he said.

"You embarrass me," she whispered.

"I want to hold you," he said.

"Ahhh."

"I want to kiss you."

She moved into his arms. "What's this?" she whispered.

"Nothing."

"Nothing?" she whispered. "Oh, it's something. Oh, I can *tell* it's something. Oh, I'm *sure* it's something. Oh yes. Yes, yes, that's it, yes."

"Molly, Molly . . ."

"Ooooh, kiss you," she whispered. "Ooooh, hold you, kiss you, kiss you."

"Beautiful," he whispered, "beautiful."

Her scarf was in the bottom drawer of the dresser. He walked to the dresser now and opened the drawer and took out the scarf and held it in his hands. It was a pale-blue scarf, light, almost transparent, made of nylon, he supposed, he didn't really know. It was the only article of her clothing left behind in the apartment. He had discovered it afterward near the closet door, he supposed it had dropped from the hanger when he'd gone to get her coat.

He looked at the scarf and wondered what he should do with it. Suppose those two detectives came back to ask more questions, suppose they search the room? Well, no, they needed a warrant to do that, didn't they? Or did they? Suppose they came back while he was out with Amelia? He'd have to get rid of the scarf, that was for sure. Or else, he could simply take it with him when he went to the police station to tell them about it, yes, that would make things a lot simpler, sure. He would go there with the scarf and that would make it easier to talk about Molly. He would ask for the detective with the deaf-mute wife. He hadn't really liked any of the others, not Parker in the luncheonette, and not those two who had just been here, either, although they weren't too bad – still, he preferred the one with the beautiful wife.

Amelia, he thought.

I'd better get rid of this scarf, first, he thought, and wondered how he should do it.

I suppose I can cut it into little pieces and flush it down the toilet. That would probably be best. Only trouble is I haven't got a scissors, nor even a knife. I can tear it in my hands, I suppose.

He looked at the scarf again.

He grasped it firmly in both hands and tried to rip it, but it wouldn't start because there was a tight, strong welting all around the edge of it. He put the end of the scarf into his mouth and tore the welting with his teeth, and then ripped it in half along a jagged line, and then decided throwing it down the toilet wouldn't be any good. Suppose the damn toilet got stuffed, that would be just great.

He went to the dresser. A book of matches was lying in the ash tray near the lamp. He picked up the matches and went to the bathroom with the scarf. He struck a match, and then held the scarf hanging from one hand over the toilet bowl, almost touching the water. He brought the other hand, with the lighted match, toward the dangling end of the scarf and was about to set fire to it when he heard someone calling him.

He recognized Mrs. Dougherty's voice, and wondered how in hell she had known he was about to set fire to a scarf in her bathroom. He shook out the match and dropped it into the bowl, and went back to his room. There he wadded the scarf into a ball and put it into the bottom dresser drawer again.

Mrs. Dougherty was still yelling his name in the hallway. "Mr. Broome, Mr. Broome, Mr. Broome!"

He went to the door and opened it.

"Yes," he said, "what is it?"

"Mr. Broome, there's a phone call for you."

"What?" he said.

"The telephone," she said.

"Who is it?" he asked.

"I don't know. It's a woman."

My mother, he thought, and wondered how she had got the number.

"I'll be right down," he said. He closed the door, went back into the room, opened the bottom dresser drawer, and shoved the blue scarf all the way to the back of it. Then he closed the drawer and went out into the hall. The pay phone was on the wall of the first-floor landing. Mrs. Dougherty was standing near the phone, waiting for him.

"Did the detectives talk to you?" she asked.

"Yes," he said.

"They were nice boys, weren't they?"

"Yes, they seemed very nice. Are they still in the building?"

"They're talking to Mrs. Ingersol on the fifth floor."

"Then they're almost finished, I guess," Roger said. He took the receiver from her hand. "Thank you," he said.

"Do you think they'll get my refrigerator back?" Mrs. Dougherty asked.

"I hope so," Roger said, and he smiled and put the receiver to his ear. "Hello?"

Mrs. Dougherty smiled and nodded and started down the steps to her apartment on the ground floor just as the voice at his ear said, "Roger, is it you? This is Amelia."

"Amelia? How – *Amelia*, did you say?"

"I was hoping you hadn't left yet."

"No, I'm still here. What time is it?"

"It's three-twenty. I was afraid you might have left."

"Why? What's the matter?"

"I'm going to be a little late."

"Why?"

"Something unexpected."

"Like what?"

"I'll tell you when I see you."

"How late will you be?"

"Four-thirty?" she said. "Is that *too* late?"

"No, that's fine."

"Same place?"

"Yes, outside the drugstore."

"Aren't you curious?"

"About what?"

"About how I got your phone number?"

"Yeah, how about that?" he said.

"Some memory, huh?"

"What do you mean? I never gave you the number here. I don't even know the number here myself."

"Aha," she said.

"How'd you get it?"

"Agnes Dougherty," she said.

"What?"

"The name on one of your valentines. The cards. Remember?"

"Oh, yeah, that's right," he said, smiling.

"Your landlady."

"That's right."

"Or so you said."

"She is. I'll introduce you to her, if you like."

"When?"

"Later."

"Sure," Amelia said. "You can't kid me. She's some big old blond broad you're living with, you can't kid me."

"No," he said, grinning, "she's my landlady."

"Hey, you know something?"

"What?"

"I like you."

"I like you, too, Amelia."

"Good."

"Four-thirty, okay?"

"Yes." She paused. "Roger?"

"Yes?"

"I *more* than just like you."

"Okay."

"Okay, look at the brushoff," she said, and laughed.

"What brushoff?"

"You're supposed to say you *more* than just like me, too."

"I do."

"Ah, such enthusiasm," Amelia said. "Okay, I'll see you later. You think you can keep out of trouble between now and four-thirty?"

"I'll try," Roger said.

"Yeah, try," she answered. "Try real hard."

"I will."

"You're very cute," she said, and hung up.

He stood grinning at the receiver for a moment, and then replaced it on the cradle.

He went up to the apartment then and burned Molly's scarf and flushed the ashes down the toilet, and then opened the bathroom window to let out the smoke.

11

___

The snow had stopped.

There was a silence to the city.

There was a clean silence that reached somewhere deep inside him the moment he stepped outside and began walking toward the garage. His footfalls were hushed, his breath plumed out ahead of him in visible silence, there was the normal hush of late afternoon, the whispering minutes before twilight, intensified now by the cushion of snow, deepened, the gentle rhythmic sound of skid chains, muffled. I'll have to put chains on the truck, he thought.

The thought came into his mind with a suddenness that was totally surprising because it carried with it the idea of going home; if he was planning to put chains on the truck, then he was planning to *use* the truck, to go someplace with it, and the only place he would take the truck would be home to Carey. He knew that was what he ought to do, put chains on the truck, and then call his mother and tell her he was leaving the city, probably be home this evening sometime, that was the thing to do. But there were also a few other things he knew he should do, or at least *felt* he ought to do, and suddenly everything seemed mixed up, suddenly the silence of the city was irritating to him rather than soothing. He knew he should call his mother and then head for home, and he also knew he should go to the police station and talk to that detective with the deaf-and-dumb wife, but he also knew he should meet Amelia at four-thirty because Amelia was the most beautiful woman he had ever known in his life and he had the feeling he should not allow her to get away from him, colored or otherwise. It still bothered him that she was colored, but not as much as it had bothered him earlier. He thought suddenly of Molly and how she had become beautiful all at once at two o'clock last night, but that was something different, that wasn't the way he felt about Amelia, that was something entirely different. Amelia really *was* beautiful, everything *about* her was beautiful – the way she looked, and the soft way she had of speaking, and that fine bright quickness about her, and the way she kissed, she really was a beautiful girl. His mother certainly wouldn't be able to kid about her the way she had kidded about all the ugly ducklings he took out in Carey, not by a long shot. It troubled him that he would be seeing Amelia when he knew he should be going home to his mother. After all, somebody had to take care of her now that his father was dead. But at the same time he really *did* want to see Amelia, to *know* Amelia, and this frightened him because at some point last night when he was in bed with Molly he had begun to think that he would really like to know her, too, and not just as somebody to take to bed, some ugly girl to take to bed, but as a beautiful person secret and private inside this very plain outside shell. That was when he supposed he began to get angry with her, that was when he supposed the argument started.

He did not want an argument to start with Amelia, and yet he had the feeling that if he met her later on he would argue with her, too, and all because he knew he should be home in Carey taking care of his mother and not getting involved with pretty girls in the city, especially pretty girls who were colored. He didn't see how he could get involved with a colored girl. Hell, he wouldn't even have asked her to take the afternoon off if he'd thought there was the slightest possibility of getting involved with someone who was colored. But then he hadn't thought he'd get involved with anyone as ugly as Molly, either, until he found himself really wondering about her and looking at her as if she was beautiful, and really believing she was beautiful, that was what had caused all the trouble.

So the thing he should do, he supposed, was to go to the police and tell them about Molly, and then go home to Carey. No, that wouldn't exactly work, either. Going to the police would keep him away from Amelia, would keep him from getting involved with her, or of getting angry with her the way he'd got angry with Molly, but it would also keep him away from his mother in Carey, well, maybe that wouldn't be so bad. He was suddenly very confused.

Look, he told himself, I'd better

Look, I think the police

Well, look, let me put the chains on the truck for now. Let me do that, and I'll work out the rest.

I mean, what the hell, she's sitting all the way up there, *somebody's* got to take care of her.

Buddy's just a kid.

Somebody's got to take care of her.

The garage attendant was a short fellow with curly black hair and very white teeth. He was wearing an old World War II flight jacket, the same jacket he'd been wearing the other day when Roger pulled in with the truck loaded.

"Hey," he said, "how you doing?"

"Fine," Roger said. "I just thought I'd stop by to put my chains on. I wasn't expecting this kind of snow."

"Something, huh?" the attendant said. "You could freeze your ass off in this city."

"It gets a lot colder up where I live," Roger said.

"Yeah, where you live?" the attendant asked, grinning. "Siberia? Or Lower Slobovia, which?"

Roger didn't know where Lower Slobovia was, so he just said, "Well, it gets pretty cold up there, believe me."

"I see you got rid of all your stuff," the attendant said.

"Yes. I sold it all yesterday."

"That's good, huh?"

"Yes, that's fine," Roger said.

"Late last night?" the attendant said.

"What?"

"That when you sold it?"

"No. No," Roger said. He stared at the attendant, puzzled. "I don't think I get you."

"The benches and stuff, the bowls. You know?"

"Yes?"

"Did you sell them late last night?"

"No. I sold the last of them yesterday afternoon sometime. Downtown."

"Oh."

"Why?"

"Oh, nothing," the attendant said. "Only I must've been gone when you came back, and the night man said you took the truck out again later."

"He did?"

"Yeah. He only told me about it because he wasn't sure he should have let it go out, you know, so he was just checking. To make sure he didn't pull a boner. You know?"

"Mmm," Roger said.

"That was pretty late."

"Yes."

"Three o'clock in the morning." The attendant grinned. His teeth were very white. "Or *early*, depending how you look at it, huh? Three o'clock could be very early."

"It *was* early," Roger said. "I had to carry some stuff."

"More of that wood stuff, huh?"

"No," Roger said quickly. "I . . ." He paused. "A man offered me a job. Yesterday afternoon, while I was downtown."

"Oh? Yeah?"

"Hauling some vegetables for him. From the market."

"Hey, that's a lucky break, huh?" the attendant said.

"Yes, I had to take them over the bridge to the other side of the river. Over there. I had to pick them up at the market."

"Downtown, huh?"

"Yes."

"Where? Down near Cummings?"

"What?"

"Cummings Street? The market down there?"

"Yes, the market."

"Sure, they open very early," the attendant said.

"Yes, I had to be there at three-thirty to make the pickup. And then I had to drive all way to the bridge and across the river."

"All the way to Lower Slobovia, huh?" the attendant said, and laughed. "Well, you're a hard worker, that's good. I admire guys who are willing to work to earn a buck. Christ knows I work hard enough. Your truck's over there near that '62 Caddy. You want a hand with the chains?"

"No, I think I can manage. Thanks."

"Don't mention it. You want the keys?"

"I don't know. How much space have I got?"

"I think you can get them on without moving it. But if you need the keys, they're right here on the board."

"Okay," Roger said, and walked to where the truck was parked at the far end of the garage. He glanced at the Cadillac alongside it, and then lowered the tailgate and climbed up into the back. His chains were in the right-hand forward corner of the truck, up near the cab, wrapped in burlap. He always dried them carefully each time he took them off, and then wrapped them in burlap so they wouldn't rust. He picked up the chains and was heading for the rear of the truck again when he saw the stain.

The stain was no larger than a half-dollar, circular, with a sawtooth edge and tiny spatters radiating from the rim.

That must've been from her nose, he thought.

He climbed down from the truck and dropped the chains near the left rear wheel, and then looked around the garage and saw a hose attached to a faucet, and alongside that a can. He glanced toward the front of the garage to check if the attendant was anywhere in sight. He walked to the hose and picked up the can and filled it about a quarter full, and then went back to the truck again. He put the can down near the tailgate. From under the front seat he took an old soiled rag, and he carried that with him to the back of the truck again, where he dipped it into the can of water.

He was very lucky. The blood had dripped onto one of the metal strips running the length of the truck, and had not fallen on the wooden floor of the body. It might have been difficult to remove a bloodstain from a wooden floor. Instead, he wiped the blood off the metal in as long as it took him to pass the wet cloth over it.

He rinsed the cloth out several times until it was clean. The water in the can showed hardly any discoloration, hardly any trace of red or even pink. He poured the water down the open drain near the hose attachment, and rinsed the can out several times.

He went back to the truck and put on the chains.

She was waiting for him outside the drugstore.

She spotted him as he turned the corner, and waved immediately and came running up to him.

"Hi," she said, and looped her arm through his. "You're late."

"I haven't got a watch," he said.

"Well, you're not *too* late, it's only about twenty to. Where were you?"

"Putting chains on my truck."

"Fine thing. Guy'd rather put chains on his truck than be with me."

"No, I'd rather be with you, Amelia."

"There are times, you know," she said, smiling, "when I think you have absolutely no sense of humor."

"None at all," he said, and returned her smile.

"So look at me," she said.

He looked at her.

"Well?"

"You changed your coat."

"This is my best coat. I only wear it on very special occasions. The collar is genuine fitch."

"What's fitch?"

"An animal."

"I know that, but—"

"You've never heard of rat fitch?"

"No."

"It's a close relative to rat fink. There are millions of rat finks in this city, but only very few rat fitches. One of them voluntarily donated his life to make a collar for my coat. Stunning, isn't it?"

"Stunning."

"Also, look." She unbuttoned the coat and held it open, her arms widespread. She was wearing a black skirt and a V-necked black sweater cut very low over her breasts. A string of tiny pearls circled her throat, startling white against her dark skin. "Very sexy number, huh?" she said.

"Very sexy."

"Also," she said, and winked, "black bra underneath. Men like black bras, huh?"

"Yes."

"Now, if you don't mind, I'll close the coat before I freeze everything I own, you don't mind, huh?" She closed the coat and buttoned it. "Brrrr, my hands are freezing." She put her left hand into the pocket of her coat, and then entwined the fingers of her right hand in his, and put both their hands into the pocket of his coat. "There," she said, "nice and cozy and warm, I can't stop talking, what the hell is it about you?"

"I'm a good listener," he said, "that's what it is."

"Yeah, how come?"

"In my house, I listen all the time."

"To who?"

"My mother."

"Mmm, mothers, don't talk about mothers. You should hear the lecture I got this afternoon."

"About what?"

"About *you*, what do you think?"

"Why?"

"Man, you de white man. You Mr. Charlie." Amelia giggled.

"Is that what Mr. Charlie is?"

"Well, sure. You Mr. Charlie, and you de ofay, and you sometimes just De Man, although De Man is also sometimes a plain old pusher, but he usually a *white* man, too, so I guess you synonymous, is that de word, man?"

"I don't know."

"It went on for hours, I thought she'd never stop."

"Is that why you couldn't make it at three-thirty?"

"That's why. She had my brother come over to talk to me. He's married and has two kids, and he drives a cab. So she called his garage and asked them to tell him to call his mother as soon as he checked in. He doesn't check in 'til about four, so I knew I'd be stuck there 'til at least a quarter after, his garage is on Twentieth, near the river. Anyway, he got to the house at twenty-five after, and I talked to him for about three seconds flat and then left."

"What'd he say?"

"He said, 'Amelia, you are out of your head.'"

"What did you say?"

"I said, 'Louis, go to hell.'"

"And then what?"

"He said if he caught us together he would cut off your balls."

"Will he really?"

"Louis is a fat happy cab driver who wouldn't know where to *find* your balls because he hasn't had any of his own since the day he married Mercedes in 1953, do you mind my talking this way?"

"What way?"

"Well, I swear a lot, I guess. Although, actually, I'm only repeating what my brother said. Anyway, I told him to go to hell again, and I walked out."

"I don't mind," Roger said.

"What do you mean?"

"Your swearing a lot." He paused. "We never swear in our house. My mother's pretty strict about that."

"Well, the hell with mothers, huh?" she said.

He felt a momentary spark of anger, and then he simply nodded. "What would you like to do?" he asked.

"Walk a little. I love snow. It makes me stand out."

"You stand out anyway," he said.

"Do I?"

"Yes."

"You say very sweet things, sweet-talker. Mother warned me. Oops, excuse me, we're not supposed to talk about mothers."

"Where would you like to walk?"

"Any place, who cares?"

He didn't like the way Amelia said that, but he told himself not to get angry. She was, after all, allowing him to assume the responsibility. She was saying she would follow him wherever he wanted to go. She was allowing him to be the man. It's *you* who's the man in the family now, Roger. He did not want to get angry with her the way he had got angry with Molly last night. Last night, he had begun to get angry with Molly when she started telling him about that man in Sacramento. He told himself later that she should not have begun talking about another man when she was in bed with him. That was what had got him so angry. But he had the feeling, even while he was trying to convince himself, that the *real* reason for his sudden anger had nothing at all to do with the man in Sacramento. He couldn't quite understand it, but he knew somehow he had got angry with Molly only because he was beginning to like her so much. That was the part he couldn't understand.

"There's been only one other man in my life who mattered," Molly had said last night. "Before you. Only one other."

He said nothing. They were lying naked on the bed in his room, and he felt spent and exhausted and content, listening to the February wind howling outside, wind always sounded more fierce in the dead of night, especially in a strange city.

"I met him when I was twenty, just a year after my mother passed away, do you mind my talking about this?"

"No," he said, because he really didn't mind yet, he wasn't angry with her yet, he liked her very much. He kept thinking about how his mother would make fun of him for bringing home another ugly duckling and of how he would say, "Why Mom, she's beautiful, what's the matter with you?"

"It was the first job after secretarial school, I really didn't know how to handle either the job *or* him. I never went out much with boys, boys hardly ever asked me out. I think I'd been kissed maybe half a dozen times in my life, and once a boy touched my breast when we were decorating the high school gym for a senior dance. I didn't even go to the dance because no one asked me." She paused. "His name was Theodore Michelsen, he had a brother who was a priest in San Diego. He was married and had two children, a little boy and a little girl, their pictures were on his desk. His wife's picture was on his desk, too, in the same frame, one of those frames that open like a book. His wife was on the left-hand side and his two children on the right. Do you mind my talking about this?"

"No," he said. He didn't mind. He was lying with his arm around her, and her lips close to his ear, staring up at the ceiling and thinking how soft her voice was and how warm and smooth she felt in his arms.

"I don't know how it started," Molly said. "I guess one day he just kissed me, and I guess it was the first time I'd ever really been kissed by anyone, I mean really kissed by a man. And then, I don't know, we just began, not that same day, but a few days later, I guess it was a Friday, I guess it was after everyone had gone home. We made love in his office, look, I know you don't want to hear this."

"No, that's all right," he said.

"We did it every day," she said. "I loved it," she said.

That was when he got angry.

He could hear the snow squeaking under his shoes. Amelia held his arm tightly and said, "We're heading for the river, did you know that?"

"No, I didn't."

"What were you thinking?"

"Thinking?" He shook his head. "Nothing."

"Oh, *yes* you were. Just a few minutes ago. You were a million miles away."

"I was thinking I ought to be getting home."

"I must be a real fascinating girl. You're walking with me, and all you can think about is getting home."

"I didn't mean it that way. It's just my mother's all alone up there. Not really alone, I have a younger brother, but you know."

"Yes," Amelia said.

"It's just I'm the man in the family."

"Yes."

"That's all." He shrugged.

"Still, you *are* here," she said. "You *are* with me."

"Yes, I know. I'm sorry. I shouldn't have—"

"I mean, I *am* a fairly good-looking girl, you know, what with my rat-fitch collar and my sexy black sweater." She grinned. "I mean well, you know, a girl doesn't get all dressed up so some guy can think of running back home to Gulchwater Flats."

"Carey," he said, and smiled.

"Right?"

"Right."

"So what do you intend to do about it, look, there's ice on the river, you could probably walk clear across to the other shore."

"There wasn't any ice last night," he said.

"What?"

"Nothing."

"Were you here last night?"

"Well, I meant early this morning. About three o'clock."

"What were you doing here at three in the morning?"

"I wasn't *here*."

"But you said—"

"I had to make a delivery."

"A delivery?"

"Yes. Vegetables."

"Oh."

"So I had a chance to see the river, that's all I meant."

"And there was no ice."

"No. I guess it must have been a little above freezing."

"It felt a lot colder than that yesterday," she said.

"Yes, it did. But the river wasn't frozen."

"Okay," she said. "You want to walk across to the other side?"

"No."

"Vegetables, did you say?"

"Yes, I got the job from a man, to pick up these vegetables and deliver them. With my truck."

"Oh." She nodded, and then said, "How cold do you think it is now?"

"I don't know. In the twenties, I'd guess."

"Are you cold?"

"A little."

"My feet are cold," she said.

"You want to go someplace? For coffee or something?"

"I thought you had a room," she said.

"I do."

"Let's go there."

They walked in silence for several moments. The river was frozen from shore to shore. The bridge uptown spanned the ice, rose from the ice as if it were a silvery spidery extension of it.

"I don't want to hurt you," he said.

"Hurt me? How can you hurt me?"

"I don't know," he said, and shrugged.

"Honey," she said, "I've been had by experts."

"Amelia, there are . . ." He shook his head.

"Yes? What?"

"There are a lot of things . . ." He shook his head again.

"What is it, Roger?"

"I should do."

"What?"

"Things I should do."

"Yes, like what?"

"Well . . . I want to be with you."

"Yes, I want to be with you, too."

"I want to kiss you again, I've been wanting to ever since—"

"Yes, yes—"

"But I don't want to hurt you."

"But, baby, how can you possibly—"

"I just want you to know that."

She stared at him silently. At last she said, "You're a funny person." She reached up and kissed him swiftly and then moved back from him and looked into his face and said, "Come," and took his hand.

12

The party in Roger's room started at about five-thirty when Fook Shanahan came in with a man who lived on the second floor and whom Roger didn't know at all. He and Amelia had just come into the room, had in fact barely taken off their coats when Fook knocked on the door and – without waiting for anyone to answer – opened the door and came in, followed by a very tall thin man with thick-rimmed eyeglasses and a thatch of brown hair turning white. His eyebrows were already completely white, thick and shaggy; they looked fake to Roger, as if they had been pasted on as a disguise. Fook had a bottle of bourbon in one hand, and two glasses in the other. He went immediately to the dresser where he put down the bottle and the glasses and then he turned to Roger and said, "Aren't you going to introduce us to the young lady?"

"Oh, sure," Roger said. "This is Amelia Perez. Amelia, I'd like you to meet Fook Shanahan, and I'm afraid I don't know the other gentleman's name."

"The other gentleman's name is Dominick Tartaglia," Fook said, "and he's no gentleman, believe me." Tartaglia laughed. Fook laughed with him and then said, "I gather you two have just come in from the frozen tundra out there, and would appreciate a drink."

"Well . . ." Roger said hesitantly, and then glanced at Amelia.

"Sure," Amelia said. "I'd love a drink."

"The problem is one of numerical disproportion," Fook said. "We seem to have four people and only three glasses."

"Roger and I can share a glass," Amelia said, and smiled gently at him.

"Then there's no problem," Fook said. He went to the dresser and opened the bottle. Amelia sat on the edge of the bed, crossing her legs and leaning forward, resting her elbow on her knee, one hand toying with the pearls at her throat. Tartaglia stood alongside the dresser, smiling as Fook poured the drinks. Roger glanced at Amelia to see if she minded them being here, but she seemed to be pretty happy. We'll make love as soon as they leave, he thought.

And suddenly he was frightened.

"We were waiting for you to come home, Roger," Fook said, "because we wanted to know how you made out with the bulls."

"Oh, we had a nice talk," Roger said.

"Were the police here?" Amelia asked, and she suddenly sat up straight and looked at Roger.

"Yeah," Tartaglia said. "Our landlady had a refrigerator stolen from her."

"A refrigerator?" Amelia said. "Thank you," she said to Fook as he handed her the drink.

"I apologize for the lack of ice," Fook said. "Would you like a little water in that?"

"Spoils the taste," Amelia said, and grinned.

"Ah, an Irish colored girl," Shanahan said. "The best kind." He lifted his glass. "Cheers, Miss."

Amelia sipped at her drink and then raised her eyebrows and rolled her eyes. "Whoosh!" she said, and handed the glass to Roger. Roger sniffed it, and then took a short swallow.

"So what happened?" Fook asked.

"Nothing," Roger said. "They came in and they were very polite, and they asked me where I'd been last night, and I told them. Then, let me see, I guess we talked about how much I thought the refrigerator was worth, and then they said I could go home or stay here, whichever I wanted, they had no more questions for me."

"That means they think he's clean," Tartaglia said to Fook.

"Of *course*," Fook said. "We're *all* clean. Who the hell would want to steal that old bitch's box, excuse me, Miss."

"That's all right," Amelia said, and she took another sip of the drink.

"Did you tell him about the shelves?" Tartaglia said.

"No," Fook said.

"What about the shelves?"

"They found them."

"What shelves?" Amelia asked.

"From the refrigerator. They found them near the furnace downstairs," Tartaglia said.

"Which means," Fook said, "that whoever went to the trouble of stealing that broken-down piece of machinery *also* went to the trouble of removing the shelves from it first. Now does that make any sense to you?"

"None at all," Amelia said, and finished her drink.

"Are you ready for another one, young lady?" Tartaglia asked.

"Just to take off the chill," Amelia said, and she winked.

"She's Irish, I tell you," Fook said.

Tartaglia took her glass and poured it half full. He poured more bourbon into his own glass, and then handed Amelia hers and walked to Fook with the bottle, filling his glass as Fook talked.

"What good is a refrigerator without shelves?" Fook asked. "You're not drinking, Roger. You're supposed to be sharing the young lady's drink."

"Amelia," she said.

"Yes, Amelia, of course. You're a beautiful girl, Amelia," Fook said. "May I congratulate you upon your taste, Roger?"

"Yes, you may," Roger said, and smiled.

"Congratulations," Fook said. "Isn't there another glass in this place?"

"I'm afraid not."

"I insist that you share the lady's—"

"Amelia," she said.

"Yes, I insist that you share *Amelia's* drink. *Amelia*, let the man have a sip."

"Well, I don't want to drink too much," Roger said.

"He gets violent when he's drunk," Fook said, and winked at Amelia.

"No, I don't think so," she said. "I don't think he's that kind."

"No, he's a very sweet man," Fook said, taking the glass from her gently, and handing it to Roger. "Drink," he said. "And tell me what you think about those shelves."

Roger sipped at the bourbon and then handed the glass back to Amelia. "Gee, I don't know what to make of it," he said.

"Why would anyone steal a refrigerator and leave the shelves behind?" Fook asked.

"Maybe it was too heavy to carry with the shelves in it," Tartaglia said, and burst out laughing.

"Let me get this straight," Amelia said, drinking. "A refrigerator was stolen from your landlady's apartment last night, but the shelves—"

"From the basement," Tartaglia corrected. "It was stolen from the basement."

"Oh. I see. Oh. But in any case, whoever took it first removed the shelves from inside, is this right?"

"That's right."

"Fingerprints." Amelia said.

"Of course!" Fook said.

"They'll find fingerprints on the shelves," Tartaglia said. "That's right. You're right, miss, have another drink."

"I'll get plotzed," Amelia said. "You'll get me plotzed here, I won't know what the hell I'm doing." She held out her glass.

They won't find fingerprints on the shelves, Roger thought. I was wearing gloves. They won't find fingerprints anywhere in that basement.

"But why did he take out the shelves?" Fook insisted. "That's the problem. Fingerprints aside, why did he bother to remove the shelves?"

They were all silent, thinking.

"I don't know," Amelia said at last, and took another swallow of bourbon.

"I don't know, either," Tartaglia said.

"Nor I," Fook said.

"Roger?" Amelia said. She grinned somewhat foolishly, and cocked her head to one side, as though she were having trouble keeping him in focus. "You seem to have an idea."

"No," he said.

"You seemed very thoughtful there," she said.

"No."

"Didn't he seem very thoughtful there?" she asked.

"He certainly did," Tartaglia said.

"Well, I don't have any ideas," Roger said, and smiled.

"I have the feeling he would like us to get out of here," Fook said.

"No, no . . ."

"I have that feeling, too," Tartaglia said.

"I think we've overstayed our welcome," Fook said. "I'm sure Roger and Amelia have a great many things to talk about, and couldn't care less about Mrs. Dougherty's goddamn icebox."

"Refrigerator," Tartaglia said.

"Yes, pardon me," Fook said, "and pardon me for saying goddamn, Miss."

"Amelia."

"Yes, Amelia."

"You don't have to rush off," Roger said. "Have another drink."

"No, no, we simply wanted to know how you'd made out with those two bulls they sent over from the station house. What were their names, Dominick? Do you remember their names?"

"Mutt and Jeff," Tartaglia said, and laughed. "You think they're ever going to find that refrigerator?"

"Never," Fook said.

"You know what?"

"What?"

"I'll bet somebody's got that refrigerator in his kitchen right this minute. I'll bet it's full of beer and eggs and milk and soda and cheese and apples and oranges and bananas and grapes and jelly and—"

"Oh, you should never put ba-nan-nuhs," Amelia sang, "In the re-fridge-a-ray-ter!"

"Cha-cha-cha," Fook said, and laughed.

"And this guy probably lives right across the hall from a cop," Tartaglia continued, "and tonight this cop'll go in there for a glass of beer or something, and the guy'll go to his refrigerator he swiped and the cop'll sit there and not even know it's a hot refrigerator," he said, and burst out laughing.

"How can a refrigerator be hot?" Amelia asked, and began laughing.

"We've got to go," Fook said. He went to the dresser and picked up his bottle. "We're glad the police gave you a clean bill of health, Roger. The least you could do, however, is ask whether Dominick here and myself also passed muster."

"Oh, gee, I'm sorry," Roger said. "I didn't mean to—"

"You will be delighted to learn that we are neither of us suspects. In the considered opinion of the police, this was an outside job. As a matter of fact, they think the basement door was jimmied. The short one said so."

"Good night, Amelia," Tartaglia said from the door.

"Good night," she said.

"It was a pleasure meeting you," he said.

"Thank you. You, too."

"It was a pleasure," Tartaglia said again.

"Miss," Fook said, and he stopped in front of her and made a small bow. "You are with one of the sweetest people who ever walked the face of this earth, Roger Broome, a fine man even on short acquaintance."

"I know," Amelia said.

"Good. You are a fine woman."

"Thank you."

"Good," he said. He went to the door. "Be sweet to each other," he said. "You are very sweet people. Be sweet."

He made a short bow and then went out. Tartaglia went out behind him, closing the door.

"I think you had better lock it," Amelia said thickly.

"Why?"

"Mmm," she said, and grinned wickedly. "We have things to do, Roger. We have *nice* things to do." She rose unsteadily and walked to the closet door, opening it, and then pulling back in surprise and turning to him and covering her giggle with a cupped hand. "I thought it was the john," she said. "Where's the john?"

"Down the hall."

"Would you mind if I went to wash my face?" she asked.

"No, not at all," he said.

"I'll be right back," she said. She went to the door, opened it, turned, and then said – with great dignity – "I *really* have to pee," and went out.

Roger sat on the edge of the bed.

His hands were sweating.

He had hit Molly very suddenly.

He had not known he was going to hit her until his hand came out, not in an open-palmed slap, but the fist bunched instead into a tight hard ball. He had struck out and hit her in the eye, and then had pulled back his fist and hit her again, making her nose bleed. He saw her opening her mouth to scream, everything looked very peculiar all at once, the blood starting from her nose, he instinctively knew he could not allow any blood to stain the sheets, her mouth beginning to open in what he knew would be a piercing scream, he reached out quickly and grabbed her throat in both huge hands, squeezing. The scream died somewhere back in her throat, leaving only a small clicking gasp as his fingers closed on her neck. He lifted her off the bed at the same moment, bending her back so that the blood ran from her nose to the side of her face and over her jawbone and down her throat, over his hands – he almost released her when the blood touched his hands – and then down over her collarbone and her small naked breasts, but not touching the bed or the floor, he did not want bloodstains on anything. He wondered for a split instant – as her eyes bulged in her head, and she struck out at him with weakening hands, the hands fluttering aimlessly like broken butterflies – he wondered why he was doing this, he loved her, she was beautiful, why was he doing this, he hated her. Everything was bottled inside her head, everything was bulging into her head as he continued squeezing, blood was bursting from her nose, her eyes were getting wider and wider, her mouth opened, a curious retching sound came from her, he thought she would vomit on his hands, he almost backed away from her and then everything seemed to stop. He realized she was no longer struggling. She hung limp at the ends of his hands. He lowered her slowly to the floor, taking care that he did not tilt her head, not wanting to get any blood on anything. He left her naked, lying on her back, and went into the bathroom to wash his hands.

He sat with her for perhaps a half-hour trying to figure out what he should do.

He thought maybe he should call his mother and tell her he had killed a girl. But then he had the funniest feeling his mother would just say Come home as quick as you can, son, leave her there and come home. He didn't think that was the right thing to do.

He kept looking at the girl lying naked on the floor. She looked even uglier in death, and he wondered how he could have ever thought she was beautiful, and then for a reason he could not understand, he reached down and with his forefinger he gently and tenderly traced the outline of her profile. Then he closed her staring eyes.

I'll take her to the police, he thought.

He went to the closet for her coat, thinking he couldn't carry her into a police station naked. He took the coat from the hanger and spread it on the floor beside her, and then lifted her and put her onto the coat as though it were a blanket, without making any attempt to put her arms into the sleeves. He went around the room then, picking up her clothing, the blouse, the skirt, the padded bra, the shoes she had taken off because her feet hurt from looking for a job, the panty-girdle, and folded these and put them all on her chest in a neat flat pile, leaving out only her nylons. He closed the coat over her chest. He did not button it. He took one of the nylons and slipped it under her back and her arms and then pulled it over her breasts and knotted it tightly. He wrapped the other nylon around her thighs, just above where the coat ended, and again knotted it tightly, and then looked down at the girl.

Her nose had stopped bleeding.

He couldn't just carry her in his arms, could he? In the street that way? He wondered what time it was. He supposed it was two o'clock or a little after, no, it wouldn't be right carrying her to the police station in his arms. No.

He didn't even know where the police station was.

He guessed he ought to go get the truck.

He could put her in the back of the truck.

He looked down at her once more where she lay trussed on the floor, one nylon tightly knotted over her breasts, holding the piled clothing in place under the coat, the other knotted around her thighs, her head sticking out of the top of the coat and her legs out of the bottom. He figured she'd be all right while he went to get the truck. He put on his coat and then went outside, testing the door behind him to make sure it was locked. He could hear Fook snoring in his room down the hall. He went down the steps quietly and cautiously and then came out into the street and began walking toward the garage. It was not as cold as it had been earlier. That surprised him. It was very windy, but the temperature wasn't all that bad. He walked with a quick spring in his step, the whole thing very clear in his mind. He would get the truck and back it down that alley alongside the building, into the back yard to the basement door. He knew there was a back door to the basement because he had seen the man from the electric company going down the alley to read the meter just yesterday. He had never been down in the basement, but he knew there was a door back there.

The night attendant at the garage wanted to know who he was, and he said he was Roger Broome and that he would like his truck, the '59 Chevy. The night man wasn't too keen on letting the truck go out at close to two-thirty in the morning, but Roger showed him the registration for the truck, and the night man sort of clucked his tongue and shook his head and said, Well, okay, I guess it's all right, I sure *hope* it's all right.

The streets were fairly deserted at that hour.

He backed the truck down the alley, cutting the engine at the top of the drive, and letting it roll back down, and then pulling the wheel sharply at the bottom of the drive so that the truck swung in close to the back of the building. He got out and saw the basement door at once. He tried the knob, but the door was locked. He walked back to the truck and took the lug wrench from under the front seat and then went to the door and kept prying at the area near the lock until the wood was splintered and jagged, and finally the lock snapped. He went into the basement and groped his way around until he found the steps leading to the ground floor of the building. He went up the steps without turning on any lights and felt for the lock on the door, and then opened the door and came into the hallway. He propped the door open by putting his truck keys on the floor in the narrow wedge where the door joined the jamb. Then he went upstairs to his room.

The girl was where he'd left her, lying on the floor.

He went to the bed and looked at it to see if there were any bloodstains on the sheets, and then he checked the floor for bloodstains, and then he looked around to make sure he'd got all of her clothes. He dragged her over to the door and opened it a crack and looked out into the hall. He didn't know why he was being so careful about bloodstains and clothes and looking out into the hallway, especially when his plan was to drive straight to the nearest police station and go in and tell them he'd killed this girl, that was going to be hard to do.

There was no one in the hallway, the building was asleep.

He picked her up, she was as light as a feather, and carried her into the hall, bracing her with one arm while he pulled the door shut with his free hand, and then holding her in both arms and going quickly down the steps to the basement door. He opened the door and then bent down for his truck keys, bracing the girl against his knee again. He went down the steps. The basement was illuminated with thin shafts of moonlight that glanced through the small side windows high up on the cinderblock wall. His eyes were becoming accustomed to the light. He could make out the furnace, and beyond that an old refrigerator, and beyond that a bicycle with one wheel. He carried Molly out of the basement and then put her into the back of the truck. A think trickle of blood had run from her nose to her upper lip. He was about to get into the truck cab and drive to the police station when he wondered what he would tell them. He stood in the silent back yard. Above him the clotheslines stretched from pole to pole, frantically and silently moving in the wind. Boy, it sure would be hard to go in there and tell them what had happened. He stood near the rear of the truck, staring at the girl wrapped in her own coat.

If he took her someplace

Well, he ought

Well

Well, what he ought to do was go to the police.

Still, if

No.

No, he had to get rid of her.

He kept looking at the girl.

Yes, he had to get rid of her.

He shrugged and went back into the basement. He went directly to the refrigerator he had seen and he opened the door and looked inside and knew immediately he would have to take the shelves out. The first two came out easily enough, but he had to struggle with the third one, and then the fourth came out just by lifting it. He put all four shelves alongside the furnace, and then he wrapped his arms around the refrigerator and tried to lift it. It was too heavy for him. He would never be able to carry it clear across the basement to the back door.

He wondered if he should forget about it.

Maybe he should take her to the police station after all.

He kept staring at the refrigerator.

Finally, he wrapped his arms around it again, but this time he lifted one end of the box and walked it forward and then lifted the opposite end, and kept doing that, shifting from one leg of the refrigerator to the other, walking it toward the door. At the door, he lifted it over the sill and then shoved it onto the concrete of the back yard and walked it to the tailgate of the truck. He wasn't at all tired. Walking the box out to the truck had been fairly simple, but he knew it would take all his strength to lift it up onto the tailgate and into the truck.

He looked at the girl.

He kept expecting her to move or something. Maybe open her eyes.

He bent at the knees and wrapped his arms around the refrigerator again and then braced himself and began lifting. The box slipped. He backed away from it in surprise. It made a dull heavy noise as it fell back to the concrete, upright. He gripped it again, and this time he mustered every ounce of power he possessed, straining, grunting, pulling it up onto the tailgate and allowing it to fall over backward into the truck. He pushed and shoved it over to the middle of the truck and then opened the door and lifted the girl and put her inside.

She wouldn't fit.

He put her in head first and then tried closing the door, but she wouldn't fit.

He tried turning her on her side and bending her legs behind her, but that didn't work either. He was beginning to get very nervous because he was afraid someone would turn on a light or open a window or look down into the yard and see him struggling there trying to get the girl into the refrigerator.

He broke both her legs.

He closed the door.

He got into the truck and began driving.

The city was an empty wilderness, he did not know where to go, he did not know where he could leave her. He did not want anyone to find the refrigerator because then they would find the girl and know who she was and possibly they would trace the refrigerator back to Mrs. Dougherty's rooming house and begin to ask questions. He found the river almost by accident. He knew the city was surrounded by water, but it didn't occur to him that he could just drive up to the river's edge and drop the refrigerator in. He had come across a small bridge and looked down and seen lights reflecting in water, and then realized he was looking down into a river and had taken the first left turn off the bridge and driven down to a deserted dock where a railroad car loomed alone and empty on a silent track. He backed the truck to the water's edge. He wondered how deep the water was. He went to the edge of the dock and got down on his hands and knees and looked over to see if there were any markings on the dock, but there weren't. He didn't want to go dropping the refrigerator into shallow water. They'd find it right off, and that wouldn't be too good.

He got into the truck again and drove off.

Now that he knew he wanted to drop the refrigerator in the river, he began actively looking for a place that would be deep enough. He didn't know how he would recognize a deep spot unless he just happened to come across a dock or bridge that was marked. But the chances of finding such a placed seemed

A bridge.

Actually, if he

Well, just drive onto it.

The middle of it.

The rail.

He could simply

He began looking for a bridge. He'd have to be very careful, he'd have to pretend something was wrong, yes, that was it, wait for a break, just bide his time, that refrigerator was very heavy. Yes.

Yes.

He drove crosstown, thinking a high bridge would be best, the refrigerator would drop a very long distance and then sink into the mud on the bottom of the river. Yes, a high bridge would be best. He headed automatically toward the highest and longest bridge he knew, the one connecting the city with the adjoining state, and then he started across it. The bridge seemed to sway somewhat in the strong wind. He wondered if the refrigerator would drop straight and true to the river, or if the wind would affect its fall.

He stopped the truck.

He went immediately to the front and lifted the hood.

He stood in front of the truck as though he were looking into the engine, but he was really watching the far end of the bridge and the approaching headlights. As soon as there was a break in the traffic, he would go to the back and lift the refrigerator down, and carry it behind the side of the truck so that he would be shielded from any other passing cars. He kept watching the cars in the distance. The headlights rushed past.

All at once, there was nothing.

Nothing was coming.

I hope this works, he thought.

He went quickly to the back of the truck, thinking how heavy the refrigerator was going to be and then surprised to find that it was amazingly light, he could lift it with hardly any effort at all. He felt almost a little giddy as he lifted the refrigerator, God it was light, and carried it around the side of the truck and then hoisted it up onto the guard rail. He looked down once quickly, to make sure no boats were passing under the bridge, and then he let the refrigerator drop. He watched it as it went down, leaving his hands large and white and getting smaller and smaller and hitting the water with an enormous splash that sent up a large white geyser of water. A car rushed past in the opposite direction. The water below was settling, a wide circle of white spreading, there were headlights at the far end of the bridge now. He went quickly to the front of the truck and pulled down the hood. He came around the side again and took one last look at the water below.

You could hardly tell anything had been dropped into the river.

He started the truck and drove across the bridge and into the next state. He drove about a mile past the toll booths, and then made a U-turn and headed back for the city. He dropped the truck off at the garage and walked to Mrs. Dougherty's. There was no one outside the building or in the hallway. Everyone was asleep. He went up to his room and got into bed.

He fell asleep almost instantly.

Amelia opened the door.

She had washed her face, and washed the lipstick from her mouth and now she entered the room and closed the door behind her, and carefully and slowly locked it. She put her bag on the dresser, and then turned to face him, leaning against the door with her hands behind her back.

"Hi," she said.

He looked up at her. "Hello."

"Did you miss me?"

"Yes."

"Tell me."

"I missed you."

"You've got some fancy bathroom down the hall there," she said. She did not move from the door. She kept staring at him, a faint strange smile on her face. "Blue toilet paper, very fancy."

"I didn't notice," Roger said.

"You're not a very observant person, are you?" She tripped on only the one word, observant, saying it a little thickly and almost missing it entirely. She wasn't really too drunk, she'd just had a few too many, and she stood inside the locked door with her hands behind her back and that very strange, mischievous, somehow evil smile on her face. He looked at her and thought how beautiful she was and then thought I'd better get her out of here before I hurt her.

She moved away from the door.

She came to where he was sitting on the edge of the bed and she moved very close to him, with her knees touching his, and then she reached down seriously and solemnly, with a drunken dignity, and spread her hands on either side of his head like two open fans. She tilted his face up and then bent down and kissed him on the lips, with her own mouth open. He reached up behind her to cup her buttocks in his huge hands, thinking how much he wanted to love her, and thinking how his mother would of course object even though she was very beautiful. His mother would of course point out that she was a colored girl. He wondered when it had begun to matter just what the hell his mother thought about the girls he went out with, who the hell cared *what* his mother thought? And then he realized that he'd been caring what his mother thought for a long long time and that last night when he had finally said to hell with her, when he had finally let himself go with Molly, why that was the bad part, that was why he'd had to do it to her.

To kill her.

I killed her, he thought.

Amelia's mouth was covering him, her tongue was insistently probing, her lips were thick and soft and wet and he felt himself falling back onto the bed with her on top of him, and feeling the softness of her breasts against his chest, his heart beating wildly. He began trembling. She had taken off her bra in the bathroom, he realized she had taken off her bra. His hands moved swiftly up under her sweater and over her back. He rolled onto her suddenly, moaning, and kissed her breasts, the dark swollen nipples. "Oh, Roger," she was saying, "oh Roger, I love you, I love you."

He was lost in the aroma of her and in the warmth of her and in the dizzy insistence of her mouth, but at the same time he was thinking more clearly than he had since late last night when he had dropped the refrigerator in the river. He was thinking that he had to get her out of here because he was sure he would hurt her. He had hurt Molly without even having liked her at first, had hurt her only later when she somehow got him angry, but he felt a lusting rage now for this girl who was beautiful and "She is colored," his mother would say, "Why are you bringing home a little colored whore to me," he loved her lips and the way her hands she was dangerous if he did not get rid of her they would find out about Molly. If he hurt her, if she allowed him to love her, if she allowed him to enter her the dark pulsing interior of her in his hands now warm and moving against him the smooth dark smothering breasts if she allowed him to love her you're the man in the family now he would have to kill her there would be no other way he would have to kill her, they would find out about Molly, get away from me he thought.

He drew away from her sharply.

She stared up at him.

Her sweater was pulled up over her naked breasts, her skirt was high on her thighs. He crouched over her trembling with love for her. She reached for him tenderly. Her hand came up to him slowly and with infinite gentleness, touching him, assuring him

"No!" he shouted.

"What?"

"Get— No," he said.

He moved off the bed. He turned his back to her.

"Go," he said. "Go home. Get out of here. Get out!"

"What?"

He was at the closet. He opened the door and took out her coat and brought it to the bed and put it down beside her without looking at her again, knowing she had still not pulled down the sweater, loving her and afraid he would hate her, please, please, go, please, not knowing whether he said the words aloud.

She got off the bed silently. She adjusted her sweater, and silently got into her coat. She picked up her bag from the dresser, went to the door, and unlocked it.

"I'll never as long as I live understand," she said and went out.

It was about seven o'clock when he went down for the truck and drove it over to the police station.

He parked just across the street, pulling up the hand brake and then cutting the ignition and glancing over to where the green globes were lighted now, the 87 showing on each of them, flanking the entrance doors.

He knew he was about to do the right thing.

It seemed very good to him that he had not harmed Amelia. That seemed like a very good sign. He didn't know why he hadn't done this right from the beginning, why he simply hadn't brought Molly here last night, right after he'd killed her, instead of putting her in the refrigerator and throwing her in the river where they'd never find her. He could have told it to someone right then and spared himself all the fear and

Wouldn't they?

Find her?

He sat quite still behind the wheel of the truck with darkness covering the city and with the precinct globes feebly glowing across the street, throwing a pale-green stain on the snow banked along the precinct steps. There was the sound of shovels scraping the sidewalks, tire chains rattling on snow. His breath plumed into the cold cab interior, the windshield was getting frosted.

She had only been in the city a week, no one knew she was here, except of course the hotel she was staying at. She would have signed a register, yes, what was the name of the hotel, a Spanish name. It didn't matter. They would think she'd skipped without paying her bill, that was all. They'd maybe report it to the police, or maybe not, depending on what she'd left behind, didn't she say she'd come here with only a suitcase and a little money, sure. But even if they did report her missing, even if they said Molly Nolan who was staying here at the hotel has just vanished without taking her clothes out of the dresser, well, okay, let's say they did that. Let's say they told the police.

She's at the bottom of the river, Roger thought.

She's not going to float up to the top because she's locked inside a heavy refrigerator, I could barely lift it onto the tailgate of the truck, I dropped that refrigerator maybe a hundred and fifty feet from the bridge to the water, maybe more, I was never good at judging distance. It must have sunk ten feet into the river bottom, or at least five, or even three, it didn't matter. Even if it was just laying there exposed on the bottom it was never going to be found, never. It was just going to sit there forever with Molly Nolan dead inside it, and nobody in the world would ever know she was down there. Her parents were dead, her only friend was in Hawaii, nobody had noticed Roger and her in the bar, nobody had seen them go up to his room together, no one would ever know.

All he had to do was drive away.

No one would ever know.

If he did not go into the police station across the street and tell them he had killed her, why they just would never know about it, they just would never find out.

He looked across the street.

I'd better go tell them, he thought.

He got out of the truck.

He was about to cross the street when the door opened. Two men came out of the station house. He recognized the taller one as the detective he'd followed to the restaurant that afternoon, and he thought, Good, he's the one I wanted to tell this to in the first place. The man with him was bald. Roger supposed he was a detective, too. The green precinct lights shone on his bald head. They gave him a funny appearance.

The men had reached the sidewalk.

Go ahead, Roger thought. Go tell him. He's the one you wanted to tell.

He hesitated.

The one with the bald head ran to the curb and made a snowball and threw it at the taller detective. The taller detective laughed, and then picked up a pile of snow and just flipped it at the bald-headed one in a big lump, without packing it, and they both laughed like kids.

"I'll see you tomorrow," the taller one said, laughing.

"Right, Steve. Good night," the bald-headed one said.

"Good night."

The men walked off in opposite directions.

Roger watched the taller one until he was out of sight.

He got back into the truck and turned the ignition key, starting the engine. He looked at the station house one more time, and then began driving home.

To mother.

JIGSAW

This is for Helen and Gene Federico

1
___

Detective Arthur Brown did not like being called black.

This might have had something to do with his name, which was Brown. Or his color, which was also brown. Or it might have had something to do with the fact that when he was but a mere strip of a boy coming along in this fair city, the word "black" was usually linked alliteratively with the word "bastard". He was now thirty-four years old and somewhat old-fashioned, he supposed, but he still considered the word derogatory, no matter how many civil rights leaders endorsed it. Brown didn't need to seek identity in his color or in his soul. He searched for it in himself as a man, and usually found it there with ease.

He was six feet four inches tall, and he weighed two hundred and twenty pounds in his undershorts. He had the huge frame and powerful muscles of a heavyweight fighter, a square clean look emphasized by the way he wore his hair, clipped close, clinging to his skull like a soft black cap, a style he had favored even before it became fashionable to look "natural". His eyes were brown, his nostrils were large, he had thick lips and thicker hands, and he wore a .38 Smith & Wesson in a shoulder holster under his jacket.

The two men lying on the floor at his feet were white. And dead.

One of them was wearing black shoes, blue socks, dark blue trousers, a pale blue shirt open at the throat, a tan poplin zippered jacket, a gold Star-of-David on a slender gold chain around his neck, and two bullet holes in his chest. The other one was dressed more elegantly – brown shoes, socks and trousers, white shirt, green tie, houndstooth-check sports jacket. The broken blade of a switch knife was barely visible in his throat, just below the Adam's apple. A Luger was on the floor near his open right hand.

The apartment was a shambles.

It was not a great apartment to begin with; Brown had certainly seen better apartments, even in the ghetto where he had spent the first twenty-two years of his life. This one was on the third floor of a Culver Avenue tenement, two rooms and a bathroom, rear exposure, meaning that it faced on a back yard with clotheslines flapping Wednesday's wash. It was now close to 10 p.m., six minutes after the building's landlady had stopped the cop on the beat to say she had heard shots upstairs, four minutes after the patrolman had forced the door, found the stiffs, and called the station house. Brown, who had been catching, took the squeal.

The Homicide cops had not yet arrived, which was just as well. Brown could never understand the department regulation that made it mandatory for Homicide to check in on every damn murder committed in this city, even though the case was invariably assigned to the precinct answering the call. He found most Homicide cops grisly and humorless. His wife, Caroline, was fond of telling him that he himself was not exactly a very comical fellow, but Brown assumed that was merely a case of the prophet going unappreciated in his native land. In fact, *he* thought he was hilarious at times. As now, for example, when he turned to the police photographer and said, "I wonder who did the interior decorating here." The police photographer apparently shared Caroline Brown's opinion. Without cracking a smile, he did his little dance around the two corpses, snapping, twisting for another angle, snapping again, shifting now to this side of the dead men, now to the other, while Brown waited for his laugh.

"I said . . ." Brown said.

"I heard you, Artie," the photographer said, and clicked his camera again.

"This is certainly not the Taj Mahal," Brown said.

"Hardly anything is," the photographer answered.

"What are you so grumpy about?" Brown asked.

"Me? Grumpy? Who's grumpy?"

"Nobody," Brown said. He glanced at the corpses again, and then walked to the far side of the room, where two windows overlooked the back yard. One of the windows was wide open. Brown checked the latch on it, and saw immediately that it had been forced. Okay, he thought, that's how one of them got it. I wonder which one. And I also wonder *why*? What did he expect to steal in this dump?

Brown leaned over the window sill. There was nothing but an empty milk carton, a crumpled wad of waxed paper, and a flower pot on the fire escape outside. The flower pot had a dead plant in it. Brown looked down into the yard below. A woman was dumping her garbage into one of the cans adjacent to the alley wall. She accidentally dropped the lid of the can, clearly and resoundingly said, "Oh, shit!" and stooped to retrieve it. Brown turned away from the window.

Monoghan and Monroe, the detectives from Homicide, were just coming through the doorway. They were dressed almost identically, both wearing the blue serge confirmation suits, brown shoes, and gray fedoras. Monroe was wearing a maroon knit tie. Monoghan wore a yellow silk tie. Their shields were pinned to the breast pockets of their suit jackets. Monroe had recently begun growing a mustache, and the sparse collection of hairs over the lip seemed to embarrass him. He kept blowing his nose into his handkerchief, even though he didn't have a cold, as though trying to hide his unsightly brush behind the white cotton square. Monoghan seemed even more embarrassed by the mustache than Monroe did. It seemed to him that after fifteen years of working together with a man, the man should not suddenly start growing a mustache one morning without first consulting his partner. Monoghan hated Monroe's mustache. He considered it unesthetic. It embarrassed him. It offended his eye. And because it offended his eye, he constantly stared at it. And the more often he stared at it, the more often Monroe took out his handkerchief and blew his nose, hiding his mustache.

"Well, well, what have we got here?" Monroe said, blowing his nose. "Hello, Brown."

"Hello, Brown," Monoghan said.

"Now this is what I call a thorough job," Monroe said, pocketing his handkerchief. "Whoever went through this place was an expert."

"A professional," Monoghan said.

"It almost looks like the *police* shook it down."

"Or the firemen," Monoghan said, and looked at his partner's mustache. Monroe took out his handkerchief again.

"Must have wanted something pretty bad," he said, and blew his nose.

"What could anybody want in *this* joint?" Monoghan asked. "You know what you find in a joint like this?"

"What?" Brown asked.

"Cockroaches," Monoghan said.

"Bedbugs," Monroe added.

"Cockroaches and bedbugs,' Monoghan summarized.

Monroe put away his handkerchief.

"*Look* at this joint," Monoghan said, and shook his head.

Brown looked at the joint. The bed had been stripped, the mattress slashed on both sides, cotton batting strewn all over the floor. The same thorough job had been done on the bed pillows and on the seat cushion, arms and back of the single easy chair in the room. Fademarks on the walls showed where several framed prints had been hanging, but the pictures had been yanked down, their backs probably examined, and then thrown carelessly onto the floor. The contents of all the dresser drawers were similarly tossed all over the room, and the drawers themselves had been pulled out of the dresser and then flung aside. The one floor lamp in the room, overturned, had had its shade removed and discarded. Through the bathroom doorway, Brown could see the open medicine cabinet, its contents thrown into the sink. The top of the toilet tank had been taken off. Even the toilet paper had been removed from its roller. In the kitchen, the refrigerator door was open, and food had been hurled haphazardly onto the floor. The one drawer in the kitchen table had been emptied onto the white enamel tabletop, utensils scattered everywhere. As Monroe had wisely commented, someone must have wanted something pretty bad.

"You know who the stiffs are?" Monoghan asked Brown.

"Not yet."

"You figure it for an interrupted burglary?"

"Right."

"How'd he get in?"

"Through the fire escape window. Tool marks on the frame."

"Other guy came home unexpectedly, and *bingo!*"

"Think he got what he came after?"

"Haven't checked him out," Brown said.

"What're you waiting for?"

"Lou's still taking pictures. And the M.E. isn't here yet."

"Who reported the crime?" Monroe asked.

"The landlady. She heard shots, stopped Kiely on the beat."

"Get her up here," Monoghan said.

"Right," Brown answered. He went to the door, told the patrolman there to go get the landlady, and then saw Marshall Davies hurrying down the hallway toward the apartment.

"I'm sorry I'm late, Artie," he said. "I had a goddamn flat."

"There was a call for you," Brown said.

"Who from?"

"Lieutenant Grossman."

"What'd he want?"

"Said you should go right back to the lab."

"The lab? What for? Who's going to handle *this* if I go back to the lab?"

"Don't know," Brown said.

"You know what he's probably got waiting for me downtown? Some nice little surprise, that's what. Some nice hit-and-run victim. Some guy who got run over by a trailer truck. I'll be down there picking headlight splinters out of his ass all night. Boy oh boy, what a day."

"It's hardly started," Brown said.

"It started for me at seven o'clock this morning," Davies said. He sighed heavily, "Okay, I'm heading back. If he should call me again, tell him I'm on my way. I don't know who's going to handle this for you, Artie. The M.E. been here yet?"

"No, not yet."

"Situation normal," Davies said, and walked out.

The patrolman came upstairs with the landlady not five minutes later. By that time, the Assistant Medical Examiner had arrived and was checking out the corpses. Brown and the two Homicide detectives took the landlady into the kitchen, where they could talk to her without the fascinating distraction of two bodies lying on the floor. She was a woman in her late forties, not unattractive, her blond hair pulled into a bun at the back of her head. She had wide Irish eyes, as green as County Cork, and she spoke with the faintest hint of a brogue. Her name was Mrs. Walter Byrnes.

"No kidding?" Monoghan said. "You any relation to the lieutenant?"

"What lieutenant?"

"Runs the Eight-seven," Monroe said.

"The Eighty-seventh squad," Monoghan said.

"He's a cop," Monroe said.

"I'm not related to any cops," Mrs. Byrnes said.

"He's a very good cop," Monoghan said.

"I'm not related to him," Mrs. Byrnes said, firmly.

"You want to tell us what happened, Mrs. Byrnes?" Monroe said.

"I heard shots. I went right outside and yelled for the police."

"Did you come up here?"

"Nope."

"Why not?"

"Would *you*?"

"Mrs. Byrnes," Brown said, "when you came in just now, did you happen to notice the bodies in the other room?"

"I'd have to be deaf, dumb, and blind not to, wouldn't I?" she said.

"Do you know either of those two men?"

"One of them, yes."

"Which one?"

"The one wearing the sports jacket," she said. Unflinchingly, she added, "The one with the knife blade sticking out of his throat."

"And who is he, Mrs. Byrnes?"

"His name is Donald Renninger. He's been living here in the building for more than two years."

"And the other man? The one wearing the Jewish star?"

"Never saw him before in my life."

"He's the one who broke in, I guess," Monroe said.

"We've had a *lot* of burglaries around here," Mrs. Byrnes said, and looked at the detectives reproachfully.

"Well, we try to do our best," Monoghan said dryly.

"Sure you do," Mrs. Byrnes said, even more dryly.

"Any idea what Mr. Renninger did for a living?" Brown asked.

"He worked at a filling station."

"Would you know where?"

"In Riverhead someplace. I don't know exactly where."

"Is he married?"

"No."

"He was a bachelor, right?" Monroe asked.

"If he wasn't married, why yes, I guess he was a bachelor," Mrs. Byrnes said sarcastically, and then looked at Monroe's mustache.

Monroe took out his handkerchief. Apologetically, he blew his nose and said, "He *could* have been divorced."

"That's true," Monoghan said.

Monroe smiled at him, and put away his handkerchief.

"But you never saw the other man?" Brown said.

"Never."

"Not here in the building..."

"No."

"...or in the neighborhood either?"

"No place," she said.

"Thank you, Mrs. Byrnes."

The landlady went to the door. She turned before she went out, and said, "What's his first name?"

"Whose?"

"The lieutenant's?"

"Peter."

"We don't have a Peter Byrnes in our family," she said, and went out, satisfied.

The M.E. was finished with the bodies. As he passed the detectives, he said, "We'll give you written reports soon as the autopsies are made. You want some guesses for now?"

"Sure," Brown said.

"Looks like the first bullet hit the guy in the poplin jacket a little low, probably got deflected off a rib. Anyway, it didn't stop him right away. Left fist is clenched, he probably threw a punch and still had time to stick his knife in the other's guy's throat, probably just as the gun went off a second time. *That* shot went clear through the heart, I'd guess. The guy in the poplin jacket started to drop, and the knife blade broke off as he fell. The other guy went down, too, probably died within minutes. Looks to me as if the knife caught his jugular, awful lot of blood in there. Okay?"

"Okay, thanks," Brown said.

"You handling this, Artie?"

"Looks like I'm stuck with it."

"Well, it's open and shut. I'll get the reports up to you tomorrow morning, that soon enough?"

"Nobody's going any place," Brown said.

"Toodle-oo," the M.E. said, and waggled his fingers and went out.

"So what'd the burglar *want* here?" Monoghan asked.

"Maybe *this*," Monroe said. He was crouched near the corpse in the poplin jacket. He pried open the dead man's clenched left hand to reveal what had appeared to be a portion of a glossy photograph clutched into the palm. He lifted the photo scrap and handed it to Brown. "Take a look at it," he said.

2

"What is it?" Detective Steve Carella asked.

"Piece of a snapshot," Brown said.

They were in a corner of the squadroom, Brown sitting behind his desk, Carella perched on one end of it. Early morning June sunshine streamed into the office. A mild breeze filtered through the wire grilles covering the open windows. Carella, sitting on the edge of the desk, sniffed of the late spring air, and wished he were sleeping in the park someplace. A tall, wiry man with wide shoulders and narrow hips, he gave the impression of being an athlete in training, even though the last time he'd engaged in any sportlike activity was the snorkeling he'd done in Puerto Rico on his last vacation. Unless one wished to count the various footraces he had run with criminals of every stripe and persuasion. Carella did not like to count those. A man could get winded just counting those. He brushed a strand of longish brown hair off his forehead now, squinted his brown eyes at the photo scrap, and wondered if he needed glasses.

"What does it look like to you?" he asked.

"A dancing girl in a leotard," Brown answered.

"Looks more like a bottle of Haig & Haig Pinch to me," Carella said. "What do you suppose this furry stuff is?"

"What furry stuff?"

"This textured stuff, whatever-the-hell-it-is."

"Mud, I would guess."

"Or part of a wall. A stucco wall." Carella shrugged, and dropped the scrap onto the desktop. "You really think this is why ... *what's* his name?"

"According to the identification in his wallet, his name was Eugene Edward Ehrbach."

"Ehrbach. Anything on him?"

"I'm running a check with the I.B. right now. On *both* of them."

"You think Ehrbach really broke into the apartment to get *this*?" Carella asked, and tapped the photograph segment with a pencil.

"Well, why else would it be in his hand, Steve? I can't see him going up there with a piece of snapshot in his hand, can you?"

"I guess not."

"Anyway, I'll tell you the truth, I don't see as it makes a hell of a lot of difference. The M.E. said it's open and shut, and I'm inclined to agree with him. Ehrbach broke into the apartment, Renninger suddenly came home and surprised him, and we get a neat double homicide."

"And the photograph?"

"Well, let's say Ehrbach *was* after it. So what? He could just as easily have been after Renninger's wrist watch. Either way, they're both dead. The snapshot doesn't change the disposition of the case either way."

"No, it doesn't."

"Soon as we get those autopsy reports, I'm going to type this up as closed. You see any other way?"

"No, it looks pretty clear."

"M.E. promised them for this morning." Brown looked at his watch. "Well, it's still a little early."

"I wonder what kind of customers we're dealing with here," Carella said.

"How do you mean?"

"Two nice ordinary citizens, one of them carrying a Luger, and the other one carrying a switch knife with an eight-inch blade."

"Whatever Ehrbach was, he wasn't a nice ordinary citizen. He opened that window like a pro."

"And Renninger?"

"Landlady says he worked at a filling station."

"I wish the I.B. would get off its dead ass," Carella said.

"Why?"

"I'm curious."

"Let's say they *have* got records," Brown said. "It still wouldn't change anything, would it?"

"You sound anxious to close this out," Carella said.

"I got a caseload up to my eyeballs, but that's not why I want to close it. There's just no reason to keep it *open*," Brown said.

"Unless there's a third party in that apartment," Carella said.

"There's no indication of that, Steve."

"Or unless..."

"Unless what?"

"I don't know. But why would anyone risk a burglary rap just to get a piece of a snapshot?"

"Excuse me," a voice called from across the squadroom. Both detectives turned simultaneously toward the slatted wooden railing at the far end of the office. A tall hatless man in a gray nailhead suit stood just outside the gate. He was perhaps thirty-five years old, with a thatch of black hair and a thick black handle-bar mustache that would have caused serious pangs of envy in someone like Monroe. His eyebrows were thick and black as well, raised now in polite inquiry over startlingly blue eyes that glinted in the squadroom sunshine. His speech stamped him immediately as a native of the city, with not a little trace of Calm's Pointese in it. "The desk sergeant said I should come right up," he said. "I'm looking for Detective Brown."

"That's me," Brown said.

"Okay to come in?"

"Come ahead."

The man searched briefly for the latch on the inside of the gate, found it, and strode into the office. He was a big man with big hands, the left one clutched around the handle of a dispatch case. He held the case very tightly. Brown had the feeling it should have been chained to his wrist. Smiling pleasantly, he extended his right hand and said, "Irving Krutch. Nice to meet you." His teeth were dazzling, the smile framed by a pair of dimples, one on either side of his mouth. He had high cheekbones, and a straight unbroken nose, and he looked like the lead in an Italian Western. The only thing he needed to attain instant stardom on the silver screen, Brown thought, was a change of name. Irving Krutch did nothing for his image. Steve Stunning, Hal Handsome, Geoff Gorgeous, any of those might have suited him better.

"How do you do?" Brown said, and took his hand briefly. He did not bother introducing Carella; cops rarely observed such formalities during business hours.

'Okay to sit down?" Krutch said.

"Please," Brown said, and indicated a chair to the right of his desk. Krutch sat. Carefully preserving the knife-crease in his trousers, he crossed his legs, and unleashed the dazzling smile again.

"So," he said, "looks like you got yourselves a little murder, huh?"

Neither of the cops answered him. They *always* had themselves a little murder, and they weren't in the habit of discussing homicides, little or otherwise, with strange, handsome, mustached, well-dressed smiling civilians who barged into the squadroom.

"The two guys over on Culver Avenue," Krutch said. "I read about them in the paper this morning."

"What about them?" Brown asked.

"I guess I should tell you I'm an insurance investigator," Krutch said. "Trans-American Insurance."

"Mm-huh," Brown said.

"Do you know the company?"

"The name sounds familiar."

"I've been with them for twelve years now, started there when I got out of college." He paused, then added, "Princeton." He waited for some response, saw that mention of his illustrious alma mater was not generating too much excitement, and then said, "I've worked with this squad before. Detective named Meyer Meyer. He still with you?"

"He's still with us," Brown said.

Carella, who had been silent until now, said, "What were you working on?"

"The National Savings & Loan Association holdup," Krutch said. "Six years ago."

"In what capacity?"

"I told you. I'm an insurance investigator. They're one of our clients." He smiled again. "Took us for a bundle on that one."

The men were silent again.

"So?" Brown said at last.

"So," Krutch said, "I read about your two corpses in the paper this morning, and I thought I'd better get up here right away."

"Why?"

"Lend you a hand," Krutch said, smiling. "Or maybe vice versa."

"You know something about those killings?" Brown asked.

"Yep."

"What do you know?"

"The newspaper said you found a piece of a photograph in Ehrbach's hand," Krutch said. His blue eyes shifted dramatically toward the photo scrap lying on Brown's desk. "Is that it?"

"What about it?" Brown asked.

"I've got another piece. And if you shake down Ehrbach's pad, I'm pretty sure you'll find a *third* piece."

"Do you want to tell it, or do we have to pull teeth?"

"I'm ready to tell it."

"Then tell it."

"Sure. Will you help me?"

"To do what?"

"First, to get the piece in Ehrbach's place."

"Why do you want it?"

"Three pieces are better than one, no?"

"Look, Mr. Krutch," Brown said, "if you've got something to say, say it. Otherwise, it's been nice meeting you, and I hope you sell a lot of insurance policies."

"I don't sell insurance, I investigate claims."

"Fine. I wish you lots of luck. Yes or no? Shit or get off the pot."

Krutch smiled at Carella, as though sharing with him his aversion to such crude language. Carella ignored the smile. He was agreeing with Brown. He hated coy disclosures. The 87th Squad ran a nice little store up here on the second floor of the building, and so far the only thing Krutch was spending in it was time. *Their* time.

Sensing the impatience of the two detectives, Krutch said, "Let me fill you in."

"Please do," Brown said.

"Fade in," Krutch said. "Six..."

'What?" Brown asked.

"That's a movie expression. Fade in."

"You involved with movies?" Brown asked, ready to confirm the suspicion he'd harbored from the moment Krutch walked in.

"No."

"Then why the movie expression?"

"Everybody says, 'Fade in,'" Krutch explained.

"*I* don't say 'Fade in,'" Brown replied.

"Okay, so we *won't* fade in," Krutch said, and shrugged. "Six years ago, in this city, in broad daylight on a rainy afternoon in August, four men held up the Culver Avenue branch of N.S.L.A. and got away with seven hundred and fifty thousand dollars. That's a lot of kale. The branch, incidentally, is located in this precinct."

"Go on," Carella said.

"You remember the case now?" Krutch asked. "Meyer and O'Brien were working on it."

"I remember it," Carella said. "Go ahead."

"Do *you* remember it, Detective Brown?"

"Yes," Brown said.

"I don't think I got your name," Krutch said, turning to Carella.

"Carella."

"Nice to meet you. Are you Italian?"

"Yes."

"The leader of the gang was Italian. Fellow named Carmine Bonamico, record as long as your arm. In fact, he'd just got out of Castleview after serving a five-and-dime there. First thing he did, while he was still on parole, was knock over the bank. You remember any of this?"

"I remember *all* of it," Carella said.

"Are my facts correct so far?"

"They are."

"My facts are *always* correct," Krutch said, and smiled. Nobody smiled with him. "The wheelman was a young punk named Jerry Stein, a Jewish kid from Riverhead, his first job. The two guns were both ex-cons, Lou D'Amore from Majesta and Pete Ryan, also from Riverhead, a regular little United Nations they had on that job. They came in just before closing time, grabbed as much as they could from the vault, shot one of the tellers, and then drove off, presumably heading for Calm's Point, which is where Bonamico lived with his wife. It was raining; did I mention it was raining?"

"You mentioned it."

"They got onto the River Road, and had almost reached the Calm's Point Bridge, when the car went into a skid, hit another car, and caused a traffic tie-up. Two patrolmen from the Three-six pulled up in a squad car, and Bonamico and his pals opened fire. All four of them were killed inside of five minutes. The great mystery is why they began shooting at all. The car was clean. It was later searched from top to bottom, but the bank loot wasn't in it. Not a dime of it," Krutch paused. "Okay, dissolve..."

Brown looked at him.

"Trans-American gets called in, Irving Krutch investigating." He grinned. "That's me. Result? Two years of intensive search for that money, and no trace of it. We finally settled the claim in full, seven hundred and fifty G's from our coffers to N.S.L.A.'s." Krutch paused. "That's bad. I don't have to tell you how bad that is."

"How bad is it?" Brown asked.

"*Bad.* Bad for Trans-American, and especially bad for Irving Krutch who couldn't find the money. Irving Krutch was up for a promotion at the time. Instead, Irving Krutch is now handling minor claims, at the same salary he was getting six years ago. Krutch is an ambitious fellow. He doesn't like dead-end jobs."

"Why doesn't Krutch *change* his job?" Carella suggested.

"Because the field's a narrow one, and losing seven hundred and fifty thousand dollars is the kind of word that gets around very fast. Besides, Krutch has an inordinate amount of pride in his work."

"Do you always talk about yourself in the third person?" Carella asked. "Like your own biographer?"

"It helps me to be objective. It's hard to be objective about losing seven hundred and fifty thousand dollars for the company, especially when the case has been officially closed by your squad."

"Who told you that?" Carella asked.

"You got the thieves, didn't you?"

"The case is still in our Open File."

"How come?"

"Let's say we *also* have an inordinate amount of pride in our work," Carella said. "The money wasn't in the car. Okay, the River Road is some three miles from the bank. Which means that somewhere along the escape route, the money could have changed hands. If that happened, then the rest of the gang is still at large, just itching to spend all that cash. We'd like to get them."

"Forget it."

"What do you mean?"

"The money wasn't turned over to *anybody*. If you're keeping the case open in hope of finding the rest of the gang, forget it. There were only four of them, and they're all dead."

"Do you know that for a fact?"

"Yes. I got it from Bonamico's sister-in-law." Krutch paused. "You mind if I tell it in order?"

"Any order you like," Brown said, "so long as you *tell* it."

"Okay, dissolve. Krutch is still bugged by the loss of that money. It keeps him awake nights. His company has settled the claim, not to mention his future, but it still bugs him. Where can the money be? Who's got it? Bonamico is no master criminal, mind you, but neither is he stupid enough to throw that kind of cash out the window of a getaway car. So where the hell is it? Krutch keeps wondering about it. Krutch keeps tossing and turning at night..."

"Krutch should be writing mystery stories," Carella said.

"...obsessed with the thought of locating that cash and becoming a contender again."

"A contender?"

"At Trans-American."

"Oh, I thought maybe you also did a little boxing on the side," Brown said.

"Matter of fact, I used to box in the Navy," Krutch said. "Middleweight division." He paused, eyed them both shrewdly, and said, "You guys don't like me much, do you?"

"We're civil servants," Brown said, "soliciting information from a private citizen who may or may not possess knowledge of a crime. We are patiently waiting. If we have to wait much longer, we'll be forced to rent you office space."

"I like your sense of humor," Krutch said, and smiled.

"My wife doesn't," Brown said. "We're still waiting, Mr. Krutch. We are getting old and gray waiting."

"Okay. Two months ago, I got lucky."

"You mean you were still working on this thing?"

"Not officially. Only on my own time. Pride, remember? Ambition. Tenacity. Krutch the would-be contender. I opened the paper one morning two months ago and learned that a woman named Alice Bonamico had died of cancer at the Sacred Heart Hospital in Calm's Point. No one would have noticed her passing, of course, if she hadn't incidentally been the widow of one Carmine Bonamico who had knocked over a bank six years earlier and caused the loot to magically disappear. I knew the lady because I'd talked to her often when I was investigating the claim. She was a nice type, quiet, pretty in a dark Sicilian way, you'd never think she'd been married to a cheap hood. Anyway, the newspaper item said that she was survived by a sister named Lucia Feroglio. I made a mental note, and later discovered she was a spinster, also living in Calm's Point."

"How much later was this?"

"A week or so. As soon as Alice Bonamico's will was filed in Surrogate's Court. It was a very interesting will. Aside from leaving her entire estate to her sister Lucia, it also left her, and I quote, 'Certain mementos, documents, photographs, and photographic segments considered to be of value by the deceased.' I immediately got on my horse and went to visit Lucia Feroglio in Calm's Point."

"This was two months ago?"

"Right. The third day of April. A Friday. Lucia Feroglio is an old lady in her seventies, memory failing, barely speaking English, partially deaf. You ever try to talk to a deaf woman?"

Carella said nothing.

"Anyway, I talked to her. I convinced her that her brother-in-law had taken out a very small policy on his wife's life, naming Lucia Feroglio as beneficiary, and that a check for one thousand dollars would be issued to her as soon as the conditions of the policy were met. I invented the conditions, of course."

"What were they?"

"That she satisfy my company that she was indeed in possession of the 'Certain mementos, documents, photographs, and photographic segments considered to be of value by the deceased.' Even deaf old ladies who hardly speak English can understand a thousand dollars. She patiently went through all the crap her sister had left her – family pictures, birth certificates, even the caul Alice had been born with, carefully wrapped in a square of pink satin; that's supposed to be good luck, you know, if you're born with a caul. And in the midst of all this crap was exactly what I hoped would be there."

"Which was?"

"A list of names. Or at least a partial list of names. And a piece of a photograph." Krutch paused. 'Would you like to see them?"

"Yes," Carella said.

Krutch opened his dispatch case. Resting on top of a sheaf of Trans-American claim forms was a legal-sized white envelope. Krutch opened the envelope and took out a scrap of paper. He put it on the desk top, and both detectives looked at it.

"Those names are in Carmine Bonamico's handwriting," Krutch said. "I'm quite familiar with it."

"Seven of them," Carella said.

"Or maybe more," Krutch answered. "As you can see, the list is torn."

"How'd it get torn?"

"I don't know. That's the way Lucia turned it over to me. It may have been accidentally damaged, or another piece of it may be in someone else's hands. Considering what Bonamico did with the photograph, that's a likely possibility."

"Let's see the picture," Carella said.

Krutch dipped into the envelope again. He took out a piece of a glossy photograph and put it on the desktop, alongside the scrap they had found clutched in Ehrbach's hand.

"How do we know these are pieces of the same photograph?" Carella asked.

"They're both cut like a jigsaw puzzle," Krutch said. "That can't be accidental. Nor can it be accidental that you found *your* piece in the hand of one of the men listed here in Bonamico's handwriting. Or that the *other* dead man is *also* on the list." Krutch paused. "Ehrbach's a better burglar than I am. I've been in and out of Renninger's place a dozen times in the past two months, and I never found a thing."

"You're admitting to breaking and entry, Mr. Krutch?"

"Shall I send for my lawyer?" Krutch asked, and grinned.

"Did you shake down Ehrbach's place as well?"

"I did. And found nothing. *His* piece is probably as carefully hidden as Renninger's was."

Carella looked at the list again. "Who's Albert Weinberg?"

"One of Stein's close buddies. Jerry Stein, the kid who drove the getaway car. Beginning to make sense?"

"Not much."

"Weinberg's a hood in his own right. So are the other two, in case you don't already know."

"Which other two?"

"Renninger and Ehrbach. Renninger was busted eight years ago for pushing junk. He was in Caramoor at the time of the holdup, got out of prison only two years ago. Ehrbach was busted twice for burglary, one more time and they'd have thrown away the key. Makes the risk he took seem even more meaningful, doesn't it? He was taking the chance of a third fall, and for what? Unless that picture means something, he was a goddamn fool to break into Renninger's place."

"You're better than the I.B.," Brown said. "Assuming this is straight goods."

"As I told you," Krutch said, smiling, "my facts are *always* correct."

"What about the other names on this list?"

"I've been through the telephone book a hundred times. You know how many Geraldines there are? Don't ask. As for Dorothy, she could be Dorothy *Anybody*. And the R-o-b? That could be Robert, or Roberta, or Robin, or even Robespierre, who knows? It was easy to fill in the 'Renninger' because the name was almost complete. And I doped out the 'Ehrbach' because of the 'Eugene E.' They're both listed in the Isola directory. Alice is Alice Bonamico, of course. But I have no idea who the others are, and no idea whether there are more than seven. I hope not. *Seven* pieces of a puzzle are more than enough."

"And when you assemble this puzzle, Mr. Krutch, what then?"

"When I assemble this puzzle," Krutch said, "I will have the exact location of the seven hundred and fifty thousand dollars stolen from N.S.L.A. six years ago."

"How do you know that?"

"Lucia Feroglio told me. Oh, it took some time to get it out of her, believe me. As I told you, her memory is failing, and she's partially deaf, and her English is of the *Mama mia* variety. But she *finally* remembered that her sister had told her the photograph showed where the treasure was. That was the exact word she used. Treasure."

"She said that in English?" Carella asked. "She said 'treasure'?"

"No. She said *tesoro*. In Italian."

"Maybe she was only calling you 'darling'," Carella said.

"I doubt it."

"You speak Italian, do you?"

"A girlfriend of mine told me what it meant. *Tesoro*. Treasure."

"So now there are two pieces," Brown said. "What do you want from us?"

"I want you to help me find the other *five* pieces. Or however many more there are." Krutch smiled. "I'm getting too well known, you see. Toward the end there, both Renninger and Ehrbach knew I was on to them. I wouldn't be surprised if Ehrbach *got* to Renninger merely by tailing *me*."

"You make it sound very complicated, Mr. Krutch."

"It *is* complicated. I'm sure that Weinberg knows I've been watching *him*, too. And frankly, I can't risk getting busted on a burglary rap. Which might happen if I keep breaking into places." He smiled again. The smile had lost none of its dazzle.

"So you want *us* to break into places for you, huh?"

"It's been done before."

"It's against the law, even for cops."

"*Lots* of things are against the law. There's seven hundred and fifty G's involved here. I'm sure the Eighty-seventh wouldn't mind locating it. Be quite a feather in your cap, after all these years."

"Yes, it might be," Carella said.

"So do it," Krutch said simply.

"Do *what*?" Brown asked.

"First of all, go over Ehrbach's place with a fine comb. You can do that legally. He's the victim of a homicide, and you're conducting an investigation."

"Okay, let's say we shake down Ehrbach's place."

"Yes, and you find the third piece of that picture."

"Assuming we do, *then* what?"

"Then you go after Weinberg."

"How? What's our legal excuse *there*, Krutch?"

"You don't have one. You couldn't approach him as fuzz, anyway. He's been in trouble before. He's not likely to co-operate with The Law."

"What kind of trouble?"

"Assault. He beat a woman half to death with his fists. He's enormous, must weigh at least two hundred and fifty pounds. He could break either one of you in half with just a dirty look, believe me." Krutch paused. "What do you say?"

"It might be worth our time," Carella said.

"We'll have to talk it over with the lieutenant."

"Yeah, you talk it over with him. I think *he* might understand how nice it would be to recover that bank loot." Krutch smiled again. "Meanwhile, I'll leave the list and the picture with you?"

"Won't you need them?"

"I've got copies," Krutch said.

"How come somebody so smart needs our help?" Carella asked.

"That smart I ain't," Krutch said. He took a card from his wallet and placed it on the desk. "That's my home number," he said. "Don't try to reach me at Trans-American. Let me know what you decide."

"We will indeed," Carella said.

"Thank you," Krutch said. He offered his hand to Brown. "Detective Brown?" He retrieved his hand, shook hands next with Carella. "Detective Carella?" Then he smiled his dazzling smile and went out of the squadroom.

"What do you think?" Brown said.

"I don't know. What do *you* think?" Carella said.

"I don't know. Let's see what the lieutenant thinks."

3

Lieutenant Byrnes looked at the list of names, and then turned his attention to the two pieces of the photograph:

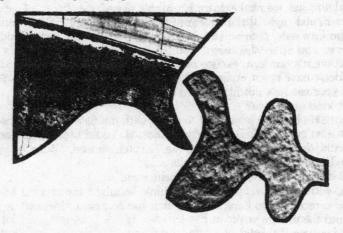

"Don't even look like they *belong* together," he muttered.

They had filled him in on Krutch's story, and he had listened intently, head cocked slightly to one side, blue eyes shifting from Carella's face to Brown's as they alternately picked up threads of the narrative. He was a thickset man, Byrnes, with heavy hands, the backs of which were sprinkled with liver spots. His hair was going white, and he had a bald patch barely beginning to show at the back of his head. But there was a sense of contained power about him, the certain knowledge that he had broken many a hood's nose before being promoted to his present desk job. Impatiently, he looked at the photograph segments again, turning each one on his desktop, trying to fit them together, and then giving up the job.

"Guy comes in here with a story," Byrnes said, "what does he expect us to do? Drop everything and go on a goddamn treasure hunt?"

"Well," Carella said, "there's a possibility he's right."

"A pretty *slim* possibility, if you ask me. Where'd you say he got this story? From an old lady who hardly speaks English, right?"

"That's right."

"But she told him in Italian," Brown said. "She told him the picture shows where *il tresoro* is buried."

"*Il* te*soro*," Carella corrected.

"Did she say that? Buried?"

"No. I don't know. Hidden, I think she said. What'd she say, Steve?"

"Just that the picture shows where the treasure *is*, I think. That's all."

"She didn't say buried, huh?"

"I don't think so."

"I just hate to put a man on this, and then..." Byrnes shook his head. "It's not as if we've got nothing else to do around here, you know."

The detectives were silent.

"Let's say we search Ehrbach's place," Byrnes said. "And let's say we *do* find a third piece of this picture, then what?"

"Then Krutch's story begins to sound a little better," Carella said.

"Yes, but where do we go from there?" Byrnes asked. "I'm willing to put you on it ... okay, we don't find anything, we've only wasted a day. But suppose we *do* find something, *then* what? This fellow ... what's his name?" Byrnes consulted the list again. "Weinberg. Albert Weinberg. He's the next logical step. But Krutch says the man's got an assault record, which means he can smell The Law six blocks away. Whoever we send after him would have to use a cover, and I'd need a second man for a contact and drop. That's two men out of action, maybe on a wild-goose chase." He shook his head again. "I don't know." He looked down at the photograph segments and then up at Carella. "What's your caseload like, Steve?"

"I've got that dry-cleaning store holdup, and the muggings over on Ainsley ... six in the past two weeks, same m.o. I've also got a lead I want to run down on the pusher who's been working the junior high school on Seventeenth. And there're two cases coming to trial this month. I have to be in court on Tuesday, matter of fact."

"What about you, Artie?"

"I forgot to mention..." Carella said.

"Yeah?"

"Couple of burglaries over in Smoke Rise. We've been getting a lot of static on those because the sister of a municipal judge lives in the neighborhood."

"Yeah, so let Hizzoner go find the burglar," Byrnes said dryly. "Artie?"

"A hit-and-run, a jewelry store holdup, and a knifing. I'm supposed to be in court tomorrow on the knifing. It'll be a quick trial – the guy stabbed his wife when he found her in bed with another man."

"You want to take a crack at this Weinberg character? Assuming we find anything in Ehrbach's apartment?"

"Sure," Brown said.

"Does Weinberg live in the precinct? Would he be likely to spot you as a cop?"

"I don't know."

"Check him out with the I.B., see if they've got an address for him."

"Right."

"You'd better find out where he's operated, too, which cities, and pick your cover accordingly. Don't make it anything too big, Artie, don't say you're a mob gun from Chicago or anything like that. Be too simple for him to check if he's got any connections at all. Make it a numbers runner, a small-time pusher, something unimportant. You stumbled on your piece of the picture, you think Weinberg's got another piece, and you want to team up with him. Keep it as simple as that."

"Right."

"Steve, you'll have to be the outside man at the skunk works."

"Fine."

"Arrange a drop, and keep your contacts as few as possible. This guy Weinberg doesn't sound like a customer to fool around with. And let's not go overboard on this thing, okay? Let's handle it in easy stages. If we don't turn up anything at Ehrbach's place, that's it, back to the salt mines. If we hit pay dirt, we move on to Weinberg, stay with him a day or two. If it looks like he's got a piece of the picture, we stick with him. Otherwise, we thank Krutch for his information and we drop the whole damn thing." He looked up at the two men. "Anything else?"

"Just one thing," Carella said. "The I.B. called a few minutes ago and verified everything Krutch said about the two dead men."

"So?"

"So maybe he's right about what we'll find in Ehrbach's apartment, too."

"Maybe," Byrnes said.

Judging from Eugene Edward Ehrbach's apartment, the man had been a highly successful burglar. One could, of course, argue that anyone who had already taken two falls for burglary could not, by any stretch of the imagination, be considered a *successful* burglar. But the fact remained that Ehrbach lived in a luxury apartment close to Silvermine Oval; neither of the detectives who shook down the place could have afforded anything even remotely similar to it on their salaries.

The doorman was not pleased to see them.

He had been hired to check on any and all strangers entering the building, his job being to prevent tenants from getting strangled in the elevator, and incidentally to call taxis for them on rainy nights. It didn't matter that *these* two strangers identified themselves as detectives from the 87th Squad. The doorman liked detectives as much as he liked stranglers or burglars. He had no way of knowing, naturally, that Eugene Edward Ehrbach had been a burglar, and undoubtedly a highly successful one. He told the detectives that he would have to check with the manager of the building, and even though they told him they were investigating a murder, he insisted on making his telephone call. When he got off the phone, he said, "It's okay, but don't go making a mess up there," which was exactly what they *intended* to make up there.

Ehrbach had lived on the tenth floor of the building, in an apartment at the end of the corridor. There were three other apartments on the floor. Ehrbach's was the choice apartment since it overlooked the River Harb. There were two rivers flanking Isola, the Harb on the north and the Dix on the south. Apartments overlooking either of these waterways were considered very desirable, even though the view of the next state across the Harb featured a big housing development and the roller coaster of an amusement park, and the view of the Dix revealed a grimy gray hospital on an island, mid-river, a collection of spiny bridges leading to Calm's Point and Sands Spit, and a house of detention on another island out beyond Devil's Causeway. From Ehrbach's living room window (in addition to the roller coaster, the housing development, and an insistently blinking SPRY sign), you could also see all the way uptown to the Hamilton Bridge.

Carella and Brown entered the apartment with a passkey provided by the doorman, and found themselves in a carpeted foyer. Their reflected images looked back at them from a gilt-framed mirror hanging on the wall facing the door. A long narrow table was against that wall, just below the mirror. The apartment ran off to the right and left of the foyer. They made a perfunctory check of the place, discovering that there were four rooms in all: living room, kitchen, den, and bedroom. A small bathroom was off the entrance foyer, and another bathroom adjoined the bedroom. That was it, and very nice indeed. They divided the apartment in half, Carella taking the foyer, the small bedroom, the kitchen and the den; Brown taking the bedroom, the living room, and the second bathroom. With all the expertise and *sang-froid* of a demolition crew, they started searching for the scrap of photo Irving Krutch was certain Ehrbach had possessed. They began the job at noon. At midnight, they were still looking.

They had made two trips downstairs for sandwiches and coffee, Carella going out at 2 p.m. and Brown going out at seven. Aside from slashing up the mattresses and upholstered furniture, a license not granted to them, they had done a thorough and painstaking job, but had found nothing. They sat now in the living room, exhausted, Brown in an easy chair near a standing floor lamp, Carella straddling the piano bench. The lamp was on, it cast a warm and cozy glow over the moss-green wall-to-wall carpeting.

"Maybe we ought to take it up," Brown said.

"Take what up?" Carella asked.

"The carpet."

"That's a big job."

"The way they lay this stuff," Brown said, "is they've got these strips of wood with tacks sticking up out of it. They nail that to the floor all around the room, and then hook the carpet onto it. You ever see these guys at work?"

"Yeah," Carella said.

"You got wall-to-wall carpeting in your house?" Brown asked.

"No."

"Me, neither. A hood like Ehrbach has wall-to-wall carpeting, and all I've got is a ten-by-twelve in the living room. How do you figure it?"

"Guess we're in the wrong racket," Carella said. "Did you check out all these books?"

"Every page."

"How about the switch plates? Did you unscrew them?"

"Yep."

"Nothing scotch-taped to the backs, huh?"

"Nothing."

Carella glanced at the floor lamp. "Did you take off that shade?"

"Yeah, zero. It'd show, anyway, with the light on."

"That's right, yeah."

"How about the ball in the toilet tank?" Brown asked. "They're hollow, you know. He might have..."

"I pried it open," Carella said. "Nothing."

"Maybe we *ought* to take up this damn carpet," Brown said.

"Be here all night," Carella said. "If we have to do that, we'd better get a crew in tomorrow. Did you look in the piano?"

"Yeah, *and* the piano bench."

"How about the clock-radio in the bedroom?"

"Unscrewed the back. Nothing. The television in the den?"

"Same thing." Carella smiled. "Maybe we ought to do what my son does when he loses one of his toys."

"What does he do?"

"Well, he starts by saying, 'Where would *you* be if you were a fire truck?'"

"Okay, where would *you* be if you were a photograph?"

"In an album," Carella said.

"You find any picture albums around?"

"Nope."

"So where *else* would you be?"

"We're looking for something maybe this big," Carella said, curling his thumb and forefinger into a C some two inches wide. "Maybe even smaller. He could have hidden it anywhere."

"Um-huh," Brown said, and nodded. "Where?"

"Did you look in those cereal boxes in the kitchen?"

"All of them. He sure likes cornflakes."

"Maybe it *is* under the carpet," Carella said.

"Would *you* put it under the carpet?"

"No. Too much trouble checking on it."

"That's what I figure. Have to move the furniture around and pull up the whole damn rug everytime you wanted to make sure the picture was still there."

"So where *would* you be?" Carella said.

"Home asleep," Brown answered.

"Okay, where *wouldn't* you be?"

"I wouldn't be in plain sight of two cops coming to look for me."

"It sure as hell ain't in plain sight," Carella said.

"Probably right under our noses, though, and we haven't yet spotted it," Brown said. "Maybe we need a little more light on the subject." He rose from the easy chair, sighed heavily, and walked to the piano. A lamp with a brass base rested on the burled walnut top. Brown switched it on. "There," he said, "how's that?"

"The better to see you with, my dear," Carella said.

"You want to look around a little more, or shall we come back in the morning and rip up the carpet?"

"Let's give it another whirl," Carella said. He got off the piano bench, walked to the middle of the room, looked around, and said, "So where the hell is it?"

"You don't think he could have rolled it up and stuck it inside a cigarette or something?" Brown asked.

"Why not? Did you check out that cigarette box?"

"I looked inside it, but I didn't slit any of the cigarettes."

"Try it," Carella said. "We may get lucky." He walked to the standing floor lamp and started to unscrew the shade.

"I've already done that," Brown said.

"Right, I'm getting punchy," Carella said. He looked down into the lamp, said, "One of the bulbs is out," and then walked across the room to where Brown was slitting cigarettes open with his thumbnail.

"Just 'cause the man's a burglar," Brown said, "that don't mean he's got to be a bulb-snatcher, too."

"Course not," Carella said. "How we doing there?"

"I may get cancer of the thumb," Brown said.

He looked up at Carella. Their eyes met, and instant recognition flashed onto both their faces at the same moment, leaping the distance between them like heat lightning.

"Yeah!" Carella said, and started moving back toward the floor lamp.

"You thinking what I'm thinking?" Brown said, following him instantly.

"Oh, you *know* it," Carella said.

There were three electric light bulbs in the lamp. Two of them were illuminated, and the third one was out. Carella reached in through the open top of the shade and unscrewed the one bulb that was not burning.

"There it is," he said. "Unplug this damn thing before we electrocute ourselves."

"Talk about a light bulb going on over a man's head," Brown said, and pulled the plug. Carella reached into the open socket with his thumb and forefinger. Neatly folded in half and then in half again, nestled into the bottom of the socket where it had been hidden by the light bulb screwed in on top of it, was the piece of the photo Krutch had promised they would find.

4

The Bureau of Criminal Identification was located at Headquarters, downtown on High Street. It was open twenty-four hours a day, its sole reason for existence being the collection, compilation, and cataloguing of any and all information descriptive of criminals. The I.B. maintained a Fingerprint File, a Criminal Index File, a Wanted File, a Degenerate File, a Parolee File, a Released Prisoner File, and Known Gamblers, Known Rapists, Known Muggers, Known You-Name-It files. Its Modus Operandi File alone contained more than 100,000 photographs of known criminals. And since all persons charged with and convicted of a crime were photographed and fingerprinted as specified by law, the file was continually growing and continually being brought up to date. The I.B. received and classified some 206,000 sets of prints yearly, and answered requests for more than 250,000 criminal records from police departments all over the country. Arthur Brown's request for information on Albert Weinberg was one of those. The package from the I.B. was waiting on his desk when he got to work that Friday morning.

As Krutch had faithfully reported, Weinberg had indeed been busted several years back. According to the supplementary information enclosed with his yellow sheet, he had started a fist fight in a bar, and then – for no apparent reason – suddenly attacked a little old lady who was sitting on a stool at the end of the bar, knocking her senseless and taking seventeen dollars and eighty-four cents from her purse. He had pleaded guilty to all charges and had served his time at Castleview Prison upstate, from which he had been released two years back. He had not been in any trouble with the law since.

Brown studied the information carefully, glanced up at the clock on the squadroom wall, and decided he had better get his ass down to the Criminal Courts Building. He told Carella where he was going, advised him that he would probably try to contact Weinberg later that day, and then left the office. He thought of the snapshot all the way downtown. There were now three pieces: the one they had found clenched in the dead Ehrbach's fist, and which was shaped somewhat like a dancing girl; the one Irving Krutch had voluntarily delivered to the squadroom, and which was obviously a corner piece; and now the one they had found hidden in Ehrbach's floor lamp, shaped like a drunken amoeba. He kept thinking of those pieces all during the trial.

His testimony was relatively simple. He explained to the assistant district attorney that at the time of the arrest, the defendant Michael Lloyd had been sitting in the kitchen of his home with a bloody bread knife in his hand. His wife was in the bedroom, stabbed in the shoulder. Her lover was no place to be found; he had apparently left in a great hurry, leaving behind his shoes and his socks. Brown testified that the defendant Michael Lloyd had not resisted arrest, and that he had told the arresting officers that he had tried to kill his wife and hoped the bitch was dead. On the basis of his statement and the evidence of the bloody knife in his hands and the wounded woman in the bedroom, he had been charged with attempted murder. In the cross-examination, the defense lawyer asked a lot of questions about Lloyd's "alleged" statement at the time of his arrest, wanting of course to know whether the prisoner had been properly advised of his rights, and Brown testified that everything had been conducted according to Miranda-Escobedo, and the district attorney excused him without a redirect, and called his next witness, the patrolman who had been present in the apartment when Lloyd had made his statement about having wanted to kill his wife. Brown left the Criminal Courts Building at three that afternoon.

Now, at 6 p.m., he sat at a table near the plate-glass front window of a cafeteria called The R&R, and knew that he was being cased from the street outside by none other than Albert Weinberg himself in person. Weinberg was even bigger than Krutch had described him, and certainly bigger than he had looked in the I.B.'s mug shot. At least as tall as Brown, heavier, with tremendous shoulders and powerful arms, a huge barrel chest and massive hands, he walked past the plate-glass window four times before deciding to come into the restaurant. He was wearing a plaid, long-sleeved sports shirt, the sleeves rolled up past his thick wrists. His reddish-blond hair was curly and long, giving his green-eyed face a cherubic look that denied the brute power of his body. He came directly to Brown's table, approaching him with the confident stride most very strong men possess, stood staring down at him, and immediately said, "You look like fuzz."

"So do you," Brown answered.

"How do I know you're not?"

"How do I know *you're* not?" Brown said. "Why don't you sit down?"

"Sure," Weinberg answered. He pulled out a chair, adjusted his body to the seat and back as though he were maneuvering a bulldozer into a tight corner, and then folded his huge hands on the tabletop. "Let's hear it again," he said.

"From the top?"

"From the top," Weinberg said, and nodded. "First, your name."

"Artie Stokes. I'm from Salt Lake City, you ever been there?"

"No."

"Nice city," Brown said. "Do you ski? Supposed to be great powder skiing at Alta."

"Did you call me to talk about the Olympics, or what?" Weinberg said.

"I thought you might be a skier," Brown answered.

"Are *you*?"

"How many Negroes have you ever seen on the ski slopes?"

"I've never been *on* the ski slopes."

"But you get my point."

"I'm still waiting for your story, Stokes."

"I already gave it to you on the phone."

"Give it to me again."

"Why?"

"Let's say we had a poor connection."

"Okay," Brown said, and sighed. "Couple of weeks ago, I bought a piece of a picture and a couple of names from a guy in Salt Lake. I paid two grand for the package. Guy who sold it to me was fresh out of Utah State, and strapped for cash."

"What's his name?"

"Danny Firth. He was doing eight years for armed robbery, got out in April and needed a stake to set up his next job. That's why he was willing to part with what he had."

"What'd he have?"

"I just told you. Two names and a piece of a snapshot."

"And you were willing to pay two grand for *that*?"

"That's right."

"Why?"

"Because Firth told me I could get seven hundred and fifty thousand dollars just by fitting my piece of the snapshot into the whole picture."

"He told you that, huh?"

"That's what he told me."

"I'm surprised he didn't sell you the Calm's Point Bridge while he was at it."

"This ain't the Calm's Point Bridge, Weinberg, and you know it."

Weinberg was silent for a few moments. He kept looking down at his clasped hands. Then he raised his eyes to Brown's and said, "You've a piece of the snapshot, huh?"

"That's right."

"And two names, huh?"

"That's right."

"What're the two names?"

"Yours is one of them."

"And the other one?"

"I'll tell you that after we make a deal."

"And what're these names supposed to be?"

"They're supposed to be the names of two people who've *also* got pieces of that picture."

"And two names, huh?"

"That's right."

"You're nuts," Weinberg said.

"I told you most of this on the phone," Brown said. "If you think I'm nuts, what're you doing here?"

Weinberg studied him again. He unclasped his hands, took a cigarette from a package in his pocket, offered one to Brown, and then lighted both of them. He let out a stream of smoke, leaned back in his chair, and said, "Did your pal Danny Firth say *how* you could get seven hundred and fifty G's for pasting a picture together?"

"He did."

"How?"

"Weinberg ... *you* know, and *I* know the full picture shows where Carmine Bonamico dropped the N.S.L.A. loot."

"I don't know what you're talking about."

"You know *exactly* what I'm talking about. Now how about it? You want to keep playing cute, or you want to talk a deal?"

"I want some more information."

"Like what?"

"Like how'd your pal Danny Firth come across his piece?"

"He got it from a guy at Utah State. The guy was doing life, no chance of getting out unless he *busted* out, which he wasn't about to do. Danny promised to look after his wife and kids if he recovered the loot."

"So Danny gets out, and turns right around and sells you his piece, huh?"

"That's right."

"Nice guy, Danny."

"What do you expect?" Brown said, and smiled. "Honor among thieves?"

"Which brings us to you," Weinberg said, returning the smile. "What's *your* bag?"

"I'm in and out of a lot of things."

"Like what?"

"The last thing I was in and out of was San Quentin," Brown said, and smiled again. "I did five years for hanging some paper. It was a bum wrap."

"It's *always* a bum wrap," Weinberg said. "Let's get back to the picture for a minute. How many pieces *are* there, do you know?"

"I was hoping you'd know."

"I don't."

"We can talk a deal, anyway."

"Maybe," Weinberg said. "Who else knows about this?"

"Nobody."

"You sure you didn't tell your brother all about it? Or some broad?"

"I haven't *got* a brother. And I never tell broads nothing." Brown paused. "Why? Who'd *you* tell?"

"Not a soul. You think I'm crazy? There's big money involved here."'

"Oh, all at once you *know* there's big money involved, huh?"

"What's the other name on your list?"

"Do we have a deal?"

"Only if it's a name I don't already have."

"How many do you have?"

"Just one."

"That makes us even."

"Unless it's the same name."

"If it's the same name, neither of us have lost anything. Here's the deal, Weinberg, take it or leave it. I put up the name and the piece *I've* got, you put up the name and the piece *you've* got. If we find the loot, we split it fifty-fifty – *after* deducting expenses. I've already laid out two grand, you know."

"That's your headache," Weinberg said. "I'm willing to share whatever expenses we have from now on, but don't expect me to pay for a *bar mitzvah* when you were thirteen."

"Okay, forget the two grand. Have we got a deal?"

"We've got a deal," Weinberg said, and extended his hand across the table. Brown took it. "Let's see your piece of the picture," Weinberg said.

"Amateur night in Dixie," Brown said, shaking his head. "You didn't *really* think I'd have it with me, did you?"

"No harm trying," Weinberg said, and grinned. "Meet me later tonight. We'll put it all on the table then."

"Where?"

"My place?" Weinberg asked.

"Where's that?"

"220 South Kirby. Apartment 36."

"What time?"

"Eleven o'clock okay with you?"

"I'll be there," Brown said.

220 South Kirby was in a slum as rank as a cesspool. Arthur Brown knew such slums well. The overflowing garbage cans in front of the building were quite familiar to him. The front stoop held no surprises; cracked cement steps, the middle riser of which was lettered in white paint with the words NO SITTING ON STOOP; rusted wrought-iron railings; a shattered pane of glass in the entrance door. The locks on the mailboxes in the foyer, where welfare checks were deposited each month, were broken. There was no light in the foyer and only a single naked bulb illuminated the first-floor landing. The hallway smelled of cooking, breathing, eliminating. The stench that assailed Brown as he climbed to the third floor brought back too many memories of a lanky boy lying in bed in his underwear, listening to the sounds of rats foraging in the kitchen. His sister, in the bed next to his, in the same bedroom shared by his mother and father, would whisper in the darkness, "Are they here again, Artie?" and he would nod wide-eyed and say reassuringly, "They'll go away, Penny."

One night, Penny said, "Suppose they don't, Artie?"

He could find no answer. In his mind's eye, he saw himself walking into the kitchen the next morning to discover the room swarming with long-tailed rats, their sharp fangs dripping blood.

Even now, he shuddered at the thought.

Suppose they don't, Artie?

His sister had died at the age of seventeen, from an overdose of heroin administered in a cellar club by a teenage girl who, like Penny, was one of the debs in a street gang called The Warrior Princes. He could remember a time when one of the boys painted the name of the gang in four-foot high letters on the brick wall of a housing project – THE WARIOR PRINCES.

In the darkness of the third-floor landing, Brown rapped on the door to 36, and heard Weinberg say from within, "Yes, who is it?"

"Me," he answered. "Stokes."

"It's open, come in," Weinberg said.

He opened the door.

Something warned him a second too late. As he opened the door, he could see through into the kitchen, but Weinberg was nowhere in sight. And then the warning came, the knowledge that Weinberg's voice had sounded very near to the closed door. He turned to his right, started to bring up his hand in protection against the coming blow – but too late. Something hard hit him on the side of his head, just below the temple. He fell sideways, almost blacked out, tried to get to his knees, stumbled, and looked up into the muzzle of a .38 Special.

"Hello there, Stokes," Weinberg said, and grinned. "Keep your hands flat on the floor, don't make a move or I'll kill you. That's it."

He stepped gingerly around Brown, reached under his jacket from behind, and pulled his gun from the shoulder holster there.

"I hope you've got a license for this," he said, grinned again, and tucked the gun into the waistband of his trousers. "Now get up."

"What do you hope to accomplish?" Brown said.

"I hope to get what I want without having to make any cockamamie deals."

"And when you've got it? Then what?"

"I move on to bigger and better things. With*out* you."

"You'd better move far and fast," Brown said, "I'm sure as hell going to find you."

"Not if you're dead, you won't."

"You'd cool me in your own apartment? Who're you trying to kid?"

"It's *not* my apartment," Weinberg said, and grinned again.

"I checked the address with..." Brown started, and shut his mouth before he'd said, "the Identification Bureau."

"Yeah, with what?"

"With your name in the phone book. Don't try to con me, Weinberg. This is your pad, all right."

"*Used* to be, only *used* to be. I moved out two months ago, kept the same phone number."

"Then how'd you get in here tonight?"

"The super's a wino. A bottle of Thunderbird goes a long way in this building."

"What about whoever lives here now?"

"He's a night watchman. He leaves here at ten and doesn't get home until six in the morning. Any other questions?"

"Yeah," Brown said. "What makes you think I'm in this alone?"

"What difference does it make?"

"I'll tell you what difference it makes. You can take my piece of the snapshot – oh, sure, I've got it with me – but if I *am* in this with another guy, or *two* other guys, or a *dozen* other guys, you can bet your ass they've all got prints of it. So where does that leave you? I'm dead, and you've got the picture, but so have they. You're right back where you started."

"*If* there's anybody else in it with you."

"Right. And if there's anybody else, they know who you are, pal, believe me. You pull that trigger, you'd better start running. Fast."

"You told me nobody knew about this."

"Sure. You told *me* we had a deal."

"Maybe you're full of shit this time, too."

"Or maybe not. You ready to chance it? You know the kind of heat you'd be asking for? Oh, not only from the cops – homicide's still against the law, you know. But also from..."

"The cops don't bother me. They'll go looking for the guy who lives here."

"Unless one of my friends tells them you and I had a meeting here to-night."

"It sounds very good, Stokes. But only if you've *really* got some friends out there. Otherwise, it ain't worth a nickel."

"Consider another angle then. You kill me, and you get my piece of the picture, sure. But you don't get that name you want. That's up *here*, Weinberg." He tapped his temple with his forefinger.

"I hadn't thought of that," Weinberg said.

"Think about it now," Brown said. "I'll give you five minutes."

"*You'll* give *me* five minutes?" Weinberg said, and burst out laughing. "*I'm* holding the gun, and *you're* giving me five minutes."

"Always play 'em like you've got 'em, my daddy used to tell me," Brown said, and smiled.

"Your daddy ever get hit with a slug from a .38?"

"No, but he *did* get hit with a baseball bat one time," Brown said, and Weinberg burst out laughing again.

"Maybe you wouldn't make such a bad partner after all," he said.

"So what do you think?"

"I don't know."

"Put up the gun. Give mine back, and we'll be on equal terms again. Then let's cut the crap and get on with the goddamn business."

"How do I know you won't try to cold-cock me?"

"Because maybe *you've* got friends, too, same as me."

"Always play 'em like you've got 'em," Weinberg said, and chuckled.

"Yes or no?"

"Sure," Weinberg said. He took Brown's gun from his waistband and handed it to him muzzle first. Brown immediately put it back into his holster. Weinberg hesitated a moment, and then put his own gun into a holster on his right hip. "Okay," he said. "Do we shake hands all over again?"

"I'd like to," Brown said.

"The two men shook hands.

"Let's see your piece of the picture," Weinberg said.

"Let's see yours," Brown said.

"The Mutual Faith and Trust Society," Weinberg said. "Okay, we'll do it together."

Together, both men took our their wallets. Together, both men removed from plastic compartments the glossy segments of the larger photograph. The piece Brown placed on the tabletop was the one he and Carella had found hidden in Ehrbach's floor lamp. The piece Weinberg placed beside it was a corner piece unlike any the police already had in their possession.

Both men studied the pieces. Weinberg began moving them around on the tabletop. A grin cracked across his face. "We're gonna make good partners," he said. "Look at this. They *fit*."

Brown looked.

Then he smiled. He smiled because the pieces sure as hell did fit. But he also smiled because, heh-heh, unbeknownst to his new partner and straight man, there were two additional pieces of the picture in the top drawer of his desk back at the squadroom, and two and two make four, and who knew what *these* two pieces and *those* two pieces together might reveal, who indeed? So Brown smiled and Weinberg smiled, and everybody was having just a wonderful old time putting together pieces of this old jigsaw puzzle.

"Now the names," Weinberg said, sounding very much like the M.C. at the Annual Academy Awards Presentations.

"Eugene Edward Ehrbach," Brown said, smiling.

"Geraldine Ferguson," Weinberg said, smiling.

"Ehrbach's dead," Brown said, and the smile dropped from Weinberg's face.

"What?" he shouted. "What the hell kind of...?"

"He was killed Wednesday night. The cops found..."

"Dead?" Weinberg shouted. "*Dead?*"

"Dead," Brown said. "But the cops found..."

"Is this a double cross? Is that what this is? Some kind of a double cross?"

"You've got to learn to calm down," Brown said.

"*I'll* calm down! I'll break your head in a million pieces, that's what I'll do."

"He was carrying a piece of the picture," Brown said softly.

"What? Who?"

"Ehrbach."

"A piece of *our* picture?"

"That's right."

"Why didn't you say so? Where is it?"

"The cops have it."

"The cops! Jesus Christ, Stokes..."

"Cops can be bought," Brown said, "same as anybody else. Ehrbach's dead and anything they found on him is probably in a brown paper bag someplace being watched by a police clerk. All we got to do is find out where, and then cross a few palms."

"I don't like negotiating with fuzz," Weinberg said.

"Who does? But to survive in this city, you *got* to deal with them every now and then."

"Biggest fuckin' thieves in the world," Weinberg said.

"Look," Brown said, "if even a felony can be squared for a couple of bills, we should be able to lay our hands on Ehrbach's piece for maybe fifty, sixty bucks. All we got to do is find out where it is."

"How do we do that? Call the cops and ask?"

"Maybe. I got to think about it a little. Now what about this Geraldine what's-her-name?"

"Ferguson. She runs an art gallery on Jefferson Avenue. I've busted her apartment maybe six or seven times already, couldn't find the picture. I wouldn't be surprised she stuck it up her twat," Weinberg said, and burst out laughing. Brown laughed with him. They were still good old buddies and still thrilled and amazed by the fact that their two separate pieces fit together as neatly as Yin and Yang.

"Have you got a print of this?" Brown asked.

"Naturally," Weinberg said. "And you?"

"Naturally."

"You want to exchange pieces, is that it?"

"That's it."

"Done," Weinberg said, and picked up the section Brown had placed on the tabletop. Brown picked up the remaining section, and both men grinned again. "Now let's go down for a drink," Weinberg said. "We got a lot of strategy to work out."

"Right," Brown said. As they went toward the front door, he said – casually, he thought – "By the way, how'd you happen to *get* your piece of the snapshot?"

"Be happy to tell you," Weinberg said.

"Good."

"As soon as you tell me how you *really* got yours," Weinberg added, and began chuckling.

Brown suddenly wondered which of them was the straight man.

5

——

It was all happening too quickly and too easily.

If getting seven hundred and fifty thousand dollars was always this simple, Brown was definitely in the wrong racket. He almost wished that he and Weinberg were truly partners. There was something about the big man that Brown liked, despite the fact that he was a felon. He did not leave Weinberg until two o'clock the next morning. By that time, each of the men had consumed a fifth of Scotch between them, and were calling each other Artie and Al. They had also decided that Brown should be the one who made the next approach to Geraldine Ferguson. Weinberg had been to her gallery several times with offers to buy the segment he was certain she possessed, but each time she had professed ignorance of the photograph, segmented or otherwise. Weinberg told Brown that he *knew* the girl had the goods they were after, but he would not reveal *how* he knew. Brown said that was a hell of a way to start a partnership, and Weinberg said Brown had started in an even *worse* way, giving him all that bullshit about a lifer at Utah State, man, that was straight out of Mickey Mouse, had Brown expected him to believe it? Brown said Well, I guess we both got our reasons for not wanting our sources known, and Weinberg said Well, maybe when we get to know each other better, and Brown said I hope so, and Weinberg said Man, I never thought I'd be partners with a spade.

Brown looked at him.

It was hip these days, he knew, for white men to call Negroes "spades", but to Brown this was simply another of the words which had once been considered – and which he *still* considered – derogatory. Weinberg was smiling in a boozy happy friendly way, and Brown was certain the slur had been unintentional. And yet, the word rankled, the whole fucking thing rankled.

"That bother you?" he asked.

"What bother me?" Weinberg said.

"My being a *spade*," Brown said, hitting the word hard.

Weinberg looked him square in the eye. "Did I say that? Did I call you that?"

"You did," Brown said, and nodded.

"Then I'm sorry. I didn't mean it." He extended his hand across the table. "I'm sorry, Artie," he said.

Brown took his hand. "Forget it."

"I may be a shit," Weinberg said. "I may go around beating up people and doing rotten things, but I like you, Artie, and I wouldn't hurt you by saying no dumb thing like that."

"Okay."

Weinberg was just gathering steam. "I may be the crumbiest guy ever walked the earth, I may have done some filthy things, but one thing I wouldn't do is call you no spade, Artie, not if I wasn't so piss-ass drunk and didn't know what I was saying that might hurt a good friend of mine and a partner besides."

"Okay," Brown said.

"Okay, excuse it, Artie. Excuse it. I mean it."

"Okay."

"Okay," Weinberg said. "Let's go home, Artie. Artie, I think we better go home. I always get in fights in bars, and I don't want to get in no trouble when we got our little deal cooking, okay?" He winked. "Okay?" He winked again. "Tomorrow morning, you got to go visit little Geraldine Ferguson. Tell her she don't give us that picture, we'll come around and do something terrible to her, okay?" Weinberg smiled. "I can't think of nothing terrible right now, but I'll think of something in the morning, okay?"

On Saturday morning, Brown put the new photo scrap into an envelope together with Geraldine Ferguson's name and address, sealed the envelope, and dropped it into a mailbox in the hallway of 1134 Culver Avenue, three blocks from the precinct. The name on the box was Cara Binieri, which was Steve Carella's little joke, *carabinieri* meaning fuzz in Italian. They had decided between them that Brown was to stay away from the squadroom, and whereas he hoped to call Carella later in the day, he wanted the information to be waiting for him in the mailbox this morning, when he would pick it up on his way to work.

Brown's own day started somewhat more glamorously.

It also ended in a pretty glamorous way.

Geraldine Ferguson was a white woman, petite, with long straight black hair and brown eyes and a generous mouth. She was in her early thirties, wearing purple bellbottom slacks and a man-tailored shirt done in lavender satin. She had big golden hoops looped into her ear lobes, and she greeted Brown with a smile nothing less than radiant.

"Good morning," she said. "Isn't it a *beautiful* morning?"

"It's a lovely morning," Brown said.

"Are you here for the Gonzagos?" she asked.

"I don't think so," Brown said. "What *are* the gonzagos?"

"Luis Gonzago," she said, and smiled again. "He's a painter. I thought you might have wanted to see his stuff, but we've already taken it down. Will you be going to Los Angeles?"

"No, I hadn't planned to," Brown said.

"Because he'll be having a show at the Herron Gallery out there starting next Tuesday. On Sepulveda."

"No, I won't be going to Los Angeles."

"That's a shame," she said, and smiled.

She was perhaps five-two or five-three, with a perfectly proportioned figure for her size. She moved with a swift feminine grace that he found delightful, her brown eyes flashing in the sunlight that streamed through the front plate-glass window, the smile breaking as sharp and as fast as a curve ball. She threw her arms wide, and said, "But we've got loads of other stuff, so if you'd like me to help you, I'd be happy to. Or you can just look around on your own, if you like. What were you interested in? Paintings or sculpture?"

"Well," Brown said, and hesitated, wondering exactly how he should play this. "Is this your own gallery?" he asked, stalling.

"Yes, it is," she said.

"Then you're Miss Ferguson. I mean, this *is* the Ferguson Gallery, so I guess..."

"Well, *Mrs.* Ferguson, really," she said. "But *not* really," she added, and the smile broke again, swift and clean. "I was married to Mr. Ferguson, Mr. *Harold* Ferguson, but Mr. Ferguson and I are no longer sharing bed and board, and so whereas I'm still Geraldine Ferguson, I am no longer *Mrs.* Ferguson. Oh hell," she said, "why don't you just call me Gerry? What's *your* name?"

"Arthur Stokes," he said.

"Are you a cop, Arthur?" she asked flatly.

"No," he said. "What gave you that idea?"

"You're big like a cop," she said, and shrugged. "Also, you carry a gun."

"Do I?"

"Mm-huh. Right here," she said, and pointed.

"I didn't think it showed."

"Well, Harold was in the diamond business, and he had a carry-permit, and he used to wear this *enormous* revolver in a shoulder holster, right where yours is. So I guess when your husband wears a gun all the time, you get used to the way it looks, and that's how I spotted yours right away. Why do you wear a gun, Arthur? Are you in the diamond business?"

"No," he said, "I'm in the insurance business."

He figured that was a fair enough beginning, even though he had borrowed the occupation from Irving Krutch who, to his knowledge, did *not* carry a gun.

"Oh, do insurance men wear guns?" Gerry asked. "I didn't know that."

"Yes," he said, "if they're insurance investigators."

"Don't *tell* me!" she squealed. "Someone's had a painting stolen! You're here to check on authenticity."

"Well, no," he said. "Not exactly."

"Arthur," she said, "I think you're a cop, I really do."

"Now why would a cop be visiting *you*, Miss Ferguson?"

"Gerry. Maybe because I charge such exorbitant prices," she said, and smiled. "I don't really. Yes, I do really. Would you like to see some pictures while you decide if you're a cop or not?"

She led him around the gallery. The walls were white, with recessed overhead lighting fixtures that illuminated the hanging paintings and standing pieces of sculpture. Her taste in paintings was a bit far-out for Brown, wildly colorful, non-objective geometric tangles that overpowered the eye and defied analysis. The sculpture was of the junkyard variety, automobile headlights welded to Stillson wrenches, a plumber's red-cupped plunger wired to the broken handle and frayed-straw brush of a broom.

"I can see we're hardly eliciting any wild response," Gerry said, and smiled. "What kind of art do you like?"

"Well, I did have a specific picture in mind," Brown said.

"Did someone see it here?" she asked. "Would it have been in the Gonzago exhibit?"

"I don't think so."

"What kind of a painting is it?"

"It isn't a painting. It's a photograph."

Gerry shook her head. "It couldn't have been here. We've never had a photographic show, not since I've owned the gallery, anyway – and that's close to five years."

"It's not even a whole photograph," Brown said, and watched her.

"Oh-*ho*," she said. This time, she didn't smile. "What happened to the other guy?"

"What other guy?"

"The guy who's been in here three or four thousand times in the past two months. He's *yay* tall, and he's got blondish curly hair, and he said his name was Al Reynolds the first time he came in, and then forgot what he'd told me and said his name was Al *Randolph* the second time around. Is *he* a cop?"

"We're neither of us cops."

"Mr. Stark . . ."

"Stokes," Brown said.

"Just checking," Gerry said, and grinned. "Mr. Stokes . . ."

"Arthur . . ."

"Arthur, I don't have what you're looking for. Believe me. If I had it, I'd sell it to you. Assuming the price was right."

"The price can be made right."

"How right is right?"

"You name a figure," Brown said.

"Well, do you see that Albright on the wall there? It's approximately four feet square, and the gallery gets ten thousand dollars for it. The smaller painting next to it, the Sandrovich, costs five thousand. And the tiny *gouache* on the far wall costs three thousand. How large is your photograph, Arthur?"

"I have no idea. Are we talking about the *whole* picture now, or just the piece you have?"

"The whole picture."

"Five by seven? Six by eight? I'm guessing."

"Then you've never seen the whole picture?"

"Have you?"

"I haven't even seen the tiny piece you're after."

"Then how do you know it's tiny?" Brown asked.

"How much is it worth to you and your friend, Arthur? Tiny or otherwise?"

"Have you got it?"

"If I told him no, why should I tell you yes?"

"Maybe I'm more persuasive."

"Sure, look at Superspade," Gerry said, and smiled. "Faster than a rolling watermelon, able to leap tall honkies in a single bound . . ."

". . . who is in reality," Brown continued, "mild-mannered Arthur Stokes of *Ebony* magazine."

"Who are you *really* in reality, Arthur?"

"An insurance investigator, I told you."

"Your friend Reynolds or Randolph or whoever-the-hell doesn't look or sound like an insurance investigator."

"No two insurance investigators look or sound alike."

"That's right. Only cops and crooks look and sound alike. Are you and your friend cops, Arthur? Or crooks? Which?"

"Maybe one of us is a cop and the other's a crook."

"Either way, I don't have what you want."

"I think you have."

"You're right," a voice said from the rear of the gallery. "She has."

"Oh, hell," Gerry said.

Brown turned to where a blue door had opened in the otherwise white wall. A blond man in a brown suit stood in the open doorway, his hand still on the knob. He was about five feet ten inches tall, wearing a vest under the suit jacket, gold-rimmed eyeglasses, a brown-and-gold striped tie. He walked briskly to where they were standing, offering his hand to Brown and said, "Bramley Kahn, how do you do?"

"Bram, you're a pain in the ass," Gerry said.

"Arthur Stokes," Brown said. "Pleased to meet you."

"If we're going to talk business ..."

"We are *not* going to talk business," Gerry interrupted.

"I suggest," Kahn continued in his mild voice, "that we go into the office." He paused, glanced at Gerry, looked back at Brown, and said, "Shall we?"

"Why not?" Brown said.

They walked to the rear of the gallery. The office was small and simply decorated – a Danish modern desk, a single naturalistic painting of a nude on the wall opposite the desk, a thick gray rug, white walls, a white Lucite hanging light globe, several leather-and-chrome easy chairs. Gerry Ferguson, pouting, sat nearest Kahn's desk, folding her legs up under her and cupping her chin in her hand. Brown took the seat opposite Kahn, who sat behind the desk in an old-fashioned swivel chair that seemed distinctly out of place in such svelte surroundings.

"I'm Gerry's partner," Kahn explained.

"Only in the *gallery*," Gerry snapped.

"I'm also her business adviser."

"I've got some advice for *you*," Gerry said heatedly. "Keep your nose..."

"Gerry has a temper," Kahn said.

"Gerry has a jerk for a partner," Gerry said.

"Oh, my," Kahn said, and sighed.

Brown watched him, trying to determine whether he was a fag or not. His manner was effete, but not quite feminine; his voice was gently modulated, but there was no evidence in it of characteristic homosexual cadences; his gestures were small and fluid, but he neither dangled a limp wrist, nor used his hands and shoulders like a dancer's. Brown couldn't tell. The biggest queen he'd ever known had been built like a wrestler and moved with all the subtle grace of a longshoreman.

"What about the picture?" Brown asked.

"She has it," Kahn said.

"I *haven't*," Gerry said.

"Maybe I ought to leave you two alone for a while," Brown said.

"How much are you willing to pay for it, Mr. Stokes?" Kahn asked.

"That depends."

"On what?"

Brown said nothing.

Kahn said, "On whether or not it's a piece you already have, isn't that the answer?"

Brown still said nothing.

"You *do* have a piece, don't you? Or *several* pieces?"

"Is it for sale or not?" Brown asked.

"No," Gerry said.

"Yes," Kahn said. "But you still haven't made an offer, Mr. Stokes."

"Let me see it first," Brown said.

"No," Kahn said.

"No," Gerry said, just a beat behind him.

"How many pieces do you have, Mr. Stokes?"

No answer.

"Is the other gentleman your partner? Do you have more than one piece?"

No answer.

"Do you know what the picture is supposed to reveal?"

"Let *me* ask a few," Brown said.

"Please," Kahn said, and offered him the floor with an open-handed, palm-up gesture.

"Miss Ferguson..."

"I thought it was Gerry."

"Gerry ... where did you get the piece you now have?"

"You're both dreaming," Gerry said. "I don't know what either one of you is talking about."

"My client..."

"Your client, my ass," Gerry said. "You're a cop. Who are you trying to kid, Arthur?"

"*Are* you a policeman, Mr. Stokes?"

"No."

"The fuzz stench is overpowering," Gerry said.

"How do you come to be so familiar with that stench?" Brown asked.

"May I answer that one?" Kahn asked

"Keep your mouth shut, Bram," Gerry warned.

"Mrs. Ferguson's sister is a girl named Patty D'Amore," Kahn said. "Does that mean anything to you?"

"Not a thing," Brown said.

"Her husband was a cheap gangster named Louis D'Amore. He was killed some six years ago, following a bank holdup."

"I don't keep track of such things," Brown said.

"No, I'll just *bet* you don't," Gerry said. "He's a cop, Bram. And *you're* a fool."

"Sicilian blood is much, *much* thicker than water," Kahn said, and smiled. "I would imagine that in your childhood, there was plenty of talk concerning the 'stench of fuzz' while the lasagna was being served, eh, Geraldine?"

"How would you like to hear a choice Sicilian expression?" Gerry asked.

"I'd love to."

"*Va fon gool,*" Gerry said.

"Even *I* know what that means," Brown said.

"Sounds Chinese," Kahn said.

"About the picture..."

"We have it, and we'll sell it," Kahn said. "That's our business. Selling pictures."

"Have you got any customers who'll buy a picture sight unseen?" Brown asked.

"Have we got any customers who'll buy a picture that doesn't even exist?" Gerry asked.

"Well," Brown said, "why don't you give me a ring when you've settled this between you, huh?"

"Where can we reach you, Mr. Stokes?"

"I'm staying at the Selby Arms. It's a fleabag on North Founders, just off Byram Lane."

"Are you an out-of-towner, Mr. Stokes?"

"Room 502," Brown said.

"You didn't answer my question."

"You didn't answer any of mine, either," Brown said. He smiled, rose, turned to Gerry and said, "I hope you'll reconsider, Miss Ferguson."

This time, she didn't ask him to call her Gerry.

On the street outside, Brown looked for a phone booth. The first phone he tried had the dial missing. The receiver on the next phone had been severed from its metal-covered cord, undoubtedly cut with a wire cutter. The third booth he found seemed okay. He put a dime into the phone and got nothing, no dial tone, no static, no nothing. He jiggled the hook. His dime did not come back. He hung up the receiver. His dime did not come back. He hit the phone with his fist. Nothing. He went out of the booth swearing, wondering when the city was going to crack down on the illegal gambling devices the telephone company had installed all over the city and labeled "Public Telephones." He supposed a Gaylord Ravenal type would have enjoyed this kind of action – you put your money in the slot and either lost it, or else hit the jackpot and a shower of coins came out of the return chute – but Brown merely wanted to make a telephone call, and the Las Vegas aspects of such an endeavor left him absolutely cold. He finally found a working telephone in a restaurant off Tyler. With a glance heavenward, he put his dime into the slot. He got a dial tone immediately.

The number he dialed was Albert Weinberg's. Weinberg had given him his new address the night before, a rooming house on North Colman, close to Byram Lane, which was why Brown had checked into the Selby Arms, only three blocks away from Weinberg's place. When Weinberg came on the line, Brown related his encounter with the owners of the Ferguson Gallery and said he hoped to hear from them later in the day, was in fact heading back to the hotel right this minute.

"That's the Selby Arms, right?" Weinberg said.

"Yeah, on North Founders. How'd *you* make out?"

"I've been doing a little asking around," Weinberg said, "and the way I understand it, whenever some guy's been knocked off, the cops take his clothes and his belongings downtown to what they call the Property Clerk's Office. The stuff can be claimed by a relative after the medics, and the lab, and the bulls on the case are finished with it. You think I could pass for Ehrbach's brother?"

"*I* sure as hell couldn't," Brown said.

"Might be worth a try, save ourselves a few bucks."

"A fix is safer," Brown said.

"Let me go on the earie a bit longer," Weinberg said, "try to find out who runs that office."

"Okay. You know where to reach me."

"Right. Let me know if Ferguson or her pansy partner get in touch."

"I will," Brown said, and hung up.

In the cloistered stillness of the squadroom (telephones jangling, typewriters clanging, teletype clattering, a prisoner screaming his head off in the detention cage across the room), Steve Carella spread the four pieces of the photograph on his desktop and tried to fit them together.

He was not very good at working jigsaw puzzles.

The way he looked at it, and there were *many* ways of looking at it, the right-angle pieces were obviously corner pieces, which meant that either of them could go in any one of four places, most rectangles having four and only four corners, brilliant deduction. The simplest of these two corner pieces looked like nothing more than a dark rough surface with something jutting into it from above or below, depending on whether the corner was a top corner or a bottom corner. The something jutting into the dark rough surface strongly resembled a phallus with string around it. (He doubted very much that it was actually a phallus. If it was, they had an entirely different kind of case on their hands.) The second corner piece, the one with the sweeping curves, seemed to be a section of a wall or a building or a handball court. Which brought him to the two remaining pieces, both with the same rough gray surface. It was the surface that troubled Carella. The more he looked at it, the more it looked like water – but how could that tie in with the wall or building or handball court in the corner piece?

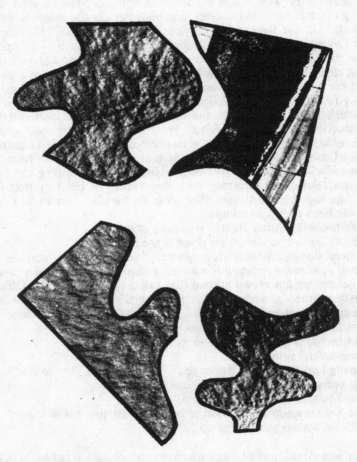

He was not very good at working jigsaw puzzles.

After ten minutes of study, he finally managed to fit two of the pieces together, a task Albert Weinberg had completed in thirty seconds. Ten minutes later, he had fitted another piece into the puzzle. Twenty minutes after that, he was convinced that the fourth piece did not fit against any of the other three. He looked at what he now had:

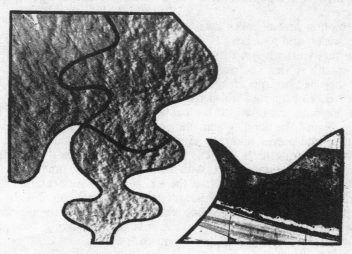

It could have been anything, anywhere.

In the city June worked its balmy Saturday afternoon magic.

On Third and Folger, two seventeen-year-old boys stopped a younger boy and asked him if he had any money. This being Saturday, the younger boy had no school carfare, and no lunch money. All he had was an overriding fear that transmitted itself to the older boys like animal musk in a virgin forest. When they discovered he was broke, they beat him up. It is probable that all they wanted to do was beat him up in the first place. They left him senseless, his nose shattered, four teeth knocked out of his mouth. All they took from him was a Ban-the-bomb button he was wearing on his jacket. Then they went to a movie where John Wayne was starring in *The Green Berets*.

June.

In Grover Park, an old lady sat on a bench feeding the pigeons. She was wearing a flowered housedress and a woolen shawl. She kept feeding the pigeons and cooing to them gently. Her bag was on the bench beside her. From its open top, a half-completed gray sweater and a pair of knitting needles protruded. A college student with long hair and a straggly beard ambled over, and sat on the bench beside her. He was wearing blue jeans and a sweat shirt and scuffed desert boots. He opened a copy of Plato's *Republic* and began reading in the sunshine.

The old lady glanced at him.

She threw a handful of bread crumbs to the pigeons, cooed at them, and glanced again at the boy, who was absorbed in his book.

"Don't you look at *me* that way," she said suddenly.

The boy looked sharply to his right, not sure at first that he was being addressed.

"You heard me, you little shit," the old lady said. "Don't look at *me* that way, you bastard."

The boy stared at the woman for a moment, decided she was crazy, closed his book and was rising from the bench when she reached into her bag, pulled out one of the knitting needles and stuck it clear through his eye to the back of his neck. At her feet, the pigeons pecked at the bread crumbs and gently cooed.

June, croon.

On a rooftop several miles away, the sunshine beat down on tar already growing sticky, and four boys held the twelve-year-old girl down against the black melting stuff while a fifth boy pulled off her panties and stuffed them into her mouth so that she could not scream. The girl could not move either, because they had her spreadeagled, arms and legs wide. A boy standing near the closed door of the roof whispered, "Hurry it up, Doc," and the boy named Doc, the one who had taken off her panties and who now stood over her, tall and large against the blinding sun, unzipped his fly, displayed his masculinity to her terror-ridden eyes, and then plunged himself deep inside her, against the protest of her tearing flesh. The boy standing near the closed door danced an impatient jig while they took turns with the little girl. By the time it was his turn, they decided they'd better get out of there before somebody caught them. The little girl, bleeding and unconscious, still lay spreadeagled against the melting tar, her panties in her mouth. The boy who had been lookout complained all the way down the stairs to the street. "You bastards," he kept saying, "you promised I'd get some, too, you promised, you promised."

June, croon, spoon.

As the afternoon waned, a sweet intoxicating breeze blew in off the River Harb and insinuated itself through the narrow canyons of the city. Dusk was upon the horizon now, the sounds of the day were beginning to blend with the sounds of approaching night. The sky to the west turned blood-red and then swam the color spectrum through purple to blue to black. A thin sliver of moon curled against the stars like a pale lemon rind. In an apartment on a side street not far from the river, a man sat in undershirt and trousers, watching television. His wife, wearing a half-slip and a brassiere padded in from the kitchen carrying two open bottles of beer and two glasses. She put one beer and one glass down in front of the man, and then poured the other beer into a glass for herself. The crescent moon shone palely through the open back-yard window. The woman looked at the television screen and said, "*That* again?"

"Yeah," the man said, and picked up his bottle of beer.

"I hate that show," his wife said.

"I like it," he said.

Without a word, the woman went to the set, and turned the channel selector. Without a word, her husband got out of his chair, walked up to her swiftly and hit her eleven times with his beer bottle, twice while she was standing, twice as she slumped to the floor, and another seven times after she was unconscious and bleeding. He turned the television back to the channel he'd been watching, and he did not call the police until the show was over, forty-five minutes later.

June, croon, spoon, moon.

In a hotel room at the Selby Arms, sixteen blocks to the west, Arthur Brown made three telephone calls in succession, and then sat back to wait for contact from Ferguson and/or Kahn. The first call he made was to his wife Caroline who deplored the fact that they'd had to cancel a dinner date, and then went on to tell Brown that she missed him and that their daughter Connie was coming down with a cold. Brown told his wife he missed her also, to which she replied, "So why don't you come home and do something about it?"

"Duty calls," he said.

"Foo," she answered.

They hung up billing and cooing and humming June, croon, spoon, moon songs.

Brown opened his notebook to the page on which he had jotted Weinberg's address and telephone number. Weinberg answered on the third ring. As soon as they had exchanged hellos, Weinberg said, "Anything?"

"Not yet."

"You think they'll try to reach you?"

"I'm still hoping."

"I ain't had much luck, either," Weinberg said. "You know that Property Clerk's Office I was telling you about?"

"Yeah?"

"First of all, there must be forty or fifty guys working there, most of them civilians. They get crap from all over the city, anything that's been involved in accidents or crimes, anything not claimed at station houses – it's like a regular goddamn warehouse down there."

"No kidding," Brown said, as if he didn't already know.

"Yeah. There's also *cops* working there, because naturally they got a lot of weapons in the place, you dig?"

"Um-huh."

"In order to claim anything after they're done with it, you got to be a *prime* relative. It doesn't matter if you're a third cousin, as long as you're the closest living relative, you dig?"

"That sounds good for us," Brown said. "You could easily pass yourself off as . . ."

"Wait a second. You got to get a release from the D.A. first. You got to go to the D.A.'s *office* and get a goddamn *release*."

"That's bad," Brown said.

"That stinks," Weinberg said.

"Who runs the whole show down there?"

"I don't know yet."

"Try to find out. He's the man we've got to reach." Brown paused. "Unless you'd like to try breaking in some night."

"Ha!" Weinberg said. "Call me later, will you? Let me know if anything happens."

"Will you be there all night?"

"All night. I got a sweet bottle of bourbon, and I intend to kill it."

"Don't let it kill *you*," Brown said, and hung up.

The next person he called was Irving Krutch.

"Well, well," Krutch said, "this is a pleasant surprise."

"We've decided to make the investigation," Brown said.

"I thought you would," Krutch answered. "You found what you were looking for in Ehrbach's apartment, didn't you?"

"Yes. But even better than that."

"What do you mean?"

"We made contact with Weinberg. He has another piece of the picture, and he gave me a copy of it."

"That's *marvellous*!" Krutch said. "When can I have a look?"

"Not tonight. Can you drop by the squadroom tomorrow morning?"

"The squadroom?"

"Yes. Why? What's wrong with the squadroom?"

"Nothing. I just forgot for a minute that you guys work on Sunday."

"Ten o'clock or thereabouts," Brown said. "I won't be there, but Carella can show you the stuff."

"Fine," Krutch said. "Where can I reach *you* if I need you?"

"I'm at the Selby Arms, room 502."

"I'll jot that down, just in case." There was a pause on the line. "Selby Arms," Krutch repeated, obviously writing, "room 502, fine. Well," he said, "we're certainly off to a good start. I can't tell you how much I appreciate this."

"We all stand to gain," Brown said. "I've got to get off the phone, I'm expecting a call."

"Oh? Another lead?"

"Yes. The 'Geraldine' on your list is a Geraldine Ferguson, sister-in-law of the late Louis D'Amore. She runs an art gallery on Jefferson Avenue."

"Who gave you that?"

"Weinberg."

"Has she got anything?"

"I think so, but I'm not sure. That's what I'm waiting to hear."

"Will you let me know?"

"As soon as anything jells."

"Good. Listen, thanks again for calling. This is great news, really."

"Right, so long," Brown said, and hung up.

His telephone did not ring that night, nor did Saturday end glamorously for him until close to midnight. He had dozed in the armchair near the telephone when a knock sounded at the door. He was instantly awake.

"Yes?" he said.

"Mr. Stokes?"

"Yes."

"Desk clerk. Woman just delivered a message for you downstairs."

"Just a second," he answered. He had taken off his shoes and socks, and he padded to the door now in his bare feet and opened it just a crack.

The door flew wide, and the glamorous part of Saturday night began.

The man was wearing a glamorous nylon stocking pulled up over his face, flattening his nose, distorting his features. He was holding a glamorous pistol in his gloved right hand and as he shoved the door open with his left shoulder, he swung the gun at Brown's head, hitting him over the eye and knocking him to the floor. The man was wearing glamorous, highly polished black shoes, and he kicked Brown in the head the moment he was down. A glamorous shower of rockets went off inside Brown's skull, and then he went unconscious.

6

It is bad to get hit on the head, any doctor can tell you that. It is even worse to get kicked in the head after you have been hit on the head, even your *mother* can tell you that. If a person gets hit on the head and loses consciousness, the doctors examining him will usually insist that he remain in the hospital for a period of at least one week, since unconsciousness precludes concussion, and concussion *can* mean internal hemorrhaging.

Brown regained consciousness twenty minutes later, and went into the bathroom to vomit. The room was a mess. Whoever had creamed him had also shaken down the place as thoroughly as the late Eugene Edward Ehrbach had shaken down the apartment of the late Donald Renninger. Brown was not too terribly concerned with the wreckage, not at the moment. Brown was concerned with staggering to the telephone, which he managed, and lifting the receiver, which he also managed. He gave the desk clerk Steve Carella's home number in Riverhead, waited while the phone rang six times, and then spoke to Fanny, the Carella housekeeper, who advised him that Mr. Carella was in Isola with his wife and was not expected home until one o'clock or thereabouts. He left a message for Carella to call him at the Selby Arms, hung up, thought he had better contact the squad immediately, and was trying to get the desk clerk again when a wave of dizziness washed over him. He stumbled over to the bed, threw himself full-length upon it, and closed his eyes. In a little while, he went into the bathroom to throw up a second time. When he got back to the bed, he closed his eyes and was either asleep or unconscious again within the next minute.

The morning hours of the night were beginning.

Steve Carella reached him a half-hour later. He knocked on the door to room 502, got no answer, and opened it immediately with a skeleton key. He picked his way through the debris on the floor, went directly to the bed where Brown lay unconscious on the slashed and mutilated mattress, saw the swollen lump over his partner's eye, said "Artie?", received no reply, and went directly to the telephone. He was waiting for the desk clerk to answer the switchboard when Brown mumbled, "I'm okay."

"Like hell you are," Carella said, and jiggled the receiver-rest impatiently.

"Cool it, Steve. I'm okay."

Carella replaced the receiver, went back to the bed, and sat on the edge of it. "I want to get a meat wagon over here," he said.

"And put me out of action for a week, huh?"

"You're growing another head the size of your first one," Carella said.

"I hate hospitals," Brown said.

"How do you like comas?" Carella asked.

"I'm not in a coma. Do I look like I'm in a coma?"

"Let me get some ice for that lump. Jesus, that's some lump."

"The man hit me with a truck," Brown said.

Carella was jiggling the receiver-rest again. When the desk clerk came on, he said, "I didn't wake you, did I?"

"What?" the desk clerk said.

"Get some ice up here on the double. Room 502."

"Room service is closed," the desk clerk said.

"Open it. This is the police."

"Right away," the desk clerk said, and hung up.

"Some people sure pick ratty dumps to stay in," Carella said.

"Some people try to lend credence to their cover," Brown said, and attempted a smile. It didn't work. He winced in pain, and closed his eyes again.

"Did you see who did it?"

"I saw him, but he had a stocking over his face."

Carella shook his head. "Ever since the first movie where a guy had a stocking over his face, we get nothing but guys with stockings over their faces." He looked around the room. "Did a nice job on the room, too."

"Beautiful," Brown said.

"We're lucky he left you alive."

"Why wouldn't he? He wasn't after me, he was after the picture."

"Who do you think it was, Artie?"

"My partner," Brown said, "Albert Weinberg."

A knock sounded on the door. Carella went to answer it. The desk clerk was standing there in his shirt sleeves, a soup dish full of ice cubes in his hands. "I had to go to the restaurant up the block for these," he complained.

"Great, thanks a lot," Carella said.

The desk clerk kept standing there. Carella reached into his pocket and handed him a quarter.

"Thanks," the desk clerk said sourly.

Carella closed the door, went into the bathroom, wrapped a towel around the ice cubes and then went back to Brown. "Here," he said, "put this on that lump."

Brown nodded, accepted the ice pack, pressed it to his swollen eye, and winced again.

"How do you know it was Weinberg?"

"I don't, for sure."

"Was he a big guy?"

"They all look big when they're about to hit you," Brown said.

"What I mean is did you get a good look at him?"

"No, it all happened..."

"...in a split second," Carella said, and both men smiled. Brown winced again. "So what makes you think it was Weinberg?"

"I had him on the phone tonight," Brown said. "Told him we'd scored."

"Who else did you talk to?"

"Irving Krutch."

"So it could have been Krutch."

"Sure. It also could have been my wife Caroline. I talked to her, too."

"She pretty good with a blunt instrument?"

"As good as most," Brown said.

"How's that eye feel?"

"Terrible."

"I think I'd *better* get a meat wagon."

"No, you don't," Brown said. "We've got work to do."

"You're not the only cop in this city," Carella said.

"I'm the only one who got clobbered in this room tonight," Brown said.

Carella sighed. "One consolation, anyway," he said.

"What's that?"

"He didn't get what he came after. *That's* in my desk drawer, back at the ranch."

It was decided over Brown's protests (actually Brown only did the protesting; Carella did all the deciding) that he would be taken to Saint Catherine's Hospital a dozen blocks away, for examination and treatment in the Emergency Room. Carella left him there at 2 a.m., still grumbling, and caught a taxi over to Weinberg's apartment on North Colman. At that hour of the morning, the neighborhood resembled a lunar landscape. Weinberg's rooming house was the only building on the street that had not already been abandoned by its owners, those entrepreneurs having decided the buildings were too expensive to maintain in accordance with the city's laws; those respectable businessmen also having discovered that no one was willing to buy such white elephants; those wheeler-dealers having merely pulled out, leaving a row of run-down tenements as a gift to the city, lucky city.

There was a time, and this not too long ago, when hippies and runaways had moved into these buildings en masse, painting their colorful flower designs on the brick fronts, sleeping on mattresses spread wall-to-wall, puffing pot, dropping acid, living the happy carefree life of the commune-dweller. The regular residents of this run-down slum area, forced to live here because of certain language and racial barriers the city raised against some of its citizens, could not understand why anyone would come to live here of his own free will and choice – but they certainly knew pigeons when they saw them. The hippies, the runaways, the carefree happy commune-dwellers had no need for telephones, being in touch as they were with nature. The only time they might have needed Mr. Bell's invention was when the restless natives of the ghetto came piling into the apartment to beat up the boys and rape the girls and take whatever meagre possessions were worth hocking. The hippies and the runaways decided that perhaps this wasteland was not for them, it becoming more and more difficult to repeat the word "Love" when a fist was being crashed into the mouth or a girl was screaming on the mattress in the other room. The ghetto regulars had struck back at a society that forced them to live in such surroundings, little realizing that the people they were harassing had themselves broken with the same society, a society that *allowed* such ghettos to exist. It was a case of poor slob beating up on poor slob, while five blocks away, a fashionable discotheque called Rembrandt's bleated its rock-and-roll music, and ladies in sequined slacks and men in dancing slippers laughed away the night. The hippies were gone now, the flower designs on the building fronts faded by the sun or washed away by the rain. The slum dwellers had reclaimed their disputed turf, and now their only enemies were the rats that roamed in the deserted tenement shells.

Weinberg lived in a rooming house on a street that looked as if it had suffered a nuclear attack. It stood with shabby pride in the middle of the block, a single light burning on the second floor of the building. Aside from that, its somber face was dark. Carella climbed to the top floor, trying to ignore the rustle of rats on the staircase, the hackles rising at the back of his neck. When he reached the fourth floor, he struck a match, found 4C at the far end of the hall and put his ear to the door, listening. To any casual passerby unfamiliar with the working ways of the police – and there were likely to be, oh, just *scores* of such passersby on a pitch-black landing at two o'clock in the morning – Carella might have looked like an eavesdropper, which is just what he was. He had been with the police department for a good many years, though, and he could not recall *ever* knocking on a door behind which there might be a criminal without first listening. He listened now for about five minutes, heard nothing, and only then knocked.

There was no answer.

He had decided together with Brown that his visit to Weinberg should not come as a visit from a cop. Instead, he was to pose as one of the "friends" that Brown had hinted at, here to seek retribution for the beating Weinberg had possibly administered. The only problem seemed to be that no one was answering the door. Carella knocked again. Weinberg had earlier told Brown that he was about to curl up with a bottle of bourbon. Was it possible he had gone over to the Selby Arms, kicked Brown and the room around a little, and then returned here to his own little palace to knock off the bottle of cheer? Carella banged on the door a third time.

A door at the other end of the hall opened.

"Who is it there?" a woman's voice said.

"Friend of Al's," Carella answered.

"What you doing knocking down the door in the middle of the night?"

"Have to see him about something," Carella said. The landing was dark, and no light came from the woman's apartment. He strained to see her in the gloom, but could make out only a vague shape in the doorway, clothed in what was either a white nightgown or a white robe.

"He's probably asleep," the woman said, "same as everybody else around here."

"Yeah, why don't you just go do that yourself, lady?" Carella said.

"Punk," the woman replied, but she closed the door. Carella heard a lock being snapped, and then the heavy bar of a Fox lock being wedged against the door, solidly hooked into the steel plate that was screwed to the floor inside. He fished into his pocket, took out a penlight, flashed it onto Weinberg's lock, and then pulled out his ring of keys. He tried five keys before he found the one that opened the door. He slipped the key out of the lock, put the ring back into his pocket, gently eased the door open, went into the apartment, closed the door softly behind him, and stood breathing quietly in the darkness.

The room was as black as the landing had been.

A water tap dripped into a sink somewhere off on his left. On the street outside, a fire engine siren wailed into the night. He listened. He could see nothing, could hear nothing. Cupping his penlight in his hand, he flashed it only a few feet ahead of him and began moving into the room, vaguely making out a chair, a sofa, a television set. At the far end of the room, there was a closed door, presumably leading to the bedroom. He turned off the flash, stood silent and motionless for several moments while his eyes readjusted to the darkness, and then started for the bedroom door. He had moved not four feet when he tripped and fell forward, his hands coming out immediately to break his fall. His right hand sank to the wrist into something soft and gushy. He withdrew it immediately, his left hand thumbing the flash into light. He was looking into the wide-open eyes of Albert Weinberg. The something soft and gushy was a big bloody hole in Weinberg's chest.

Carella got to his feet, turned on the lights, and went into the small bathroom off the kitchen. When he turned on the lights there, an army of cockroaches scurried for cover. Fighting nausea, Carella washed his bloody right hand, dried it on a grimy towel hanging on a bar over the sink, and then went into the other room to call the precinct. A radio motor-patrol car arrived some five minutes later. Carella filled in the patrolmen, told them he'd be back shortly, and then headed acrosstown and uptown to Irving Krutch's apartment. He did not get there until 3:15 a.m., two and a half hours before dawn.

Krutch opened the door the moment Carella gave his name. He was wearing pajamas, his hair was tousled, even his mustache looked as if it had been suddenly awakened from a very deep sleep.

"What's the matter?" he asked.

"Just a few questions, Mr. Krutch," Carella said.

"At three in the morning?"

"We're both awake, aren't we?"

"I wasn't two minutes ago," Krutch said. "Besides ..."

"This won't take long," Carella said. "Did you speak to Arthur Brown tonight?"

"I did. Why? What ...?"

"When was that?"

"Must have been about ... eight o'clock? Eight-thirty? I really can't say for sure."

"What'd you talk about, Mr. Krutch?"

"Well Brown told me you'd found a piece of that photograph in Ehrbach's apartment, and he said you'd also got another piece from Weinberg. I was supposed to come up to the squadroom tomorrow morning to see them. In fact, *you* were supposed to show them to me."

"But you couldn't wait, huh?"

"What do you mean, I couldn't ..."

"Where'd you go after you spoke to Brown?"

"Out to dinner."

"Where?"

"The Ram's Head. The top of 777 Jefferson."

"Anybody with you?"

"Yes."

"Who?"

"A friend of mine."

"Man or woman?"

"A girl."

"What time'd you leave the restaurant?"

"About ten-thirty, I guess."

"Where'd you go?"

"For a walk. We looked in the store windows along Hall Avenue. It was a beautiful night and ..."

"Where were you along about midnight, Mr. Krutch."

"Here," Krutch said.

"Alone?"

"No."

"The girl came back here with you?"

"Yes."

"So she was with you between what time and what time?" Carella said.

"She was here when Brown called at eight – or whenever it was." Krutch paused. "She's still here."

"Where?"

"In bed."

"Get her up."

"Why?"

"One man's been assaulted and another's been killed," Carella said. "I want her to tell me where you were when all this was happening. That all right with you?"

"Who was killed?" Krutch asked.

"You sound as if you *know* who was *assaulted*," Carella said quickly.

"No. No, I don't."

"Then why'd you only ask who was killed? Aren't you interested in who was beaten up?"

"I'm..." Krutch paused. "Let me get her. She can clear this up in a minute."

"I hope so," Carella said.

Krutch went into the bedroom. Carella heard voices behind the closed door. The bedsprings creaked. There were footsteps. The door opened again. The girl was a young blonde, her long hair trailing down her back, her brown eyes wide and frightened. She was wearing a man's bathrobe belted tightly at the waist. Her hands fluttered like butterflies on an acid trip.

"This is Detective Carella," Krutch said. "He wants to know..."

"*I'll* ask her," Carella said. "What's your name, Miss?"

"Su ... Su ... Suzie," she said.

"Suzie what?"

"Suzie Endicott."

"What time did you get here tonight, Miss Endicott?"

"About ... seven-thirty," she said. "Wasn't it seven-thirty, Irving?"

"About then," Krutch said.

"What time did you go out to dinner, Miss Endicott?"

"Eight or eight-thirty."

"Where'd you eat?"

"The Ram's Head."

"And where'd you go afterwards?"

"We walked for a little while, and then came here."

"What time was that?"

"I guess we got here at about eleven."

"Have you been here since?"

"Yes," she said.

"Did Mr. Krutch leave you at any time between seven-thirty and now?"

"Yes, when he went to the men's room at the restaurant," Suzie said.

"Happy now?" Krutch asked.

"Overjoyed," Carella answered. "Are you familiar with timetables, Mr. Krutch?"

"What do you mean? *Train* timetables?"

"No, *investigating* timetables. You're an insurance investigator, I thought you might..."

"I'm not sure I'm following you."

"I want you to work up a timetable for me. I want you to list everything you did and the exact time you did it from 6 p.m. until right this minute," Carella said, and paused. "I'll wait," he added.

7

There's nothing like a little homicide to give an investigation a shot in the arm. Or the chest, as the case may be. Albert Weinberg had been shot in the chest at close range with a .32-caliber pistol. His demise caused Brown to have a heated argument with the hospital intern who kept insisting he should be kept there under observation, and who refused to give him back his trousers. Brown called Carella, who brought his partner a pair of pants, a clean shirt, and his own spare gun. The two men had a hurried consultation while Brown dressed, deciding that Carella should go out to Calm's Point for a chat in Italian with Lucia Feroglio, the late Carmine Bonamico's sister-in-law. In the meantime, Brown would go over to the Ferguson Gallery, presumably closed on a Sunday, let himself into the place (against the law, but what the hell), and do a little snooping around. The nurse came in as Brown was zipping up his fly.

"What are you doing out of bed?" she asked.

"I'll get back in, if you'll join me," Brown said, grinning lecherously, and the nurse fled down the corridor, calling for the intern. By the time the intern got to the room, the detectives were in the main lobby downstairs, setting up plans for contacting each other later in the day. They nodded to each other briefly, and went out into the June sunshine to pursue their separate pleasures.

Carella's pleasure was the Church of the Holy Spirit on Inhurst Boulevard in Calm's Point. He had first stopped at Lucia Feroglio's garden apartment where he was told by her neighbors that the old lady went to nine o'clock Mass every Sunday morning. He had then driven over to the church, where Mass was in progress, and asked the sexton if he knew Lucia Feroglio, and if he would mind pointing her out when Mass broke. The sexton seemed not to understand any English until Carella put five dollars in the box in the narthex. The sexton then admitted that he knew Lucia Feroglio very well, and would be happy to identify her when she came out of the church.

Lucia must have been a beauty in her youth; Carella could not understand how or why she had remained a spinster. A woman in her seventies now, she still walked with a tall, erect pride, her hair snowy white, her features recalling those of ancient Roman royalty, the aquiline nose, the full sensuous mouth, the high brow and almond-shaped eyes. The sexton nodded toward her as she came down the broad sunwashed steps. Carella moved to her side immediately and said, *"Scusi, Signorina Feroglio?"*

The woman turned with a faint half-smile on her mouth, her eyebrows lifting in mild curiosity. *"Sì, che cosa?"* she asked.

"Mi chiamo Steve Carella," he answered. *"Sono un agente investigativo, dal distretto ottanta-sette."* He opened his wallet and showed her his detective's shield.

"Sì che vuole?" Lucia asked. "What do you want?"

"Possiamo parlare?" Carella asked. "Can we talk?"

"Certo," she said, and they began to walk away from the church together.

Lucia seemed to have no aversion to holding a conversation with a cop. She was warm, open, and co-operative, speaking in a Sicilian dialect Carella understood only incompletely, promising him she would tell him everything she knew about the photographic segment she had inherited from her sister. As it turned out, though, she knew nothing at *all* about it.

"I do not understand," Carella said in Italian. "Did you not tell the insurance investigator that the full picture reveals where the treasure is?"

"Ma che tesoro?" Lucia asked. "What treasure?"

"The treasure," Carella reported. "Did you not tell Mr. Krutch about a treasure? When you gave him the list and the photograph?"

"I know nothing of a treasure," Lucia said. "And *what* list? I gave him only the little piece of picture."

"You did *not* give him such a list with names on it?"

"No. Nor has Mr. Krutch given me the thousand dollars he promised. Do you know this man?"

"Yes, I know him."

"Would you ask him, please, to send me my money? I gave him the picture, and now it is only fair to expect payment. I am not a wealthy woman."

"Let me understand this, Miss Feroglio," Carella said. "Are you telling me that you did *not* give Mr. Krutch a list of names?"

'Never. *Mai*. Never."

"And you did *not* tell Mr. Krutch about a treasure?"

"If I did not know it, how could I have told him?" She turned to him suddenly, and smiled warmly and quite seductively for a woman in her seventies. *Is* there a treasure, *signore*?" she asked.

"God only knows, *signorina*," Carella answered, and returned the smile.

The best burglars in the world are cops.

There are three types of alarm systems in general use, and the one on the back door of the Ferguson Gallery was a closed-circuit system, which meant that it could not be put out of commission merely by cutting the wires, as could be done with the cheapest kind. A weak current ran constantly through the wires of the closed-circuit system; if you cut them, breaking the current, the alarm would sound. So Brown cross-contacted the wires, and then opened the door with a celluloid strip. It was as simple as that, and it took him no longer than ten minutes. In broad daylight.

The gallery was empty and still.

Sunshine slanted silently through the wide plate-glass windows fronting Jefferson Avenue. The white walls were pristine and mute. The only screaming in the place came from the colorful paintings on the walls. Brown went immediately to the blue door on the far wall, opened it and stepped into Bramley Kahn's office.

He started with Kahn's desk. He found letters to and from artists, letters to patrons, a rough mock-up of a brochure announcing the gallery's one-man show to come in August, memos from Kahn to himself, a letter from a museum in Philadelphia, another from the Guggenheim in New York, a hardbound copy of *Story of O* (the first few pages of which Brown scanned, almost getting hooked, almost forgetting why he had come here), a trayful of red pencils and blue pencils, and in the bottom drawer a locked metal cashbox – and a .32-caliber Smith & Wesson. Brown tented his handkerchief over the revolver, picked it up by the butt, and sniffed the barrel. Despite the fact that Albert Weinberg, his late partner, had been slain with a .32-caliber weapon, this gun did not seem to have been fired lately. Brown rolled out the cylinder. There were six cartridges in the pistol, one in each chamber. He closed the gun, put it back into the drawer, and was reaching for the cashbox when the telephone rang. He almost leaped out of Steve Carella's borrowed trousers. The phone rang once, twice, again, again, again. It stopped suddenly.

Brown kept watching the instrument.

It began ringing again. It rang eight times. Then it stopped.

Brown waited.

The phone did not ring again.

He lifted the gray metal cashbox from the bottom drawer. The lock on it was a simple one; he opened the cashbox in thirty seconds. It contained anything but cash. He found a partnership agreement between Kahn and Geraldine Ferguson, a certificate for two hundred shares of IBM stock. Kahn's last will and testament, three United States Savings Bonds in fifty-dollar denominations, and a small, white, unmarked, unsealed envelope.

Brown opened the envelope. There was a slip of white paper in it:

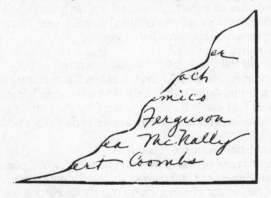

However lousy a bank robber Carmine Bonamico may have been, he was sure good at cutting out paper dolls. If this wasn't the second half of the list Krutch had brought to the squadroom, Brown would eat the list, the photograph, the first chapter of *Story of O*, and maybe O herself. He quickly copied the names in his notebook, replaced the fragment in its envelope, put the envelope and everything else into the cashbox, locked the box, and replaced it in the bottom drawer of the desk. His attention was captured by the painting of the nude on the opposite wall. He went to it, lifted one edge, and peeked behind it. Reaching up with both hands, he took the heavy painting off the wall. There was a small black safe behind it. Brown knew that people who used safes or combination locks with any frequency would often leave the dial just a notch or two to the right or left of the last number. This facilitated constant opening, since all you then had to do was give the dial a single twist each time, rather than going through the whole, boring rigmarole. He was moving the dial a notch to the left of the number showing when he heard the back door of the gallery being opened. Swiftly, he moved behind the door of Kahn's office, and threw back his jacket.

The butt of Carella's borrowed .38 protruded from a holster at his waist. He drew the gun now and stood silently listening to the footsteps that clattered across the white tile floor toward Kahn's office. The footsteps stopped just outside the open door. Brown held his breath. The man was in the doorway now, his shadow falling into the room across the gray rug. Brown did not want the man to be Bramley Kahn. Breaking and entry was breaking and entry, and Brown did not want a suit filed against the city; Brown did not want to get kicked off the force; Brown did not want to be smothered again by the ghetto he had escaped.

The first things that registered were the thick handlebar mustache and the glinting blue eyes.

"Hello Krutch," Brown said.

Irving Krutch whirled.

"Hey," he said. "Hi."

"Didn't you see that decal on the back door? 'These premises are protected by the Buckley Alarm System.'"

"I cross-contacted the wiring," Krutch said.

"That makes two of us. Was it you who called ten minutes ago?"

"Yes. I wanted to make sure nobody was here."

"Somebody *was* here," Brown said.

"So I see."

"What do you want, Krutch?"

"The same thing you want. We're in this together, remember?"

"I thought you were letting *us* handle it."

"I figured you might need a hand."

Brown holstered the gun, went to the safe again, moved the dial a notch to the left, then two notches, then three, trying to open it after each move, and getting no results. He tried the same sequence to the right, and when he got nothing, he turned to Krutch and said, "I *do* need a hand. Grab one end of this painting."

"Have you found anything?" Krutch asked.

Brown hesitated. "No," he said.

They lifted the painting and hung it in place. Brown stepped back from it, walked over to the wall again, and tilted one corner of the frame.

"A little to the other side," Krutch said.

"How's that?"

"Perfect."

"Let's go," Brown said.

"I'd sure like to know what's in that safe," Krutch said.

"So would I. What's your guess?"

"A little piece of a picture."

"How are you on safecracking?"

"Lousy."

"So am I. Let's go."

"Where are we going?" Krutch asked.

"*You're* going to fix those alarm wires. *I'm* going to visit Geraldine Ferguson."

"Fix the wires? I can get arrested if I'm caught doing that."

"I may arrest you anyway," Brown said. "You're in here illegally."

"So are you."

"An off-duty cop on the prowl. Cruising by, saw the back door ajar, came in and discovered a burglary in progress."

"I'm your *partner*," Krutch protested.

"I had another partner, too. Albert Weinberg, who right now is on ice downtown."

"I had nothing to do with that," Krutch said.

"Who suggested you did?"

"Carella."

"Well, maybe he's just a suspicious person," Brown said.

"How about *you*? What do *you* think?"

"I think you were with that young lady named Suzie Endicott from seven-thirty until whenever it was Carella came to see you. That's what you told him, isn't it?"

"Yes."

"So why would I have any reason to doubt you?"

"Look Brown . . ."

"I'm looking."

"I want that lost N.S.L.A. money; I want it very badly. But not badly enough to kill for it. *Nothing's* worth that much. Not even my career."

"Okay."

"I just want to get that straight between us."

"It's straight," Brown said. "Now let's get the hell out of here."

Geraldine Ferguson was in her pajamas when she opened the door.

"Oh, hell," she said.

"That's right, Miss Ferguson," Brown said. "Here come de fuzz."

"He's *admitting* it," she said in surprise, and then smiled. "Come in. I admire honest men."

The living room resembled an annex to the gallery – white walls, muted furniture, huge canvases glaring with color, twisted sculptured shapes on pedestals. Gerry swayed across the rug like a dancer, tight little behind jiggling in the blue silk pajama bottoms, black hair caught in a pony tail that bounced between her shoulder blades.

"Would you like a drink?" she asked. "Or is it too early?"

"It's almost one o'clock," Brown said.

"Name it."

"I'm on duty."

"So? When did cops get so lily-white, you should pardon the expression?"

"I like to keep a clear head when I'm working," Brown said.

"Okay, keep a clear head," Gerry said, and shrugged. "*I'll* have a drink, though, if you don't mind. I find Sundays very boring. Once I've read the comics and Martin Levin, there's just nothing exciting left to do."

"Who's Martin Levin?" Brown asked.

Gerry went to a bar over which hung a white canvas slashed with jagged black streaks of paint. She poured a liberal shot of bourbon onto the ice in a short glass, lifted the glass, said, "Here's to improved race relations," and drank, eying him steadily over the glass.

"Miss Ferguson . . ."

"Gerry," she corrected.

"Gerry, a man was killed last night . . ."

"Who?" she said immediately, and put the glass down on the bar top.

"The man who visited you several times. The one who said he was Al Reynolds. Or Al Randolph."

"What was his real name?"

"Albert Weinberg." Brown paused. 'Ever hear of him?"

"No," Gerry said, and picked up her glass again. "What's *your* real name?"

"Arthur Brown."

"You're putting me on," she said, and smiled.

"No, that's it. Detective Second/Grade, 87th Squad, Want to see my shield?"

"Why?"

"You're supposed to ask for identification."

"I don't like to do anything I'm *supposed* to do," Gerry said.

"On Wednesday night..."

"How'd we get back to Wednesday?"

"I just took us there," Brown said impatiently. "On Wednesday night, two men killed each other in a brawl..."

"Who?"

"That's not important, Gerry. What *is* important is that one of them had a piece of a photograph in his hand..."

"Are we going to start on *that* again? I already told you..."

"Miss Ferguson," Brown said, "I've got some questions to ask you concerning murder and armed robbery. I'd like to ask those questions here in comfortable surroundings, but I can just as easily ask them uptown, in the squadroom."

"What's that, a threat?"

"No, it's a realistic appraisal of the situation."

"After I was nice enough to offer you a drink," Gerry said, and smiled. "Go on, I promise to be quiet."

"Thank you. We have good reason to believe that the fragment in the dead man's hand was part of a larger photograph showing the location of the money stolen from the National Savings & Loan Association six years ago. We also have good reason to believe that *you* have another piece of that picture, and *we* want it. It's as simple as that."

"What smoked you out, Arthur?" she asked. "What made you drop the phoney cover? Are you afraid somebody else might get killed?"

"It's possible, yes."

"Me?"

"Possibly. *Whoever's* got a piece of that picture is in danger. For your own safety..."

"Bullshit," Gerry said.

"I beg your pardon?"

"The day the cops start worrying about anybody's *safety* is the day..." She banged the glass down on the bar top. "Who do you think you're kidding, Arthur?"

"Miss Ferguson, I'm not..."

"And make up your goddamn mind! It's either Miss Ferguson or it's Gerry. You can't have it both ways."

"Then I think I'd prefer Miss Ferguson."

"Why? Are you afraid of me or something? Big strong Superspade afraid of a snippety little girl?"

"Let's knock off the 'Superspade' crap, shall we?" Brown said.

"You ever been to bed with a white girl?" Gerry asked suddenly.

"No."

"Want to try?"

"No."

"Why not?"

"Believe it or not, Miss Ferguson, my fantasies don't include a big black Cadillac and a small white blonde."

"I'm not blonde."

"I know that. I was merely ..."

"Stop getting so nervous. I'll bet your palms are wet."

"My palms are dry," Brown said evenly.

"Mine aren't," Gerry said, and turned away from him to pour herself another drink. The living room was silent. "You married?" she asked.

"I am."

"That's okay. I've been to bed with married spades, too."

"I don't like that expression, Miss Ferguson."

"Which? Married?" she asked, and turned to face him, leaning on the bar. "Grow up, Arthur."

Brown rose from the sofa. "I think maybe we'd *better* head uptown," he said. "You want to get dressed, please?"

"No, I don't," Gerry said, and smiled, and sipped at her bourbon. "What'll the charge be? Attempted rape?"

"I don't have to charge you with anything, Miss Ferguson. I'm conducting a murder investigation, and I'm entitled ..."

"All right, all right, don't start spouting legalities. Sit down, Arthur. Oh, *do* sit down. I'd much rather talk here than in some stuffy old squadroom."

Brown sat.

"There, isn't that better? Now – what would you like to know?"

"*Do* you have a piece of the photograph?"

"Yes."

"Where'd you get it?"

"My brother-in-law gave it to me."

"Louis D'Amore?"

"Yes."

"When?"

"Just before the holdup."

"What'd he say about it?"

"Only that I should hold on to it."

"How come he gave it to you, and not your sister?"

"My sister's a scatterbrain, always was. Lou knew who the smart one was."

"Did he give you the list, too?"

"What list?"

"The list of names."

"I don't know anything about a list of names."

"That's a lie, Gerry."

"No, I swear. What list?"

"A list that has your name on it, among others."

"I've never seen it."

"You're lying Gerry. Your partner has half of that list. Where'd he get it?"

"I don't know anything *about* a list. What's it supposed to be?"

"Forget it," Brown said. "Where's your part of the snapshot?"

"In the gallery safe."

"Will you turn it over to us?"

"No."

"I thought you said..."

"I said I'd answer your questions. Okay. I've done that. There's no law that says I have to give personal property to the police."

"I can think of one," Brown said.

"Yeah, which one?"

"How about Section 1308 of the Penal Law? *A person who conceals, withholds, or aids in concealing or withholding any property, knowing the same to have been stolen...*"

"Is the photograph stolen property?"

"It indicates the *location* of stolen property."

"How do I know that? Lou gave me a tiny little corner of a photograph and asked me to hold onto it. That's all I know."

"Okay, I'm *telling* you the photograph shows the location of the N.S.L.A. loot. Now you know."

"Can you prove it?" Gerry said, and smiled. "I don't think so, Arthur. Until you find the money, you can't say for sure it even *exists*. And you *won't* find the money until you put the whole picture together. Tch, tch, such a dilemma. Why don't we go into the other room and ball a little?"

"I'd rather not, thanks."

"I'd drive you out of your mind, Arthur."

"You already have," Brown said, and left.

8

—

The dilemma was not quite so horned as Geraldine Ferguson imagined. All Brown had to do was find himself a Supreme Court judge, swear to the judge that upon reliable information and personal knowledge, there was probable cause to believe that a safe at the Ferguson Gallery at 568 Jefferson Avenue contained evidence that could lead to the solution of a crime, and request from the judge a warrant and order of seizure to open the safe, search it, and appropriate the evidence. He couldn't do that today because it was Sunday, and in the city for which Brown worked, Supreme Court judges were entitled to a day of rest; only the direst of emergencies would have been considered cause for shaking a man out of his bed and requesting a search warrant. Brown was confident, though, that Gerry would not rush down to the gallery and take the photograph out of the safe. He had done nothing to disabuse her notion that he was helpless to open that safe, and he felt certain the photograph would still be there come morning when, armed with his legal paper, he would force her to produce it.

At 3 p.m. Sunday afternoon, he met with Carella in the squadroom and went over what they now had. By combining Krutch's half of the list (which *he* claimed to have received from Lucia Feroglio, but which *she* claimed not to have given him) with the half found in Kahn's cashbox (which Geraldine Ferguson claimed she knew nothing about), they were able to piece together seven names:

ALBERT WEINBERG
DONALD RENNINGER
EUGENE E. EHRBACH
ALICE BONAMICO
GERALDINE FERGUSON
DOROTHEA McNALLY
ROBERT COOMBS

The first four people on the list were already dead. The fifth person had admitted having a piece of the photograph, and they hoped to get that from her in the morning. Now, with the telephone directories for the five sections of the city spread open before them, they began searching for the remaining two names.

There was a Robert Coombs in Riverhead, and another Robert Coombs in Bethtown.

There were a hundred and sixty-four McNallys scattered all over the city, more than enough to have started a revival of the clan, but none of them were named Dorothea, and there was only one listing for a *McNally, D.* – on South Homestead, off Skid Row.

"How do you want to hit them?" Carella asked.

"Let's save Bethtown till tomorrow morning. Have to take a ferry over there, and God knows how they run on Sundays."

"Okay," Carella said. "Why don't I take the Coombs in Riverhead, and go straight home from there?"

"Fine. I'll take the McNally woman."

"How come you're getting all the girls lately?"

"It's only fair," Brown said, "We *never* get them on television."

It was a city of contrasts.

Follow Esplanade Avenue uptown to where the Central & Northeastern railroad tracks came up out of the ground and, within the length of a city block, the neighborhood crumbled before your eyes, buildings with awnings and doormen giving way to grimy brick tenements, well-dressed affluent citizens miraculously transformed into shabby, hungry, unemployed victims of poverty. Take any crosstown street that knifed through the 87th Precinct, follow it across Mason, and Culver, and Ainsley, and you passed through slums that spread like cancers and then abruptly shriveled on the fringes of fancy Silvermine Road, with luxurious, exclusive, wooded, moneyed Smoke Rise only a stone's throw away. Head all the way downtown to The Quarter, and find yourself a bustling middle-class bohemian community with its fair share of faggots and artsy-craftsy leather shops, its little theaters and renovated brownstones glistening with sandblasted facades and freshly painted balustrades and fire escapes, shuttered windows, cobblestoned alleys, spring flowers hanging in gaily colored pots over arched doorways with shining brass knobs and knockers. Then follow your nose west into Little Italy, a ghetto as dense as those uptown, but of a different hue, take a sniff of coffee being brewed in *espresso* machines, savor the rich smells of a transplanted Neapolitan cuisine merged with the aroma of roasting pork wafting over from Chinatown, not a block away, where the telephone booths resembled miniature pagodas and where the phones – like their uptown cousins – rarely worked. (How nice to have an emergency number with which to dial the police, three fast digits and a cop was on your doorstep – if only the phones would work.) Then walk a few blocks south, crossing the wide avenue where the elevated train structure used to stand, its shadow gone now, the flophouses and soup kitchens, the wholesale lighting fixture, restaurant supply, factory reject, party favor, and office equipment establishments draped with winos and exposed in all their shabby splendor to the June sunshine.

D. McNally lived in a building two blocks south of the wide avenue that ran for better than half a mile, the city's skid row, a graveyard for vagrants and drunks, a happy hunting ground for policemen anxious to fill arrest quotas – pull in a bum, charge him with vagrancy or disorderly conduct, allow him to spend a night or two or more in jail, and then turn him out into the street again, a much better person for his experience. Brown walked past two drunks who sat morosely on the front stoop. Neither of the men looked up at him. Sitting on the curb in front of the building, his feet in the gutter, was a third man. He had taken off his shirt, black with lice, and he delicately picked the parasites from the cloth now, squashing them with his thumbnail against the curbstone. His skin was a pale sickly white in the glare of the sunshine, his back and arms covered with sores.

The entryway was dark; after the brilliant sunshine outside, it hit the eyes like a closed fist. Brown studied the row of broken mailboxes and found one with a hand-crayoned card that read D. McNally, Apt. 2A. He climbed the steps, listened outside the apartment door for several moments, and then knocked.

"Yes?" a woman's voice said.

"Miss McNally?"

"Yes?" she said, and before Brown could announce that he was The Law, the door opened. The woman standing in the doorway was perhaps fifty years old. Her hair had been dyed a bright orange, and it exploded about her chalk-white face like Fourth-of-July fireworks, erupting from her scalp in every conceivable direction, wildly unkempt, stubbornly independent. Her eyes were a faded blue, their size emphasized by thick black eyeliner. Her lashes had been literally stroked with mascara, her brows had been darkened with pencil, her mouth had been enlarged with lipstick the color of human blood. She wore a silk flowered wrapper belted loosely at the waist. Pendulous white breasts showed in the open top of the wrapper. Near the nipple of one breast, a human bite mark was clearly visible, purple against her very white skin. She was a short, dumpy woman with an overabundance of flabby flesh, and she looked as though she had deliberately dressed for the role of the unregenerate old whore in the local amateur production of *Seven Hookers East*.

"I don't take niggers," she said immediately, and started to close the door. Brown stuck his foot out, and the closing door collided with his shoe. Through the narrow open crack, D. McNally said again, emphatically this time, "I told you I don't take niggers." Brown didn't know whether to laugh himself silly or fly into an offended rage. Here was a run-down old prostitute who would probably flop with anyone and everyone for the price of a bottle of cheap wine, but she would not take Negroes. He decided to find it amusing.

"All I want's a blow job," he said.

"No," D. McNally said, alarmed now. "No. Go away!"

"A friend of mine sent me," he said.

From behind the door, D. McNally's voice lowered in suspicion. "Which friend?" she asked. "I don't suck no niggers."

"Lieutenant Byrnes," Brown said.

"A soldier?"

"No, a policeman," Brown said, and decided to end the game. "I'm a detective, lady, you want to open this door?"

"You ain't no detective," she said.

Wearily, Brown dug into his pocket and held his shield up to the crack between door and jamb.

"Why didn't you say so?" D. McNally asked.

"Why? Do you suck nigger *detectives*?"

"I didn't mean no offense," she said, and opened the door. "Come in."

He went into the apartment. It consisted of a tiny kitchen and a room with a bed. Dishes were piled in the sink, the bed was unmade, there was the stale stink of human sweat and cheap booze and cheaper perfume.

"You the Vice Squad?" she asked.

"No."

"I ain't hooking no more," she said. "That's why I told you to go away. I been out of the game, oh, must be six, seven months now."

"Sure," Brown said. "Is your name Dorothea McNally?"

"That's right. I put 'D. McNally' in the phone book and in the mailbox downstairs because there's all kind of crazy nuts in this city, you know? Guys who call up and talk dirty, you know? I don't like that kind of dirty shit."

"No, I'll bet you don't."

"When I was hooking, I had a nice clientele."

"Mm-huh."

"Gentlemen."

"But no niggers."

"Look, you didn't take offense at that, did you?"

"No, of course not. Why should I take offense at a harmless little remark like that?"

"If you're going to make trouble just because I said..."

"I'm not going to make any trouble, lady."

"Because if you *are*, look, I'll go down on you right this minute, you know what I mean? A cock's a cock," Dorothea said, "white *or* black."

"Or even purple," Brown said.

"Sure, even purple. Just don't make trouble for me, that's all." She paused. "You want me to?"

"No. Thanks a lot," Brown said.

"Well," she said, and shrugged, "if you should change your mind..."

"I'll let you know. Meanwhile, I'm here to talk about a photograph."

"Yeah, well come on in," she said, gesturing toward the bedroom. "No sense standing here with the dirty dishes, huh?"

They walked into the other room. Dorothea sat on the bed and crossed her legs. Brown stood at the foot of the bed, looking down at her. She had allowed the silk wrapper to fall open again. The bite mark near her nipple looked angry and swollen, the outline of the teeth stitched across her flabby breast in a small elongated oval.

"A photograph, huh?" Dorothea said.

"That's right."

"Man, you guys sure know how to bring up ancient history," she said. "I thought you weren't going to make trouble for me."

"I'm not."

"I musta posed for those pictures twenty years ago. You mean to tell me one of them's still around?" She shook her head in amazement. "I was *some* little piece in those days. I had guys coming to see me all the way from San Francisco. They'd get in town, pick up the phone, 'Hello there, Dorothea, this is old Bruce, you ready to go, honey?' I was always ready to go in those days. I knew how to show a man a good time." She looked up at Brown. "I *still* do, I mean I'm not exactly what you'd call an old hag, you know. Not that I'm in the game, any more. I mean, I'm just saying."

"When was your last arrest for prostitution?" Brown asked.

"I told you, musta been six or seven..."

"Come on, I can check it."

"All right, last month. But I've been clean since. This is no kind of life for a person like me. So, you know, when you come around bringing up those pictures, Jesus, I can get in real trouble for something like that, can't I?" She smiled suddenly. "Why don't you just come on over here, sweetie, and we'll forget all about those pictures, okay?"

"The picture I'm talking about isn't pornography," Brown said.

"No? What then?"

"A picture that may have come into your possession six years ago."

"Jesus, who can remember six years ago?"

"You just now had no trouble remembering *twenty* years ago."

"Yeah, but that was . . . you know, a girl remembers something like that. That's the only time I ever done anything like that, you know, pose for pictures with some guy. I only let them take one roll, that was all, just *one*, and I got fifty bucks for it, which was more than I'd have got if I was just turning a trick without them taking pictures, you understand?"

"Sure," Brown said. "What do you know about the National Savings & Loan Association holdup six years ago?"

"Oh, man, now we're jumping around real fast," Dorothea said. "First it's hooking, then it's dirty pictures, now it's armed robbery. The stakes keep getting higher all the time."

"What do you know about that holdup?"

"I think I remember reading about it."

"What do you remember reading?"

"Look . . . I got your word you ain't going to make trouble?"

"You've got it."

"My nephew was one of the guys who pulled that job."

"What's his name?"

"Peter Ryan. He's dead now. They *all* got killed on that job, some bank robbers," she said, and grimaced.

"And the picture?"

"*What* picture. I don't know what . . ."

"A piece of the snapshot. From what you've just told me, your nephew might have given it to you. Before the job. Would you remember anything like that?"

"Jesus, that was six years ago."

"Try to remember."

"When was the job? Do you remember what month it was?"

"August."

"August. Six years ago. Let me see . . ." She grimaced again. "I wasn't even living here at the time. God knows *where* the hell I was."

"Think, Dorothea."

"I think better when I'm drinking," she said.

"Have you got anything in the house?"

"Yeah, but that's like my insurance, you know? The Johns are few and far between these days."

Brown reached into his wallet. "Here's ten dollars," he said. "Drink up your insurance and get yourself another bottle later."

"And if I remember about the picture?"

"What about it?"

"How much is it worth to you?"

"Another twenty."

"Make it fifty. You're taking up a lot of my time, you know."

"I don't see a line of guys outside the door," Brown said.

"Well, they come and go, come and go," Dorothea said. "I'd hate to have to send a trick away just because I'm busy in here with a cop." She paused, and then smiled. "Fifty?"

"Thirty-five."

"It's a deal." She went into the kitchen, took a bottle of cheap rye from the shelf, poured herself a half tumblerful, looked up, and said, "You want some of this piss? Makes you go blind, I understand."

"No, thanks," Brown said.

"Here's looking up your whole family," Dorothea said, and drained the glass. "Whooo," she said, "that's poison, absolute poison." She poured the glass full to the brim and carried it back into the bedroom with her. "I don't remember any snapshot," she said, shaking her head.

"Where were you living at the time?"

"Up on the North Side, I think. I think I had a room in a hotel up there." She sipped at the rye thoughtfully. "Six years ago. That's like a whole century, you know?"

"Think."

"I'm thinking, just shut up. My nephew was in and out all the time; who remembers whether he ever gave me a snapshot?"

"This would be just a *portion* of a snapshot. Not the whole picture."

"Better yet," Dorothea said. "Even if he *did* give it to me, you know how many times I moved in the past six years? Don't ask. Between The Law and the rent collector, I'm a very busy lady."

"Where do you keep your valuables?"

"*What* valuables?"

"Where do you keep important papers?"

"Are you kidding me?"

"Things like your birth certificate, your Social Security card..."

"Oh, yeah, I got them around someplace," Dorothea said, and sipped at the drink again.

"Where?"

"I don't keep much junk, you know. I don't like memories. Too many fucking memories," she said, and this time she took a healthy swallow of the drink, draining the glass. She got up from the bed, walked into the kitchen, and poured the glass full again. "You ever hear of a fighter named Tiger Willis?" she asked, coming back into the bedroom.

"No."

"This was before your time, I guess. Twenty-five years ago, maybe even longer. He was a middleweight."

"What about him?"

"I used to live with him. He had a *shlong* on him, man, it musta been a yard long." Dorothea shook her head. "He got killed in the ring. This kid from Buenos Aires killed him. Hit him so hard, he ... I was there that night, at ringside, you know. Freddie – that was his real name, Freddie Willis, the 'Tiger' shit was just for the ring – Freddie always got me a ringside seat for his fights, I was something in those days, I was real merchandise. This kid from Buenos Aires, he brought one up from the floor, almost knocked Freddie's head off. And Freddie went down, he went down like a stone, he hit that canvas so hard..." She swallowed more rye and looked away from Brown. "Well, those are the old times," she said.

"About the photograph," Brown said gently.

"Yeah, yeah, the fucking photograph. Let me see what's in the closet here."

She went across the room, and opened the door to the closet. A black cloth coat hung on a wire hanger. Beside it was a blue satin dress. Nothing else was hanging on the wooden bar. On the floor of the closet, there were two pairs of high-heeled pumps. A cardboard box and a candy tin were on the shelf over the bar. Dorothea reached up, and came back to the bed with the candy tin in her hands. She pried off the lid.

"Not much here," she said. "I don't like to keep things."

There was a birth certificate, a marriage certificate (Dorothea Pierce to Richard McNally), a snip of hair in a cheap gold-plated locket, a *Playbill* for an opening night long long ago, a photograph of a very young girl sitting on a swing behind a clapboard house, a faded valentine card, and a copy of *Ring* magazine with a picture of Tiger Willis on the cover.

"That's all of it," Dorothea said.

"Want to dump it all on the bed here?" Brown suggested. "What we're looking for may be very small." He picked up the *Playbill* and shook out its pages. Nothing. He picked up the copy of *Ring* magazine.

"Be careful with that," Dorothea warned.

He gave it a single shake. The pages fluttered apart, and a glossy black-and-white photograph scrap fell onto the soiled sheets.

"Is that what you're looking for?" Dorothea asked.

"That's what I'm looking for," Brown said.

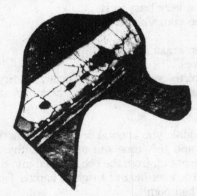

"It resembles Donald Duck," she said. "Or Woody Woodpecker."

"Or the extinct dodo bird," Brown said.

"I don't remember Petey giving it to me," Dorothea said, and shook her head. "I suppose he must have, but I really don't remember." Her look hardened. She held out her hand to Brown, and said, "That's thirty-five bucks, mister."

The address for the Robert Coombs who lived in Riverhead was 6451 Avondale, two miles from Carella's house. Carella got there at about four-thirty, pulling into the tree-lined street just behind a Good Humor ice-cream truck, the first he had seen this season. The houses on the block were mostly two-family homes. The community gave an appearance of neat lower-middle-class respectability. This was Sunday afternoon, and the Riverhead burghers were out on their front stoops reading their newspapers or listening to transistor radios. Carella counted twelve kids on bicycles as he drove up the street searching for 6451.

The house was on the corner of Avondale and Birch, a big brick-and-clapboard building on a comfortable plot. As Carella stepped out of the car, he smelled the aroma of cooking steak. He had eaten only a hamburger for lunch, and he was hungry as hell. A small black sign on the front lawn was lettered in white with the name R. COOMBS. Carella went up the walk to the front door, rang the bell, and waited. There was no answer. He rang again. He waited several moments more, and then walked around towards the back of the house. A man in a white apron was standing near an outdoor grille, a long fork in his right hand. Another man and two women were sitting at a redwood picnic table opposite the grille. The foursome was in conversation as Carella came around the side of the house, but they stopped talking the moment they saw him.

"I'm looking for Robert Coombs," Carella said.

"Yes, I'm Coombs," the man at the grille said.

"Sorry to intrude like this, Mr. Coombs," Carella said, walking over to him. "I'm Detective Carella of the 87th Squad. I wonder if I might talk to you privately."

"What is it, Bobby?" one of the women said, and rose immediately from where she was sitting at the picnic table. She was a tall woman wearing a blond fall, a snug blue cashmere sweater, tight navy-blue slacks. Her eyes were a shade lighter than the sweater, and she squinted them in suspicion, if not open hostility, as she approached the grille. "I'm *Mrs.* Coombs," she said, as if she were announcing exactly who ran this household. "What is it you want?"

"He's a detective, hon," Coombs said.

"A detective? What is it? What's the matter?"

"Nothing, Mrs. Coombs," Carella said. "I simply wanted to ask your husband some questions."

"What about? Are you in some kind of trouble, Bobby?"

"No, no, hon, I . . ."

"He's not in any trouble, Mrs. Coombs. This has to do with . . ."

"Then it can wait," Mrs. Coombs said. "The steaks are almost done. You just come back later, Detective . . ."

"Coppola," Coombs said.

"Carella," Carella said.

"We're about to eat," Mrs. Coombs said. "You come back later, do you hear?"

"Can you come back in an hour?" Coombs asked gently.

"Make it an hour and a half," Mrs. Coombs snapped.

"Honey, an hour's more time than . . ."

"I don't want to rush through my Sunday dinner," Mrs. Coombs said flatly. "An hour and a half, Detective Coppola."

"Carella," he said, *"bon appétit,"* and walked out of the yard, the aroma of the cooking steak nearly destroying him forever. He found an open luncheonette on Birch, ordered a cup of coffee and a cheese Danish, and then went out for a stroll around the neighborhood. Four little girls on the sidewalk ahead were skipping rope, chanting their ritualistic ditty, "Double-ee-Dutch, double-ee-Dutch," and from the open lot on the corner, there came the crack of a bat against a baseball, and a shout went up from the middle-aged men in shirt sleeves who were watching their sons play. The sky, magnificently blue all day long, virtually cloudless, was succumbing to the pale violet of dusk. The balmy afternoon breeze was turning a bit cooler. All up and down the street, he could hear mothers calling their children in to dinner. It was the time of day when a man wanted to be home with his family. Carella looked at his watch and sighed.

*   *   *

Isabel Coombs was a ventriloquist, of that Carella was certain.

The Coombs's guests had gone indoors the moment he'd returned, and he could see them now through the rear sliding glass doors of the house, standing near the record player and browsing through the album collection. He sat with Mr. and Mrs. Coombs at the redwood table and even though Robert Coombs occasionally tried to answer a question, he was really only the dummy in the act, and Isabel Coombs was doing most of the talking.

"Mr. Coombs," Carella said, "I'll make this as brief as I can. We found your name on a list allegedly ..."

"His name?" Isabel said. "You found *Bobby's* name on some list?"

"Yes, ma'am," Carella said, "a list ..."

"*His* name is not on any list," Isabel said.

"Well, maybe it is, hon," Robert said.

"It is *not*," Isabel said. "Detective Caretta ..."

"Carella."

"Yes, perhaps before we talk any further, we'd better get a lawyer."

"Well, that's entirely up to you, of course," Carella said, "but there's no intention here of charging your husband with any crime. We're merely seeking information about ..."

"Then why is his name on a *list*?" Isabel demanded.

Carella's wife was a deaf mute. He looked at Isabel Coombs now, wearing her blond fall and her brassy voice, and silently contrasted her with Teddy – black hair and brown eyes, voiceless, gentle, beautiful.

Mrs. Coombs's blue eyes flashed. "Well?" she said.

"Mrs. Coombs," Carella said patiently, "maybe it'd be better if you just let me *ask* the questions before you decide what they're going to be."

"What's that supposed to mean?"

"It's supposed to mean that this can take ten minutes or ten hours. We can do it right here in your back yard, or I can request that your husband accompany me ..."

"You're going to *arrest* him?"

"No, ma'am, I'm only going to ask him some questions."

"Then why don't you?"

Carella was silent for a moment. Then he said only, "Yes, ma'am," and fell silent again. He had forgotten for a moment just what it was he wanted to ask Coombs. He kept thinking of Teddy and wishing he were home in bed with her. "Well," he said, "Mr. Coombs, would you have any knowledge of a robbery that took place ...?"

"I thought you said there wasn't any crime being investigated," Isabel said.

"I didn't say that. I said we had no intention of charging your *husband* with any crime."

"You just mentioned a robbery."

"Yes, six years ago." He turned to Robert and said, "Would you know anything about such a robbery, Mr. Coombs?"

"I don't know," Robert said. "Who was robbed?"

"The National Savings & Loan Association."

'What's that?"

"A bank."

"Where?"

"In this city," Carella said. "Downtown."

"Six years ago," Isabel said flatly, "we were living in Detroit."

"I see," Carella said. "and when did you move here?"

"Just before Christmas," Robert said.

"That'd be ... about six months ago."

"Almost six months ago exactly," Robert said.

"Mr. Coombs, did anyone ever give you or did you ever come into possession in any way whatsoever..."

"This has to do with the robbery, doesn't it?" Isabel said shrewdly.

"...a piece of a photograph?" Carella continued, ignoring her.

"What do you mean?" Robert asked.

"A section of a picture."

"A picture of *what*?" Isabel asked.

"We don't know. That is, we're not sure."

"Then how would my husband know whether or not he has it?"

"If he has it, I guess he would know he has it," Carella said. "Do you have it?"

"No," Robert said.

"Do any of these names mean anything to you? Carmine Bonamico, Louis D'Amore..."

"No."

"Jerry Stein..."

"No."

"Pete Ryan?"

"No."

"Never heard of any of them?"

"No. Who are they?"

"How about these names? Albert Weinberg, Donald Renninger, Alice Bonamico..."

"No, none of them."

"Dorothea McNally? Geraldine Ferguson?"

Robert shook his head.

"Eugene Ehrbach?"

"No, I'm sorry."

"Well, then," Carella said. "I guess that's it. Thank you very much for your time." He rose, nodded briefly at Isabel Coombs, and started out of the yard."

Behind him, Isabel said, "Is that all?"

She sounded disappointed.

Carella did not get home until eight o'clock that night.

His wife Teddy was sitting at the kitchen table with Arthur Brown. She smiled as he entered, brown eyes engulfing him, one delicate hand brushing a strand of black hair away from her face.

"Hey, this is a surprise," he said to Brown. "Hello, honey," he said to Teddy, and bent to kiss her.

"How'd you make out?" Brown asked.

"He's not our man. Moved here from Detroit six months ago, doesn't know a thing about the photograph, and never even *heard* of National Savings & Loan." Carella suddenly turned to his wife. "I'm sorry honey," he said, "I didn't realize my back was turned." He repeated what he had just told Brown, watching Teddy's eyes for confirmation that she was reading his lips. She nodded when he had finished, and then rapidly moved her fingers in the hand alphabet he understood, telling him that Arthur had found another section of the photograph.

"Is that right?" Carella said, turning to Brown. "You've got another piece?"

"That's why I'm here, baby," Brown said. He reached into his jacket pocket, pulled out a glassine envelope, opened it, and emptied five pieces of the snapshot onto the tabletop. The men stared blankly at the collection. Teddy Carella – who lived in a soundless, speechless, largely visual and tactile universe – studied the twisted shapes on the tabletop. Her hands moved out swiftly. In less time than it had taken Carella to assemble the four pieces that had been in their possession yesterday, she now put together the five pieces before her:

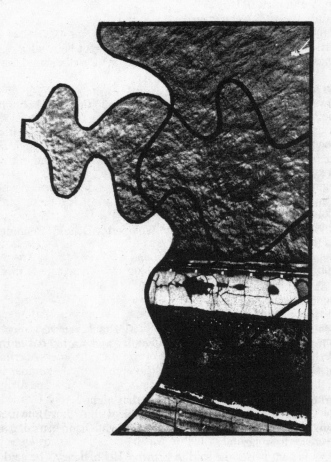

"Hey!" Brown said. "*Now* we're getting there!"

"Yeah," Carella said, "but where?"

9

Never let it be bruited about that just because a homicide victim also happens to be an ex-con, the police will devote less time and energy to finding out who has done him in. Perish the thought! In this fair and democratic land of ours, the rich and the poor, the powerful and the meek, the honest citizen and the wrongdoer are all afforded equal protection under the law, even after they're dead. So, boy oh boy, did those guys work hard trying to find out who had left the hole in Albert Weinberg's chest!

To begin with, there are a lot of people who have to be informed when someone inconsiderately gets himself knocked off. Just *informing* all these different people takes a lot of time. Imagine having to call the Police Commissioner, *and* the Chief of Detectives, *and* the District Commander of the Detective Division, *and* Homicide, *and* the Squad and Precinct Commanding Officers of the precinct where the body was found, *and* the Medical Examiner, *and* the District Attorney, *and* the Telegraph, Telephone and Teletype Bureau at Headquarters, *and* the Police Laboratory, not to mention the police photographers and stenographers – the list alone is longer than the average laundry list, and just try phoning in a dirty shirt to the local laundryman. All that vast machinery of law enforcement ground into immediate action the moment it was discovered that Albert Weinberg had a hole in his chest; all those oiled gears smoothly meshed and rotated in the cause of justice; all those relentless preventers of crime and pursuers of criminals called upon their enormous reservoir of physical courage and stamina, their mental acumen, their experience, intelligence, their *brilliance* even – and all in an attempt to discover who had shot and killed the man who once upon a time had beat up a little old lady for the sum of seventeen dollars and eighty-four cents.

Actually, most of the physical courage and stamina, the mental acumen, the experience, intelligence and brilliance was being expended by Detectives Meyer Meyer and Cotton Hawes of the 87th Squad; Carella (who had discovered the corpse) being elsewhere occupied. Meyer and Hawes did not have much trouble taking apart the apartment; whoever killed Weinberg had already done a very good job of that. They decided after a thorough search of the place that Brown's surmise was a correct one. The killer had been after Weinberg's pieces of the photograph, and had apparently been successful in finding them. Meyer and Hawes questioned all of the tenants in the building and discovered that three of them had heard a very loud noise shortly after midnight. None of these people thought it either necessary or advisable to call the police. In this neighborhood, policemen were not exactly looked upon as benefactors of the people, and besides the sounds of gunfire were somewhat commonplace, day *or* night. So both detectives went back to the squadroom to consult the timetable Irving Krutch had so thoughtfully typed up for Steve Carella:

6:00 P.M.	-- ARRIVED HOME FROM WORK. TALKED TO DOORMAN DOWNSTAIRS ABOUT FINE WEATHER.
6:05 P.M.	-- ENTERED APARTMENT. CALLED SUZANNE ENDICOTT, REMINDED HER OF OUR DATE.
6:15 P.M.	-- RAN BATH, MIXED MARTINIS, CAUGHT LAST PART OF SIX O'CLOCK NEWS ON TELEVISION WHILE WAITING FOR TUB TO FILL.
6:30 P.M. to 7:30 P.M.	-- BATHED, SHAVED, DRESSED, MIXED ANOTHER PITCHERFUL OF MARTINIS.
7:30 P.M.	-- SUZIE ARRIVED AT APARTMENT. WE EACH HAD TWO MARTINIS.
8:00 P.M.	-- ARTHUR BROWN CALLED TO ADVISE ME OF NEW DEVELOPMENTS ON CASE.
8:25 P.M.	-- CALLED DOWNSTAIRS, ASKED DOORMAN TO GET ME A TAXICAB.
8:30 P.M.	-- SUZIE AND I WENT DOWNSTAIRS, TAXI WAITING, TOOK TAXI TO THE RAM'S HEAD, 777 JEFFERSON AVENUE. (RESERVATION FOR 8:45 P.M. MADE BY MY SECRETARY, DONNA HOGAN, EARLIER IN DAY.)
8:45 P.M. to 10:30 P.M.	-- DINNER AT THE RAM'S HEAD. HEADWAITER MAURICE SUGGESTED THE CHATEAU BOUSCAUT '64.
10:30 P.M. to 11:30 P.M.	-- WALKED UP HALL AVENUE LOOKING IN SHOP WINDOWS, AND FINALLY HAILED TAXI.
11:45 P.M.	-- TAXI DROPPED US AT APARTMENT. CAME UPSTAIRS. I HAD A COGNAC, SUZIE HAD A CREME DE MENTHE ON THE ROCKS. WATCHED JOHNNY CARSON FOR APPROXIMATELY A HALF-HOUR. BUDDY HACKETT GUEST STAR.
12:15 A.M.	-- WENT TO BED.
3:15 A.M.	-- AWAKENED BY KNOCKING ON DOOR. DETECTIVE STEVE CARELLA IN HALLWAY OUTSIDE.
3:15 A.M. to 3:25 A.M.	-- TALKED TO DETECTIVE CARELLA.
3:25 A.M.	-- TYPED TIMETABLE FOR DETECTIVE CARELLA.
3:30 A.M.	-- DETECTIVE CARELLA LEFT. WENT BACK TO BED.

The day doorman outside Krutch's apartment building corroborated that Krutch had come home from work at about 6 p.m., and that they had had a brief discussion about the wonderful weather, when the city was sweltering in the grip of a ninety-degree heat wave. He put Meyer and Hawes in touch with the night doorman who stated that Krutch had called down for a taxi at approximately eight-thirty, and had left the building with a young lady shortly thereafter. He had personally given Krutch's destination to the cab driver: The Ram's Head at 777 Jefferson Avenue. He further reported that Krutch and the young lady had come back to the apartment shortly before midnight and that he had not seen either of them leaving again at any time during his tour of duty, which ended at 8 a.m., Meyer and Hawes went over the building's entrances very carefully, though, and discovered that anyone who chose not to be seen by either the doorman or the elevator operator had only to take the service steps down to the basement and leave the building through the side-street exit door, where the garbage cans were stacked.

The reservations book for The Ram's Head noted a reservation for "Irving Krutch, 2" at 8:45 p.m. on the night Albert Weinberg was murdered. The headwaiter, a man named Maurice Duchene recalled Mr. Krutch and a young lady being there, and also recalled recommending the Chateau Bouscaut '64 to them. He said that Mr. Krutch had ordered a bottle and had commented that the wine was delicious. Mr. Krutch had tipped him three dollars when he left the restaurant at about ten-thirty.

A call to the local affiliate of the National Broadcasting Company ascertained the fact that one of Johnny Carson's guests that night had been Buddy Hackett and that he had come on almost immediately after the monologue, sometime before midnight.

There was nothing left to do but talk to Suzanne Endicott.

Ask any cop whom he would rather interview, an eighty-year-old lady with varicose veins or a twenty-two-year-old blonde wearing a see-through blouse, just ask any cop.

Suzanne Endicott worked in a swinging boutique called The Nickel Bag, and she was wearing a leather mini-skirt and a blouse through which her breasts were clearly visible. Her attire was very disconcerting, especially to policemen who were rather more used to eighty-year-old ladies with varicose veins. Detective Meyer Meyer was a married man. Cotton Hawes was a single man, but he, too, seemed to be having difficulty concentrating on the questions. He kept thinking he should ask Suzanne Endicott to go to a movie with him. Or something. The shop was thronged with young girls similarly though not identically dressed, mini-skirts and tights, headbands and shiny blouses, a veritable aviary of chirping young birds – Meyer Meyer hadn't even enjoyed the Hitchcock film. Suzanne Endicott fluttered here and there, helping this young lady with a pants suit, that one with a crocheted dress, the next with a sequined vest. Between flutterings and chirpings and quick glimpses of nipples and thighs, the detectives tried to ask their questions.

"You want to tell us exactly what happened that night?" Meyer asked.

"Oh, sure, I'd be happy to," Suzie said. She had the faintest trace of a Southern accent in her speech, Hawes noticed.

"Where are you from originally?" he asked, thinking to put her at ease, and also thinking he would definitely ask her to go to a movie or something.

"Oh my, does my accent still show?" Suzie said.

"Just a little," Hawes said, and tried a gentle understanding smile which did not seem appropriate to his massive height, nor his fiery red mane, nor the white streak in the hair over his left temple, the result of a knifing many years back.

"I'm from Georgia," she said. "The Peach State."

"It must be lovely down there in Georgia," Hawes said.

"Oh yes, just lovely," Suzie said. "Excuse me, just one teeny little minute, won't you?" she said, and dashed off to where a striking brunette was coming out of one of the dressing rooms. The brunette had on bright red velvet hip-huggers. Hawes thought he might go over and ask *her* to go to a movie or something.

"I feel as if I'm backstage at the Folies-Bergère," Meyer whispered.

"Have you ever *been* backstage at the Folies-Bergère?" Hawes whispered back.

"No, but I'm sure it's just like this."

"Better," Hawes said.

"Have *you* ever been?"

"Never."

"Well, here I am, back again," Suzie said, and smiled, and tossed her long blond hair and added, "I think they were a bit too snug, don't you?"

"What's that?" Meyer said.

"The pants she had on."

"Oh, sure, a little too snug," Meyer said. "Miss Endicott, about the night Weinberg was killed ..."

"Oh, yes, that was just dreadful, wasn't it?" Suzie said.

"Yes, it was," Hawes said gently and tenderly.

"Although I understand he was a criminal. Weinberg, I mean."

"Who told you that?"

"Irving did. *Was* he a criminal?"

"He paid his debt to society," Hawes said tenderly and gently.

"Oh, yes, I suppose he did," Suzie answered. "But still."

"In any event," Meyer said, passing a hand over his bald pate and rolling his china-blue eyes, "he *was* killed, and we're conducting an investigation into his murder, and we'd like very much to ask you questions about that night, if it's not too much trouble, Miss Endicott."

"Oh, it's no trouble at all," Suzie said. "Would you please excuse me for just one teeny minute?" she said, and went over to the cash register where a leggy redhead was standing with several sweaters in her arms, waiting to pay for them.

"We'll *never* get out of this joint," Meyer said.

"That wouldn't be too bad," Hawes said.

"For *you*, maybe it wouldn't be too bad. For *me*, if I don't get home in time for dinner, Sarah'll kill me."

"Why don't you run on along then?" Hawes said, and grinned. "I think I can handle this alone."

"Oh, I'm sure you can," Meyer said. "Trouble is, you see, we're supposed to find out who killed Weinberg. That's the trouble, you see."

"Well, here I am back again," Suzie said, and smiled, and tossed her long blond hair. "I've asked Michelle to spell me, so I don't think we'll be interrupted again."

"That's very kind of you, Suzie," Hawes said.

"Oh, not at all," she answered, and smiled again.

"About that night ..."

"Yes," she said, alert, and responsive, and eager to co-operate. "What would you like to know?"

"First, what time did you get to Irving Krutch's apartment?"

"It must have been about seven-thirty," Suzie said.

"How long have you known Mr. Krutch?" Hawes said.

"We've practically been living together for four years," Suzie answered, her big brown eyes opened wide.

"Oh," Hawes said.

"Yes."

"I see."

"We have separate apartments, of course."

"Of course."

Meyer cleared his throat. "What ... uh ... what was I saying?" he said, turning to Hawes.

"Time she got there," Hawes said.

"Oh yes. Seven-thirty, is that right?"

"That's right," Suzie said.

"And what did you do when you got there?"

"Irving gave me a martini. Two martinis, in fact. I love martinis. Don't you just adore martinis?" she asked Hawes.

"Mmm," Hawes said.

"Were there any visitors while you were there?"

"None."

"Any phone calls?"

"Yes."

"Would you happen to know from whom?"

"From a detective. Irving seemed very happy when he hung up."

"Are you engaged or something?" Hawes asked. "Is that it?"

"To be married, do you mean?"

"Yes, to be married."

"Oh, no, don't be silly," Suzie said.

Meyer cleared his throat again. "What time did you *leave* the apartment?" he asked.

"About eight-thirty. I think it was eight-thirty. It could have been a teeny bit earlier or a teeny bit later. But I think it was *around* eight-thirty."

"And where did you go?"

"To The Ram's Head." She smiled up at Hawes. "That's a restaurant. Have you ever been there?"

"No. No, I haven't."

"It's very nice."

"What time did you leave the restaurant, Miss Endicott?"

"About ten-thirty. Again, as I said, it might have been a teeny bit ..."

"Yes, but it was *around* ten-thirty."

"Yes."

"And then what did you do?"

"We went for a walk on Hall Avenue, and looked in all the store windows. We saw some marvelous lounging pajamas in Kilkenny's. Italian, I think they were. Just, oh so colorful."

"How long did you walk on Hall Avenue?"

"An hour or so? I guess it was an hour or so."

"And then what did you do?"

"We went back to Irving's apartment. What we do, you see, is we either go to Irving's apartment or to my apartment. I live downtown in The Quarter," she said, looking up at Hawes. "Do you know Chelsea Street?"

"Yes, I do," Hawes said.

"12½ Chelsea Street," she said, "apartment 6B. That's because of hard luck."

"What is?"

"The 12½. It should be 13, but the owner of the building is superstitious."

"Yes, there are lots of buildings in the city like that," Hawes said.

"Lots of buildings don't even have a thirteenth *floor*," Suzie said. "That is, they *have* a thirteenth floor, but it's called the *fourteenth* floor."

"Yes, I know."

"12½ Chelsea Street," she said, "apartment 6B, Hampton 4-8100." She paused. "That's my telephone number."

"So you went back to Mr. Krutch's apartment at about eleven-thirty," Meyer said, "and then what did you do?"

"We watched television for a while. Buddy Hackett was on. He's a scream. Don't you just adore Buddy Hackett?" she said, looking up at Hawes.

"I adore him, yes," Hawes said, and Meyer gave him a peculiar look. "He's very comical," Hawes said, ignoring the look.

"He's just adorable," Suzie said.

"What did you do after watching television?" Meyer said.

"We made love," Suzie said.

Meyer cleared his throat.

"Twice," Suzie added.

Meyer cleared his throat again.

"Then we went to sleep," she said, "and in the middle of the night this Italian detective knocked on the door and started asking all sorts of questions about where we were and what we were doing. Is he allowed to do something like that, come around in the middle of the night, and bang on the door, and ask dumb questions?"

"Yes, he is," Hawes said.

"I think that's awful," Suzie said. "Don't you think that's awful?" she asked Hawes.

"Well, it's a job," Hawes said, and smiled weakly, and tried to avoid Meyer's glance again.

"Did either of you leave the apartment at any time between 11:30 and 3 a.m.?" Meyer asked.

"Oh, no. I told you. First we watched television, and then we made love, and then we went to sleep."

"You were there all the time?"

"Yes."

"*Both* of you?"

"Yes."

"Mr. Krutch didn't leave the apartment at all?"

"No."

"If you were asleep, how do you know whether he left or not?"

"Well, we didn't go to sleep until maybe two o'clock. Things take *time*, you know."

"You were awake until 2 a.m.?"

"Yes."

"And Mr. Krutch did not leave the apartment?"

"No."

"Did he leave the bedroom?"

"No."

"Not at any time during the night?"

"Not at any time during the night."

"Okay," Meyer said. "You got anything else, Cotton?"

"Is that your name?" Suzie asked. "I had an uncle named Cotton."

"That's my name," Hawes said.

"After Cotton Mather?"

"That's right."

"Isn't that a coincidence?" Suzie asked. "I think that's a marvelous coincidence."

"You got anything else to ask?" Meyer said again.

"Well . . . yes," Hawes said, and looked at Meyer.

"I'll wait for you outside," Meyer said.

"Okay," Hawes said.

He watched as Meyer picked his way through the milling girls in the shop, watched as Meyer opened the front door and stepped out onto the sidewalk.

"I have only one further question, Suzie," he said.

"Yes, what's that?"

"Would you like to go to a movie with me? Or something?"

"Oh, no," Suzie said. "Irving wouldn't like that." She smiled and looked up at him with her big brown eyes. "I'm terribly sorry," she said, "really I am, but Irving simply wouldn't like that at all."

"Well, uh, thanks a lot for your co-operation, Miss Endicott," Hawes said. "Thank you very much, I'm sorry we – uh – broke into your day this way, thanks a lot."

"Not at all," Suzie said, and rushed off to another beautiful brunette who was emerging from yet another dressing room. Hawes looked at the brunette, decided not to risk further rejection, and went outside to where Meyer was waiting on the sidewalk.

"Did you score?" Meyer asked.

"Nope."

"How come? I thought it was a sure thing."

"So did I. I guess she thinks Krutch is just adorable."

"I think *you're* just adorable," Meyer said.

"Up yours," Hawes answered, and both men went back to the squadroom. Hawes typed up the report and then went out to talk to a grocery store owner who had a complaint about people stealing bottles of milk from boxes stacked up in the back of the store, this in the wee hours of the morning before the store was opened for business. Meyer went to talk to an assault victim and to show him some mug shots for possible identification. They had worked long and hard on the Weinberg case, yeah, and it was now in the Open file, pending further developments.

Meanwhile, on the ferry to Bethtown, two other cops were working very hard at sniffing the mild June breezes that blew in off the River Harb. Coatless, hatless, Carella and Brown stood at the railing and watched Isola's receding skyline, watched too the busy traffic on the river, tugboats and ocean liners, a squadron of Navy destroyers, barges and scows, each of them tooting and chugging and sounding bells and sending up steam and leaving a boiling, frothy wake behind.

"This is still the cheapest date in the city," Brown said. "Five cents for a forty-five minute boat ride – who can beat it?"

"I wish *I* had a nickel for all the times I rode this ferry with Teddy, before we were married," Carella said.

"Caroline used to love it," Brown said. "She never wanted to sit inside, winter or summer. We always stood here on the bow, even if it meant freezing our asses off."

"The poor man's ocean cruise," Carella said.

"Moonlight and sea breezes . . ."

"Concertina playing . . ."

"Tugboats honking . . ."

"Sounds like a Warner Brothers movie."

"I sometimes thought it *was*," Brown said wistfully. "There were lots of places I couldn't go in this city, Steve, either because I couldn't afford them or because it was made plain to me I wasn't wanted in them. On the Bethtown ferry, though, I could be the hero of the movie. I could take my girl out on the bow and we could feel the wind on our faces, and I could kiss her like a colored Humphrey Bogart. I love this goddamn ferry, I really do."

"Yeah," Carella said, and nodded.

"Sure," Robert Coombs said, "I used to have a piece of that picture."

"*Used* to have?" Brown asked.

"*Used* to have, correct," Coombs said, and spat on the sidewalk in front of the hot-dog stand. He was a man of about sixty, with a weather-beaten face, spikes of yellow-white hair sticking up out of his skull like withered stalks of corn, an altogether grizzled look about him as he sat on one of the stools in front of his establishment (Bob's Roadside) and talked to the two detectives. The hot-dog stand was on Route 24, off the beaten path; it was unlikely that a dozen automobiles passed the place on any given day, in either direction.

"Where'd you get it?" Carella asked.

"Petey Ryan give it to me before the holdup," Coombs said. His eyes were a pale blue, fringed with blond lashes, overhung with blond-white brows. His teeth were the color of his brows. He spat again on the sidewalk. Brown wondered what it was like to eat food prepared at Bob's Roadside.

"Why'd Ryan give it to you?" Carella asked.

"We was good friends," Coombs said.

"Tell us all about it," Brown suggested.

"What for? I already told you I ain't got the picture no more."

"Where is it now?"

"Christ knows," Coombs said, and shrugged, and spat.

"How long before the holdup?" Carella asked.

"How long *what*?"

"When he gave you the picture."

"Three days."

"Petey came to you . . ."

"Correct."

"And handed you a piece of a snapshot . . ."

"Correct."

"And said what?"

"Said I should hang onto it till after the hit."

"And then what?"

"Then he'd come and collect it from me."

"Did he say why?"

"In case he got busted."

"He didn't want to have the picture on him if the police caught him, is that it?"

"Correct."

"What did you think about all that?" Brown asked.

"What should I think? A good friend asks me to do a favor, I do it. What was there to think?"

"Did you have any idea what the picture meant?"

"Sure."

"What did it mean?"

"It showed where they was ditching the loot. You think I'm a dope?"

"Did Petey say how many pieces there were in the complete photograph?"

"Nope."

"Just told you to hang onto this little piece of it until he came to collect it?"

"Correct."

"Okay, where's the piece now?"

"I threw it in the garbage," Coombs said.

"Why?"

"Petey got killed. Cinch he wasn't going to come back for the piece, so I threw it out."

"Even though you knew it was part of a bigger picture? A picture that showed where they were dropping the N.S.L.A. loot?"

"Correct."

"When did you throw it out?"

"Day after the hit. Soon as I read in the paper that Petey got killed."

"You were in a pretty big hurry to get rid of it, huh?"

"A pretty big hurry, correct."

"Why?"

"I didn't want to get hooked into the holdup. I figured if the picture was hot, I didn't want no part of it."

"But you accepted if from Petey to begin with, didn't you?"

"Correct."

"Even though you knew it showed where they planned to hide the proceeds of a robbery."

"I only *guessed* that. I didn't know for sure."

"When did you find out for sure?"

"Well, I *still* don't know for sure."

"But you became sufficiently alarmed *after* the robbery to throw away the scrap Petey had given you."

"Correct."

"This was six years ago, right, Mr. Coombs."

"Correct."

"You threw it in the garbage."

"In the garbage, correct."

"Where was the garbage?"

"Where was the *what*?"

"The garbage."

"In the back."

"Out back there?"

"Correct."

"You want to come back there with us, and show us where you threw it in the garbage?"

"Sure," Coombs said, and got off the stool, and spat, and then led them around to the rear side of the hot-dog stand. "Right there," he said, pointing. "In one of them garbage cans."

"You carried that little tiny piece of the photograph out back here, and you lifted the lid of the garbage can and dropped it in, is that right?"

"Correct."

"Show us how you did it," Brown said.

Coombs looked at him curiously. Then he shrugged, pinched an imaginary photograph segment between his thumb and forefinger, carried it to the nearest garbage can, lifted the lid, deposited the non-existent scrap inside the can, covered the can, turned to the cops, and said, "Like that. That's how I done it."

"You're lying," Brown said flatly.

Neither of the two detectives, of course, knew whether or not Coombs was lying, nor had their little charade with the garbage can proved a damn thing. But public relations has a lot to do with criminal investigation and detection. There is not a red-blooded citizen of the U.S. of A. who does not know through constant exposure to television programs and motion pictures that cops are always asking trick questions and doing trick things to trap a person in a lie. Coombs had seen his share of movies and television shows, and he knew now, knew with heart-stopping, face-blanching, teeth-jarring certainty that he had done something wrong when he walked over to the garbage can, and lifted the lid, and dropped in the imaginary photo scrap, something that instantly told these two shrewd investigators that he was lying.

"Lying?" he said. "Me? Lying?" He tried to spit again, but his throat muscles wouldn't respond, and he almost choked, and then began coughing violently.

"You want to come along with us?" Carella said, sternly and pompously, and in his most legal-sounding voice.

"Wh ... wh ... wh...?" Coombs said, and coughed again, his face turning purple, and then put one hand flat against the rear wall of the hot-dog stand, head bent, and leaned against it, and tried to catch his breath and recover his wits. They had him cold, he knew, but he couldn't figure what the charge would be, and he tried to buy time now while the big black cop reached into his back pocket and pulled out a pair of handcuffs with vicious-looking saw-toothed edges – oh Jesus, Coombs thought, I am busted. But for what?

"What's the crime," he said, "the charge," he said, "what's the, what's the, what did I do?"

"You know what you did, Mr. Coombs," Carella said, coldly. "You destroyed evidence of a crime."

"That's a felony," Brown said, lying.

"Section 812 of the Penal Law," Carella said.

"Look, I..."

"Come along, Mr. Coombs," Brown said, and held out the handcuffs.

'What if I ... what if I hadn't thrown out the thing, the picture?" Coombs asked.

"Did you?"

"I didn't. I got it. I'll give it to you. Jesus, I'll give it to you."

"Get it," Brown said.

*　　*　　*

A ferryboat is a good place for speculation. It is also a good place for listening. So on the way back to Isola, Carella and Brown each did a little speculating and a little listening.

"Four guys in the holdup," Brown said. "Carmine Bonamico, who master-minded the job..."

"Some mastermind," Carella said.

"Jerry Stein, who drove the getaway heap, and two guns named Lou D'Amore and Pete Ryan. Four altogether."

"So?"

"So figure it out. Pete Ryan gave one piece of the snapshot to his aunt Dorothea McNally and another piece to his good old pal Robert Coombs..."

"Of Bob's Famous Roadside Emporium," Carella said.

"Correct," Brown said. "Which means, using a method known as arithmetical deduction, that Ryan was at one time in possession of *two* pieces of the snapshot."

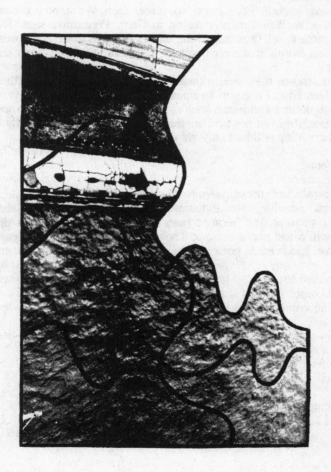

"Correct," Carella said.

"Is it not reasonable to assume, therefore, that *each* member of the gang was *likewise* in possession of two pieces of the snapshot?"

"It is reasonable, but not necessarily exclusive," Carella said.

"How do you mean, Holmes?"

"Elementary. You are assuming there are only *eight* pieces of the full photograph. However, using other multiples of four, we can equally reason that there are twelve pieces, or sixteen pieces, or indeed . . ."

"My guess is eight," Brown said.

"Why the magic number eight?"

"If you were planning a heist, would you go cutting a picture into twelve parts? Or sixteen?"

"Or twenty?" Carella said.

"*Would* you?"

"I think it's a goofy idea to begin with," Carella said. "I wouldn't cut up a photograph at *all.*"

"My guess is eight. Four guys, two pieces each. We've now got six of them. My guess is we'll find number seven in Gerry Ferguson's safe. That'll leave only one piece to go. One, baby. One more piece and we're home free.

As Robert Burns, that sage Scottish poet once remarked, however, the best laid plans . . .

That afternoon, they went down to the Ferguson Gallery with a warrant obliging Geraldine Ferguson to open her safe. And though they searched it from top to bottom and found a lot of goodies in it, none of which were related to any crime, they did *not* find another piece of the photograph. By the end of that Monday, they still had only six pieces.

Six.

Count 'em.

Six.

As they studied these assembled pieces in the midnight silence of the squadroom, something struck them as being terribly wrong. There was no sky in the picture. And because there was no sky, neither was there an up nor a down, a top nor a bottom. They were looking at a landscape without perspective, and it made no sense.

10

The nylon stocking was wrapped tightly around her throat, embedded in the soft flesh of her neck. Her eyes were bulging, and she lay grotesque in death upon the turquoise-colored rug in her bedroom, wearing a baby-doll nightgown and bikini panties, the bedsheets trailing off the bed and tangled in one twisted leg.

Geraldine Ferguson would never again swear in Italian, never again proposition married spades, never again charge exorbitant prices for a painting or a piece of sculpture. Geraldine Ferguson lay robbed of life in a posture as angularly absurd as the geometric designs that had shrieked from the walls of her gallery, death silent and shrill in that turquoise-matted sanctuary, the bedroom a bedlam around her, a tired reprise of the havoc wreaked in the rooms of Donald Renninger and Albert Weinberg, the searcher run amok, the quest for seven hundred and fifty G's reaching a climax of desperation. The police had not found what they'd wanted in Gerry's safe, and they wondered now if whoever had demolished Gerry's apartment and strangled her into the bargain had had any better luck than they.

Arthur Brown went out into the hallway and, oddly, wondered if Gerry had ever roller-skated on a city sidewalk.

They picked up Bramley Kahn in a gay bar that night.

He was wearing a brocade Nehru jacket over white linen hip-huggers. His hand was resting on the shoulder of a curly-haired young man in a black leather jacket. A sculpted gold ring set with a gray freshwater pearl was on Kahn's left pinky.

He was slightly drunk, and decidedly campy, and he seemed surprised to see the police. Everywhere around him, men danced with men, men whispered to men, men embraced men, but Kahn was nonetheless surprised to see the police because this was the most permissive city in the world, where private homosexual clubs could expressly prohibit policemen from entering (unless of course they, too, were members) and where everyone looked the other way unless a six-year-old boy was being buggered by a flying queen in a dark alley. This was just a run-of-the-mill gay bar, never any trouble here, never any strident jealous arguments, never anything more than consenting adults quietly doing their thing – Kahn was very surprised to see the police.

He was even more surprised to learn that Geraldine Ferguson was dead.

He kept telling the police how surprised he was.

This was a Tuesday, he kept telling the police, and Tuesday was normally Gerry's day off; she took Tuesdays, he took Wednesdays. He had not expected to see her at the gallery and was not surprised when she did not show up for work. He had closed the gallery at six, had gone for a quiet dinner with a close friend, and then had come down here to The Quarter for a nightcap before turning in. Arthur Brown asked him if he would mind coming uptown to the squadroom, and Kahn said he had better first consult his lawyer. Brown said he was entitled to a lawyer, and in fact didn't have to answer any questions at all if he didn't want to, lawyer or no lawyer, and then went into the whole Miranda-Escobedo bit, advising Kahn of his rights while Kahn listened intently, and then decided that he had *better* call his lawyer and have him come up to the squadroom to be present during the interrogation, murder being a somewhat serious occurrence, even in a city as permissive as this one.

The lawyer was a man named Anatole Petitpas, and he asked Brown to do the whole Miranda-Escobedo song and dance one more time for the benefit of the people in the cheaper seats. Brown patiently explained Kahn's rights to him again, and Kahn said that he understood everything, and Petitpas seemed satisfied that all was being conducted in a proper legal manner, and then he signaled to the detectives that it was now all right to ask his client whatever questions they chose to ask. There were four detectives standing in a loose circle around Kahn, but their weight of numbers was offset by the presence of Petitpas, who could be counted on to leap into the fray if ever the questioning got too rough. This was murder they were fooling around with here, and nobody was taking any chances.

They asked all the routine questions (almost putting even themselves to sleep) such as WHERE WERE YOU AT 2 a.m. LAST NIGHT? (the time established by the M.E. as the probable time of Gerry's death) and WHO WAS WITH YOU? and WHERE DID YOU GO? and WERE YOU SEEN BY ANYONE?, all the usual police crap, the questions coming alternately from Brown, Carella, Meyer, and Hawes working smoothly and efficiently as a team. And then finally they got back to the photograph, everything always got back to the photograph because it was obvious to each of the cops in that squadroom that four people had been killed so far and that all of them had been in possession of a piece or pieces of a picture showing the location of the N.S.L.A. loot, and if a motive were any more evident than that, each of them would have tripped over it with his big flat feet.

"When I talked to you at the gallery Saturday," Brown said, "you told me Gerry Ferguson was in possession of a certain piece of a photograph. When you said this, were you..."

"Just a second," Petitpas interrupted. "Have you talked to my client before this?"

"I talked to him, yes."

"Did you advise him of his rights?"

"I was conducting a field investigation," Brown said wearily.

"He didn't tell me he was a cop," Kahn said.

"Is that true?" Petitpas asked.

"It's true."

"It may be significant."

"Not necessarily," Brown said, and smiled. The other detectives smiled with him. They were thinking of thousands of social agency reports in triplicate where, for example, a young man would be described as having been arrested at the age of fourteen for possession of narcotics, at sixteen for possession with intent to sell, and at eighteen for smuggling in twelve kilos of heroin in a brown paper bag, all of which damning criminal history would be followed by the words, typewritten in upper case,

NOT NECESSARILY SIGNIFICANT.

"Go on," Petitpas said.

"I wanted to ask your client whether he knew for certain that Miss Ferguson had a piece of that photograph."

"I knew for certain," Kahn said.

"Miss Ferguson told us the piece was in the gallery safe," Carella said. "Was that your impression as well?"

"It was my impression."

"As you know, however, when we opened the safe, we did not find the photograph."

"I know that."

"Where do you think it was then?" Hawes asked.

"I don't understand your question."

"When you found out it wasn't in the safe, when we opened the safe yesterday and the picture wasn't in it, where did you think it might be?"

"I had no idea."

"Did you think it was in Miss Ferguson's apartment?" Meyer asked.

"He has already told you he had no idea where it was," Petitpas said. "You're asking him to speculate..."

"Let's save it for the courtroom, counselor," Carella said. "There's nothing out of line here so far, and you know it. A woman's been killed. If your client can satisfy us on certain points, he'll walk out of here in ten minutes. If not..."

"Yes, Mr. Canella?"

"Carella. If not, I think you're as well aware of the possibilities as we are."

"Are you threatening him with a murder charge?"

"Did anyone mention a murder charge?"

"The implication was clear."

"So was Detective Meyer's question. Mr. Kahn, did you or did you not think the photograph might be in Miss Ferguson's apartment?"

"May I answer that?" Kahn asked his lawyer.

"Yes, go ahead, go ahead," Petitpas said, annoyed.

"I guess I thought it could have been there, yes."

"Did you go there looking for it?" Brown asked.

"That's it, I'm afraid," Petitpas said. "I feel I must advise my client at this point that it would not be to his benefit to answer any further questions."

"Do you want us to book him, counselor, is that it?"

"You may do as you wish. I know I don't have to remind you that murder is a serious..."

"Oh, man, what bullshit," Brown said. "Why don't you just play ball with us, Petitpas? Has your man got something to hide?"

"I've got nothing to hide, Anatole," Kahn said.

"Then let him answer the goddamn questions," Carella said.

"I can answer the questions," Kahn said, and looked at Petitpas.

"Very well, go ahead," Petitpas said.

"I didn't kill her, Anatole."

"Go ahead, go ahead."

"I really didn't. I have nothing to hide."

"Okay, counselor?"

"I have already indicated that he may answer your questions."

"Thank you. Did you go to Gerry Ferguson's apartment last night?"

"No."

"Or any time yesterday?"

"No."

"Did you see her yesterday?"

"Yes, at the gallery. I left before she did. This was sometime after you'd opened the safe."

"Sometime after you knew the picture wasn't in the safe?"

"That's right, yes."

"And sometime after you thought it might be in Miss Ferguson's apartment?"

"Yes."

"Let's talk about the list, Mr. Kahn."

"What?"

"The list."

"What list?"

"The torn list of names you keep in the little cashbox in the bottom drawer of your office desk."

"I . . . I don't know what you mean," Kahn said.

"Four people on that list have already been killed, Mr. Kahn."

"What list does he mean?" Petitpas asked.

"I don't know."

"It's a list of names, Mr. Petitpas," Brown said, "presumably of people who possess or once possessed portions of a photograph alleging to show the location of certain monies stolen from the National Savings & Loan Association six years ago. Does that clearly identify the nature of the list, Mr. Kahn?"

Petitpas stared at his client. Kahn stared back.

"Well, answer it," Petitpas said.

"It clearly identifies the nature of the list, yes," Kahn said.

"Then the list *does* exist?"

"It exists."

"And a torn portion of it is indeed in your cashbox?"

"It is, yes, but how . . ."

"Never mind how. Where'd you get that list?"

"Gerry gave it to me for safekeeping."

"Where'd *she* get it?"

"I don't know."

"Mr. Kahn, try to help us," Meyer said gently.

"I didn't kill her," Kahn said.

"Somebody did," Carella said.

"It wasn't me."

"We're not suggesting it was."

"All right. As long as you know."

"Who gave her the list?"

"Carmine."

"Bonamico?"

"Yes. Carmine Bonamico. He gave half of the list to his wife, and half to Geraldine."

"Why Geraldine?"

"They were having a thing."

"They were lovers?"

"Yes."

"Did he also give her a piece of the photograph?"

"No. She got that from her brother-in-law, Lou D'Amore. There were four men on the holdup. Bonamico cut the picture into eight parts, a wiggly line across the middle horizontally, three wiggly lines vertically, eight pieces in all. He gave two pieces to each of the men, and kept two for himself. He asked the men to distribute the pieces to people they could trust. It was an insurance policy, so to speak. The beneficiaries were the people who held sections of the photograph. The trustees were Alice Bonamico and Gerry Ferguson, the only two people who could put together the list and collect the photograph segments and uncover the loot."

"Who told you all this?"

"Gerry."

"How'd she know?"

"Pillow talk. Bonamico told her everything. I don't think his wife knew who had the other half of the list. But Gerry sure as hell knew."

"So Gerry was in possession of half of the list as well as one piece of the photograph."

"Yes."

"Why didn't she put the list together and go after the other pieces?"

"She tried to."

"What stopped her?"

"Alice." Kahn paused. "Well, after all, would *your* wife co-operate with your mistress?"

"I don't have a mistress," Carella said.

"Here's a typewritten copy of the list," Brown said. "Take a look at it."

"Is it all right to look at it?" Kahn asked his lawyer.

"Yes," Petitpas said. He turned to the police stenographer and said, "let the record indicate that Mr. Kahn is being shown a list with such-and-such names on it; record all the names as they appear on the list."

"May I see the list?" the stenographer asked.

Brown handed it to him. The stenographer studied it, noted the names, and then handed it back to Brown.

"All right, Mr. Kahn, would you now please look at this list?"

Kahn accepted the list.

ALBERT WEINBERG

DONALD RENNINGER

EUGENE E. EHRBACH

ALICE BONAMICO

GERALDINE FERGUSON

DOROTHEA McNALLY

ROBERT COOMBS

"I've looked at it," he said, and handed it back to Brown.

"Which of those names are familiar to you?"

"Only three of them."

"Which?"

"Gerry, of course, Alice Bonamico, and Donald Renninger. He's the other person who got a piece of the picture from Lou D'Amore."

"How come?"

"They were cellmates at Caramoor. In fact, Lou mailed the piece to him there. He was still behind bars at the time of the robbery."

"What about these other names?"

"I don't know any of them."

"Robert Coombs?"

"Don't know him."

"His name was on the half of the list you had in your possession. Didn't you ever try to contact him?"

"Gerry may have. I didn't."

"You weren't at all curious about him, is that right?"

"Oh, I was *curious*, but not curious enough to go all the way out to..." Kahn suddenly stopped.

"Out to where, Mr. Kahn."

"All right, Bethtown. I *did* go to see him. He wouldn't give up the piece. I offered him twelve hundred dollars for it, but he wouldn't give it up."

"How about some of these other names? Did you ever try to contact any of them?"

"How could I? I only had half the list."

"There are only seven names on this list, Mr. Kahn."

"Yes, I noticed that."

"You said the picture had been divided into eight pieces."

"That's what Gerry told me."

"Who's got the eighth piece?"

"I don't know."

"How about this first name on the list, Mr. Kahn? Albert Weinberg? Are you trying to say you've never heard of him?"

"Never."

"Don't you read the newspapers?"

"Oh, you mean his murder. Yes, of course, I read about his murder. I thought you were referring..."

"Yes?"

"To my having some knowledge of him *before* them."

"Did you kill Albert Weinberg?"

"Just a second, Mr. Brown..."

"It's all right, Anatole," Kahn said. "No, I did *not* kill him, Mr. Brown. In fact, before the night of his murder, I didn't even know he *existed*."

"I see," Brown said. "Even though he'd been in the gallery several times to inquire about the photograph?"

"Yes, but always using an assumed name."

"I see."

"I had nothing to do with either murder."

"Did you have anything to do with beating me up?"

"I should say not!"

"Where were you at the time?"

"Home in bed!"

"When?"

"The night you were beat up."

"How do you know it happened at night?"

"Just a second, Mr. Brown..."

"No, it's all right, Anatole," Kahn said. "Gerry told me."

"Who told Gerry?"

"Why, *you* I would guess."

"No, I didn't tell her anything about it."

"Then she must have known some other way. Maybe she was involved in it. Maybe she hired someone to go to your hotel..."

"How do you know that's where it happened?"

"She ... she said so."

"She said I'd been attacked by two men in my hotel room?"

"Yes, she told me about it the next day."

"She couldn't have told you there were *two* men, Mr. Kahn, because I just made that up. There was only *one* man, wearing a stocking over his face."

"Well, it wasn't *me!*" Kahn shouted.

"Then who was it?" Brown shouted back. "You just said you learned about Albert Weinberg on the night of his murder. How?"

"The morning after, I meant. The newspapers..."

"You said 'the *night* of his murder,' you said you didn't even know he existed until that night. How'd you find *out* about his existence, Mr. Kahn? From my open notebook just by the telephone?"

"Just a second, just a second," Petitpas shouted.

"I didn't kill him!" Kahn shouted.

"What'd you do, go after him the minute you left me?"

"No!"

"Just a second!"

"Walk the three blocks to his room..."

"No!"

"You killed him, Kahn, admit it!"

"No!"

"You attacked me..."

"Yes, no, NO!"

"Yes or no?"

Kahn had half-risen from his chair, and now he collapsed back into it, and began sobbing.

"Yes or no, Mr. Kahn?" Carella asked gently.

"I didn't want to ... to hit you, I deplore violence," Kahn said, sobbing, not looking up at Brown. "I intended only to ... to force you to give me the piece you had ... to ... to threaten you with the gun. And then ... when you opened the door, I ... you looked so *big* ... and ... and in that split second, I ... I decided to ... to strike out at you. I was very frightened, so frightened. I ... I was afraid you might hurt me."

"Book him," Brown said. "First Degree Assault."

"Just a second," Petitpas said.

"Book him," Brown said flatly.

11

It was time to put on that old thinking cap.

It was time for a little plain and fancy deduction.

Nothing can confuse a person (cops included) more than a lot of names and a lot of pieces and a lot of corpses. Stop any decent law-abiding citizen on the street and ask him which he would prefer, a lot of names and pieces and corpses or a simple hatchet murder, and see what he says. Oh, you can safely bet six-to-five he'll take that hatchet in the head any day of the week, Thursday included, and Thursdays are no prizes, except when they fall on Thanksgiving.

Here's the way they saw it.

Fact: Renninger killed Ehrbach and Ehrbach killed Renninger – a simple uncomplicated mutual elimination, which was only fair.

Fact: Bramley Kahn kayoed Arthur Brown in one point four seconds of the first round, using the .32 Smith & Wesson Brown later found in the bottom drawer of Kahn's desk, and using as well his own feet – not for nothing was Kahn renowned as one of the fanciest dancers in gay bars all along The Quarter's glittering Kublenz Square.

Fact: Somebody killed Albert Weinberg.

NOT NECESSARILY SIGNIFICANT.

Fact: Somebody killed Geraldine Ferguson.

NOT NECESSARILY SIGNIFICANT.

(The "somebody," it was decided after intensive questioning was definitely *not* Bramley Kahn, who had gone directly home to the arms of a forty-four-year-old closet queen after battering Brown senseless.)

Fact(s): There were seven names on the list in Carmine Bonamico's handwriting. Carmine had skillfully dissected the list, giving one-half of it to his late wife, Alice Bonamico, and the other half to his late mistress, Geraldine Ferguson. Thoughtful fellow he, sharing his bed, his board, and also his contemplated ill-gotten gains with the two fairest flowers in his life. More's the pity the two broads could not have put their heads and their halves together and thereafter reaped the rewards of Carmine's professional acumen. Crime does not pay if you're fooling around with another woman.

Fact(s): There were eight pieces to the picture that revealed the location of the N.S.L.A. loot. Carmine had given two pieces to each of his associates, and had presumably kept two pieces for himself, he being the founder and beloved leader of the doomed band of brigands.

Fact: Petey Ryan, a gun on the ill-fated caper, had given one of his pieces to Dorothea McNally, woman about town, and another to Robert Coombs, restaurateur extraordinaire.

Fact: Lou D'Amore, the second gun, had given one of his pieces to Geraldine Ferguson, art appreciator, and the other to Donald Renninger, ex-cellmate.

Fact: Carmine Bonamico, mastermind, had given one of his pieces to Alice, his aforementioned wife.

Theory: Was it possible that Jerry Stein, Jewish driver of the misbegotten getaway car, had given one of his pieces to Albert Weinberg, and another to Eugene Edward Ehrbach, both of them likewise Jewish, rather than handing them over, say, to some passing Arab?

NOT NECESSARILY SIGNIFICANT.

Question: To whom had Carmine Bonamico given the eighth piece of the picture, the piece for which no name had been listed?

Or (to break things down into list form, which the police were very fond of doing):

PETE RYAN	-- DOROTHEA MCNALLY	(1)
	ROBERT COOMBS	(2)
LOU D'AMORE	-- GERALDINE FERGUSON	(3)
	DONALD RENNINGER	(4)
JERRY STEIN	-- ALBERT WEINBERG-?	(5)
	EUGENE E. EHRBACH-?	(6)
CARMINE BONAMICO	-- ALICE BONAMICO	(7)
	??????????????	(8)

But there was more, oh there was yet more, a policeman's lot is not a happy one. For example, was it not Irving Krutch, the *provocateur*, who had told the police that Alice Bonamico's piece, together with a torn list of names, had been willed to her sister, Lucia Feroglio, from whose dainty Sicilian hands Krutch had acquired both items, having faithlessly promised that good lady a thousand dollars in return for them? And had he not also said that Lucia had told him the assembled photograph would reveal the location of *"il tesoro,"* and had not Lucia delicately denied ever having said this to him? Or, for that matter, ever having given him a list of names? Ah so. And if he had *not* received his information from Lucia, then from whom exactly had it come? The person in possession of the eighth piece? The person who had gone unlisted by Carmine Bonamico?

On the night of Weinberg's murder, Brown had talked to three people: his wife Caroline, whom he could safely discount as a suspect; Weinberg, himself, who had been speedily dispatched to that great big photo lab in the sky; and Irving Krutch, to whom he had reported having struck pay dirt with Weinberg.

It seemed about time to talk to Irving Krutch again.

If Krutch was lying about having received the list of names from Lucia Feroglio, he could also be lying about having spent that night of the murder in his apartment with Suzanne Endicott. It was worth a try. When you're running out of suspects, it's even worth talking to the local Welsh terrier. Brown put on his sunglasses in preparation for the insurance investigator's dazzling smile.

Krutch was not smiling.

"The old bag's lying," he said. "It's as simple as that."

"Or maybe you are," Brown said.

"Why should I be? For Christ's sake, I'm the one who *came* to you with all this stuff. I'm as anxious to locate that money as you are. It's my *career* here that's at stake, don't you realize that?"

"Okay, I'll ask you again," Brown said patiently. "Why would a nice old deaf lady who hardly speaks English and who's incidentally waiting for you to fork over a thousand bucks . . ."

"I'll pay her, don't you worry. Krutch doesn't welsh."

"Why would this nice old lady deny having told you anything about a treasure? Or about having given you a list of names?"

"How do I know? Go ask *her*. I'm telling you she gave me the list, a piece of the picture, and the information that tied them together."

"She says she only gave you the picture."

"She's a liar. Sicilians are born liars."

"Okay, Krutch," Brown said, and sighed. "One other thing I'd like to know."

"What's that?"

"I want to know where you were on Monday night when Geraldine Ferguson got killed."

"What? Why the hell do you want to know *that*?"

"Because we'd already told you we struck out on Gerry's safe. And maybe you decided to have a look around her apartment, the way you've had a look around a few other apartments."

"No," Krutch said, and shook his head. "You've got the wrong customer."

"Okay, so tell me where you were."

"I was in bed with Suzanne Endicott."

"You're *always* in bed with Suzanne Endicott, it seems."

"Wouldn't *you* be?" Krutch said, and flashed his brilliant grin.

"And, of course, she'll corroborate that."

"Go ask her. I've got nothing to hide," Krutch said.

"Thanks, partner," Brown said.

When he got back to the squadroom, Carella told him that there had been a call from Bramley Kahn, who had been arraigned, released on bail, and – while awaiting trial – was back selling art at the same old stand. Brown returned his call at once.

"I want to talk a deal," Kahn said.

"I'll be right over," Brown answered.

When he got to the gallery, Kahn was waiting in his office, seated in the old-fashioned swivel chair behind his desk, facing the painting of the nude on the wall opposite. Brown took a seat in one of the leather-and-chrome chairs. Kahn took a long time getting started. Brown waited. At last, Kahn said, "Suppose . . ." and hesitated.

"Yes, suppose what?"

"Suppose I know where Gerry's piece of the picture is?"

"Do you?"

"I'm saying suppose."

"Okay, suppose you do?"

"Suppose I didn't tell you everything I know about that picture?"

"Okay, go ahead, we're still supposing."

"Well, what would it be worth to you?"

"I can't make any promises," Brown said.

"I understand that. But you *could* talk to the district attorney, couldn't you?"

"Oh, sure. He's a very nice fellow, the D.A., always eager for a little chat."

"I've heard that the D.A.'s office is the bargain basement of the law," Kahn said. "Well, I want a bargain."

"Your lawyer pleaded 'Not Guilty' to Assault One, didn't he?"

"That's right."

"Okay, let's suppose you're willing to co-operate, and let's suppose I can catch the D.A.'s ear, and let's suppose he would allow you to plead guilty to a lesser charge, how would that sound to you?"

"A lesser charge like what?"

"Like Assault Two."

'What's the penalty for that?"

"A maximum of five years in prison, or a thousand-dollar fine, or both."

"That's steep," Kahn said.

"The penalty for Assault One is even steeper."

"What is it?"

"A maximum of ten years."

"Yes, but Anatole feels I can win my case."

"Anatole's dreaming. You confessed to a crime in the presence of your own lawyer, four detectives, and a police stenographer. You haven't got a chance in hell of beating this rap, Kahn."

"Still, he feels we can do it?"

"In which case, I would suggest that you change your lawyer."

"How about *Third* Degree Assault? Is there such a thing?"

"Yes, there is, but forget it. The D.A. wouldn't even listen to such a suggestion."

"Why not?"

"He's got a sure conviction here. He may not even want to reduce it to Second Degree. It all depends on how valuable your information is. And on whether or not he had a good breakfast on the morning I go to talk to him."

"I think my information is *very* valuable," Kahn said.

"Let me hear it, and I'll tell you how valuable it is."

"First, what's the deal?"

"I told you, I can't make any promises. If I think your information is really worth something, I'll talk to the D.A. and see what he thinks. He may be willing to accept a plea of guilty to Assault Two."

"That sounds very nebulous."

"It's all I've got to sell," Brown said, and shrugged. "Yes or no?"

"Suppose I told you . . ." Kahn said, and hesitated.

"I'm listening."

"Let's start with the picture."

"Okay, let's start with the picture."

"There are eight pieces, right?"

"Right."

"But only seven names on the list."

"Right."

"Suppose I know where that eighth piece went?"

"Let's stop supposing," Brown said. "*Do* you know?"

"Yes."

"Okay, where'd it go?"

"To Alice Bonamico."

"We already know that, Kahn. Her husband gave her half of the list and one piece of the photograph. If that's all you're ..."

"No, he gave her *two* pieces of the photograph."

"Two," Brown said.

"Two," Kahn repeated.

"How do you know?"

"Gerry tried to bargain with her, remember? But Alice was dealing from a position of strength. Her husband had given his *mistress* only half of the list. But to Alice, his *wife*, he had given the other half of the list plus two pieces of the photo. That can make a woman feel very important."

"Yes, that was very thoughtful of him," Brown said. He was remembering that Irving Krutch claimed to have received half of the list and only one piece of the picture from Lucia Feroglio. If Alice Bonamico had indeed possessed *two* pieces of the picture, why had she willed only *one* of those pieces to her sister? And where was the missing piece now, the eighth piece? He decided to ask Kahn.

"Where *is* that eighth piece now?" he asked.

"I don't know," Kahn said.

"Well, that's certainly very valuable information," Brown said. "When I talk to the D.A. he might even be able to reduce the charge to Spitting On The Sidewalk, which is only a misdemeanor."

"But I *do* know where Gerry's piece is," Kahn said, unperturbed. "And believe me, it's a *key* piece. I don't think Bonamico realized how important a piece it was, or he wouldn't have entrusted it to a dumb gunsel like D'Amore."

"Okay," Brown said, "where *is* Gerry's piece?"

"Right behind you," Kahn said.

Brown turned and stared at the wall.

"We've already looked in the safe," he said.

"*Not* in the safe," Kahn said.

"Then where?"

"Give me a hand, will you?" Kahn said, and walked to the painting of the nude. Together, they lifted the painting from the wall, and placed it face-down on the rug. The canvas was backed with what appeared to be brown wrapping paper. Kahn lifted one corner of the backing and plucked a shining black-and-white scrap from where it was wedged between the frame and the canvas.

"*Voilà*," he said, and handed the scrap to Brown.

"Well," Kahn said, "what do you think now?"

"I think you're right," Brown answered. "It *is* a key piece."

* * *

It was a key piece because it gave perspective to the photograph. There was no sky, they now realized, because the picture had been taken from *above*, the photographer shooting *down* at what now revealed itself as a road running beside a footpath. The Donald Duck segment of the picture, now that the perspective was defined, showed three benches at the back of the fowl's head, a broken patch in the cement forming the bird's eye, a series of five fence posts running vertically past its bill. The bill jutted out into...

Not mud, not cement, not stucco, not fur, but *water*.

Cool, clear water.

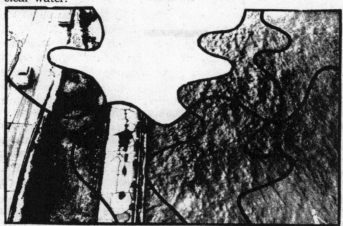

Or, considering the fact that Carmine Bonamico and his inept band had tried to make their escape along the River Road, perhaps water that was *not* quite so clear, perhaps water that was slightly polluted, but water nonetheless, the water of the River Dix that ran along the southern bank of Isola. Carella and Brown had a hurried conversation in the squadroom, and decided between them that Donald Duck should be easy to spot from the air.

He was not all that easy to spot.

They boarded a police helicopter at the heliport downtown and flew above the River Road for close to three hours, up and down its winding length, swooping low wherever a side street entered the road. The upper left-hand corner of the picture indicated just such a side street entering *somewhere*, and they hoped now to find the elusive duck with its telltale eye just below one of those entrances. The footpath with its benches and its guardrail ran the length of the river. There were thirty-four side streets entering the road, spaced at ten-block intervals. Their only hope of finding the *right* side street was to find the broken patch of cement.

But the robbery had taken place six years ago.

And whereas the city was sometimes a trifle slow in repairing broken sections of footpaths, they had done a damn good job on Donald Duck's eye.

Without the missing eighth piece, nobody knew where *nothing* was.

12

You can sometimes solve a mystery by the simple process of elimination, which is admittedly undramatic, but where does it say that a cop has to get hit on the head every day of the week? Cops may be dumb, but not *that* dumb. When everything has already narrowed itself down into the skinny end of the funnel, when nearly everybody's either dead or obviously innocent, then it merely becomes a matter of trying to figure out who is lying and why. There are lots of things cops don't understand, but lies they understand very well.

They don't understand, for example, why thieves will spend so much time and energy devising and executing a crime (with all its attendant risks) when that same amount of time and energy devoted to a legal pursuit would probably net much larger returns in the long run. It was the belief of every detective on the 87th Squad that the *real* motive behind half the crimes being committed in the city was *enjoyment*, plain and simple – the *fun* of playing Cops and Robbers. Forget gain or profit as motivation, forget passion, forget hostility or rebellion, it all came down to Cops and Robbers.

What had Carmine Bonamico been doing, if not playing Cops and Robbers? Took his little camera, dear boy, and went out to photograph the River Road from an airplane or something, and then drew his squiggly little lines across the print, and cut it apart, and handed out pieces to his gang, all hush-hush, top-secret, tip-toey, clever-crook stuff – Cops and Robbers. Why the hell hadn't he just whispered the location to each of his hoods, and asked them to whisper it in turn to their friends and loved ones? Ah, but no. That would have taken from the crime one of its essential elements, known to gumshoes far and wide as The Game Aspect. Take the fun out of criminal activity, and all the prisons in the world would be empty. Who can figure crooks? Certainly not cops. They couldn't even figure why Irving Krutch had had the audacity to come to them for assistance in locating the loot, unless this too was tied in with The Game Aspect, the sheer enjoyment of playing Cops and Robbers.

They *did* figure, however, that Krutch was not telling them the truth about his whereabouts on the nights Albert Weinberg and Geraldine Ferguson were murdered; when a man's lying, it comes over like a supersonic missile streaking through the atmosphere, and you don't have to be working for NASA to spot it. Krutch's alibi, of course, was a broad he'd been laying since the year One, hardly the most reliable sort of witness to bring to your defense in a courtroom.

But Suzanne Endicott's credibility as a witness was academic unless they could get Krutch *into* a courtroom. Logical deduction aside, the fact remained that he claimed to have been in bed with Suzie while both murders were being committed, and Suzie backed his story, and it is quite a trick to be out killing people while you are home in your apartment making love to a sweet li'l ol' Georgia peach. These days, it was getting more and more difficult to arrest a person even if you caught him with a hacksaw in his bloody hands, standing over a dissected corpse. How could you arrest a mustache-twirling villain who had an alibi as long as a peninsula?

How indeed?

It was Carella who first got the idea.

He discussed it with Hawes, and Hawes thought it was too risky. Carella insisted that it was a good idea, considering the fact that Suzie Endicott was from Georgia. Hawes said he thought Brown might take offense if they even *suggested* the idea to him, and Carella said he thought Brown would go along with the idea wholeheartedly. Hawes again protested that the notion was pretty far-out to begin with: Suzie had been living in the north for at least four years now, spending half that time in bed with Krutch (to hear her tell it), and had probably been pretty well assimilated into the culture; it was a bad idea. Carella informed Hawes that certain prejudices and stereotyes died very hard deaths, as witness Hawes' own reluctance to even *broach* the idea to Brown. Hawes took offense at that, saying he was as tolerant a man as ever lived, in fact, it was his very tolerance that *caused* his reluctance, he simply didn't want to offend Brown by suggesting an idea that probably wouldn't work anyway. Carella raised his voice and demanded to know how they could possibly crack Suzie's story; *he* had tried to crack it, *Hawes* had tried to crack it, the only way they could get to her was to scare hell out of her. Hawes shouted that Brown's feelings were more important to him and to the well-being of the squad than solving any goddamn murder case, and Carella shouted back that prejudice was certainly a marvelous thing when a white man couldn't even explore an excellent idea with a Negro for fear of hurting his feelings.

"Okay, *you* ask him," Hawes said.

"I will," Carella answered.

They came out of the Interrogation Room together and walked to where Brown was sitting at his desk, studying the photograph for the seven-hundredth time.

"We've got an idea, Artie," Carella said.

"*He's* got an idea," Hawes said. "It's *his* idea, Artie."

"What's the idea?" Brown said.

"Well, you know," Carella said, "we're all pretty much agreed on this Krutch character, right?"

"Right."

"I mean, he wants that seven hundred and fifty G's so bad, his hands are turning green. And you can't tell me his *career* has anything to do with it."

"Me neither," Brown said.

"He wants that *money*, period. The minute he gets it, he'll probably take Suzie and head straight for Brazil."

"Okay, how do we get to him?" Brown asked.

"We go to Suzie."

"We've *been* to Suzie," Brown said. "*You* talked to her, *Meyer* talked to her, *Cotton* talked to her. She alibis Krutch right down the line."

"Sure, but she's been sleeping with the guy for four years," Hawes said, still annoyed by the thought."

"Another three years, and they're man and wife in the eyes of the law," Carella said. "You expect her *not* to back his alibis?"

"Okay, let's say she's lying," Brown said.

"Let's say she's lying. Let's say Krutch *did* leave that apartment, once to kill Weinberg, and again to kill Gerry Ferguson."

"Okay, let's say it. How we going to prove it?"

"Well, let's say that we drop in on Krutch sometime tonight and ask him a few more questions. Just to keep him busy, you understand? Just to make sure he doesn't climb into the sack with li'l Suzie again."

"Yeah?"

"Yeah, and let's say about two o'clock in the morning, somebody knocks on li'l Suzie's door and starts getting rough with her."

"Come on, Steve, we can't do that," Brown said.

"I don't mean we actually push her around," Carella said.

"I told you he wouldn't buy it," Hawes said.

"I mean we just let her *think* we're getting rough."

"Well, why would she think that?" Brown asked. "If we're *not* going to push her around ..."

"She's from Georgia," Carella said.

The squadroom went silent. Hawes looked at his shoes.

"Who's going to hit Krutch?" Brown asked.

"I thought Cotton and I might do that."

"And who'll go to scare Suzie?"

The squadroom went silent again. The clock on the wall was ticking too loudly.

"Don't tell me," Brown said, and broke into a wide grin. "Man, I love it."

Hawes glanced at Carella uncertainly.

"You'll do it?" Carella asked.

"Oh, man, I *love* it," Brown said, and fell into a deliberately broad dialect. "We goan send a big black nigger man to scare our Georgia peach out'n her skin! Oh, man it's delicious!"

Prejudice is a wonderful thing.

Stereotypes are marvelous.

At two o'clock in the morning, Suzie Endicott opened her door to find that the most terrifying of her Southern fantasies had materialized in the gloom, a Nigra come to rape her in the night, just as her mother had warned her time and again. She started to close the door, but her rapist suddenly shouted, "You jes' hole it right there, Missy. This here's the law! Detective Arthur Brown of d'87th Squad. I got some questions to ask you."

"Wh ... wh ... it's ... the middle of the night," Suzie said.

Brown flashed his shield. "This hunk o' tin here doan respec' no time o' day nor night," he said, and grinned. "You goan let me in, Missy, or does I start causin' a ruckus here?" Suzie hesitated. Brown suddenly wondered if he were playing it too broadly, and then decided he was doing just fine. Without waiting for an answer, he shoved past her into the apartment, threw his fedora onto the hall table, looked around appreciatively, whistled, and said, "Man, this's *some* nice place you got here. Ain't never *been* inside no fancy place like this one."

"Wh ... wh ... what did you want to ask me?" Suzie said. She was wearing a robe over her nightgown, and her right hand was clutched tightly into the collar of the robe.

"Well now, ain't no hurry, is there?" Brown asked.

"I ... I have to go to work in the mor ... morning," Suzie said. "I ... I ... I ... have to get some sleep," she said, and realized instantly she had made a mistake by even mentioning anything even remotely suggesting bed. "I mean ..."

"Oh, I *knows* whut you mean," Brown said, and grinned lewdly. "Sit down, Missy."

"Wh ... what did you want to ask?"

"I *said* sit down! You jes' do whut I tells you to do, okay, an' we goan get along fine. Otherwise ..."

Suzie sat instantly, tucking the flaps of her robe around her.

"Those're nice legs," Brown said. He narrowed his eyes. "Mighty fine white legs, I can tell you that, honey."

Suzie wet her lips and then swallowed. Brown was suddenly afraid she might pass out cold before he got to the finale of his act. He decided to push on regardless.

"We busted yo' li'l playmate half an hour ago," he said. "So if you're thinkin *he* goan help you, you can jes' f'get it."

"Who? What? What did you say?"

"Irving Krutch, yo' lover boy," Brown said. "You shunt'a lied to us, Missy. That ain't goan sit too well with the D.A."

"I didn't lie to ... to ... anybody," Suzie said.

"'Bout bein' in bed there all the time? 'Bout making love there when two people was being murdered. Tsk, tsk, Missy, them was outright lies. I'm really sprised at you."

"We did, we were, we did do that, we ..." Suzie started, and realized they were talking about making love, and suddenly looked into Brown's eyes, and saw the fixed, drooling stare of a sex-crazed maniac and wondered how she would ever get out of this alive. She should have listened to her mother who had warned her never to wear a tight skirt walking past any of these people because it was so easy to arouse animal lust in them.

"You in serious trouble," Brown said.

"I didn't ..."

"Real serious trouble."

"... lie to anybody, I swear."

"Only one way to get out of that trouble now," Brown said.

"But I didn't ..."

"Only *one* way, Missy."

"... really. I didn't lie, really. Really, officer," she heard herself saying to this black man, "officer, I really didn't, I swear. I don't know what Irving told you, but I honestly did not lie to anyone, if anyone was lying, it was him. I had no idea of anything, of it, of anything. I mean that, officer, you can check that out if you want to. I certainly wouldn't lie to the police, not to those nice policemen who ..."

"Only *one* way to save yo' sweet ass now," Brown said, and saw her face go pale.

"Wh ... what's that?" Suzie said. "*What* way? What?"

"You can tell d'troof," Brown said, and rose out of his chair to his full monstrous height, muscles bulging, eyes glaring, shoulders heaving, rose like a huge black gorilla, and hulked toward her with his arms dangling at his sides, hands curled like an ape's, towered over her where she sat small and white and trembling on the edge of her chair, and repeated in his most menacing nigger-in-the-alley voice, "You can tell d'troof *now*, Missy, unless you cares to work it out some *other* way!"

"Oh my good Lord Jesus," Suzie shouted, "he left the apartment, he left both times, I don't know where he went, I don't know anything else, if he killed these people, I had nothing to do with it!"

"Thank you, Miss Endicott," Brown said. "Would you put on some clothes now, I'd like you to accompany me to the squadroom."

She stared at him in disbelief. Where had the rapist gone? Who was this polite nuclear physicist standing in his place? And then his charade dawned upon her, and her eyes narrowed, and her lips drew back over her teeth, and she said, "Boy, you say *please* when you ask *me* to go any place."

"Go to *hell*," Brown said. "Please."

"The rotten bitch," Krutch said.

He could have been talking about Suzie Endicott, but he wasn't. He was railing, instead, against the late Alice Bonamico. The departed gang leader's departed wife, it seemed, had cheated Krutch. In his investigation of the robbery, he had learned from Carmine's widow that she was in possession of "certain documents and photographic segments" purporting to show the hiding place of the N.S.L.A. loot. He had bargained with her for months, and they had finally agreed on a purchase price. She had turned over to him the half of the list in her possession as well as the piece of the photo he had originally shown the police.

"But I didn't know she had yet *another* piece," Krutch said. "I didn't learn that until I read about her will, and contacted her sister. That's when I got *this* piece. The eighth piece of the puzzle. The *important* one. The one that bitch held out on me."

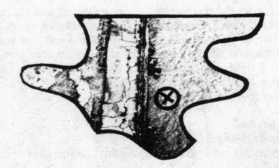

"Which, naturally, you didn't give to us," Brown said.

"Naturally. It shows the exact location of the loot. Do you think I'm an idiot?"

"Why'd you come to us in the first place?"

"I *told* you why. Krutch needed help. Krutch couldn't handle it alone any more. Krutch figured what better way to get help on an investigation than by calling in experts?"

"You got more than you bargained for," Brown said.

"Except from Alice Bonamico, that bitch. I paid her ten thousand dollars for half of the list and a meaningless piece of the picture. Ten thousand bucks! It was every penny I had."

"But, of course, you were going for very big money."

"It was an investment," Krutch said. "Krutch looked upon it as an investment."

"Well," Brown said, "now Krutch can look upon it as a capital loss. Why'd you kill Weinberg?"

"Because you told me he had another piece, and I wanted it. Look, I was running a race with you guys. I knew I was ahead of you because *I* had the piece with the X on it, but suppose you got cute somewhere along the line and refused to show me anything else? I'm in the insurance business, you know. Getting Weinberg's piece was insurance, plain and simple."

"And Gerry Ferguson's?"

"Same thing. Insurance. I went in there looking for it because you'd already told me it wasn't in the safe. So where *else* could it be? Had to be in her apartment, right? I wasn't going to kill her, but she started screaming the minute I came in. I was too close then to let anybody stop me. You don't *know* how close I came to putting this whole thing together. You guys were helping me more than you realized. I almost had it made."

"You've got balls, all right," Brown said, shaking his head. "You come to the police for help in locating the proceeds from a bank robbery. That takes real balls."

"Real *brains*," Krutch corrected.

"Oh, yes," Brown said.

"It wasn't easy to think this up."

"You'll have plenty of time to do a lot more thinking," Brown said.

"What do you mean?"

"You figure it out."

"In prison, do you mean?" Krutch asked.

"Now you've got the picture," Brown said.

This time, the helicopter ride was a joyous one. For whereas there were thirty-four side streets entering the River Road, only one of those side streets was opposite a twin cluster of offshore rocks. Coincidentally, the rocks were just west of the Calm's Point Bridge, from which vantage point Bonamico must have snapped the picture, standing on the bridge's walkway some fifty feet above the surface of the water. They landed the chopper close to where Donald Duck's eye must have been before the city's Highway Maintenance Department had repaired it, and then they walked towards the rocks and looked down into the filthy waters of the River Dix and saw nothing. Carmine Bonamico's "X" undoubtedly marked the spot, but water pollution triumphed over the naked eye, and there was nary a treasure to be seen. They did not uncover the loot until they dredged the river close to the bank, and found an old leather suitcase, green with slime, water-logged, badly deteriorated. Seven hundred and fifty thousand dollars in good American currency was ensconced in that bag, slightly damp to be sure, but nonetheless negotiable.

It was a good day's pay.

Arthur Brown got home in time for dinner.

His wife met him at the door and said, "Connie's got a fever. I had the doctor here a half-hour ago."

"What'd he say?"

"He thinks it's just the flu. But she's *so* uncomfortable, Artie."

"Did he give her anything?"

"I'm waiting for it now. The drug store said they'd deliver."

"She awake?"

"Yes."

"I'll go talk to her. How're *you*?" he said, and kissed her.

"Forgot what you looked like," Caroline answered.

"Well, here's what I look like," he said and smiled.

"Same old handsome devil," Caroline said.

"That's me," he said, and went into the bedroom.

Connie was propped against the pillows, her eyes wet, her nose running. "Hello, Daddy," she said in her most miserable-sounding voice.

"I thought you were sick," he said.

"I *am*," she answered.

"You can't be sick," he said, "you look too beautiful." He went to the bed and kissed her on the forehead.

"Oh, Daddy, please be careful," Connie said, "you'll catch the bug."

"I'll catch him and stomp him right under my foot," Brown said, and grinned. Connie giggled.

"How would you like me to read you a story?" he asked.

"Yes," she said. "Please."

"What would you like to hear?"

"A good mystery," Connie said. "One of the Nancy Drews."

"One of the Nancy Drews it is," Brown said, and went to the bookcase. He crouched over, searching the shelves for Connie's favorite, when he heard the urgent shriek of a police siren on the street outside.

"Do you like mysteries, Daddy?" Connie asked.

Brown hesitated a moment before answering. The siren faded into the distant city. He went back to the bed and gently touched his daughter's hair, and wondered again, oddly, if Geraldine Ferguson had ever roller-skated on a city sidewalk. Then he said, "No, honey, I don't care for mysteries too much," and sat on the edge of the bed, and opened the book, and began reading aloud.

HAIL, HAIL, THE GANG'S ALL HERE!

This modest volume is dedicated to the Mystery Writers of America, who, if they do not award it the Edgar for the best *ten* mystery novels of the year should have their collective mysterious heads examined.

(COERCION: *A person who with a view to compel another person to do or abstain from doing an act which such other person has a legal right to do or to abstain from doing wrongfully and unlawfully, is guilty of a misdemeanor. Section 530, New York State Penal Law.*)

1

Nightshade

The morning hours of the night come imperceptibly here.

It is a minute before midnight on the peeling face of the hanging wall clock, and then it is midnight, and then the minute hand moves visibly and with a lurch into the new day. The morning hours have begun, but scarcely anyone has noticed. The stale coffee in soggy cardboard containers tastes the same as it did thirty seconds ago, the spastic rhythm of the clacking typewriters continues unabated, a drunk across the room shouts that the world is full of brutality, and cigarette smoke drifts up toward the face of the clock, where, unnoticed and unmourned, the old day has already been dead for two minutes. The telephone rings.

The men in this room are part of a tired routine, somewhat shabby about the edges, as faded and as gloomy as the room itself, with its cigarette-scarred desks and its smudged green walls. This could be the office of a failing insurance company were it not for the evidence of the holstered pistols hanging from belts on the backs of wooden chairs painted a darker green than the walls. The furniture is ancient, the typewriters are ancient, the building itself is ancient – which is perhaps only fitting since these men are involved in what is an ancient pursuit, a pursuit once considered honorable. They are law enforcers. They are, in the words of the drunk still hurling epithets from the grilled detention cage across the room, rotten prick cop bastards.

The telephone continues to ring.

The little girl lying in the alley behind the theater was wearing a belted white trench coat wet with blood. There was blood on the floor of the alley, and blood on the metal fire door behind her, and blood on her face and matted in her blond hair, blood on her miniskirt and on the lavender tights she wore. A neon sign across the street stained the girl's ebbing life juices green and then orange, while from the open knife wound in her chest, the blood sprouted like some ghastly night flower, dark and rich, red, orange, green, pulsing in time to the neon flicker, a grotesque psychedelic light show, and then losing the rhythm, welling up with less force and power. She opened her mouth, she tried to speak, and the scream of an ambulance approaching the theater seemed to come instead from her mouth on a fresh bubble of blood. The blood stopped, her life ended, the girl's eyes rolled back into her head. Detective Steve Carella turned away as the ambulance attendants rushed a stretcher into the alley. He told them the girl was already dead.

"We got here in seven minutes," one of the attendants said.

"Nobody's blaming you," Carella answered.

"This is Saturday night," the attendant complained. "Streets are full of traffic. Even *with* the damn siren."

Carella walked to the unmarked sedan parked at the curb. Detective Cotton Hawes, sitting behind the wheel, rolled down his frost-rimed window and said "How is she?"

"We've got a homicide," Carella answered.

The boy was eighteen years old, and he had been picked up not ten minutes ago for breaking off car aerials. He had broken off twelve in the same street, strewing them behind him like a Johnny Appleseed planting radios; a cruising squad car had spotted him as he tried to twist off the aerial of a 1966 Cadillac. He was drunk or stoned or both, and when Sergeant Murchison at the muster desk asked him to read the Miranda-Escobedo warning signs on the wall, printed in both English and Spanish, he could read neither. The arresting patrolman took the boy to the squadroom upstairs, where Detective Bert Kling was talking to Hawes on the telephone. He signaled for the patrolman to wait with his prisoner on the bench outside the slatted wooden rail divider, and then buzzed Murchison at the desk downstairs.

"Dave," he said, "we've got a homicide in the alley of the Eleventh Street Theater. You want to get it rolling?"

"Right," Murchison said, and hung up.

Homicides are a common occurrence in this city, and each one is treated identically, the grisly horror of violent death reduced to routine by a police force that would otherwise be overwhelmed by statistics. At the muster desk switchboard downstairs, while upstairs Kling waved the patrolman and his prisoner into the squadroom, Sergeant Murchison first reported the murder to Captain Frick, who commanded the 87th Precinct, and then to Lieutenant Byrnes, who commanded the 87th Detective Squad. He then phoned Homicide, who in turn set into motion an escalating process of notification that spread cancerously to include the Police Laboratory, the Telegraph, Telephone and Teletype Bureau at Headquarters, the Medical Examiner, the District Attorney, the District Commander of the Detective Division, the Chief of Detectives, and finally the Police Commissioner himself. Someone had thoughtlessly robbed a young woman of her life, and now a lot of sleepy-eyed men were being shaken out of their beds on a cold October night.

Upstairs, the clock on the squadroom wall read 12:30 a.m. The boy who had broken off twelve car aerials sat in a chair alongside Bert Kling's desk. Kling took one look at him and yelled to Miscolo in the Clerical Office to bring in a pot of strong coffee. Across the room, the drunk in the detention cage wanted to know where he was. In a little while, they would release him with a warning to try to stay sober till morning.

But the night was young.

They arrived alone or in pairs, blowing on their hands, shoulders hunched against the bitter cold, breaths pluming whitely from their lips. They marked the dead girl's position in the alleyway, they took her picture, they made drawings of the scene, they searched for the murder weapon and found none, and then they stood around speculating on sudden death. In this alleyway alongside a theater, the policemen were the stars and the celebrities, and a curious crowd thronged the sidewalk where a barricade had already been set up, anxious for a glimpse of these men with their shields pinned to their overcoats – the identifying *Playbills* of law enforcement, without which you could not tell the civilians from the plainclothes cops.

Monoghan and Monroe had arrived from Homicide, and they watched dispassionately now as the Assistant Medical Examiner fluttered around the dead girl. They were both wearing black overcoats, black mufflers, and black fedoras, both heavier men than Carella, who stood between them with the lean look of an overtrained athlete, a pained expression on his face.

"He done some job on her," Monroe said.

"Son of a bitch," Monoghan added.

"You identified her yet?"

"I'm waiting for the M.E. to get through," Carella answered.

"Might help to know what she was doing here in the alley. What's that door there?" Monroe asked.

"Stage entrance."

"Think she was in the show?"

"I don't know, " Carella said.

"Well, what the hell," Monoghan said, "they're finished with her pocketbook there, ain't they? Why don't you look through it? You finished with that pocketbook there?" he yelled to one of the lab technicians.

"Yeah, anytime you want it," the technician shouted back.

"Go on, Carella, take a look."

The technician wiped the blood off the dead girl's bag, and handed it to Carella. Monoghan and Monroe crowded in on him as he twisted open the clasp.

"Bring it over to the light," Monroe said.

The light, with a metal shade, hung over the stage door. So violently had the girl been stabbed that flecks of blood had even dotted the enameled white underside of the shade. In her bag they found a driver's license identifying her as Mercy Howell of 1113 Rutherford Avenue, Age 24, Height 5'3", Eyes Blue. They found an Actors Equity card in her name, as well as credit cards for two of the city's largest department stores. They found an unopened package of Virginia Slims, and a book of matches advertising an art course. They found a rat-tailed comb. They found seventeen dollars and forty-three cents in cash. They found a package of Kleenex, and an appointment book. They found a ball-point pen with shreds of tobacco clinging to its tip, an eyelash curler, two subway tokens, and an advertisement for a see-through blouse, clipped from one of the local newspapers.

In the pocket of her trench coat, when the M.E. had finished with her and pronounced her dead from multiple stab wounds in the chest and throat, they found an unfired Browning .25 caliber automatic. They tagged the gun and the handbag, and they moved the girl out of the alleyway and into the waiting ambulance for removal to the morgue. There was now nothing left of Mercy Howell but a chalked outline of her body and a pool of her blood on the alley floor.

"You sober enough to understand me?" Kling asked the boy.

"I was never drunk to begin with," the boy answered.

"Okay then, here we go," Kling said. "In keeping with the Supreme Court decision in *Miranda* v. *Arizona*, we are not permitted to ask you any questions until you are warned of your right to counsel and your privilege against self-incrimination."

"What does that mean?" the boy asked. "Self-incrimination?"

"I'm about to explain that to you now," Kling said.

"This coffee stinks."

"First, you have the right to remain silent if you so choose," Kling said. "Do you understand that?"

"I understand it."

"Second, you do not have to answer any police questions if you don't want to. Do you understand that?"

"What the hell are you asking me if I understand for? Do I look like a moron or something?"

"The law requires that I ask whether or not you understand these specific warnings. *Did* you understand what I just said about not having to answer . . . ?"

"Yeah, yeah, I understood."

"All right. Third, if you *do* decide to answer any questions, the answers may be used as evidence against you, do you . . . ?"

"What the hell did I do, break off a couple of car aerials? Jesus!"

"Did you understand that?"

"I understood it."

"You also have the right to consult with an attorney before or during police questioning. If you do not have the money to hire a lawyer, a lawyer will be appointed to consult with you."

Kling gave this warning straight-faced even though he knew that under the Criminal Procedure Code of the city for which he worked, a public defender could not be appointed by the courts until the preliminary hearing. There was no legal provision for the courts *or* the police to appoint counsel during questioning, and there were certainly no police funds set aside for the appointment of attorneys. In theory, a call to the Legal Aid Society should have brought a lawyer up there to the old squadroom within minutes, ready and eager to offer counsel to any indigent person desiring it. But in practice, if this boy sitting beside Kling told him in the next three seconds that he was unable to pay for his own attorney and would like one provided, Kling would not have known just what the hell to do – other than call off the questioning.

"I understand," the boy said.

"You've signified that you understand all the warnings," Kling said, "and now I ask you whether you are willing to answer my questions without an attorney here to counsel you."

"Go shit in your hat," the boy said. "I don't want to answer nothing."

So that was that.

They booked him for Criminal Mischief, a Class-A Misdemeanor defined as intentional or reckless damage to the property of another person, and they took him downstairs to a holding cell, to await transportation to the Criminal Courts Building for arraignment.

The phone was ringing again, and a woman was waiting on the bench just outside the squadroom.

The watchman's booth was just inside the metal stage door. An electric clock on the wall behind the watchman's stool read 1:10 a.m. The watchman was a man in his late seventies who did not at all mind being questioned by the police. He came on duty, he told them, at seven-thirty each night. The company call was for eight, and he was there at the stage door waiting to greet everybody as they arrived to get made up and in costume. Curtain went down at eleven-twenty, and usually most of the kids was out of the theater by quarter to twelve, or, latest, midnight. He stayed on till nine the next morning, when the theater box office opened.

"Ain't much to do during the night except hang around and make sure nobody runs off with the scenery," he said, and chuckled.

"Did you happen to notice what time Mercy Howell left the theater?" Carella asked.

"She the one got killed?" the old man asked.

"Yes," Hawes said. "Mercy Howell. About this high, blond hair, blue eyes."

"They're *all* about that high, with blond hair and blue eyes," the old man said and chuckled again. "I don't know hardly none of them by name. Shows come and go, you know. Be a hell of a chore to have to remember all the kids who go in and out that door."

"Do you sit here by the door all night?" Carella asked.

"Well, no, not all night. What I do, is I lock the door after everybody's out and then I check the lights, make sure just the work light's on. I won't touch the switchboard, not allowed to, but I can turn out lights in the lobby, for example, if somebody left them on, or down in the toilets, sometimes they leave lights on down in the toilets. Then I come back here to the booth, and read or listen to the radio. Along about two o'clock, I check the theater again, make sure we ain't got no fires or nothing, and then I come back here and make the rounds again at four o'clock and six o'clock, and again about eight. That's what I do."

"You say you lock this door . . ."

"That's right."

"Would you remember what time you locked it tonight?"

"Oh, must've been about ten minutes to twelve. Soon as I knew everybody was out."

"How do you know when they're out?"

"I give a yell up the stairs there. You see those stairs there? They go up to the dressing rooms. Dressing rooms are all upstairs in this house. So I go to the steps, and I yell, 'Locking up! Anybody here?' And if somebody yells back, I know somebody's here, and I say 'Let's shake it, honey,' if it's a girl, and if it's a boy, I say, 'Let's hurry it up, sonny.'" The old man chuckled again. "With *this* show, it's sometimes hard to tell which's the girls and which's the boys. I manage though," he said and again chuckled.

"So you locked that door at ten minutes to twelve?"

"Right."

"And everybody had left the theater by that time?"

"'Cept me, of course."

"Did you look out into the alley before you locked the door?"

"Nope. Why should I do that?"

"Did you hear anything outside while you were locking the door?"

"Nope."

"Or at anytime *before* you locked it?"

"Well, there's always noise outside when they're leaving, you know. They got friends waiting for them or else they go home together, you know, there's always a lot of chatter when they go out."

"But it was quiet when you locked the door."

"Dead quiet," the old man said.

*   *   *

The woman who took the chair beside Detective Meyer Meyer's desk was perhaps thirty-two years old, with long straight black hair trailing down her back, and wide brown eyes that were terrified. It was still October, and the color of her tailored coat seemed suited to the season, a subtle tangerine with a small brown fur collar that echoed an outdoors trembling with the colors of autumn.

"I feel sort of silly about this," she said, "but my husband insisted that I come."

"I see," Meyer said.

"There are ghosts," the woman said.

Across the room, Kling unlocked the door to the detention cage and said "Okay, pal, on your way. Try to stay sober till morning, huh?"

"It ain't one-thirty yet," the man said, "the night is still young." He stepped out of the cage, tipped his hat to Kling, and hurriedly left the squadroom.

Meyer looked at the woman sitting beside him, studying her with new interest because, to tell the truth, she had not seemed like a nut when she first walked into the squadroom. He had been a detective for more years than he chose to count, and in his time had met far too many nuts of every stripe and persuasion. But he had never met one as pretty as Adele Gorman with her well-tailored, fur-collared coat, and her Vassar voice and her skillfully applied eye makeup, lips bare of color in her pale white face, pert and reasonably young and seemingly intelligent – but apparently a nut besides.

"In the house," she said. "Ghosts."

"Where do you live, Mrs. Gorman?" he asked. He had written her name on the pad in front of him, and now he watched her with his pencil poised and recalled the lady who had come into the squadroom only last month to report a gorilla peering into her bedroom from the fire escape outside. They had sent a patrolman over to make a routine check, and had even called the zoo and the circus (which was coincidentally in town, and which lent at least *some* measure of possibility to her claim) but there had been no ape on the fire escape, nor had any simians recently escaped their cages. The lady came back the next day to report that her visiting gorilla had put in another appearance the night before, this time wearing a top hat and carrying a black cane with an ivory head. Meyer had assured her that he would have a platoon of cops watching her building that night, led her personally out of the squadroom and down the iron-runged steps, and through the high-ceilinged muster room, and onto the sidewalk outside the station house. Sergeant Murchison, at the muster desk, shook his head after the lady was gone, and muttered, "More of them outside than in."

Meyer watched Adele Gorman now, remembered what Murchison had said, and thought *Gorillas in September, ghosts in October.*

"We live in Smoke Rise," she said. "Actually, it's my father's house, but my husband and I are living there with him."

"And the address?"

"374 MacArthur Lane. You take the first access road into Smoke Rise, about a mile and a half east of Silvermine Oval. The name on the mailbox is Van Houten. That's my father's name. Willem Van Houten." She paused and studied him, as though expecting some reaction.

"Okay," Meyer said, and ran a hand over his bald pate, and looked up, and said, "Now, you were saying, Mrs. Gorman..."

"That we have ghosts."

"Um-huh. What kind of ghosts?"

"Ghosts. Poltergeists. Shades. I don't know," she said, and shrugged. "What kinds of ghosts *are* there?"

"Well, they're *your* ghosts, so suppose you tell me," Meyer said.

The telephone on Kling's desk rang. He lifted the receiver and said, "Eighty-seventh Squad, Detective Kling."

"There are two of them," Adele said.

"Male of female?"

"One of each."

"Yeah," Kling said into the telephone, "go ahead."

"How old would you say they were?"

"Centuries, I would guess."

"No, I mean . . ."

"Oh, how old do they *look*? Well, the man . . ."

"You've *seen* them?"

"Oh, yes, many times."

"Um-huh," Meyer said.

"I'll be right over," Kling said into the telephone. "You stay there." He slammed down the receiver, opened his desk drawer, pulled out a holstered revolver, and hurriedly clipped it to his belt. "Somebody threw a bomb into a storefront church. 7133 Culver Avenue. I'm heading over."

"Right," Meyer said. "Get back to me."

"We'll need a couple of meat wagons. The minister and two other people were killed, and it sounds as if there're a lot of injured."

"Will you tell Dave?"

"On the way out," Kling said, and was gone.

"Mrs. Gorman," Meyer said, "as you can see, we're pretty busy here just now. I wonder if your ghosts can wait till morning."

"No, they can't." Adele said.

"Why not?"

"Because they appear precisely at two forty-five a.m., and I want someone to see them."

"Why don't you and your husband look at them?" Meyer said.

"You think I'm a nut, don't you?" Adele said.

"No, no, Mrs. Gorman, not at all."

"Oh, yes you do," Adele said. "I didn't believe in ghosts, either, until I saw these two."

"Well, this is all very interesting, I assure you, Mrs. Gorman, but really we do have our hands full right now, and I don't know what we can do about these ghosts of yours, even if we did come over to take a look at them."

"They've been stealing things from us," Adele said, and Meyer thought *Oh, we have got ourselves a prime lunatic this time.*

"What sort of things?"

"A diamond brooch that used to belong to my mother when she was alive. They stole that from my father's safe."

"What else?"

"A pair of emerald earrings. They were in the safe, too."

"When did these thefts occur?"

"Last month."

"Isn't it possible the jewelry was mislaid someplace?"

"You don't mislay a diamond brooch and a pair of emerald earrings that are locked inside a wall safe."

"Did you report any of these thefts?"

"No."

"Why not?"

"Because I knew you'd think I was crazy. Which is just what you're thinking right this minute."

"No, Mrs. Gorman, but I'm sure you can appreciate the fact that we, uh, can't go around arresting ghosts," Meyer said, and tried to smile.

Adele Gorman did not smile back. "Forget the ghosts," she said. "I was foolish to mention them, I should have known better." She took a deep breath, looked him squarely in the eye, and said, "I'm here to report the theft of a diamond brooch valued at six thousand dollars, and a pair of earrings worth thirty-five hundred dollars. Will you send a man to investigate tonight, or should I ask my father to contact your superior officer?"

"Your father? What's he got to...?"

"My father is a retired Surrogate's Court judge," Adele said.

"I see."

"Yes, I hope you do."

"What time did you say these ghosts arrive?" Meyer asked, and sighed heavily.

Between midnight and two o'clock, the city does not change very much. The theaters have all let out, and the average Saturday night revelers, good citizens from Bethtown or Calm's Point, Riverhead or Majesta, have come into the Isola streets again in search of a snack or a giggle before heading home to their separate beds. The city is an ant's nest of after-theater eateries ranging from chic French cafés to pizzerias to luncheonettes to coffee shops to hot dog stands to delicatessens, all of them packed to the ceilings because Saturday night is not only the loneliest night of the week, it is also the night to howl. And howl they do, these good burghers who have put in five long hard days of labor and who are anxious now to relax and enjoy themselves before Sunday arrives, bringing with it the attendant boredom of too damn much leisure time, anathema for the American male. The crowds shove and jostle their way along The Stem, moving in and out of bowling alleys, shooting galleries, penny arcades, strip joints, night clubs, jazz emporiums, souvenir shops, lining the sidewalks outside plate glass windows in which go-go girls gyrate, or watching with fascination as a roast beef slowly turns on a spit. Saturday night is a time for pleasure, and even the singles can find satisfaction, briefly courted by the sidewalk whores standing outside the shabby hotels in the side streets off The Stem, searching out homosexuals in gay bars on the city's notorious North Side or down in The Quarter, thumbing through dirty books in the myriad "back magazine" shops, or slipping into darkened screening rooms to watch 16mm films of girls taking off their clothes, good people all or most, with nothing more on their minds than a little fun, a little enjoyment of the short respite between Friday night at five and Monday morning at nine.

But along around 2 a.m., the city begins to change.

The citizens have waited to get their cars out of parking garages (more damn garages than there are barbershops) or have staggered their way sleepily into subways to make the long trip back to the outlying sections, the furry toy dog won in the Pokerino palace clutched limply in arms that may or may not later succumb to less than ardent embrace, the laughter a bit thin, the voice a bit croaked, a college song being sung on a rattling subway car, but without much force or spirit, Saturday night has ended, it is really Sunday morning already, the morning hours are truly upon the city now, and the denizens appear.

The hookers brazenly approach any straying male, never mind the "Want to have a good time, sweetheart?", never mind the euphemisms now. Now it's "Want to fuck, honey?", yes or no, a quick sidewalk transaction and the attendant danger of later getting mugged and rolled or maybe killed by a pimp in a hotel room stinking of Lysol while your pants are draped over a wooden chair. The junkies are out in force, too, looking for cars foolishly left unlocked and parked on the streets, or – lacking such fortuitous circumstance – experienced enough to force a side vent with a screwdriver, hook the lock button with a wire hanger, and open the door that way. There are pushers peddling their dream stuff, from pot to hoss to speed, a nickel bag or a twenty-dollar deck; fences hawking their stolen goodies, anything from a transistor radio to a refrigerator, the biggest bargain basement in town; burglars jimmying windows or forcing doors with a Celluloid strip, this being an excellent hour to break into apartments, when the occupants are asleep and the street sounds are hushed. But worse than any of these people (for they are, after all only citizens engaged in commerce of a sort) are the predators who roam the night in search of trouble. In cruising wedges of three or four, sometimes high but more often not, they look for victims – a taxicab driver coming out of a cafeteria, an old woman poking around garbage cans for hidden treasures, a teenage couple necking in a parked automobile, it doesn't matter. You can get killed in this city at any time of the day or night, but your chances for extinction are best after 2 a.m. because, paradoxically, the night people take over in the morning. There are neighbourhoods that terrify even cops in this lunar landscape, and certain places they will not enter unless they have first checked to see that there are two doors, one to get in by, and the other to get out through fast, should someone decide to block the exit from behind.

The Painted Parasol was just such an establishment.

They had found in Mercy Howell's appointment book a notation that read Harry, 2 a.m., The Painted Parasol, and since they knew this particular joint for exactly the kind of hole it was, and since they wondered what connection the slain girl might have had with the various unappetizing types who frequented the place from dusk till dawn, they decided to hit it and find out. The front entrance opened on a long flight of stairs that led down to the main room of what was not a restaurant, and not a club, though it combined features of both. It did not possess a liquor license, and so it served only coffee and sandwiches, but occasionally a rock singer would plug in his amplifier and guitar and whack out a few numbers for the patrons. The back door of the – hangout? – opened onto a side-street alley. Hawes checked it out, reported back to Carella, and they both made a mental floor plan in case they needed it later.

Carella went down the long flight of steps first, Hawes immediately after him. At the bottom of the stairway, they moved through a beaded curtain and found themselves in a large room overhung with an old Air Force parachute painted in a wild psychedelic pattern. A counter upon which rested a coffee urn and trays of sandwiches in Saran Wrap was just opposite the hanging beaded curtain. To the left and right of the counter were perhaps two dozen tables, all of them occupied. A waitress in a black leotard and black high-heeled patent leather pumps was swiveling among and around the tables, taking orders. There was a buzz of conversation in the room, hovering, captured in the folds of the brightly painted parachute. Behind the counter, a man in a white apron was drawing a cup of coffee from the huge silver urn. Carella and Hawes walked over to him.

Carella was almost six feet tall, and he weighed a hundred and eighty pounds, with wide shoulders and a narrow waist and the hands of a street brawler. Hawes was six feet two inches tall, and he weighed a hundred and ninety-five pounds bone-dry and his hair was a fiery red with a white streak over the left temple, where he had once been knifed while investigating a burglary. Both men looked like exactly what they were: fuzz.

"What's the trouble?" the man behind the counter asked immediately.

"No trouble," Carella said. "This your place?"

"Yeah. My name is Georgie Bright, and I already been visited, thanks. Twice."

"Oh? Who visited you?"

"First time a cop named O'Brien, second time a cop named Parker. I already cleared up that whole thing that was going on downstairs."

"What whole thing going on downstairs?"

"In the men's room. Some kids were selling pot down there, it got to be a regular neighborhood supermarket. So I done what O'Brien suggested, I put a man down there outside the toilet door, and the rule now is only one person goes in there at a time. Parker came round to make sure I was keeping my part of the bargain. I don't want no narcotics trouble here. Go down and take a look if you like. You'll see I got a man watching the toilet."

"Who's watching the man watching the toilet?" Carella asked.

"That ain't funny," Georgie Bright said, looking offended.

"Know anybody named Harry?" Hawes asked.

"Harry who? I know a lot of Harrys."

"Any of them here tonight?"

"Maybe."

"Where?"

"There's one over there near the bandstand. The big guy with the blond hair."

"Harry what?"

"Donatello."

"Make the name?" Carella asked Hawes.

"No," said Hawes.

"Neither do I."

"Let's talk to him."

"You want a cup of coffee or something?" Georgie Bright asked.

"Yeah, why don't you send some over to the table?" Hawes said, and followed Carella across the room to where Harry Donatello was sitting with another man. Donatello was wearing grey slacks, black shoes and socks, a white shirt open at the throat, and a double-breasted blue blazer. His long blond hair was combed straight back from the forehead, revealing a sharply defined widow's peak. He was easily as big as Hawes, and he sat with his hands folded on the table in front of him, talking to the man who sat opposite him. He did not look up as the detectives approached.

"Is your name Harry Donatello?" Carella asked.

"Who wants to know?"

"Police officers," Carella said, and flashed his shield.

"I'm Harry Donatello, what's the matter?"

"Mind if we sit down?" Hawes asked, and before Donatello could answer, both men sat, their backs to the empty bandstand and the exit door.

"Do you know a girl named Mercy Howell?" Carella asked.

"What about her?"

"Do you know her?"

"I know her. What's the beef? She underage or something?"

"When did you see her last?"

The man with Donatello, who up to now had been silent, suddenly piped, "You don't have to answer no questions without a lawyer, Harry. Tell them you want a lawyer."

The detectives looked him over. He was small and thin, with black hair combed sideways to conceal a receding hairline. He was badly in need of a shave. He was wearing blue trousers and a striped shirt.

"This is a field investigation," Hawes said drily, "and we can ask anything we damn please."

"Town's getting full of lawyers," Carella said. "What's *your* name, counselor?"

"Jerry Riggs. You going to drag *me* in this, whatever it is?"

"It's a few friendly questions in the middle of the night," Hawes said. "Anybody got any objections to that?"

"Getting so two guys can't even sit and talk together without getting shook down," Riggs said.

"You've got a rough life, all right," Hawes said, and the girl in the black leotard brought their coffee to the table, and then hurried off to take another order. Donatello watched her jiggling behind as she swiveled across the room.

"So when's the last time you saw the Howell girl?" Carella asked again.

"Wednesday night," Donatello said.

"Did you see her tonight?"

"No."

"Were you *supposed* to see her tonight?"

"Where'd you get that idea?"

"We're full of ideas," Hawes said.

"Yeah, I was supposed to meet her here ten minutes ago. Dumb broad is late, as usual."

"What do you do for a living, Donatello?"

"I'm an importer. You want to see my business card?"

"What do you import?"

"Souvenir ashtrays."

"How'd you get to know Mercy Howell?"

"I met her at a party in The Quarter. She got a little high, and she done her thing."

"What thing?"

"The thing she does in that show she's in."

"Which is what?"

"She done this dance where she takes off all her clothes."

"How long have you been seeing her?"

"I met her a couple of months ago. I see her on and off, maybe once a week, something like that. This town is full of broads, you know, a guy don't have to get himself involved in no relationship with no specific broad."

"What was your relationship with *this* specific broad?"

"We have a few laughs together, that's all. She's a swinger, little Mercy," Donatello said, and grinned at Riggs.

"Want to tell us where you were tonight between eleven and twelve?"

"Is this still a *field* investigation?" Riggs asked sarcastically.

"Nobody's in custody yet," Hawes said, "so let's cut the legal crap, okay? Tell us where you were, Donatello."

"Right here," Donatello said. "From ten o'clock till now."

"I suppose somebody saw you here during that time."

"A *hundred* people saw me."

A crowd of angry black men and women were standing outside the shattered window of the storefront church. Two fire engines and an ambulance were parked at the curb. Kling pulled in behind the second engine, some ten feet away from the hydrant. It was almost 2:30 a.m. on a bitterly cold October night, but the crowd looked and sounded like a mob at an afternoon street-corner rally in the middle of August. Restless, noisy, abrasive, anticipative, they ignored the penetrating cold and concentrated instead on the burning issue of the hour, the fact that a person or persons unknown had thrown a bomb through the plate glass window of the church. The beat patrolman, a newly appointed cop who felt vaguely uneasy in this neighborhood even during his daytime shift, greeted Kling effusively, his pale white face bracketed by earmuffs, his gloved hands clinging desperately to his nightstick. The crowd parted to let Kling through. It did not help that he was the youngest man on the squad, with the callow look of a country bumpkin on his unlined face, it did not help that he was blond and hatless, it did not help, that he walked into the church with the confident youthful stride of a champion come to set things right. The crowd knew he was fuzz, and they knew he was Whitey, and the knew, too, that if this bombing had taken place on Hall Avenue crosstown and downtown, the Police Commissioner himself would have arrived behind a herald of official trumpets. This, however, was Culver Avenue, where a boiling mixture of Puerto Ricans and Negroes shared a disintegrating ghetto, and so the car that pulled to the curb was not marked with the Commissioner's distinctive blue-on-gold seal, but was instead a green Chevy convertible that belonged to Kling himself, and the man who stepped out of it looked young and inexperienced and inept despite the confident stride he affected as he walked into the church, his shield pinned to his overcoat.

The bomb has caused little fire damage, and the firemen already had the flames under control, their hoses snaking through and around the overturned folding chairs scattered about the small room. Ambulance attendants picked their way over the hoses and around the debris, carrying out the injured – the dead could wait.

"Have you called the Bomb Squad?" Kling asked the patrolman.

"No," the patrolman answered, shaken by the sudden possibility that he had been derelict in his duty.

"Why don't you do that now?" Kling suggested.

"Yes, *sir*," the patrolman answered, and rushed out. The ambulance attendant went by with a moaning woman on a stretcher. She was still wearing her eyeglasses, but one lens had been shattered and blood was running in a steady rivulet down the side of her nose. The place stank of gunpowder and smoke and charred wood. The most serious damage had been done at the rear of the small store, furthest away from the entrance door. Whoever had thrown the bomb must have possessed a damn good pitching arm to have hurled it so accurately through the window and across the fifteen feet to the makeshift altar. The minister lay across his own altar, dead, one arm blown off in the explosion. Two women who had been sitting on folding chairs closest to the altar lay upon each other on the floor now, tangled in death, their clothes still smoldering. The sounds of the injured filled the room, and then were suffocated by the overriding siren-shriek of the arriving second ambulance. Kling went outside to the crowd.

"Anybody here witness this?" he asked.

A young man, black, wearing a beard and a natural hair style, turned away from a group of other youths, and walked directly to Kling.

"Is the minister dead?" he asked.

"Yes, he is," Kling answered.

"Who else?"

"Two women."

"Who?"

"I don't know yet. We'll identify them as soon as the men are through in there." He turned again to the crowd. "Did anybody see what happened?" he asked.

"I saw it," the young man said.

"What's your name, son?"

"Andrew Jordan."

Kling took out his pad. "All right, let's have it."

"What good's this going to do?" Jordan asked. "Writing all this shit in your book?"

"You said you saw what..."

"I saw it, all right. I was walking by, heading for the poolroom up the street, and the ladies were inside singing, and this car pulled up, and a guy got out, threw the bomb, and ran back to the car."

"What kind of a car was it?"

"A red VW."

"What year?"

"Who can tell with those VWs?"

"How many people in it?"

"Two. The driver and the guy who threw the bomb."

"Notice the license plate?"

"No. They drove off too fast."

"Can you describe the man who threw the bomb?"

"Yeah. He was white."

"What else?" Kling asked.

"That's all," Jordan replied. "He was *white*."

There were perhaps three dozen estates in all of Smoke Rise, a hundred or so people living in luxurious near seclusion on acres of valuable land through which ran four winding, interconnected, private roadways. Meyer drove between the wide stone pillars marking Smoke Rise's western access road, entering a city within a city, bounded on the north by the River Harb, shielded from the River Highway by stands of poplars and evergreens on the south – exclusive Smoke Rise, known familiarly and derisively to the rest of the city's inhabitants as 'The Club.'

374 MacArthur Lane was at the end of the road that curved past the Hamilton Bridge. The house was a huge gray stone structure with a slate roof and scores of gables and chimneys jostling the sky, perched high in gloomy shadow above the Harb. As he stepped from the car, Meyer could hear the sounds of river traffic, the hooting of tugs, the blowing of whistles, the eruption of a squawk box on a destroyer midstream. He looked out over the water. Reflected lights glistened in shimmering liquid beauty, the hanging globes on the bridge's suspension cables, the dazzling reds and greens of signal lights on the opposite shore, single illuminated window slashes in apartment buildings throwing their mirror images onto the black surface of the river, the blinking wing lights of

an airplane overhead moving in watery reflection like a submarine. The air was cold, a fine piercing drizzle had begun several minutes ago. Meyer shuddered, pulled the collar of his coat higher on his neck, and walked toward the old gray house, his shoes crunching on the driveway gravel, the sound echoing away into the high surrounding bushes.

The stones of the old house oozed wetness. Thick vines covered the walls, climbing to the gabled, turreted roof. He found a doorbell set over a brass escutcheon in the thick oaken doorjamb, and pressed it. Chimes sounded somewhere deep inside the house. He waited.

The door opened suddenly.

The man looking out at him was perhaps seventy years old, with piercing blue eyes, bald except for white thatches of hair that sprang wildly from behind each ear. He wore a red smoking jacket and black trousers, a black ascot around his neck, red velvet slippers.

"What do you want?" he asked immediately.

"I'm Detective Meyer of the Eighty-seventh ..."

"Who sent for you?"

"A woman named Adele Gorman came to the ..."

"My daughter's a fool," the man said. "We don't need the police here," and slammed the door in his face.

Meyer stood on the doorstep feeling somewhat like a horse's ass. A tugboat hooted on the river. A light snapped on upstairs, casting an amber rectangle into the dark driveway. He looked at the luminous dial of his watch. It was 2:35 a.m. The drizzle was cold and penetrating. He took out his handkerchief, blew his nose, and wondered what he should do next. He did not like ghosts, and he did not like lunatics, and he did not like nasty old men who did not comb their hair and who slammed doors in a person's face. He was about to head back for his car when the door opened again.

"Detective Meyer?" Adele Gorman said. "Do come in."

"Thank you," he said, and stepped into the entrance foyer.

"You're right on time."

"Well, a little early actually," Meyer said. He still felt foolish. What the hell was he doing in Smoke Rise investigating ghosts in the middle of the night?

"This way," Adele said, and he followed her through a somberly paneled foyer into a vast, dimly lighted living room. Heavy oaken beams ran overhead, velvet draperies hung at the window, the room was cluttered with ponderous old furniture. He could believe there were ghosts in this house, he could suddenly believe it. A young man wearing dark glasses rose like a specter from the sofa near the fireplace. His face, illuminated by the single standing floor lamp, looked wan and drawn. Wearing a black cardigan sweater over a white shirt and dark slacks, he approached Meyer unsmilingly with his hand extended – but he did not accept Meyer's hand when it was offered in return.

Meyer suddenly realized that the man was blind.

"I'm Ralph Gorman," he said, his hand still extended. "Adele's husband."

"How do you do, Mr. Gorman," Meyer said, and took his hand. The palm was moist and cold.

"It was good of you to come," Gorman said. "These apparitions have been driving us crazy."

"What time is it?" Adele asked suddenly, and looked at her watch. "We've got five minutes," she said. There was a tremor in her voice. She seemed suddenly very frightened.

"Won't your father be here?" Meyer asked.

"No, he's gone up to bed," Adele said. "I'm afraid he's bored with the whole affair, and terribly angry that we notified the police."

Meyer made no comment. Had he known that Willem Van Houten, former Surrogate's Court judge, had *not* wanted the police to be notified, Meyer would not have been here in the first place. He debated leaving now, but Adele Gorman had begun talking again, and it was impolite to depart in the middle of another person's sentence.

"... is in her early thirties, I would guess. The other ghost, the male, is about your age – forty or forty-five, something like that."

"I'm thirty-seven," Meyer said.

"Oh."

"The bald head fools a lot of people."

"Yes."

"I was bald at a very early age."

"Anyway," Adele said, "their names are Elisabeth and Johann, and they've probably been..."

"Oh, they have names, do they?"

"Yes. They're ancestors, you know. My father is Dutch, and there actually *were* and Elisabeth and Johann Van Houten in the family centuries ago, when Smoke Rise was still a Dutch settlement."

"They're Dutch, um-huh, I see," Meyer said.

"Yes. They always appear wearing Dutch costumes. And they also speak Dutch."

"Have *you* heard them, Mr. Gorman?"

"Yes," Gorman said. "I'm blind, you know..." he added, and hesitated, as though expecting some comment from Meyer. When none came, he said "But I *have* heard them."

"Do you speak Dutch?"

"No. My father-in-law speaks it fluently, though, and he identified the language for us, and told us what they were saying."

"What *did* they say?"

"Well, for one thing, they said they were going to steal Adele's jewelry, and they damn well did."

"Your *wife's* jewelry? But I thought..."

"It was willed to her by her mother. My father-in-law keeps it in his safe."

"*Kept*, you mean."

"No, keeps. There are several pieces in addition to the ones that were stolen. Two rings and also a necklace."

"And the value?"

"Altogether? I would say about forty thousand dollars."

"Your ghosts have expensive taste."

The floor lamp in the room suddenly began to flicker. Meyer glanced at it and felt the hackles rising at the back of his neck.

"The lights are going out, Ralph," Adele whispered.

"Is it two forty-five?"

"Yes."

"They're here," Gorman whispered.

Mercy Howell's roommate had been asleep for close to four hours when they knocked on her door. But she was a wily young lady, hip to the ways of the big city, and very much awake as she conducted her own little investigation without so much as opening the door a crack. First she asked them to spell their names slowly. Then she asked them their shield numbers. Then she asked them to hold their shields and their I.D. cards close to the door's peephole, where she could see them. Still unconvinced, she said through the locked door, "You just wait there a minute." They waited for closer to five minutes before they heard her approaching the door again. The heavy steel bar of a Fox lock was pushed noisily to the side, a safety chain rattled on its track, the tumbler of one lock clicked open, and then another, and finally the girl opened the door.

"Come in," she said. "I'm sorry I kept you waiting. I called the station house and they said you were okay."

"You're a very careful girl," Hawes said.

"At this hour of the morning? Are you kidding?" she said.

She was perhaps twenty-five, with her red hair up in curlers, her face cold-creamed clean of makeup. She was wearing a pink quilted robe over flannel pajamas, and although she was probably a very pretty girl at 9 a.m., she now looked about as attractive as a Buffalo nickel.

"What's your name, miss?" Carella asked.

"Lois Kaplan. What's this all about? Has there been another burglary in the building?"

"No, Miss Kaplan. We want to ask some questions about Mercy Howell? Did she live here with you?"

"Yes," Lois said, and suddenly looked at them shrewdly. "What do you mean *did*? She still *does*?"

They were standing in the small foyer of the apartment, and the foyer went so still that all the night sounds of the building were clearly audible all at once, as though they had not been there before but had only been summoned now to fill the void of silence. A toilet flushed somewhere, a hot water pipe rattled, a baby whimpered, a dog barked, someone dropped a shoe. In the foyer now filled with noise, they stared at each other wordlessly, and finally Carella drew a deep breath and said, "Your roommate is dead. She was stabbed tonight as she was leaving the theater."

"No," Lois said, simply and flatly and unequivocally. "No, she isn't."

"Miss Kaplan..."

"I don't give a damn what you say, Mercy isn't dead."

"Miss Kaplan, she's dead."

"Oh Jesus," Lois said, and burst into tears, "oh Jesus, oh damn damn, oh Jesus."

The two men stood by feeling stupid and big and awkward and helpless. Lois Kaplan covered her face with her hands and sobbed into them, her shoulders heaving, saying over and over again, "I'm sorry, oh Jesus, please, I'm sorry, please, oh poor Mercy, oh my God," while the detectives tried not to watch. At last the crying stopped and she looked up at them with eyes that had been knifed, and said softly, "Come in. Please," and led them into the living room. She kept staring at the floor as she talked. It was as if she could not look them in the face, not these men who had brought her the news.

"Do you know who did it?" she asked.

"No. Not yet."

"We wouldn't have waked you in the middle of the night..."

"That's all right."

"But very often, if we get moving on a case fast enough, before the trail gets cold . . ."

"Yes, I understand."

"We can often . . ."

"Yes, before the trail gets cold," Lois said.

"Yes."

The apartment went silent again.

"Would you know if Miss Howell had any enemies?" Carella asked.

"She was the sweetest girl in the world," Lois said.

"Did she argue with anyone recently, were there . . . ?"

"No."

". . . any threatening telephone calls or letters?"

Lois Kaplan looked up at them.

"Yes," she said. "A letter."

"A *threatening* letter?"

"We couldn't tell. It frightened Mercy, though. That's why she bought the gun."

"What kind of gun."

"I don't know. A small one."

"Would it have been a .25 caliber Browning?"

"I don't know guns."

"Was this letter mailed to her, or delivered personally?"

"It was mailed to her. At the theater."

"When?"

"A week ago."

"Did she report it to the police?"

"No."

"Why not?"

"Haven't you seen *Rattlesnake*?" Lois said.

"What do you mean?" Carella said.

"*Rattlesnake*. The musical. Mercy's show. The show she was in."

"No, I haven't."

"But you've *heard* of it."

"No."

"Where do you live, for God's sake? On the moon?"

"I'm sorry, I just haven't . . ."

"Forgive me," Lois said immediately. "I'm not usually . . . I'm trying very hard to . . . I'm sorry. Forgive me."

"That's all right," Carella said.

"Anyway, its . . . it's a big hit now but . . . there was trouble in the beginning, you see . . . are you *sure* you don't know about this? It was in all the newspapers."

"Well, I guess I missed it," Carella said. "What was the trouble about?"

"Don't *you* know about this either?" she asked Hawes.

"No, I'm sorry."

"About Mercy's dance?"

"No."

"Well, in one scene, Mercy danced the title song without any clothes on. Because the idea was to express . . . the *hell* with what the idea was. The point is that the dance wasn't at all prurient, it wasn't even sexy! But the police *missed* the point, they closed the show down two days after it opened.

The producers had to go to court for a writ to get the show opened again."

"Yes, I remember it now," Carella said.

"What I'm trying to say is that nobody involved with *Rattlesnake* would report *anything* to the police. Not even a threatening letter."

"If she bought a pistol," Hawes said, "she would have *had* to go to the police. For a permit."

"She didn't have a permit."

"Then how'd she get the pistol? You can't buy a handgun without first ..."

"A friend of hers sold it to her."

"What's the friend's name?"

"Harry Donatello."

"An importer," Carella said drily.

"Of souvenir ashtrays," Hawes said.

"I don't know what he does for a living," Lois said. "But he got the gun for her."

"When was this?"

"A few days after she received the letter."

"What did the letter say?" Carella asked.

"I'll get it for you," Lois said, and went into the bedroom. They heard a dresser drawer opening, the rustle of clothes, what might have been a tin candy box being opened. Lois came back into the room. "Here it is," she said.

There didn't seem much point in trying to preserve latent prints on a letter that had already been handled by Mercy Howell, Lois Kaplan, and God knew how many others. But Carella nonetheless accepted the letter on a handkerchief spread over the palm of his hand, and then looked at the face of the envelope. "She should have brought this to us immediately," he said. "It's written on hotel stationery, we've got an address without lifting a finger."

The letter had indeed been written on stationery from The Addison Hotel, one of the city's lesser-known fleabags, some two blocks north of the Eleventh Street Theater, where Mercy Howell had worked. There was a single sheet of paper in the envelope. Carella unfolded it. Lettered in pencil were the words:

Put on Your
Close, Miss!

The Avenging Angel

The lamp went out, the room was black.

At first there was no sound but the sharp intake of Adele Gorman's breath. And then, indistinctly, as faintly as though carried on a swirling mist that blew in wetly from some desolated shore, there came the sound of garbled voices, and the room grew suddenly cold. The voices were those of a crowd in endless debate, rising and falling in cacophonous cadence, a mixture of tongues that rattled and rasped. There was the sound too, of a rising wind, as though a door to some forbidden landscape had been sharply and suddenly blown open (How cold the room was!) to reveal a host of corpses incessantly pacing, involved in formless dialogue. The voices rose in volume now, carried on that same chill penetrating wind, louder, closer, until they seemed to overwhelm the room, clamoring to be released from whatever unearthly vault contained them. And then, as if two and only two of those disembodied voices had succeeded in breaking away from the mass of unseen dead, bringing with them a rush of bone-chilling air from some world unknown, there came a whisper at first, the whisper of a man's voice, saying the single word "Ralph!" sharp-edged and with a distinctive foreign inflection, "Ralph!" and then a woman's voice joining it, "Adele!" pronounced strangely and in the same cutting whisper, "Adele!" and then "Ralph!" again, the voices overlapping, unmistakably foreign, urgent, rising in volume until the whispers commingled to become an agonizing groan and the names were lost in the shrilling echo of the wind.

Meyer's eyes played tricks in the darkness. Apparitions that surely were not there seemed to float on the crescendo of sound that saturated the room. Barely perceived pieces of furniture assumed amorphous shapes as the male voice snarled and the female voice moaned above it in contralto counterpoint. And then the babel of other voices intruded again, as though calling these two back to whatever grim mossy crypt they had momentarily escaped. The sound of the wind became more fierce, and the voices of those numberless pacing dead receded, and echoed, and were gone.

The lamp sputtered back into dim illumination. The room seemed perceptibly warmer, but Meyer Meyer was covered with a cold clammy sweat.

"*Now* do you believe?" Adele Gorman asked.

Detective Bob O'Brien was coming out of the men's room down the hall when he saw the woman sitting on the bench just outside the squadroom. He almost went back into the toilet, but he was an instant too late; she had seen him, there was no escape.

"Hello, Mr. O'Brien," she said, and performed an awkward little half-rising motion, as though uncertain whether she should stand to greet him or accept the deference due a lady. The clock on the squadroom wall read 3:02 a.m., but the lady was dressed as though for a brisk afternoon hike in the park, brown slacks and low-heeled walking shoes, brief beige car coat, a scarf around her head. She was perhaps fifty-five or thereabouts, with a face that once must have been pretty, save for the over-long nose. Green-eyed, with prominent cheekbones and a generous mouth, she executed her abortive rise, and then fell into step beside O'Brien as he walked into the squadroom.

"Little late in the night to be out, isn't it, Mrs. Blair?" O'Brien asked. He was not an insensitive cop, but his manner now was brusque and dismissive. Faced with Mrs. Blair for perhaps the seventeenth time in a month, he tried not to empathize with her loss because, truthfully, he was unable to assist her, and his inability to do so was frustrating.

"Have you seen her?" Mrs. Blair asked.

"No," O'Brien said. "I'm sorry, Mrs. Blair, but I haven't."

"I have a new picture, perhaps that will help."

"Yes, perhaps it will," he said.

The telephone was ringing. He lifted the receiver and said, "Eighty-seventh Squad, O'Brien here."

"Bob, this's Bert Kling over on Culver, the church bombing."

"Yeah, Bert."

"Seems I remember seeing a red Volkswagen on that hot car bulletin we got yesterday. You want to dig it out and let me know where it was snatched?"

"Yeah, just a second," O'Brien said, and began scanning the sheet on his desk.

"Here's the new picture," Mrs. Blair said. "I know you're very good with runaways, Mr. O'Brien, the kids all like you and give you information. If you see Penelope, all I want you to do is tell her I love her and am sorry for the misunderstanding."

"Yeah, I will," O'Brien said. Into the phone, he said, "I've got *two* red VWs, Bert, a '64 and a '66. You want them both?"

"Shoot," Kling said.

"The '64 was stolen from a guy named Art Hauser. It was parked outside 861 West Meridian."

"And the '66?"

"Owner is a woman named Alice Cleary. Car was stolen from a parking lot on Fourteenth."

"North or South?"

"South. 303 South."

"Right. Thanks, Bob," Kling said, and hung up.

"And ask her to come home to me," Mrs. Blair said.

"Yes, I will," O'Brien said. "If I see her, I certainly will."

"That's a nice picture of Penny, don't you think?" Mrs. Blair asked. "It was taken last Easter. It's the most recent picture I have. I thought it would be most helpful to you."

O'Brien looked at the girl in the picture, and then looked up into Mrs. Blair's green eyes, misted now with tears, and suddenly wanted to reach across the desk and pat her hand reassuringly, the one thing he could *not* do with any honesty. Because whereas it was true that he was the squad's runaway expert, with perhaps fifty snapshots of teenage boys and girls crammed into his bulging notebook, and whereas his record of finds was more impressive than any other cop's in the city, uniformed or plainclothes, there wasn't a damn thing he could do for the mother of Penelope Blair, who had run away from home last June.

"You understand . . ." he started to say.

"Let's not go into *that* again Mr. O'Brien," she said, and rose.

"Mrs. Blair . . ."

"I don't want to hear it," Mrs. Blair said, walking quickly out of the squadroom. "Tell her to come home. Tell her I love her," she said, and was gone down the iron-runged steps.

O'Brien sighed and stuffed the new picture of Penelope into his notebook. What Mrs. Blair did not choose to hear again was the fact that her runaway daughter Penny was twenty-four years old, and there was not a single agency on God's green earth, police or otherwise, that could force her to go home again if she did not choose to.

Fats Donner was a stool pigeon with a penchant for Turkish baths. A mountainous white Buddha of a man, he could usually be found at one or another of the city's steam emporiums at any given hour of the day, draped in a towel and reveling in the heat that saturated his flabby body. Bert Kling found him in an all-night place called Steam-Fit. He sent the masseur into the steam room to tell Donner he was there, and Donner sent word out that he would be through in five minutes, unless Kling wished to join him. Kling did not wish to join him. He waited in the locker room, and in seven minutes' time, Donner came out, draped in his customary towel, a ludicrous sight at *any* time, but particulary at close to 3:30 a.m.

"Hey!" Donner said. "How you doing?"

"Fine," Kling said. "How about yourself?"

"*Comme ci, comme ça*," Donner said, and made a see-sawing motion with one fleshy hand.

"I'm looking for some stolen heaps," Kling said, getting directly to the point.

"What kind?" Donner said.

"Volkswagens. A '64 and a '66."

"What colour are they?"

"Red."

"Both of them?"

"Yes."

"Where were they heisted?"

"One from in front of 861 West Meridian. The other from a parking lot on South Fourteenth."

"When was this?"

"Both last week sometime. I don't have the exact dates."

"What do you want to know?"

"Who stole them."

"You think it's the same guy on both?"

"I doubt it."

"What's so important about these heaps?"

"One of them may have been used in a bombing tonight."

"You mean the church over on Culver?"

"That's right."

"Count me out," Donner said.

"What do you mean?"

"There's a lot of guys in this town who're in *sympathy* with what happened over there tonight. I don't want to get involved in none of this black-white shit."

"Who's going to know whether you're involved or not?" Kling asked.

"The same way *you* get information, *they* get information."

"I need your help Donner."

"Yeah, well, I'm sorry on this one," Donner said, and shook his head.

"In that case, I'd better hurry downtown to High Street."

"Why? You got another source down there?"

"No, that's where the D.A.'s office is."

Both men stared at each other, Donner in a white towel draped around his belly, sweat still pouring from his face and his chest even though he was no longer in the steam room, Kling looking like a slightly tired advertising executive rather than a cop threatening a man with revelation of past deeds not entirely legal. They stared at each other with total understanding, caught in the curious symbiosis of law breaker and law enforcer, an empathy created by neither man, but essential to the existence of both. It was Donner who broke the silence.

"I don't like being coerced," he said.

"I don't like being refused," Kling said.

"When do you need this?"

"I want to get going on it before morning."

"You expect miracles, don't you?"

"Doesn't everybody?"

"Miracles cost."

"How much?"

"Twenty-five if I turn up one heap, fifty if I turn up both."

"Turn them up first. We'll talk later."

"And if somebody breaks my head later?"

"You should have thought of that before you entered the profession," Kling said. "Come on, Donner, cut it out. This is a routine bombing by a couple of punks. You've got nothing to be afraid of."

"No?" Donner asked. And then, in a very professorial voice, he uttered perhaps the biggest understatement of the decade. "Racial tensions are running very high in this city right now."

"Have you got my number at the squadroom?"

"Yeah, I've got it," Donner said glumly.

"I'm going back there now. Let me hear from you soon."

"You mind if I get dressed first?" Donner asked.

The night clerk at The Addison Hotel was alone in the lobby when Carella and Hawes walked in. Immersed in an open book on the desk in front of him, he did not look up as they approached. The lobby was furnished in faded Gothic: a threadbare oriental rug, heavy curlicued mahogany tables, ponderous stuffed chairs with sagging bottoms and soiled antimacassars, two spittoons resting alongside each of two mahogany-paneled supporting columns. A real Tiffany lampshade hung over the registration desk, one leaded glass panel gone, another badly cracked. In the old days, The Addison had been a luxury hotel. It now wore its past splendor with all the style of a two-dollar hooker in a moth-eaten mink she'd picked up in a thrift shop.

The clerk, in contrast to his ancient surroundings, was a young man in his mid-twenties, wearing a neatly pressed brown tweed suit, a tan shirt, a gold-and-brown silk rep tie, and eyeglasses with tortoiseshell rims. He glanced up at the detectives belatedly, squinting after the intense concentration of peering at print, and then he got to his feet.

"Yes, gentlemen," he said "May I help you?"

"Police officers," Carella said. He took his wallet from his pocket, and opened it to where his detective's shield was pinned to a leather flap.

"Yes, sir."

"I'm Detective Carella, this is my partner Detective Hawes."

"How do you do? I'm the night clerk, my name is Ronnie Sanford."

"We're looking for someone who may have been registered here two weeks ago," Hawes said.

"Well, if he was registered here two weeks ago," Sanford said, "chances are he's still registered. Most of our guests are residents."

"Do you keep stationery in the lobby here?" Carella asked.

"Sir?"

"Stationery. Is there any place here in the lobby where someone could walk in off the street and pick up a piece of stationery?"

"No, sir. There's a writing desk there in the corner, near the staircase, but we don't stock it with stationery, no, sir."

"Is there stationery in the rooms?"

"Yes, sir."

"How about here at the desk"

"Yes, of course, sir."

"Is there someone at this desk twenty-four hours a day?"

"Twenty-four hours a day, yes, sir. We have three shifts. Eight to four in the afternoon. Four to midnight. And midnight to eight a.m."

"You came on at midnight did you?"

"Yes, sir."

"Any guests come in after you started your shift?"

"A few, yes, sir."

"Notice anybody with blood on his clothes?"

"Blood? Oh, no, sir."

"*Would* you have noticed."

"What do you mean?"

"Are you generally pretty aware of what's going on around here?"

"I try to be, sir. At least, for most of the night. I catch a little nap when I'm not studying, but usually ..."

"What do you study?"

"Accounting."

"Where?"

"At Ramsey U."

"Mind if we take a look at your register?"

"Not at all, sir."

He walked to the mail rack and took the hotel register from the counter there. Returning to the desk, he opened it, and said, "All our present guests are residents, with the exception of Mr. Lambert in 204, and Mrs. Grant in 701."

"When did they check in."

"Mr. Lambert checked in ... last night, I think it was. And Mrs. Grant has been here for four days. She's leaving on Tuesday."

"Are these the actual signatures of your guests?"

"Yes, sir. All guests are asked to sign the register, as required by state law."

"Have you got that note, Cotton?" Carella asked, and then turned again to Sanford. "Would you mind if we took this over to the couch there?"

"Well, we're not supposed..."

"We can give you a receipt for it, if you like."

"No, I guess it'll be all right."

They carried the register to a couch upholstered in faded red velvet. With the book supported on Carella's lap, they unfolded the note Mercy Howell had received, and began comparing the signatures of the guests with the only part of the note not written in block letters, the words "The Avenging Angel."

There were fifty-two guests in the hotel. Carella and Hawes went through the register once, and then started through it a second time.

"Hey," Hawes said suddenly.

"What?"

"Look at this one."

He took the note and placed it on the page so that it was directly above one of the signatures:

PUT ON YOUR CLOSE, MISS!

The Avenging Angel

Timothy Allen Ames

"What do you think?" he asked.

"Different handwriting," Carella said.

"Same initials," Hawes said.

Detective Meyer Meyer was still shaken. He did not like ghosts. He did not like this house. He wanted to go home. He wanted to be in bed with his wife Sarah. He wanted her to stroke his hand and tell him that such things do not exist, there was nothing to be afraid of, a grown man? How could he believe in poltergeists, shades, Dutch spirits? Ridiculous.

But he had heard them, and he had felt their chilling presence, and had almost thought he'd seen them, if only for an instant. He turned with fresh shock now toward the hall staircase and the sound of descending footsteps. Eyes wide, he waited for whatever new manifestation might present itself. He was tempted to draw his revolver, but he was afraid such an act would appear foolish to the Gormans. He had come here a skeptic, and he was now at least *willing* to believe, and he waited in dread for whatever was coming down those steps with such ponderous footfalls – some ghoul trailing winding sheets and rattling chains? Some specter with a bleached skull for a head and long bony clutching fingers dripping the blood of babies?

Willem Van Houten, wearing his red velvet slippers and his red smoking jacket, his hair still jutting wildly from behind each ear, his blue eyes fierce and snapping, came into the living room and walked directly to where his daughter and son-in-law were sitting.

"Well?" he asked. "Did they come again?"

"Yes, Daddy," Adele said.

"What did they want this time?"

"I don't know. They spoke Dutch again."

"Bastards," Van Houten said, and then turned to Meyer. "Did you see them?" he asked.

"No, sir, I did not," Meyer said.

"But they were *here*," Gorman protested, and turned his blank face to his wife. "I heard them."

"Yes, darling," Adele assured him. "We *all* heard them. But it was like that other time, don't you remember? When we could hear them even though they couldn't quite break through."

"Yes, that's right." Gorman said, and nodded. "This happened once before, Detective Meyer." He was facing Detective Meyer now, his head tilted quizzically, the sightless eyes covered with their black reflecting glasses. When he spoke, his voice was like that of a child seeking reassurance. "But you *did* hear them, didn't you, Detective Meyer?"

"Yes," Meyer said. "I heard them, Mr. Gorman."

"And the wind?"

"Yes, the wind, too."

"And felt them? It ... gets so cold when they appear. You *did* feel their presence, didn't you?"

"I felt something." Meyer said.

Van Houten suddenly asked, "Are you satisfied?"

"About what?" Meyer said.

"That there are ghosts in this house? That's why you're here, isn't it? To ascertain ..."

"He's here because I asked Adele to contact the police," Gorman said.

"Why did you do that?"

"Because of the stolen jewelry," Gorman said. "And because ..." He paused. "Because I ... I've lost my sight, yes, but I wanted to ... to make sure I wasn't losing my mind as well."

"You're quite sane, Ralph," Van Houten said.

"About the jewelry ..." Meyer said.

"*They* took it," Van Houten said.

"Who?"

"Johann and Elisabeth. Our friendly neighborhood ghosts, the bastards."

"That's impossible, Mr. Van Houten."

"Why is it impossible?"

"Because ghosts ..." Meyer started, and hesitated.

"Yes?"

"Ghosts, well, ghosts don't go around stealing jewelry. I mean, what use would they have for it?" he said lamely, and looked at the Gormans for corroboration. Neither of them seemed to be in a supportive mood. They sat on the sofa near the fireplace, looking glum and defeated.

"They want us out of this house," Van Houten said. "It's as simple as that."

"How do you know?"

"Because they said so."

"When?"

"Before they stole the necklace and the earrings."

"They told this to you?"

"To me and to my children. All three of us were here."

"But I understand the ghosts speak only Dutch."

"Yes, I translated for Ralph and Adele."

"And then what happened?"

"What do you mean?"

"When did you discover the jewelry was missing?"

"The very instant they were gone."

"You mean you went to the safe..."

"Yes, and opened it, and the jewelry was gone."

"We had put it in the safe not ten minutes before that," Adele said. "We'd been to a party, Ralph and I, and we got home very late, and Daddy was still awake, reading, sitting in that chair you're in this very minute. I asked him to open the safe, and he did, and he put the jewelry in, and closed the safe and ... and then *they* ... came and ... and made their threats."

"What time was this?"

"The usual time. The time they always come. Two forty-five in the morning."

"And you say the jewelry was put into the safe at what time?"

"About two-thirty," Gorman said.

"And when was the safe opened again?"

"Immediately after they left. They only stay a few moments. This time they told my father-in-law they were taking the necklace and the earrings with them. He rushed to the safe as soon as the lights came on again..."

"Do the lights always go off?"

"Always," Adele said. "It's always the same. The lights go off, and the room gets very cold, and we hear these ... strange voices arguing." She paused. "And then Johann and Elisabeth come."

"Except that *this* time they didn't come," Meyer said.

"And one other time," Adele said quickly.

"They want us out of this house," Van Houten said, "that's all there is to it. Maybe we *ought* to leave. Before they take *everything* from us."

"Everything? What do you mean?"

"The rest of my daughter's jewelry. Some stock certificates. Everything that's in the safe."

"Where *is* the safe?" Meyer asked.

"Here. Behind this painting." Van Houten walked to the wall opposite the fireplace. An oil painting of a pastoral landscape hung there in an ornate gilt frame. The frame was hinged to the wall. Van Houten swung the painting out as though opening a door, and revealed the small, round, black safe behind it. "Here," he said.

"How many people know the combination?" Meyer asked.

"Just me," Van Houten said.

"Do you keep the number written down anywhere?"

"Yes."

"Where?"

"Hidden."

"Where?"

"I hardly think that's any of your business, Detective Meyer."

"I'm only trying to find out whether some other person could have got hold of the combination somehow."

"Yes, I suppose that's possible," Van Houten said. "But highly unlikely."

"Well," Meyer said, and shrugged. "I don't really know what to say. I'd like to measure the room, if you don't mind, get the dimensions, placement of doors and windows, things like that. For my report." He shrugged again.

"It's rather late, isn't it?" Van Houten said.

'Well, I *got* here rather late," Meyer said, and smiled.

"Come, Daddy, I'll make us all some tea in the kitchen," Adele said. "Will you be long, Detective Meyer?"

"I don't know. It may take a while."

"Shall I bring you some tea?"

"Thank you, that would be nice."

She rose from the couch and then guided her husband's hand to her arm. Walking slowly beside him, she led him past her father and out of the room. Van Houten looked at Meyer once again, nodded briefly, and followed them out. Meyer closed the door behind them and immediately walked to the standing floor lamp.

The woman was sixty years old, and she looked like anybody's grandmother, except that she had just murdered her husband and three children. They had explained her rights to her, and she had told them she had nothing to hide and would answer any questions they chose to ask. She sat in a straight-backed squadroom chair, wearing a black cloth coat over bloodstained pajamas and robe, her handcuffed hands in her lap, her hands unmoving on her black leather pocketbook. O'Brien and Kling looked at the police stenographer, who glanced up at the wall clock, noted the time of the interrogation's start as 3:55 a.m., and then signaled that he was ready whenever they were.

"What is your name?" O'Brien asked.

"Isabel Martin."

"How old are you, Mrs. Martin?"

"Sixty."

"Where do you live?"

"On Ainsley Avenue,"

"Where on Ainsley?"

"657 Ainsley."

"With whom do you live there?"

"With my husband Roger, and my son Peter, and my daughters Annie and Abigail."

"Would you like to tell us what happened tonight, Mrs. Martin?" Kling asked.

"I killed them all," she said. She had white hair, a fine aquiline nose, brown eyes behind rimless spectacles. She stared straight ahead of her as she spoke, looking neither to her right nor to her left, ignoring her questioners completely, seemingly alone with the memory of what she had done not a half-hour before.

"Can you give us some details, Mrs. Martin?"

"I killed *him* first, the son of a bitch."

"Who do you mean, Mrs. Martin."

"My husband."

"When was this?"

"When he came home."

"What time was that, do you remember?"

"A little while ago."

"It's almost four o'clock now," Kling said. "Would you say this was at, what, three-thirty or thereabouts?"

"I didn't look at the clock," she said. "I heard his key in the latch, and I went in the kitchen, and there he was."

"Yes?"

"There's a meat cleaver I keep on the sink. I hit him with it."

"Why did you do that, Mrs. Martin?"

"Because I wanted to."

"Were you arguing with him, is that it?"

"No. He was locking the door, and I just went over to the sink and picked up the cleaver, and then I hit him with it,"

"Where did you hit him, Mrs. Martin?"

"On his head and on his neck and I think on his shoulder."

"You hit him three times with the cleaver?"

"I hit him a lot of times, I don't know how many times."

"Were you aware that you were hitting him?"

"Yes, I was aware."

"You knew you were striking him with a cleaver."

"Yes, I knew."

"Did you intend to kill him with the cleaver?"

"I intended to kill him with the cleaver."

"And afterwards, did you know you had killed him?"

"I knew he was dead, yes, the son of a bitch."

"What did you do then?"

"My oldest child came into the kitchen. Peter. My son. He yelled at me, he wanted to know what I'd done, he kept yelling at me. I hit him, too, to get him to shut up. I hit him only once, across the throat."

"Did you know what you were doing at the time?"

"I knew what I was doing. He was *another* one, that Peter. Little bastard."

"What happened next, Mrs. Martin?"

"I went in the back bedroom where the two girls sleep, and I hit Annie with the cleaver first, and then I hit Abigail."

"Where did you hit them, Mrs. Martin?"

"On the face. Their faces."

"How many times?"

"I think I hit Annie twice, and Abigail only once."

"Why did you do that, Mrs. Martin?"

"Who would take care of them after I was gone?" Mrs. Martin asked of no one.

"Is there anything else you want to tell us?" Kling asked.

"There's nothing more to tell. I done the right thing."

The detectives walked away from the desk. They were both pale. "Man," O'Brien whispered.

"Yeah," Kling said. "We'd better call the night D.A. right away, get him to take a full confession from her."

"Killed four of them without batting an eyelash," O'Brien said, and shook his head, and went back to where the stenographer was typing up Mrs. Martin's statement.

The telephone was ringing. Kling walked to the nearest desk and lifted the receiver. "Eighty-seventh Squad, Detective Kling," he said.

"This is Donner."

"Yeah, Fats."

"I think I got a lead on one of those heaps."

"Shoot."

"This would be the one heisted on Fourteenth Street. According to the dope I've got, it happened yesterday morning. Does that check out?"

"I'll have to look at the bulletin again. Go ahead Fats."

"It's already been ditched," Donner said. "If you're looking for it, try outside the electric company on the River Road."

"Thanks, I'll make a note of that. Who stole it, Fats?"

"This is strictly *entre nous*," Donner said, "I don't want *no* tie-in with it *never*. The guy who done it is a mean little bastard, rip out his mother's heart for a dime. He hates niggers, killed two of them in a street rumble four years ago, and managed to beat the rap. I think maybe some officer was on the take, huh, Kling?"

"You can't square homicide in this city, and you know it, Fats."

"Yeah? I'm surprised. You can square damn near anything else for a couple of bills."

"What's his name?"

"Danny Ryder. 3541 Grover Avenue, near the park. You won't find him there now, though."

"Where *will* I find him now?"

"Ten minutes ago, he was in an all-night bar on Mason, place called Felicia's. You going in after him?"

"I am."

"Take your gun," Donner said.

There were seven people in Felicia's when Kling got there at a quarter to five. He cased the bar through the plate glass window fronting the place, unbuttoned the third button of his overcoat, reached in to clutch the butt of his revolver, worked it out of the holster once and then back again, and went in through the front door.

There was the immediate smell of stale cigarette smoke and beer and sweat and cheap perfume. A Puerto Rican girl was in whispered consultation with a sailor in one of the leatherette booths. Another sailor was hunched over the jukebox, thoughtfully considering his next selection, his face tinted orange and red and green from the colored tubing. A tired, fat, fifty-year-old blonde sat at the far end of the bar, watching the sailor as though the next button he pushed might destroy the entire world. The bartender was polishing glasses. He looked up when Kling walked in and immediately smelled the law.

Two men were seated at the opposite end of the bar.

One of them was wearing a blue turtleneck sweater, gray slacks and desert boots. His brown hair was cut close to his scalp in a military cut. The other man was wearing a bright orange team jacket, almost luminous with the words *Orioles, S.A.C.* lettered across its back in Old English script. The one with the crew cut said something softly, and the other one chuckled. Behind the bar, a glass clinked as the bartender replaced it on the shelf. The jukebox erupted in sound, Jimi Hendrix rendering "All Along the Watchtower."

Kling walked over to the two men.

"Which one of you is Danny Ryder?" he asked.

The one with the short hair said, "Who wants to know?"

"Police officer," Kling said, and the one in the orange jacket whirled with a pistol in his hand, and Kling's eyes opened wide in surprise, and the gun went off.

There was no time to think, there was hardly any time to breathe. The explosion of the gun was shockingly close, the acrid stink of cordite rushed into his nostrils. The knowledge that he was still alive, the sweet rushing clean awareness that the bullet had somehow missed him was only a fleeting click of intelligence accompanying what was essentially a reflexive act. The .38 came free of its holster, his finger was inside the trigger guard and around the trigger, he squeezed off his shot almost before the gun had cleared the flap of his overcoat, fired into the orange jacket and threw his shoulder simultaneously against the chest of the man with the short hair, knocking him backward off his stool. The man in the orange jacket, his face twisted in pain, was leveling the gun for another shot. Kling fired again, squeezing the trigger without thought or rancor, and then whirling on the man with the short hair, who was crouched on the floor against the bar.

"Get up!" he yelled.

"Don't shoot."

"Get up, you son of a bitch!"

He yanked the man to his feet, hurled him against the bar, thrust the muzzle of his pistol at the blue turtleneck sweater, ran his hands under the armpits and between the legs while the man kept saying over and over again, "Don't shoot, please don't shoot."

He backed away from him and leaned over the one in the orange jacket.

"Is this Ryder?" he asked.

"Yes."

"Who're you?"

"Frank ... Frank Pasquale. Look, I ..."

"Shut up, Frank," Kling said. "Put your hands behind your back. Move!"

He had already taken his handcuffs from his belt. He snapped them onto Pasquale's wrists now, and only then became aware that Jimi Hendrix was still singing, the sailors were watching with pale white faces, the Puerto Rican girl was screaming, the fat faded blonde had her mouth open, the bartender was frozen in mid-motion, the tip of the bar towel inside a glass.

"All right," Kling said. He was breathing harshly. "All right," he said again, and wiped his forehead.

Timothy Allen Ames was a pot-bellied man of forty, with a thick black mustache, a mane of long black hair, and brown eyes sharply alert at five minutes past five in the morning. He answered the door as though he'd been already awake, asked for identification, and then asked the detectives to wait a moment, and closed the door, and came back shortly afterwards, wearing a robe over his striped pajamas.

"Is your name Timothy Ames?" Carella asked.

"That's me," Ames said. "Little late to be paying a visit, ain't it?"

"Or early, depending on how you look at it," Hawes said.

"One thing I can do without at five a.m. is humorous cops," Ames said. "How'd you get up here, anyway? Is the little jerk asleep at the desk again?"

"Who do you mean?" Carella asked.

"Lonnie Sanford, whatever the hell his name is."

"*Ronnie* Sanford."

"Yeah, him. Little bastard's always giving me trouble."

"What kind of trouble?"

"About broads," Ames said. "Acts like he's running a nunnery here, can't stand to see a guy come in with a girl. I notice he ain't got no compunctions about letting *cops* upstairs, though, no matter *what* time it is."

"Never mind Sanford, let's talk about you," Carella said.

"Sure, what would you like to know?"

"Where were you between eleven-twenty and twelve o'clock tonight?"

"Right here."

"Can you prove it?"

"Sure. I got back here about eleven o'clock, and I been here since. Ask Sanford downstairs ... no, never mind, he wasn't on yet. He don't come on till midnight."

"Who *else* can we ask, Ames?"

"Listen, you going to make trouble for me?"

"Only if you're *in* trouble."

"I got a broad here. She's over eighteen, don't worry. But, like, she's a junkie, you know? She ain't holding or nothing, but I know you guys, and if you want to make trouble..."

"Where is she?"

"In the john."

"Get her out here."

"Look, do me a favor, will you? Don't bust the kid. She's trying to kick the habit, she really is. I been helping her along."

"How?"

"By keeping her busy," Ames said, and winked.

"Call her."

"Bea, come out here!" Ames shouted.

There was a moment's hesitation, and then the bathroom door opened. The girl was a tall, plain brunette wearing a short terry cloth robe. She sidled into the room cautiously, as though expecting to be struck in the face at any moment. Her brown eyes were wide with expectancy. She knew fuzz, and she knew what it was like to be busted on a narcotics charge, and she had listened to the conversation from behind the closed bathroom door, and now she waited for whatever was coming, expecting the worst.

"What's your name, miss?" Hawes asked.

"Beatrice Norden."

"What time did you get here tonight, Beatrice?"

"About eleven."

"Was this man with you?"

"Yes."

"Did he leave here at any time tonight?"

"No."

"Are you sure."

"I'm positive. He picked me up about nine o'clock ..."

"Where do you live, Beatrice?"

"Well, that's the thing, you see," the girl said. "I been put out of my room."

"So where'd he pick you up?"

"At my girl friend's house. You can ask her, she was there when he came. Her name is Rosalie Dewes. Anyway, Timmy picked me up at nine, and we went to eat Chink's, and then we came up here around eleven."

"I hope you're telling us the truth, Miss Norden," Carella said.

"I swear to God, we been here all night," Beatrice answered.

"All right, Ames," Hawes said, "we'd like a sample of your handwriting."

"My *what*?"

"Your handwriting."

"What for?"

"We collect autographs," Carella said.

"Gee, these guys really break me up," Ames said to the girl. "Regular night-club comics we get in the middle of the night."

Carella handed him a pen and then tore a sheet from his pad. "You want to write this for me?" he said. "The first part's in block lettering."

"What the hell is block lettering?" Ames asked.

"He means *print* it," Hawes said.

"Then why didn't he say so?"

"Put on your clothes, miss." Carella said.

"What for?" Beatrice said. "I mean the thing is, I was in bed when you guys..."

"That's what I want him to write," Carella explained.

"Oh."

"Put on your clothes, miss," Ames repeated, and lettered it onto the sheet of paper. "What else?" he asked, looking up.

"Now sign it in your own handwriting with the following words: The Avenging Angel."

"What the hell is this supposed to be?" Ames asked.

"You want to write it, please?"

Ames wrote the words, and then handed the slip of paper to Carella. He and Hawes compared it with the note that had been mailed to Mercy Howell:

Put on your
Close, Miss!
The Avenging Angel

———————

Put on your Clothes,
Miss.
The Avenging Angel

"So?" Ames asked.

"So, you're clean," Hawes said.

"Imagine if I was dirty," Ames answered.

At the desk downstairs Ronnie Sanford was still immersed in his accounting textbook. He got to his feet again as the detectives came out of the elevator, adjusted his glasses on his nose, and then said, "Any luck?"

"Afraid not," Carella answered. "We're going to need the register for a while, if that's okay."

"Well..."

"Give him a receipt for it, Cotton," Carella said. It was late, and he didn't want a debate in the lobby of a run-down hotel. Hawes quickly made out a receipt in duplicate, signed both copies and handed one to Sanford.

"What about this torn cover?" Hawes asked belatedly.

"Yeah," Carella said. There was a small rip on the leather binding of the book, he fingered it briefly now, and then said, "Better note that on the receipt, Cotton." Hawes took back the receipt and, on both copies, jotted the words "Small rip on front cover." He handed the receipts back to Sanford.

"Want to just sign these, Mr. Sanford?" he said.

"What for?" Sanford asked.

"To indicate we received the register in this condition."

"Oh, sure," Sanford said. He picked up a ball-point pen from its desk holder, and asked, "What do you want me to write?"

"Your name and your title, that's all."

"My title?"

"Night Clerk, The Addison Hotel."

"Oh, sure," Sanford said, and signed both receipts. "This okay?" he asked. The detectives looked at what he had written.

"You like girls?" Carella asked suddenly.

"What?" Sanford asked.

"Girls," Hawes said.

"Sure. Sure, I like girls."

"Dressed or naked?"

"What?"

"With clothes or without?"

"I ... I don't know what you mean sir."

"Where were you tonight between eleven-twenty and midnight?" Hawes asked.

"Getting ... getting ready to come to ... to work," Sanford said.

"You sure you weren't in the alley of the Eleventh Street Theater stabbing a girl named Mercy Howell?"

"What? No ... no, of course ... of course not. I was ... I was ... I was home ... getting ... getting dressed ... to ... to ..." Sanford took a deep breath and decided to get indignant. "Listen, what's this all about?" he said. "Would you mind telling me?"

"It's all about *this*," Carella said, and turned one of the receipts so that Sanford could read the signature:

Ronald Sanford
Night Clerk
The Addison Hotel

"Get your hat," Hawes said. "Study hall's over."

It was twenty-five minutes past five when Adele Gorman came into the room with Meyer's cup of tea. He was crouched near the air-conditioning unit recessed into the wall to the left of the drapes, and he glanced over his shoulder when he heard her, and then rose.

"I didn't know what you took," she said "so I brought everything."

"Thank you," he said. "Just a little milk and sugar is fine."

"Have you measured the room?" she asked, and put the tray down on the table in front of the sofa.

"Yes, I think I have everything I need now," Meyer said. He put a spoonful of sugar into the tea, stirred it, added a drop of milk, stirred it again, and then lifted the cup to his mouth. "Hot," he said.

Adele Gorman was watching him silently. She said nothing. He kept sipping his tea. The ornate clock on the mantelpiece ticked in a swift whispering tempo.

"Do you always keep this room so dim?" Meyer asked.

"Well, my husband is blind, you know," Adele said. "There's really no need for brighter light."

"Mmm. But your father reads in this room, doesn't he?"

"I beg your pardon?"

"The night you came home from that party. He was sitting in the chair over there near the floor lamp. Reading. Remember?"

"Oh. Yes, he was."

"Bad light to read by."

"Yes, I suppose it is."

"I think maybe those bulbs are defective," Meyer said.

"Do you think so?"

"Mmm. I happened to look at the lamp, and there are three hundred-watt bulbs in it, all of them burning. You should be getting a lot more illumination with that kind of wattage."

"Well, I really don't know too much about..."

"Unless the lamp is on a rheostat, of course."

"I'm afraid I don't know what a rheostat is."

"It's an adjustable resistor. You can dim your lights or make them brighter with it. I thought maybe the lamp was on a rheostat, but I couldn't find a control knob anywhere in the room." Meyer paused. "You wouldn't know if there's a rheostat control someplace in the house, would you?"

"I'm sure there isn't," Adele said.

"Must be defective bulbs then," Meyer said, and smiled. "Also, I think your air conditioner is broken."

"No, I'm sure it isn't."

"Well, I was just looking at it, and all the switches are turned to the 'On' position, but it isn't working. So I guess it's broken. That's a shame too, because it's such a nice unit. Sixteen thousand BTUs. That's a lot of cooling power for a room this size. We've got one of those big old price-fixed apartments on Concord, my wife and I, with a large bedroom, and we get adequate cooling from a half-ton unit. It's a shame this one is broken."

"Yes. Detective Meyer, I don't wish to appear rude, but it *is* late . . ."

"Sure," Meyer said. "Unless, of course, the air conditioner's on a remote switch, too. So that all you have to do is turn a knob in another part of the house and it comes on." He paused. "*Is* there such a switch someplace, Mrs. Gorman?"

"I have no idea."

"I'll just finish my tea and run along," Meyer said. He lifted the cup to his lips, sipped at the tea, glanced at her over the rim, took the cup away from his mouth, and said, "But I'll be back."

"I hardly think there's any need for that," Adele said.

"Well, some jewelry's been stolen . . ."

"The ghosts . . ."

"Come off it, Mrs. Gorman."

The room went silent.

"Where are the loudspeakers, Mrs. Gorman?" Meyer asked. "In the false beams up there? They're hollow, I checked them out."

"I think perhaps you'd better leave," Adele said slowly.

"Sure," Meyer said. He put the teacup down, sighed, and got to his feet.

"I'll show you out," Adele said.

They walked to the front door and out into the driveway. The night was still. The drizzle had stopped, and a thin layer of frost covered the grass rolling away toward the river below. Their footsteps crunched on the gravel as they walked slowly toward the automobile.

"My husband was blinded four years ago," Adele said abruptly. "He's a chemical engineer, there was an explosion at the plant, he could have been killed. Instead, he was only blinded." She hesitated an instant, and then said again, "Only blinded," and there was such a sudden cry of despair in those words that Meyer wanted to put his arm around her, console her the way he might his daughter, tell her that everything would be all right come morning, the night was almost done, and morning was on the horizon. He leaned on the fender of his car, and she stood beside him looking down at the driveway gravel, her eyes not meeting his. They could have been conspirators exchanging secrets in the night, but they were only two people who had been thrown together on a premise as flimsy as the ghosts that inhabited the house.

"He gets a disability pension from the company," Adele said, "they've really been quite kind to us. And, of course, I work. I teach school, Detective Meyer. Kindergarten. I love children." She paused. She would not raise her eyes to meet his. "But . . . it's sometimes very difficult. My father, you see . . ."

Meyer waited. He longed suddenly for dawn, but he waited patiently, and heard her catch her breath as though committed to go ahead now, however painful the revelation might be, compelled to throw herself upon the mercy of the night before the morning sun broke through.

"My father's been retired for fifteen years." She took a deep breath, and then said, "He gambles, Detective Meyer. He's a horse player. He loses large sums of money."

"Is that why he stole your jewels?" Meyer asked.

"You know, don't you?" Adele said simply, and raised her eyes to his. "Of course you know. It's quite transparent, his ruse, a shoddy little show really, a performance that would fool no one but . . . no one but a blind man." She brushed at her cheek; he could not tell whether the cold air had caused her sudden tears. "I . . . I really don't care about the theft, the jewels were left to me by my mother, and after all it was my father who bought them for her, so it's . . . it's really like returning a legacy, I really don't care about that part of it. I . . . I'd have *given* the jewelry to him if only he'd asked, but he's so proud, such a proud man. A proud man who who steals from me and pretends that ghosts are committing the crime. And my husband, in his dark universe, listens to the sounds my father puts on tape and visualizes things he cannot quite believe and so he asks me to contact the police because he needs an impartial observer to contradict the suspicion that someone is stealing pennies from his blind man's cup. That's why I came to you, Detective Meyer. So that you would arrive here tonight and perhaps be fooled as I was fooled at first, and perhaps say to my husband, 'Yes, Mr. Gorman, there *are* ghosts in your house.'" She suddenly placed her hand on his sleeve. The tears were streaming down her face, she had difficulty catching her breath. "Because you see, Detective Meyer, there *are* ghosts in this house, there really and truly are. The ghost of a proud man who was once a brilliant judge and lawyer and who is now a gambler and thief; and the ghost of a man who once could see, and who now trips and falls in . . . in the darkness."

On the river, a tugboat hooted. Adele Gorman fell silent. Meyer opened the door of his car and got in behind the wheel.

"I'll call your husband tomorrow," he said abruptly and gruffly. "Tell him I'm convinced something supernatural is happening here."

"And will you be back, Detective Meyer?"

"No," he said. "I won't be back, Mrs. Gorman."

In the squadroom they were wrapping up the night. Their day had begun at 7:45 p.m. yesterday, and they had been officially relieved at 5:45 a.m., but they had not left the office yet because there were still questions to be asked, reports to be typed, odds and ends to put in place before they could go home. And since the relieving detectives were getting *their* approaching workday organized, the squadroom at 6 a.m. was busier than it might have been on any given afternoon, with two teams of cops getting in each other's way.

In the Interrogation Room, Carella and Hawes were questioning young Ronald Sanford in the presence of the assistant district attorney who had come over earlier to take Mrs. Martin's confession, and who now found himself listening to another one when all he wanted to do was go home to sleep. Sanford seemed terribly shocked that they had been able to notice the identical handwriting in "The Addison Hotel" and "The Avenging Angel," he couldn't get over it. He thought he had been very clever in mis-spelling the word "clothes," because then if they ever *had* traced the note, they would think some illiterate had written it, and not someone who was studying to be an accountant. He could not explain why he had killed Mercy Howell. He got all mixed up when he tried to explain that. It had something to do with the moral climate of America, and people exposing themselves in public, people like that shouldn't be allowed to pollute others, to foist their filth upon others, to intrude upon the privacy of others who only wanted to make a place for themselves in the world, who were trying very hard to make something, studying accounting by day and working in a hotel by night, what right had these other people to ruin it for everybody else?

Frank Pasquale's tune, sung in the Clerical Office to Kling and O'Brien, was not quite so hysterical, but similar to Sanford's nonetheless. He had got the idea together with Danny Ryder. They had decided between them that the niggers in America were getting too damn pushy, shoving their way in where they didn't belong, taking jobs away from decent hard-working people who only wanted to be left alone, what right did they have to force themselves on everybody else? So they had decided to bomb the church, just to show the goddamn boogies that you couldn't get away with shit like that, not in America. He didn't seem too terribly concerned over the fact that his partner was lying stone cold dead on a slab at the morgue, or that their little Culver Avenue expedition had cost three people their lives, and had severely injured a half-dozen others. All he wanted to know, repeatedly, was whether his picture would be in the newspaper.

At his desk, Meyer Meyer started to type up a report on the Gorman ghosts, and then decided the hell with it. If the lieutenant asked him where he'd been half the night, he would say he had been out cruising, looking for trouble in the streets. Christ knew there was enough of *that* around. He pulled the report forms and their separating sheets of carbon paper from the ancient typewriter, and noticed that Detective Hal Willis was pacing the room anxiously, waiting to get at the desk the moment he vacated it.

"Okay, Hal," he said "it's all yours."

"*Finalmente!*" Willis, who was not Italian, said.

The telephone rang.

The sun was up when they came out of the building and walked past the hanging green "87" globes and down the low flat steps to the sidewalk. The park across the street shimmered with early morning autumn brilliance, the sky above it clear and blue. It was going to be a beautiful day. They walked toward the diner on the next block, Meyer and O'Brien ahead of the others, Carella, Hawes and Kling bringing up the rear. They were tired, and exhaustion showed in their eyes and in the set of their mouths, and in the pace they kept. They talked without animation, mostly about their work, their breaths feathery and white on the cold morning air. When they reached the diner, they took off their overcoats and ordered hot coffee and cheese Danish and toasted English muffins. Meyer said he thought he was coming down with a cold. Carella told him about some cough medicine his wife had given one of the children. O'Brien, munching on a muffin glanced across the diner and saw a young girl in one of the booths. She was wearing blue jeans and a brightly colored Mexican serape, and she was talking to a boy wearing a Navy pea jacket.

"I think I see somebody," he said, and he moved out of the booth past Kling and Hawes, who were talking about the new goddamn regulations on search and seizure.

The girl looked up when he approached the booth.

"Miss Blair?" he said. "Penelope Blair?"

"Yes," the girl answered. "Who are you?"

"Detective O'Brien," he said, "the Eighty-seventh Squad. Your mother was in last night, Penny. She asked me to tell you..."

"Flake off, cop," Penelope Blair said. "Go stop a riot someplace."

O'Brien looked at her silently for a moment. He nodded then, and turned away, and went back to the table.

"Anything?" Kling asked.

"You can't win 'em all," O'Brien said.

2

Daywatch

The boy who lay naked on the concrete in the backyard of the tenement was perhaps eighteen years old. He wore his hair quite long, and he had recently begun growing a beard. His hair and his beard were black. His body was very white, and the blood that oozed onto the concrete pavement was very red.

The superintendent of the building discovered him at two minutes before 6 a.m., when he went to put his garbage in one of the cans out back. The boy was lying face down in his own blood, and the super did not recognize him. He was shocked, of course. He did not ordinarily discover naked dead men in the backyard when he went to put out his garbage. But considering his shock, and considering his advanced age (he was approaching eighty), he managed to notify the police with considerable dispatch, something not every good citizen of the city managed to do quite so well or so speedily.

Hal Willis arrived on the scene at fifteen minutes past six, accompanied by Richard Genero, who was the newest man on the squad, having been recently promoted from patrolman to Detective 3rd/Grade. Forbes and Phelps, the two men from Homicide, were already there. It was Willis' contention that any pair of Homicide cops was the same as any other pair of Homicide cops. He had never, for example, seen Forbes and Phelps in the same room with Monoghan and Monroe. Was this not undeniable proof that they were one and the same couple? Moreover, it seemed to Willis that all Homicide cops exchanged clothing regularly, and that Forbes and Phelps could on any given day of the week be found wearing suits and overcoats belonging to Monoghan and Monroe.

"Good morning," Willis said.

"Morning," Phelps said.

Forbes grunted.

"Nice way to start a goddamn Sunday, right?" Phelps asked.

"You fellows got here pretty fast," Genero said.

Forbes looked at him. "Who're you?"

"Dick Genero."

"Never heard of you," Forbes said.

"I never heard of you, neither," Genero answered, and glanced to Willis for approval.

"Who's the dead man?" Willis asked drily. "Anybody ever hear of *him*?"

"He sure as hell ain't carrying any identification," Phelps said, and cackled hoarsely.

"Not unless he's got it shoved up his ass someplace," Forbes said, and began laughing along with his partner.

"Who found the body?" Willis asked.

"Building superintendent."

"Want to get him, Dick?"

"Right," Genero said, and walked off.

"I hate to start my day like this," Phelps said.

"Grisly," Forbes said.

"All I had this morning was a cup of coffee," Phelps said. "And now *this*. Disgusting."

"Nauseating," Forbes said.

"Least have the decency to put on some goddamn clothes before he jumps off the roof," Phelps said.

"How do you know he jumped off the roof?" Willis asked.

"I don't. I'm only saying."

"What do you *think* he was doing?" Forbes asked. "Walking around the backyard naked?"

"I don't know," Willis said, and shrugged.

"Looks like a jumper to me," Phelps said. He glanced up at the rear wall of the building. "Isn't that a broken window up there?"

"Where?"

"Fourth floor there. Isn't that window broken there?"

"Looks like it," Forbes said.

"Sure looks like it to me," Phelps said.

"Hal, here's the super," Genero said, approaching with the old man. "Name's Mr. Dennison, been working here for close to thirty years."

"How do you do, Mr. Dennison? I'm Detective Willis."

Dennison nodded and said nothing.

"I understand you found the body."

"That's right."

"When was that?"

"Just before I called the cops."

"What time was that, Mr. Dennison?"

"Little after six, I guess."

"Know who it is?"

"Can't see his face," Dennison said.

"We'll roll him over for you as soon as the M.E. gets here," Genero said.

"Don't do me no favors," Dennison answered.

Unlike patrolmen, detectives – with the final approval of the Chief downtown – decide upon their own work schedules. As a result, the shifts will vary according to the whims of the men on the squad. For the past three months, and based on the dubious assumption that the night shift was more arduous than the day, the detectives of the 87th Squad had broken their working hours into two shifts, the first beginning at six in the morning and ending at eight in the evening, the second beginning then and ending at six the next day. The daywatch was fourteen hours long, the nightwatch only ten. But there were more men on duty during the day, and presumably this equalized the load. That some of these men were testifying in court or out on special assignments some of the time seemed not to bother any of the detectives, who considered the schedule equitable. At least for the time being. In another month or so, someone would come up with suggestions for a revised schedule, and they'd hold a meeting in the Interrogation Office and agree that they ought to try something new. A change was as good as a rest, provided the Chief approved.

As with any schedule, though, there were ways of beating it if you tried hard enough. Relieving the departing team at fifteen minutes before the hour was a mandatory courtesy, and one way of avoiding a 5:45 a.m. arrival at the squadroom was to plant yourself in a grocery store that did not open its doors until six-thirty. Detective Andy Parker found himself just such a grocery store on this bright October morning. The fact that the store had been robbed three times in broad daylight during the past month was only incidental. The point was that *some* detective had to cover the joint, and Andy Parker fortuitously happened to *be* that detective. The first thing he did to ingratiate himself with the owner was to swipe an apple from the fruit stand outside the store. The owner, one Silvio Corradini, who was sharp of eye for all his seventy-two years, noticed the petty larceny the moment it was committed. He was about to run out on the sidewalk to apprehend the brigand, when the man began walking directly into the store, eating the apple as he came. It was then that Silvio realized the man could be nothing but a cop.

"Good morning," Parker said.

"Good morning," Silvio replied. "You enjoy the fruit?"

"Yeah, very good apple," Parker said. "Thanks a lot." He grinned amiably. "I'm Detective Parker," he said, "I've been assigned to these holdups."

"What happened to the other detective?"

"Di Maeo? He's on vacation."

"In October?"

"We can't all get the summertime, huh?" Parker said, and grinned again. He was a huge man wearing rumpled brown corduroy trousers and a soiled tan windbreaker. He had shaved this morning before eating breakfast, but he managed to look unshaven nonetheless. He bit into the apple ferociously, juice spilling onto his chin. Silvio watching him, thought he resembled a hired gun for the Mafia.

"*Lei è italiano?*" he asked.

"What?"

"Are you Italian?"

"No, are you?" Parker said, and grinned.

"Yes," Silvio answered. He drew back his shoulders. "Yes, I'm Italian."

"Well, good, good," Parker said. "You always open the store on Sunday?"

"What?"

"I said . . ."

"I only stay open till twelve o'clock, that's all," Silvio said, and shrugged. "I get the people coming home from church."

"That's against the law in this state, you know that?"

"Nobody ever said anything."

"Well, just because somebody's willing to look the other way every now and then, that doesn't make it legal," Parker said. He stared deep into Silvio's eyes. "We'll talk about it later, huh? Meantime, fill me in on these holdups, okay?"

Silvio hesitated. He knew that talking about it later would cost him money. He was beginning to be sorry he'd ever told the police about the holdups. He sighed now and said, "It is three times in the past month."

"Same guy each time?"

"*Two* of them. I don't know if it's the same. They are wearing – *come si dice? Maschere.*"

"Masks?"

"*Si*, masks."

"Same masks each time?"

"No. Once it was stockings, another time black ones, the third time handkerchiefs."

Parker bit into the apple again. "Are they armed?" he asked.

"If they did not have guns, I would break their heads and throw them out on the sidewalk."

"Handguns?" Parker asked.

"What?"

"Pistols?"

"Yes, yes, pistols."

"Both of them armed, or just one?"

"Both."

"What time do they usually come in?"

"Different times. The first time was early in the morning when I just opened the store. The next time was at night, maybe six, six-thirty. The last time was around lunch, the store was very quiet."

"Did they take anything but cash?"

"Only cash."

"Well," Parker said, and shrugged. "Maybe they'll come back, who knows? If you don't mind, I'll just hang around, okay? You got a back room or something?"

"Behind the curtain," Silvio said. "But if they come back again, I am ready for them myself."

"What do you mean?"

"I got a gun now."

He walked behind the counter to the cash register, opened it, and removed from the drawer a .32 Smith & Wesson.

"You need a permit for that, you know," Parker said.

"I got one. A man gets held up three times, nobody argues about giving him a permit."

"Carry or premises?"

"Premises."

"You know how to use that thing?" Parker asked.

"I know how, yes."

"I've got some advice for you," Parker said. "If those hoods come back, leave your gun in the drawer. Let *me* take care of any shooting needs to be done."

A woman was coming into the store. Without answering, Silvio turned away from Parker, smiled, and said to her, "*Buon giorno, signora.*"

Parker sighed, threw the curtain back, and went into the other room.

"What do you think?" Willis asked the assistant medical examiner.

"Fell or was pushed from someplace up there," the M.E. said. "Split his skull wide open when he hit the ground. Probably dead on impact."

"Anything else?"

"What more do you want? You're lucky we haven't got an omelette here." He snapped his bag shut, rose from where he was crouched beside the body, and said, "I'm finished, you can do what you like with him."

"Thanks, Al," Willis said.

"Yeah," the M.E. answered, and walked off.

The body was now lying on its back. Genero looked down at the open skull and turned away. Dennison, the building superintendent, walked over with his hands in the pockets of his bib overalls. He looked down at the boy's bloody face and nodded.

"That's the kid in 4C," he said.

"What's his name?"

"Scott."

"That the first name or the last?"

"The last. I got his first name written down someplace inside. I got all the tenants' names written down. You want me to look it up for you?"

"Would you please?"

"Sure," Dennison said.

"Would that be 4C up there?" Willis asked. "The apartment with the broken window?"

"That's it, all right," Dennison said

The telephone on Arthur Brown's desk was ringing. He lifted the receiver, tucked it between his shoulder and his ear, said, "Eighty-seventh Squad, Detective Brown," and then glanced toward the slatted rail divider, where a patrolman was leading a handcuffed prisoner into the squadroom.

"Is this a detective?" the woman on the telephone asked.

"Yes, ma'am, Detective Brown."

"I want to report a missing person," the woman said.

"Yes, ma'am, just one second, please."

Brown opened his desk drawer, took out a block of wood to which was attached the key to the detention cage across the room, and flipped it to the patrolman, who missed the catch. The prisoner laughed. The patrolman picked up the key, led the prisoner to the cage, opened the grillwork door, and shoved him inside.

"Take it easy, man," the prisoner warned.

The patrolman locked the cage door without answering him. Then he walked to Brown's desk and sat on the edge of it, tilting his peaked cap back on his forehead and lighting a cigarette. On the telephone, Brown was saying, "Now, what's your name, please, ma'am?"

"Mary Ellingham. Mrs. Donald Ellingham."

"Would you spell that for me, please?"

"E-L-L..."

"Yep..."

"...I-N-G, H-A-M."

"And your address, Mrs. Ellingham?"

"742 North Trinity."

"All right, who's missing, Mrs. Ellingham?"

"My husband."

"That his full name? Donald Ellingham?"

"Yes. Well, no. Donald *E.* Ellingham. For Edward."

"Yes, ma'am. How long has he been gone?"

"He was gone a week this past Friday."

"Has this ever happened before, Mrs. Ellingham?"

"No. Never."

"He's never been gone before? Never any unexplained absences?"

"Never."

"And you say he's been missing since, let's see, that'd be Friday the ninth?"

"Yes."

"Did he go to work on Monday morning? The twelfth?"

"No."

"You called his office?"

"Yes, I did."

"And he wasn't there."

"He hasn't been there all week."

"Why'd you wait till today to report this, Mrs. Ellingham?"

"I wanted to give him a chance to come back. I kept extending the deadline, you see. I thought I'd give him a few days, and then it turned into a week, and then I thought I'd give him just another day, and then Saturday went by, and ... well, I decided to call today."

"Does your husband drink, Mrs. Ellingham?"

"No. That is, he drinks, but not excessively. He's not an alcoholic, if that's what you mean."

"Has there ever been any problem with ... well ... other women?"

"No."

"What I'm trying to say, Mrs. Ellingham ..."

"Yes, I understand. I don't think he's run off with another woman, no."

"What *do* you think has happened, Mrs. Ellingham?"

"I'm afraid he's been in an accident."

"Have you contacted the various hospitals in the city?"

"Yes. He's not at any of them."

"But you still think he may have been in an accident."

"I think he may be dead someplace," Mrs. Ellingham said, and began weeping. Brown was silent. He looked up at the patrolman.

"Mrs. Ellingham?"

"Yes."

"I'll try to get over there later today if I can, to get the information I'll need for the Missing Persons Bureau. Will you be home?"

"Yes."

"Shall I call first?"

"No, I'll be here all day."

"Fine, I'll see you later then. If you should hear anything meanwhile..."

"Yes, I'll call you."

"Good-bye, Mrs. Ellingham," Brown said, and hung up. "Lady's husband disappeared," he said to the patrolman.

"Went down for a loaf of bread a year ago, right?" the patrolman said.

"Right. Hasn't been heard from since." Brown gestured toward the detention cage. "Who's the prize across the room?"

"Caught him cold in the middle of a burglary on Fifth and Friedlander. On a third-floor fire escape. Jimmied open the window, and was just entering."

"Any tools on him?"

"Yep. I left them on the bench outside."

"Want to get them for me?"

The patrolman went out into the corridor. Brown walked over to the detention cage. The prisoner looked at him.

"What's your name?" Brown asked.

"What's yours?"

"Detective Arthur Brown."

"That's appropriate," the prisoner said.

"I find it so," Brown said coolly. "Now what's yours?"

"Frederick Spaeth."

The patrolman came back into the room carrying a leather bag containing a hand drill and bits of various sizes, a jimmy, a complete set of picklocks, several punches and skeleton keys, a pair of nippers, a hacksaw, a pair of brown cotton gloves, and a crowbar designed so that it could be taken apart and carried in three sections. Brown looked over the tools and said nothing.

"I'm a carpenter," Spaeth said in explanation.

Brown turned to the patrolman. "Anybody in the apartment, Simms?"

"Empty," Simms replied.

"Spaeth," Brown said, "we're charging you with burglary in the third degree, which is a felony. And we're also charging you with Possession of Burglar's Instruments, which is a Class-A Misdemeanor. Take him down, Simms."

"I want a lawyer," Spaeth said.

"You're entitled to one," Brown said.

"I want him *now. Before* you book me."

Because policemen are sometimes as confused by Miranda-Escobedo as are laymen, Brown might have followed the course pursued by his colleague Kling, who, the night before, had advised a prisoner of his rights even though cruising radio patrolmen had arrested him in the act. Instead, Brown said, "What for, Spaeth? You were apprehended entering an apartment illegally. Nobody's asking you any questions, we caught you cold. You'll be allowed three telephone calls after you're booked, to your lawyer, your mother, your bail bondsman, your best friend, whoever the hell you like. Take him down, Simms."

Simms unlocked the cage and prodded Spaeth out of it with his nightstick.

"This is illegal!" Spaeth shouted.

"So's breaking and entry," Brown answered.

The woman in the apartment across the hall from 4C was taller than both Willis and Genero, which was understandable. Hal Willis was the shortest man on the squad, having cleared the minimum five-feet-eight-inch height requirement by a scant quarter of an inch. Built like a soft shoe dancer, brown-haired and brown-eyed, he stood alongside Genero, who towered over him at five feet nine inches. Hal Willis knew he was short. Richard Genero thought he was very tall. From his father, he had inherited beautiful curly black hair and a strong Neapolitan nose, a sensuous mouth and soulful brown eyes. From his mother, he had inherited the tall Milanese carriage of all his male cousins and uncles – except Uncle Dominick, who was only five feet six. But this lady who opened the door to apartment 4B was a very big lady indeed. Both Willis and Genero looked up at her simultaneously, and then glanced at each other in something like stupefied awe. The lady was wearing a pink slip and nothing else. Barefooted, big-breasted, redheaded, green-eyed, she put her hands on her nylon-sheathed hips and said, "Yeah?"

"Police officers," Willis said, and showed her his shield.

The woman scrutinized it, and then said, "Yeah?"

"We'd like to ask you a few questions," Genero said.

"What about?"

"About the young man across the hall. Lewis Scott."

"What about him?"

"Do you know him?"

"Slightly."

"Only slightly?" Genero said. "You live directly across the hall from him..."

"So what? This is the city."

"Even so..."

"I'm forty-six years old, he's a kid of what? Eighteen? Nineteen? How do you *expect* me to know him? Intimately?"

"Well, no, ma'am but..."

"So that's how I know him. Slightly. Anyway, what about him?"

"Did you see him at any time last night?" Willis asked.

"No. Why? Something happen to him?"

"Did you hear anything unusual in his apartment anytime last night?"

"Unusual like what?"

"Like glass breaking?"

"I wasn't home last night. I went out to supper with a friend."

"What time was this?"

"Eight o'clock."

"And what time did you get back?"

"I didn't. I slept over."

"With your friend?"

"Yes."

"What's her name?" Genero asked.

"Her name is Morris Strauss, *that's* her name."

"Oh," Genero said. He glanced at Willis sheepishly.

"When *did* you get home, ma'am?" Willis asked.

"About five o'clock this morning. Morris is a milkman. He gets up very early. We had breakfast together, and then I came back here. Why? What's the matter? Did Lew do something?"

"Did you happen to see him at *any* time yesterday?"

"Yeah. When I was going to the store. He was just coming in the building."

"What time was that, would you remember?"

"About four-thirty. I was going out for some coffee. I ran out of coffee. I drink maybe six hundred cups of coffee a day. I'm always running out. So I was going up the street to the A&P to get some more. That's when I saw him."

"Was he alone?"

"No."

"Who was with him?"

"Another kid."

"Boy or girl?"

"A boy."

"Would you know who?" Genero asked.

"I don't hang around with teenagers, how would I...?"

"Well, you might have seen him around the neighborhood..."

"No."

"How old would you say he was?" Willis asked.

"About Lew's age. Eighteen, nineteen, I don't know. A big kid."

"Can you describe him?"

"Long blond hair, a sort of handlebar mustache. He was wearing a crazy jacket."

"What do you mean, crazy?"

"It was like an animal skin, with the fur inside and the, you know, what do you call it, the pelt. Is that what you call it?"

"Go ahead."

"The raw side, you know what I mean? The skin part. That was the outside of the jacket, and the fur was the inside. White fur. And there was a big orange sun painted on the back of the jacket."

"Anything else?"

"Ain't that enough?"

"Maybe it is," Willis said. "Thank you very much, ma'am."

"You're welcome," she answered. "You want some coffee? I got some on the stove."

"No, thanks, we want to take a look at the apartment here," Genero said. "Thanks a lot, though. You've been very kind."

The woman smiled so suddenly and so radiantly that it almost knocked Genero clear across the hallway to the opposite wall.

"Not at all," she said in a tiny little voice, and gently eased the door shut. Genero raised his eyebrows. He was trying to remember exactly what he had said, and in what tone of voice. He was still new at this business of questioning people, and any trick he could learn might prove helpful. The trouble was, he couldn't remember his exact words.

"What did I say?" he asked Willis.

"I don't remember," Willis answered.

"No, come on, Hal, what did I say? What made her smile that way, and all of a sudden get so nice?"

"I think you asked her if she'd like to go to bed with you," Willis said.

"No," Genero said seriously, and shook his head. "No, I don't think so."

With the passkey the superintendent had provided, Willis opened the door to 4C, and stepped into the apartment. Behind him, Genero was still pondering the subtleties of police interrogation.

There were two windows facing the entrance door. The lower pane of the window on the left was almost completely shattered, with here and there an isolated shard jutting from the window frame. Sunlight streamed through both windows, dust motes rising silently. The apartment was sparsely furnished, a mattress on the floor against one wall, a bookcase on the opposite wall, a stereo record player and a stack of LP albums beside it, a bridge table and two chairs in the kitchen alcove, where another window opened onto the fire escape. A black camp trunk studded with brass rivets served as a coffee table in the center of the room, near the record player. Brightly colored cushions lined the wall on either side of the bookcase. Two black-and-white anti-war posters decorated the walls. The windows were curtainless. In the kitchen alcove, the shelves over the stove carried only two boxes of breakfast cereal and a bowl of sugar. A bottle of milk and three containers of yogurt were in the refrigerator. In the vegetable tray, Willis found a plastic bag of what looked like oregano. He showed it to Genero.

"Grass?" Genero said.

Willis shrugged. He opened the bag and sniffed the greenish-brown, crushed leaves. "Maybe," he said. He pulled an evidence tag from his pad, filled it out, and tied it to the plastic bag.

They went through the apartment methodically. There were three coffee mugs on the camp trunk. Each of them smelled of wine, and there was a red lipstick stain on the rim of one cup. They opened the camp trunk and found it stuffed with dungarees, flannel shirts, undershorts, several sweaters, a harmonica, an army blanket, and a small metal cash box. The cash box was unlocked. It contained three dollars in change, and a high school G.O. card encased in plastic. In the kitchen they found two empty wine bottles in the garbage pail. A sprung mousetrap, the bait gone, was under the kitchen sink. On top of the closed toilet seat in the bathroom, they found a pair of dungarees with a black belt through the trouser loops, an orange Charlie Brown sweatshirt with the sleeves cut off raggedly at the elbows, a pair of white sweat socks, a pair of loafers and a woman's black silk blouse.

The blouse had a label in it.

They came into the grocery store at twenty minutes past seven, each of them wearing a Halloween mask, even though this was only the middle of the month and Halloween was yet two weeks away. They were both holding drawn guns, both dressed in black trench coats and black trousers. They walked rapidly from the front door to the counter, with the familiarity of visitors who had been there before. One of them was wearing a Wolf Man mask and the other was wearing a Snow White mask. The masks completely covered their faces and lent a terrifying nightmare aspect to their headlong rush for the counter.

Silvio's back was turned when they entered the store. He heard the bell over the door, and whirled quickly, but they were almost to the counter by then, and he had time to shout only the single word "*Ancora!*" before he punched the NO SALE key on the register and reached into the drawer for his gun. The man wearing the Snow White mask was the first to realize that Silvio was going for a gun. He did not say a word to his partner. Instead, he fired directly into Silvio's face at close range. The slug almost tore off Silvio's head and sent him spinning backward against the shelves. Canned goods clattered to the floor. The curtain leading to the back room was suddenly thrown open and Parker stood in the doorway with a .38 Police Special in his fist. The man with the Wolf Man mask had his hand in the cash drawer and was scooping up a pile of bills.

"Hold it!" Parker shouted, and the man with the Snow White mask fired again. His slug caught Parker in the right shoulder. Parker bent low and pulled off a wild shot just as the man at the cash register opened fire, aiming for Parker's belly, catching him in the leg instead. Parker grabbed for the curtain behind him, clutching for support, tearing it loose as he fell to the floor screaming in pain.

The two men in their Halloween masks ran out of the store and into the Sunday morning sunshine.

There were 186 patrolmen assigned to the 87th Precinct and on any given day of the week, their work schedule was outlined by a duty chart that required a PhD in Arabic literature to be properly understood. In essence, six of these patrolmen worked from 8 a.m. to 4 p.m., Monday through Friday, two of them serving as the Captain's clerical force, one as a highway safety patrolman, and the last two as community relations patrolman and roll call man respectively. The remaining 180 patrolmen were divided into twenty squads with nine men on each squad. Their duty chart looked like this:

TOURS OF DUTY

DAY ON CHART	12 MID. TO 8 A.M. SQUAD	8 A.M. TO 4 P.M. SQUAD	4 P.M. TO 12 MID. SQUAD
1	(1)-2-3-4-5	8-9-10-11-12	15-16-17-18-19
2	(2)-3-4-5-6	9-10-11-12-13	16-17-18-19-20
3	(3)-4-5-6-7	10-11-12-13-14	17-18-19-20-1
4	(4)-5-6-7-8	11-12-13-14-15	18-19-20-1-2
5	(5)-6-7-8-9	12-13-14-15-16	19-20-1-2-3
6	(6)-7-8-9-10	13-14-15-16-17	20-1-2-3-4
7	(7)-8-9-10-11	14-15-16-17-18	1-2-3-4-5
8	(8)-9-10-11-12	15-16-17-18-19	2-3-4-5-6
9	(9)-10-11-12-13	16-17-18-19-20	3-4-5-6-7
10	(10)-11-12-13-14	17-18-19-20-1	4-5-6-7-8
11	(11)-12-13-14-15	18-19-20-1-2	5-6-7-8-9
12	(12)-13-14-15-16	19-20-1-2-3	6-7-8-9-10
13	(13)-14-15-16-17	20-1-2-3-4	7-8-9-10-11
14	(14)-15-16-17-18	1-2-3-4-5	8-9-10-11-12
15	(15)-16-17-18-19	2-3-4-5-6	9-10-11-12-13
16	(16)-17-18-19-20	3-4-5-6-7	10-11-12-13-14
17	(17)-18-19-20-1	4-5-6-7-8	11-12-13-14-15
18	(18)-19-20-1-2	5-6-7-8-9	12-13-14-15-16
19	(19)-20-1-2-3	6-7-8-9-10	13-14-15-16-17
20	(20)-1-2-3-4	7-8-9-10-11	14-15-16-17-18

SCHEDULE OF DUTY FOR PATROLMEN § — 1969

Day on Chart	JAN.	FEB.	MAR.	APR.	MAY	JUNE	JULY	AUG.	SEPT.	OCT.	NOV.	DEC.
1	3-23	12	4-24	(13)	(3)-23	12	2-22	11-(31)	(20)	10-30	19	9-29
2	(4)-24	13	5-25	14	(4)-(24)	13	3-23	12	1-(21)	(11)-31	20	10-30
3	(5)-(25)	14	6-26	15	5-(25)	(14)	4-24	13	2-22	(12)	(1)-21	11-31
4	6-(26)	(15)	7-27	16	6-26	(15)	(5)-25	14	3-23	13	(2)-(22)	12
5	7-27	(16)	(8)-28	17	7-27	16	(6)-(26)	15	4-24	14	3-(23)	(13)
6	8-28	17	(9)-(29)	18	8-28	17	7-(27)	(16)	5-25	15	4-24	(14)
7	9-29	18	10-(30)	(19)	9-29	18	8-28	(17)	(6)-26	16	5-25	15
8	10-30	19	11-31	(20)	(10)-30	19	9-29	18	(7)-(27)	17	6-26	16
9	(11)-31	20	12	1-21	(11)-(31)	20	10-30	19	8-(28)	(18)	7-27	17
10	(12)	(1)-21	13	2-22	12	(1)-(21)	11-31	20	9-29	(19)	(8)-28	18
11	13	(2)-(22)	14	3-23	13	2-(22)	(12)	1-21	10-30	20	(9)-(29)	19
12	14	3-(23)	(15)	4-24	14	3-23	(13)	(2)-22	11	1-21	10-(30)	(20)
13	15	4-24	(16)	(5)-25	15	4-24	14	(3)-(23)	12	2-22	11	1-(21)
14	16	5-25	17	(6)-(26)	16	5-25	15	4-(24)	(13)	3-23	12	2-22
15	17	6-26	18	7-(27)	(17)	6-26	16	5-25	(14)	(4)-24	13	3-23
16	(18)	7-27	19	8-28	(18)	(7)-27	17	6-26	15	(5)-(25)	14	4-24
17	(19)	(8)-28	20	9-29	19	(8)-(28)	18	7-27	16	6-(26)	(15)	5-25
18	20	(9)	(1)-21	10-30	20	9-(29)	(19)	8-28	17	7-27	(16)	(6)-26
19	1-21	10	(2)-(22)	11	1-21	10-30	(20)	(9)-29	18	8-28	17	(7)-(27)
20	2-22	11	3-(23)	(12)	2-22	11	1-21	(10)-(30)	19	9-29	18	8-(28)

O AROUND SQUAD NUMBER INDICATES EXCUSAL EXCEPT WHEN IT CORRESPONDS WITH O AROUND DATE

O INDICATES SATURDAYS & SUNDAYS

§ TO BE USED BY: PATROL PRECINCTS, EMERGENCY SERVICE, ACCIDENT INVESTIGATION SQUAD, SGTS & PTL OF HARBOR PCT.

EFF. 1.1.66

All of which meant that patrolmen worked five tours for a forty-hour week, and then were off for fifty-six hours except when they were working the midnight to 8 a.m. shift, in which case they then worked only *four* tours and were off for eighty hours. Unless, of course, the *fifth* night tour happened to fall on a Friday or Saturday night, in which case they were required to work. All clear?

Patrolmen were supposed to be relieved on post as soon as possible after the hour by the squad that had just answered roll call in the precinct muster room. But most patrolmen began to drift back toward the station house shortly before the hour, so that seconds after the new shift trotted down the precinct steps, the old one entered the building and headed for the locker room to change into street clothes. There were a lot of cops in and around a police station when the shift was changing, and Sunday morning was no exception. If anything, the precinct was busier on Sunday because Saturday night brought thieves out like cockroaches and their resultant handiwork spilled over onto the day of rest.

This particular Sunday morning was more chaotic than usual because a cop had been shot, and nothing can galvanize a police department like the knowledge that one of their own has been gunned down. Lieutenant Peter Byrnes, who was in command of the sixteen detectives on the 87th Squad, saw fit to call in three men who were on vacation, perhaps on the theory that one wounded cop is worth at least three who were ambulatory. Not content to leave it at that, he then put in a call to Steve Carella at his home in Riverhead, ostensibly to inform him of the shooting.

Sitting behind his desk in the corner room upstairs, looking down at the front steps of the building, where the patrolmen filed out in pairs, the green globes flanking the steps and burning with sunshine as though fired from within, Byrnes must have known that Carella had worked the night shift and that the man did not now need a call from his superior officer. But he dialled the number nonetheless, and waited while the phone rang repeatedly on the other end. When at last Carella answered, Byrnes said, "Steve? Were you asleep?"

"No, I was just getting into my pajamas."

"Sorry to bother you this way."

"No, no, what is it Pete?"

"Parker just got shot in a grocery store on Ainsley."

"No kidding?"

"Yeah."

"Jesus," Carella said.

"Two hoods killed the proprietor, wounded Parker in the shoulder and leg. He's been taken to Buenavista Hospital. It looks pretty serious."

"Jesus," Carella said again.

"I've already called in Di Maeo, Levine, and Meriwether. They're on vacation, Steve, but I had to do it, I don't like it when cops get shot."

"No, neither do I."

"I just thought I'd tell you."

"Yeah, I'm glad you did, Pete."

The line went silent.

"Pete?"

"Yeah, Steve."

"What is it? Do you want *me* to come in, too?"

"Well, you had a long night, Steve."

The line went silent again.

"Well ... what do you want me to do, Pete?"

"Why don't you see how you feel?" Byrnes said. "Go to bed, get some rest, maybe you'll feel like coming in a little later, okay?" Byrnes paused. "I can use you, Steve. It's up to you."

"What time is it, anyway?" Carella asked.

Byrnes look up at the wall clock. "Little after eight. Get some rest, okay?"

"Yeah, okay," Carella said.

"I'll talk to you later," Byrnes said, and hung up. He rose from behind his desk, hooked his thumbs into his belt just above both hip pockets and walked to the window overlooking the park. He was a compact man with gray hair and flinty blue eyes, and he stood looking silently at the sun-washed foliage across the street, his face expressionless, and then turned suddenly and walked to the frosted glass door of his office, yanked it open, and went out into the squadroom.

A marine corporal was sitting with Detective Carl Kapek at the desk closest to the lieutenant's office. A swollen discolored lump the size of a baseball sat just over the marine's left eye. His uniform was rumpled and soiled, and he looked extremely embarrassed, his hands clasped in his lap rather like a schoolboy's. He spoke in a very low voice, almost a whisper, to Kapek as the lieutenant walked past them to where Brown was on the telephone at his own desk.

"Right, I'll tell him," Brown said, and replaced the phone on its cradle.

"That about Parker?" Byrnes asked.

"No, that was Delgado over on South Sixth. Guy was on his way to church, four other guys grabbed him as he came out of his building, damn near killed him. Delgado's on it now."

"Right. The hospital call back on Parker?"

"Not yet."

"Who's that in the holding cell downstairs?"

"A burglar Simms picked up on Fifth and Friedlander."

"You'd better get over to that grocery store, Artie."

"That'll leave Kapek all alone here."

"I've got some men coming in. They should be here anytime now."

"Okay then."

"I want some meat on this, Artie. I don't like my squad getting shot up."

Brown nodded, opened the top drawer of his desk, and took from it a holstered .38 Detective's Special. He fastened the holster to his belt just slightly forward of his right hip pocket, put on his jacket, and then went to the locker room to get his coat and hat. On his way out of the squadroom, he stopped at Kapek's desk and said, "I'll be at that grocery store, you need me."

"Okay," Kapek said, and turned back to the marine. "I still don't understand exactly how you got beat up," he said. "You mind going over it one more time?"

The marine looked even more embarrassed now. He was short and slender, dwarfed by Kapek, who sat beside him in his short sleeves with his tie pulled down, collar open, straight blond hair falling onto his forehead, wearing a shoulder holster from which protruded the walnut butt of a .38.

"Well, you know, I got jumped, is all," the marine said.

"How?"

"I was walking along, and I got jumped, is all."

"Where was this, Corporal Miles?"

"On The Stem."

"What time?"

"Must've been about three in the morning."

"What were you doing?"

"Just walking."

"Going any place in particular?"

"I'd just left this bar, you see? I'd been drinking in this bar on Seventeenth Street, I think it was."

"Anything happen in the bar?"

"Well, like what?"

"Any trouble? Any words?"

"No, no, it was a real nice bar."

"And you left there about three o'clock and started walking up The Stem."

"That's right."

"Where were you going?"

"Oh, just for a little walk, that's all. Before heading back to the ship. I'm on this battleship over to the Navy Yard. It's in dry dock there."

"Um-huh," Kapek said. "So you're walking along and this man jumped you."

"Mmm."

"Just one man?"

"Yeah. One."

"What'd he hit you with?"

"I don't know."

"And you came to just a little while ago, is that it?"

"Yeah. And found out the bastards had taken my wallet and watch."

Kapek was silent for several seconds. Then he said, "I thought there was only one of them."

"That's right. Just one."

"You said 'bastards'."

"Huh?"

"Plural."

"Huh?"

"How many were there actually, Corporal?"

"Who hit me, you mean? Like I said. Just one."

"Never mind who hit you or who didn't. How many were there altogether?"

"Well ... two."

"All right, let's get this straight now. It was *two* men who jumped you, not ..."

"Well, no. Not exactly."

"Look, Corporal," Kapek said, "you want to tell me about this, or you want to forget it? We're pretty busy around here right now, and I don't have time for this kind of thing, I mean it. You want us to try to recover your stuff, then give us a little help, okay? Otherwise, so long, it was nice meeting you, I hope you get back to your ship all right."

Miles was silent for several moments. Then he sighed deeply and said, "I feel like a goddamn jackass, is all."

"Why? What happened?"

"There was this girl in the bar ..."

"I figured," Kapek said, and nodded.

"In a red dress. She kept wiggling her ass at me all night long, you know? So I finally started a conversation with her, and she was real friendly and all, I mean she didn't seem to be *after* nothing, I think I maybe bought her only two drinks the whole night long."

"Yeah, go ahead."

"So a little before three, she tells me she's awful tired and wants to go home to bed, and she says good night to everybody, and then goes to the door and winks at me and gives me a kind of a little come-on move with her head, you know? Like this, you know? Like just this little movement of her head, you know? To tell me I should follow her. So I paid the check, and hurried on outside, and there she was on the corner, and she starts walking the minute she sees me, looking back over her shoulder, and giving me that same come-on again, trotting her little ass right up the avenue, and then turning off into one of the side streets. So I turned the corner after her and there's this guy standing there, and wham, he clobbers me. Next thing I know, I wake up with *this* fucking thing over my eye, and my money gone, and my watch, too. Little bitch."

"Was she black or white?"

"Black."

"And the man?"

"White."

"Would you recognize her if you saw her again?"

"I'll never forget her long as I live."

"What about the man?"

"I only got a quick look at him. He hit me the minute I come round that corner. Man, I saw stars. They musta moved me after I went out because I woke up in this hallway, you see. I mean, I was laying on the sidewalk when . . ." Miles stopped and looked down at his hands.

"Yes, Corporal?"

"What gets me is, I mean, she *kicked* me, the little bitch. When I was down on the sidewalk, she kicked me with this goddamn pointed shoe of hers. I mean, man, *that's* what put me out, not the guy hitting me. It was her kicking me with that pointed shoe of hers." Corporal Miles looked up plaintively. "Why'd she do *that*, huh? I was nice to her. I mean it. I was only nice."

The ambulance had come and gone, carrying away the man who had been attacked as he was leaving his home to go to church. It was now nine o'clock and there was still blood on the front stoop of the building. Detective 3rd/Grade Alexiandre Delgado stood on the steps with the victim's wife and two children, and tried to believe they were unaware of the blood drying in the early morning sunshine. Mrs. Huerta was a black-haired woman with brown eyes filled now with tears. Her two daughters, dressed to go to church, wearing identical green wool coats and black patent leather shoes and white ankle socks, resembled their mother except for the tears. Their brown eyes were opened wide in curiosity and fright and incomprehension. But neither of the two was crying. A crowd of bystanders kept nudging toward the stoop, despite the efforts of the beat patrolman to disperse them.

"Can you tell me exactly what happened, Mrs. Huerta?" Delgado asked. Like the woman he was questioning, he was Puerto Rican. And like her, he had been raised in a ghetto. Not this one, but a similar one (when you've seen *one* slum, you've seen them all, according to certain observers) in the shadow of Calm's Point Bridge downtown. He could have spoken to her in fluent Spanish, but he was still slightly embarrassed by his accent when he was speaking English, and as a result he tried to speak it *all* the time. Mrs. Huerta, on the other hand, was not so sure she wanted to conduct the conversation in English. Her young daughters understood and spoke English, whereas their Spanish was spotty at best. At the same time, many of Mrs. Huerta's neighbors (who were eagerly

crowding the front stoop now) spoke *only* Spanish, and she recognized that
talking to this detective in English might enable her to keep at least *some* of
her business to herself. She silently debated the matter only a moment longer,
and then decided to answer in English.

"We were going down to church," she said, "the eight o'clock mass. The church
is right up the street, it takes five minutes. We came out of the building, José
and me and the two girls, and these men came at him."

"How many men?"

"Four."

"Did you recognize any of them?"

"No." Mrs. Huerta said.

"What happened?"

"They hit him."

"With what?'

"Broom handles. Short. You know, they take the broom and saw it off."

"Did they say anything to your husband?"

"*Nada.* Nothing."

"Did he say anything to them?"

"No."

"And you didn't recognize any of them? They weren't men from the *barrio*,
the neighborhood?"

"I never saw them before."

One of the little girls looked up at her mother and then turned quickly
away.

"*Si, qué hay?*" Delgado asked immediately.

"Nothing," the little girl answered.

"What's your name?" Delgado said.

"Paquita Huerta."

"Did you see the men who attacked your father, Paquita?"

"Yes," Paquita said, and nodded.

"Did you know any of those men?"

The little girl hesitated.

"*Puede usted decirme?*"

"No," Paquita said. "I did not know any of them."

"And you?" Delgado said, turning to the other girl.

"No. None of them."

Delgado searched their eyes. The little girls watched him unblinkingly. He
turned to Mrs. Huerta again. "Your husband's full name is José Huerta?" he
asked.

"José Vicente Huerta."

"How old is he, *señora*?"

"Forty-seven."

"What does he do for a living?"

"He is a real estate agent."

"Where is his place of business, Mrs. Huerta?"

"In Riverhead. 1345 Harrison Avenue. It is called J-R Realty."

"Does he own the business?"

"Yes."

"No partners?"

"Yes, he has a partner."

"What's his partner's name?"

"Ramon Castañeda. That's how they got the J-R. From José and Ramon."

"And where does Mr. Castañeda live?"

"Two blocks from here. On Fourth Street."

"The address."

"112 South Fourth."

"All right, thank you," Delgado said. "I'll let you know if we come up with anything."

"*Por favor*," Mrs. Huerta said, and took both her daughters by their hands and led them into the building.

The black blouse found in Lewis Scott's bathroom had come from a clothing store called The Monkey Wrench, on Culver Avenue. Since this was a Sunday, the store was closed. The patrolman on the beat spotted Willis and Genero peering through the plate glass window and casually ambled over to them.

"Help you fellows?" he asked.

Both Genero and Willis looked at him. Neither of them recognized him. "You new on the beat, kid?" Genero said. The patrolman was perhaps three or four years *older* than Genero, but since his rank was lower, Genero felt perfectly free to address him in this manner. The patrolman could not decide whether he was dealing with hoods or fellow law enforcers; the distinction was sometimes difficult to make. He debated whether he should answer smart-ass or subservient. While he was deciding, Willis said, "I'm Detective Willis. This is my partner, Detective Genero."

"Oh," the patrolman said, managing to make the single word sound eloquent.

"How long you been on the beat, kid?" Genero asked.

"Just this past week. They flew me in from Majesta."

"Special assignment?"

"Yeah. This is a glass post, you know, there's been lots of breakage and looting lately. They almost doubled the force here, from what I understand."

"Where's the regular beat man?"

"He's catching a cup of coffee at the diner up the street. Anything I can help you with?"

"What's his name?"

"Haskins. You know him?"

"Yeah," Willis said. "Diner on the corner there?"

"Right."

"See you later, kid," Genero said, and both detectives walked off toward the diner. Behind them, the patrolman shrugged in a manner clearly indicating that he thought all detectives were no-good rotten bastards who were always pulling rank.

The diner at fifteen minutes before ten was empty save for Patrolman Haskins and the man behind the counter. Haskins was hunched over a cup of coffee. He looked as though he had not had much sleep the night before. Genero and Willis walked to the counter and took stools on either side of him.

"Hello, Bill," Willis said.

Haskins looked up from his coffee. "Hey, hi," he said.

"Two coffees," Genero said to the counterman.

"You looking for me," Haskins asked, "or you just happen in?"

"We're looking for you."

"What's up"

"How do you want those coffees?" the counterman asked.

"Regular," Willis said.

"One regular, one black," Genero said.

"Two regulars, one black," the counterman said.

"*One* regular, *one* black," Genero said.

"*He* wants a regular," the counterman insisted, "and *you* want a regular and a black."

"What are you, a comedian?" Genero said.

"It's all on the arm anyway, ain't it?" the counterman answered.

"Who says?"

"The day a cop pays for a cup of coffee in here, that's the day they give a parade up Hall Avenue."

None of the policemen answered him. They were not, as a matter of fact, in the habit of paying for coffee in local eateries. Neither did they enjoy being reminded of it.

"Bill, we're looking for a kid about eighteen, nineteen," Willis said. "Long blond hair, handlebar mustache. Seen anybody around like that?"

"I seen a hundred of them," Haskins said. "Are you kidding?"

"This one was wearing a jacket with the fur side inside, the skin side out." Haskins shrugged.

"Big sun painted on the back of it," Willis said.

"Yeah, that rings a bell. I think I seen that jacket around."

"Remember the kid wearing it?"

"Where the hell did I see that jacket?" Haskins asked aloud.

"He might have been with another kid his age, black beard, black hair."

"No," Haskins said, and shook his head. "An orange sun, right? Like an orange sun with rays coming out of it, right?"

"That's right, orange."

"Yeah, I seen that jacket," Haskins said. "Just the other day. Where the hell did I see it?"

"Two coffees, one regular, one black," the counterman said, and put them down.

"Jerry, you ever see a kid in here wearing a fur jacket with a sun painted on the back of it?" Haskins asked.

"No," the counterman said flatly, and walked back into the kitchen.

"White fur, right?" Haskins said to Willis. "On the inside, right? Like white fur?"

"That's right."

"Sure, I seen that goddamn jacket. Just give me a minute, okay?"

"Sure, take your time," Willis said.

Haskins turned to Genero and conversationally said, "I see you got the gold tin. Who's your rabbi?"

"I was promoted a long time ago," Genero said, somewhat offended. "Where the hell have you been?"

"I guess I don't keep up with what's happening around the station house," Haskins said, and grinned.

"You *know* I was promoted."

"Yeah, I guess it just slipped my mind," Haskins said. "How do you like the good life, Genero?"

"Beats laying bricks all to hell," Genero answered.

"What *doesn't*?" Haskins said.

"About that jacket..." Willis interrupted.

"Yeah, yeah, just give me a minute, it'll come to me," Haskins said, and lifted his coffee cup in both hands, and sipped at it and said, "That new kid covering out there?"

"He's doing fine, don't worry about him."

"The Monkey Wrench!" Haskins said, snapping his fingers. "*That's* where I seen the damn thing. In the window of The Monkey Wrench. Right up the street."

"Good," Willis said, and nodded. "Got any idea who runs that shop?"

"Yeah, these two dykes who live over on Eighth. Just around the corner from the store."

"What's their names?"

"Flora Schneider and Frieda something, I don't know what. Flora and Frieda, everybody calls them."

"What's the address on Eight?"

"327 North. The brownstone right around the corner."

"Thanks," Willis said.

"Thanks for the coffee," Genero yelled to the kitchen.

The counterman did not answer.

Detective Arthur Brown was a black man with a very dark complexion, kinky hair, large nostrils, and thick lips. He was impressively good-looking, though unfortunately not cast in the Negro mold acceptable to most white people, including liberals. In short, he did not resemble Harry Belafonte, Sidney Poitier, or Adam Clayton Powell. He resembled only himself, which was quite a lot since he was six feet four inches tall and weighed two hundred and twenty pounds. Arthur Brown was the sort of black man who caused white men to cross the street when he approached, on the theory that this mean-looking son of a bitch (mean-looking only because he was big and black) would undoubtedly mug them or knife them or do something possibly worse, God knew what. Even after Brown identified himself as a police detective, there were many white people who still harbored the suspicion that he was really some kind of desperate criminal impersonating an officer.

It was therefore a pleasant surprise for Brown to come across a witness to the grocery store shootings who did not seem at all intimidated by either his size or his color. The person was a little old lady who carried a bright blue umbrella on her arm, despite the fact that the day was clear, with that sharp penetrating bite in the air that comes only with October. The umbrella matched the lady's eyes, which were as clear and as sharp as the day itself. She wore a little flowered hat on her head. If she had been a younger woman, the black coat she was wearing might have been called a maxi. She leaped to her feet as Brown came through the front door of the grocery, and said to him in a brisk resonant voice, "Ah, at last!"

"Ma'am?" Brown said.

"You're the detective aren't you?"

"I am," Brown admitted.

"My name is Mrs. Farraday, how do you do?"

"Detective Brown," he said, and nodded, and would have let it go at that, but Mrs. Farraday was holding out her hand. Brown clasped it, shook it, and smiled pleasantly. Mrs. Farraday returned the smile and released his hand.

"They told me to wait in here, said a detective would be along any minute. I've been waiting half the morning. It's past ten-thirty now."

"Well, Mrs. Farraday, I've been talking to people in the neighborhood since a little after eight o'clock. Takes a little while to get around to all of them."

"Oh, I can well imagine," she said.

"Patrolman outside says you've got some information for me though. Is that right?"

"That's right. I saw the two men who held up the store."

"Where'd you see them?"

"Running around the corner. I was on my way home from church, I always go to six o'clock mass, and I'm generally out by seven, and then I stop at the bakery for buns, my husband likes buns with his breakfast on Sundays, or coffee cake."

"Um-huh."

"Never goes to church himself," she said, "damn heathen."

"Um-huh."

"I was coming out of the bakery – this must have been, oh, close to seven-thirty – when I saw two of them come running around the corner. I thought at first . . ."

"What were they wearing, Mrs. Farraday?"

"Black coats. And masks. One of them was a girl's face – the mask, I mean. And the other was a monster mask, I don't know which monster. They had guns. Both of them. But none of that's important, Detective Brown."

"What *is* important?"

"They took the masks *off*. As soon as they turned the corner, they took the masks off, and I got a very good look at both of them."

"Can you describe them to me now?"

"I certainly can."

"Good." Brown took out his pad and flipped it open. He reached into his pocket for his pen – he was one of the few cops on the squad who still used a fountain pen rather than a ball-point – took off the cap, and said, "Were they white or black, Mrs. Farraday?"

"White," Mrs. Farraday said.

"How old would you say they were?"

"Young."

"How young? Twenty? Thirty?"

"Oh, no. In their forties, I would say. They were young, but they were definitely not *kids*, Detective Brown."

"How tall were they?"

"One was about your height, a very big man. How tall are you?"

"Six four," Brown said.

"My, that *is* big," Mrs. Farraday said.

"And the other one?"

"Much shorter. Five eight or nine, I would guess."

"Notice the hair colour?"

"The short one was blond. The tall one had dark hair."

"I don't suppose you saw the colour of their eyes."

"They passed close enough, but I just didn't see. They went by very quickly."

"Any scars? Tattoos? Birthmarks?"

"Not that I could see."

"Both clean-shaven?"

"Do you mean did they have beards or mustaches?"

"Yes, ma'am."

"No, both clean-shaven."

"You say they took the masks off as they came around the corner, is that right?"

"Yes. They just ripped them off. It must be difficult to see through those things, wouldn't you imagine?"

"Was there a car waiting for them?"

"No, I don't think they had a car, Detective Brown. They were running too fast for that. It's my guess they were trying to make their escape on foot. Wouldn't that be your guess as well?"

"I really couldn't say yet, Mrs. Farraday. I wonder if you could show me where that bakery store is."

"Certainly. It's right around the corner."

They walked out of the grocery, and the patrolman outside said to Brown, "You know anything about when I'm supposed to be relieved here?"

"What do you mean?" Brown asked.

"I think there's some kind of foul-up. I mean, this ain't even my post."

"Where *is* your post?"

"On Grover Avenue. Near the park."

"So what're you doing here?"

"That's just it. I collared this guy around quarter to seven, must've been, and took him back to the station house to book him – he was trying to bust into a Mercedes parked on South Second. By the time I got finished there, it was like seven-fifteen, and Nealy and O'Hara are going by in a patrol car, so I hail them and ask for a lift back to my post. We're on the way when all of a sudden they catch the radio squeal about the shooting here at the grocery store. So we all rush over here, and there's a big hullabaloo, you know, Parker caught some stuff, you know, and Nealy and O'Hara take off on a Ten-Thirteen, and the sergeant tells me to stay here outside the door. So I been here all morning. I was supposed to be relieved on post at eight o'clock, but how's my relief supposed to know where I am so he can relieve me? You going back to the station house?"

"Not right away."

"Listen, I hate to leave here, because the sarge might get sore, you know. He told me to stay right here."

"I'll call in from the nearest box," Brown said.

"Would you do that? I certainly would appreciate it."

"Right away," Brown said.

He and Mrs. Farraday walked around the corner to the bakery shop. "This is where I was standing when they ran by," Mrs. Farraday said. "They were taking off the masks as they came around the corner, and they had them off by the time they passed me. Then they went racing up the street and ... oh, my goodness!" she said, and stopped.

"What is it, Mrs. Farraday?"

"I just remembered what they did with those masks, Detective Brown. They threw them down the sewer there. They stopped at the sewer grating and just threw them away, and then they started running again."

"Thank you, Mrs. Farraday," Brown said, "you've been most helpful."

"Oh, well," she said, and smiled.

Flora and Frieda did not get back to their apartment on North Eighth until seven minutes past eleven. They were both pretty women in their late twenties, both wearing pants suits and short car coats. Flora was a blonde, Frieda a redhead. Flora wore big gold hoop earrings. Frieda had a tiny black beauty spot near the corner of her mouth. They explained to the detectives that they always walked in the park on Sunday mornings, rain or shine. Flora offered them tea, and when they accepted, Frieda went upstairs to the kitchen, to put the kettle on.

Their apartment was in a brownstone that had run the gamut from luxury dwelling fifty years back, to crumbling tenement for as many years, to reconverted town house in a block of similar buildings trying desperately to raise their heads above the slime of the neighborhood. The women owned the entire building, and Flora explained now that the bedrooms were on the top floor, the kitchen, dining room and spare room on the middle floor, and the living room on the ground floor. The detectives were sitting with her in that room now, sunlight streaming through the damask-hung windows. A cat lay before the tiled fireplace, dozing. The living room ran the entire length of the ground floor, and was warmly and beautifully furnished. There was a false sense here of being someplace other than the city – some English country home in Dorset perhaps, or some Welsh manor, quiet and secluded, with gently rolling grassy hills just outside the door. But it was one thing to convert a slum building into a beautiful town house, and quite another to ignore the whirlpool surrounding it. Neither Flora nor Frieda were fools; there were iron gates over the windows facing the backyard, and a Fox lock on the front door.

"The store hasn't been burglarized, has it?" Flora asked. Her voice was somewhat throaty. She sounded very much like a torch singer holding the mike too close to her lips.

"No, no," Willis assured her. "We merely want to ask about some articles of clothing that may have been purchased there."

"Thank heavens," Flora said. Frieda had come down from the kitchen and stood now behind Flora's wingback chair, her hand delicately resting on the lace antimacassar just behind her partner's head.

"We've been burglarized four times since we opened the store," Frieda said.

"Each time they've taken, oh, less than a hundred dollars worth of merchandise. It's ridiculous. It costs us more to replace the broken glass each time. If they'd just come in the store and *ask* for the damn stuff, we'd give it to them outright."

"We've had the locks changed four times, too. That all costs money," Frieda said.

"We operate on a very low profit margin," Flora said.

"It's junkies who do it," Flora said. "Don't you think so, Flora?"

"Oh, no question," Flora said. "Hasn't that been your experience?"she asked the detectives.

"Well, sometimes," Willis said. "But not all burglars are junkies."

"Are all junkies burglars?" Frieda asked.

"Some of them."

"Most of them?"

"A lot of them. Takes quite a bit of money to support a habit, you know."

"The city ought to do something about it," Flora said.

The cat near the fireplace stirred, stretched, blinked at the detectives, and then stalked out of the room.

"Pussy's getting hungry," Flora said.

"We'll feed her soon," Frieda answered.

"What clothes did you want to ask about?" Flora said.

"Well, primarily a jacket you had in the window last week. A fur jacket with . . ."

"The llama, yes, what about it?"

"With an orange sun painted on the back?" Genero said.

"Yes, that's it."

"Would you remember who you sold it to?" Willis asked.

"I didn't sell it," Flora said. She glanced up at her partner. "Frieda?"

"Yes, I sold it," Frieda said.

"Would you remember who bought it?"

"A boy. Long blond hair and a mustache. A young boy. I explained to him that it was really a woman's coat, but he said that didn't matter, he thought it was groovy and wanted it. It has no buttons, you realize, so that wasn't any problem. A woman's garment buttons differently . . ."

"Yes, I know that."

"This particular coat is held closed with a belt. I remember him trying it *with* the belt and then *without* the belt."

"Excuse me," Genero said, "but is this a coat or a jacket?"

"Well, it's a short coat, actually. Mid-thigh. It's really designed for a woman, to go with a miniskirt. It's about that length."

"I see."

"I guess a man could wear it, though," Frieda said dubiously.

"Do you know who the boy was?"

"I'm sorry, I don't. I'd never seen him before."

"How much did the coat cost?"

"A hundred and ten dollars."

"Did he pay for it in cash?"

"No, by . . . oh, of course."

"Yes?" Willis said.

"He gave me a check. His name would be on the check, wouldn't it?" she turned to Flora. "Where are the checks we're holding for deposit tomorrow?" she asked.

"Upstairs," Flora said. "In the locked drawer." She smiled at the detectives and said, "One drawer in the dresser locks. Not that it would do any good if someone decided to break in here."

"Shall I get it for you?" Frieda asked.

"If you would." Willis said.

"Certainly. The tea must be ready, too."

She went out of the room. Her tread sounded softly on the carpeted steps leading upstairs.

"There was one other item," Willis said. "Dick, have you got that blouse?"

Genero handed him a manilla envelope. Willis unclasped it, and removed from it the black silk blouse they had found on Scott's bathroom floor, the police evidence tag dangling from one of its buttons. Flora took the blouse and turned it over in her hands.

"Yes, that's ours," she said.

"Would you know who bought it from you?"

Flora shook her head. "I really couldn't say. We sell dozens of blouses every week." She looked at the label. "This is a thirty-four, a very popular size." She shook her head again. "No, I'm sorry."

"Okay," Willis said. He put the blouse back into the envelope. Frieda was coming into the room with a tray upon which was a teapot covered with a cozy, four cups and saucers, a milk pitcher, a sugar bowl, and several sliced lemons in a low dish. A check was under the sugar bowl. Frieda put down the tray, lifted the sugar bowl and handed the check to Willis.

A name and an address were printed across the top of the check:

ROBERT HAMLING
3541 Carrier Avenue
Isola

The check was made out to the order of The Monkey Wrench for one hundred thirty-five dollars and sixty-eight cents; it was signed by Hamling in a broad, sprawling hand. Willis looked up. "I thought the coat cost a hundred and ten dollars. This check..."

"Yes, he bought a blouse as well. The blouse cost eighteen dollars. The rest is tax."

"A black silk blouse?" Genero asked.

"Yes," Frieda said.

"*This* one?" Genero asked, and pulled the blouse from its envelope like a magician pulling a rabbit from a hat.

"Yes, that's the blouse," Frieda said.

Genero nodded in satisfaction. Willis turned the check over. On the back of it were the penned words: "Drivers Lic" and the numbers "21546 68916 506607-52."

"Did you write this?" Willis asked.

"Yes," Frieda answered.

"He showed you identification, I take it."

"Oh yes, his driver's license. We never accept checks without proper identification."

"Can I see that?" Genero asked. Willis handed him the check. "Carrier Avenue," Genero said. "Where's that?"

"Downtown," Willis answered. "In The Quarter."

"What do you take in your tea, gentlemen?" Flora asked.

They sat sipping tea in the living room streaming with sunlight. Once, during a lull in the small talk over their steaming cups, Genero asked, "Why'd you name your store The Monkey Wrench?"

"Why not?" Frieda answered.

It was clearly time to go.

The curious thing about fishing in the sewer for those Halloween masks was that it filled Brown with a sense of exhilaration he had not known since he was a boy. He could remember a hundred past occasions when he and his childhood friends had removed an iron sewer grating and climbed down into the muck to retrieve a rubber ball hit by a stickball bat, or an immie carelessly aimed, or even now and then a dime or a quarter that had slipped from a clenched fist and rolled down into the curbside drain. He was too large now to squeeze through the narrow opening of the sewer, but he could see at least one of the masks some five feet below him, resting on the pipe elbow in a brownish paper-littered slime. He stretched out flat on the pavement, head twisted away from the curb and tried to reach the mask. His arm, as long as it was, was not long enough. His fingertips wiggled below, touching nothing but stagnant air. He got to his feet, brushed off the knees of his trousers and the elbows of his coat, and then looked up the block. Not a kid in sight. Never a kid around when you needed one. He began searching in his pockets. He found a paper clip holding a business card to one of the pages in his pad. He removed the clip, put the card into his wallet, and then took a sheaf of evidence tags from his inside jacket pocket. Each of the tags had a short length of string tied through a hole at one end. He unfastened the strings from ten tags, knotted them all together and came up with a five-foot-long piece of string. He opened the paper clip so that it resembled a fish hook, and then tied it to one end of the string. Weighting the line with the duplicate key to his station house locker, he grinned and began fishing in the sewer. On the twentieth try, he hooked the narrow piece of elastic clipped to the mask. Slowly, carefully, patiently, he reeled in his line.

He was looking at a somewhat soiled Snow White, but this was the Seventies, and nobody expected to find virgins in sewers anymore.

Still grinning, Brown replaced the grating, brushed himself off again, and headed back for the squadroom.

In the city for which Brown worked, the Identification Section and the Police Laboratory operated on weekends with only a skeleton force, which was only slightly better than operating with no force at all. Most cases got put over till Monday, unless they were terribly urgent. The shooting of a police detective was considered terribly urgent, and so the Snow White mask Brown dispatched to the lab downtown on High Street was given top priority. Detective-Lieutenant Sam Grossman, who ran the lab, was of course not working on a Sunday. The task of examining the mask for latent fingerprints (or indeed *any* clue as to its wearer's identity) fell to Detective 3rd/Grade Marshall Davies, who, like Genero, was a comparatively new detective and therefore prone to catching weekend duty at the lab. He promised Brown he would get back to him as soon as possible, mindful of the fact that a detective had been shot and that there might be all kinds of pressure from upstairs, and then set to work.

In the squadroom, Brown replaced the telephone on its cradle and looked up as a patrolman approached the slatted rail divider with a prisoner in tow. At his desk, Carl Kapek was eating an early lunch, preparatory to heading for the bar in which the marine had encountered the girl with the bewitching behind, bars in this city being closed on Sundays until twelve, at which time it was presumably acceptable for churchgoers to begin getting drunk. The clock on the squadroom wall read fifteen minutes to noon. The squadroom was somewhat more crowded than it might have been at this hour on a Sunday because Levine, Di Maeo and Meriwether, the three detectives who had been called in when they were supposed to be on vacation, were sitting at one of the desks waiting to see the lieutenant, who at the moment was talking to Captain Frick, commander of the precinct, about the grocery store shooting and the necessity to get some more men on it. The three detectives were naturally grumbling. Di Maeo said that next time he was going to Puerto Rico on his vacation because then the lieutenant could shove it up his ass if he wanted him to come back. Cooperman was on vacation, too, wasn't he? But he was in the Virgin Islands, and the loot sure as hell didn't call *him* down there and drag *him* in, did he? Besides, Levine pointed out, Andy Parker was a lousy cop and who the hell cared if he got shot or even killed? Meriwether, who was a mild-mannered hair-bag in his early sixties, and a detective/first to boot said, "Now, now, fellows, it's all part of the game, all part of the game," and Di Maeo belched.

The patrolman walked over to Brown's desk, told his prisoner to sit down, took Brown aside, and whispered something to him. Brown nodded and came back to the desk. The prisoner was handcuffed, sitting with his hands in his lap. He was a pudgy little man with green eyes and a pencil-line mustache. Brown estimated his age at forty or thereabout. He was wearing a brown overcoat, a brown suit and shoes, white shirt with a button-down collar, gold-and-brown striped silk tie. Brown asked the patrolman to advise the man of his rights, a job the patrolman accepted with some trepidation, while he called the hospital to ask about Parker's condition. They told him that Parker was doing fine. Brown accepted the report without noticeable enthusiasm. He hung up the phone, heard the prisoner tell the patrolman he had nothing to hide and would answer any questions they wanted to ask, swiveled his chair around to face the man, and said, "What's your name?"

The man would not look Brown in the eye. Instead, he kept staring past his left ear to the grilled windows and the sky outside.

"Perry Lyons," he said, His voice was very low. Brown could barely hear him.

"What were you doing in the park just now, Lyons?" Brown said.

"Nothing," Lyons answered.

"Speak up!" Brown snapped. There was a noticeable edge to his voice. The patrolman, too, was staring down at Lyons in what could only be described as an extremely hostile way, his brow twisted into a frown, his eyes hard and mean, his lips tightly compressed, his arms folded across his chest.

"I wasn't doing nothing." Lyons answered.

"Patrolman Brogan here seems to think otherwise."

Lyons shrugged.

"What about it, Lyons?"

"There's no law against talking to somebody."

"Who were you talking to, Lyons?"

"A kid."

"What'd you say to him?"

"Just it was a nice day, that's all."

"That's not what the kid told Patrolman Brogan."

"Well, kids, you know kids," Lyons said.

"How old was the kid, Joe?" Brown asked.

"About nine," Brogan answered.

"You always talk to nine-year-old kids in the park?" Brown asked.

"Sometimes."

"How often?"

"There's no law against talking to kids. I like kids."

"I'll bet you do," Brown said. "Tell him what the boy told you, Brogan."

Brogan hesitated a moment, and then said, "The boy said you asked him to blow you, Lyons."

"No," Lyons said. "No, I never said anything like that. You're mistaken."

"I'm not mistaken," Brogan said.

"Well then, the kid's mistaken. He never heard anything like that from me, nossir."

"You ever been arrested before?" Brown asked.

Lyons did not answer.

"Come on," Brown said impatiently, "we can check it in a minute."

"Well, yes," Lyons said. "I have been arrested before."

"How many times?"

"Twice."

"What for?"

"Well..." Lyons said, and shrugged.

"What *for*, Lyons?"

"Well, it was, uh, I got in trouble with somebody a while back."

"What kind of trouble?"

"With some kid."

"What was the charge, Lyons?"

Lyons hesitated again.

"What was the charge?" Brown repeated.

"Carnal Abuse."

"You're a child molester, huh, Lyons?"

"No, no, it was a bum rap."

"Were you convicted?"

"Yes, but that don't mean a thing, you guys know that. The kid was lying. He wanted to get even with me, he wanted to get me into trouble, so he told all kinds of lies about me. Hell, what would I want to fool around with a kid like that for? I had a girl friend and everything, this waitress, you know? A real pretty girl, what would I want to fool around with a little kid for?"

"You tell me."

"It was a bum rap, that's all. These things happen, that's all. You guys know that."

"And the second arrest?"

"Well, that..."

"Yeah?"

"Well, you see what happened, after I got paroled, you know, I went back to live in this motel I used to live in before I got put away, you know?"

"Where'd you serve your time?"

"Castleview."

"Go ahead."

"So I had this same room, you know? That I had before they locked me up. And it turned out the kid who got me into trouble before, he was living there with his mother."

"Just a coincidence, huh?"

"Well, no, not by coincidence. I mean, I can't claim it was coincidence. His mother ran the place, you see. I mean, she and her father owned it together. So it wasn't coincidence, you know. But I didn't think the kid was going to cause me no more trouble, you see what I mean? I done my time, he already got even with me, so I didn't expect no more trouble from him. Only thing is he come around to my cabin one day, and he made me do things to him. He said he'd tell his mother I was bothering him again if I didn't do these things to him. I mean, I was on parole, you know what I mean? If the kid had went to his mother, they'd have packed me off again in a minute."

"So what *did* you do, Lyons?"

"Argh, the fuckin' little bastard started yelling. They ... they busted me again."

"Same charge?"

"Well, not the same 'cause the kid was older now. You know, like there's Carnal Abuse with a kid ten years old or younger, and then there's Carnal Abuse with a kid over ten and less than sixteen. He was eight years old the first time and eleven the next time. It was a bum rap both times. Who the hell needs that kind of stuff, you think I need it? Anyway, this was a long time ago. I already served *both* sentences. You think I'd be crazy enough to risk a third fall?"

"You could've been put away for life the *second* time," Brown said.

"Don't you think I know it? So why would I take another chance?" He looked up at Brogan. "That kid must've heard me wrong, Officer. I didn't say nothing like that to him. Honest. I really didn't."

"We're booking you for Endangering the Morals of a Child, as defined in Section 483-a of the Penal Law," Brown said. "You're allowed three telephone..."

"Hey, hey, look," Lyons said, "give me a break, will you? I didn't mean no harm to the kid, I swear it. We were just sitting there talking, I swear to God. I *never* said nothing like that to him, would I say something like that to a little kid? Jesus, what do you take me for? Hey, come on, give me a break, will you? Come on, Officer, give me a break."

"I'd advise you to get a lawyer," Brown said. "You want to take him down, Brogan?"

"Hey, come on," Lyons said.

Brown watched as the patrolman led Lyons out of the squadroom. He stared at the retreating figure, and thought *The guy's sick, why the hell are we sending him away again, instead of helping him,* and then he thought *I have a seven-year-old daughter* – and then he stopped thinking because everything seemed suddenly too complex, and the telephone on his desk was ringing.

He lifted the receiver.

It was Steve Carella reporting that he was on his way to the squadroom.

José Vicente Huerta was in a bad way. Both of his legs had been broken by the four assailants who'd attacked him, and his face was swathed in bandages that covered the multiple wounds that had spilled his blood all over the front stoop of the building. He resembled a not so invisible Invisible Man, his brown eyes burning fiercely through the holes left in the bandages.

His mouth, pink against the white, showed through another hole below the eye holes, and looked like a gaping wound itself. He was conscious now, but the doctors advised Delgado that their patient was heavily sedated and might drift in and out of sleep as he talked. Delgado figured he would take his chances.

He sat in a chair by the side of Huerta's bed. Huerta, both legs in traction, his hands lying on the covers, palms up, his head turned into the pillow in Delgado's direction, the brown eyes burning fiercely, the wound of the mouth open and pathetically vulnerable, listened as Delgado identified himself, and then nodded when asked if he felt able to answer some questions.

"First," Delgado said, "do you know who the men were?"

"No," Huerta answered.

"You didn't recognize any of them?"

"No."

"Were they young men?"

"I don't know."

"You saw them as they attacked you, didn't you?"

"Yes."

"Well, how old would you say they were?"

"I don't know."

"Were they neighborhood men?"

"I don't know."

"Mr. Huerta, any information you can give us..."

"I don't know who they were," Huerta said.

"They hurt you very badly. Surely..."

The bandaged head turned away from Delgado, into the pillow.

"Mr. Huerta?"

Huerta did not answer.

"Mr. Huerta?"

Again, he did not answer. As had been promised by the doctors, he seemed to have drifted off into sleep. Delgado sighed and stood up. Since he was at Buenavista Hospital, anyway, and just so his visit shouldn't be a total loss, he decided to stop in on Andy Parker to see how he was doing. Parker was doing about as well as Huerta. He, too, was asleep. The interne on the floor informed Delgado that Parker was out of danger.

Delgado seemed as thrilled by the information as Brown had earlier been.

The trouble with being a detective in any given neighborhood is that almost everybody in the neighborhood knows you're a detective. Since detection is supposed to be undercover secret stuff at least some of the time, snooping around becomes a little difficult when 90 per cent of the people you encounter know you're a snoop. The bartender at Bar Seventeen (which was the name of the bar in which the marine had first encountered the girl who later kicked him in the head, such bar being thus imaginatively named since it was located on Seventeenth Street) knew that Carl Kapek was a bull, and Kapek knew that the bartender knew, and since they *both* knew, neither of them made any pretense of playing at cops and robbers. The bartender set up beers for Kapek, who was not supposed to drink on duty, and Kapek accepted them without offering payment, and everybody had a nice little understanding going. Kapek did not even attempt to ask the bartender about the kicking girl and her boyfriend. Nor did the bartender try to find out why Kapek was there. If he was there, he was there for a reason, and the bartender knew it, and Kapek knew he knew it, and so the two men kept a respectful distance, coming into contact only when the bartender refilled Kapek's glass from time to time. It was a cool symbiosis. The bartender merely hoped that Kapek was not there investigating some minor violation that would inevitably cost him money. He was already paying off two guys from the Fire Department, not to mention the police sergeant on the beat; one more guy with his hand out, and it would be cheaper to take care of the goddamn violations instead. Kapek, for his part, merely hoped that the bartender would not indicate to too many of his early afternoon patrons that the big blond guy sitting at the bar was a police detective. It was difficult enough these days to earn a living.

The way he decided to earn his living on this particular bright October Sunday – bright *outside*, dim and cheerless inside – was to engage a drunk in conversation. Kapek had been in the bar for close to an hour now, studying the patrons, trying to decide which of them were regulars, which of them came here infrequently, which of them recognized him from around the streets, which of them had not the faintest inkling that he was fuzz. He did all of this in what he hoped was a surreptitious manner, going to the phone booth once to pretend he was making a call, going to the men's room once, going to the jukebox three or four times, casing everyone in the place on his various excursions, and then settling down on a stool within listening distance of the bartender and a man in a dark blue suit. Kapek opened the Sunday tabloid he had carried with him into the bar, and turned to the sports section. He pretended to be pondering yesterday's racing results, working figures with a pencil in the margin of the newspaper, while simultaneously listening intently to everything the man in the blue suit said. When the bartender walked off to serve someone at the other end of the bar, Kapek made his move.

"Damn horse never delivers when he's supposed to," he said.

"I beg your pardon?" the man in the blue suit said, turning on his stool. He was already very intoxicated, having presumably begun his serious drinking at home before the bar could legally open its doors. He looked at Kapek now with the benign expression of someone anxious to be friendly with anyone at all, even if he happened to be a cop. He did not seem to know that Kapek was a cop, nor was Kapek anxious to let him in on the secret.

"You follow the ponies?" Kapek asked.

"I permit myself a tiny wager every so often," the man in the blue suit said. He had bleary blue eyes and a veined nose. His white shirt looked unironed, his solid blue tie was haphazardly knotted, his suit rumpled. He kept his right hand firmly clutched around a water tumbler full of whiskey on the bar top in front of him.

"This nag's the goddamn favorite nine times out of ten," Kapek said, "but he never wins when he's supposed to. I think the jocks got it all fixed between them."

The bartender was ambling back. Kapek shot him a warning glance: *Stay out of this pal. You work your side of the street, I'll work mine.* The bartender hesitated in mid-stride, then turned on his heel and walked over to his other customer.

"My name's Carl Kapek," Kapek said, and closed his newspaper, encouraging further conversation. "I've been playing the horses for twelve years now, I made only one decent killing in all that time."

"How much?" the man in the blue suit asked.

"Four hundred dollars on a long shot. Had two dollars on his nose. It was beautiful, beautiful," Kapek said, and grinned and shook his head remembering the beauty of this event that had never taken place. The most he had ever won in his life was a chemistry set at a church bazaar.

"How long ago was that?" the man in the blue suit asked.

"Six years ago," Kapek said, and laughed.

"That's a long time between drinks," the man said, and laughed with him.

"I don't think I got your name," Kapek said, and extended his hand.

"Leonard Sutherland," the man said. "My friends all call me Lennie."

"How do you do, Lennie?" Kapek said, and they shook hands.

"What do *your* friends call *you*?" Lennie asked.

"Carl."

"Nice meeting you, Carl." Lennie said.

"A pleasure," Kapek answered

"*My* game's poker," Lennie said. "Playing the horses, you'll pardon me, is for suckers. Poker's a game of skill."

"No question," Kapek agreed.

"Do you actually *prefer* beer?" Lennie asked suddenly.

"What?"

"I notice you have been drinking beer exclusively. If you would permit me, Carl, I'd consider it an honor to buy you something stronger."

"Little early in the day for me," Kapek said, and smiled apologetically.

"Never too early for a little rammer," Lennie said, and smiled.

"Well, I was out drinking late last night," Kapek said, and shrugged.

"I am out drinking late *every* night," Lennie said, "but it's still never too early for a little rammer." To emphasize his theory, he lifted the water glass

. and swallowed half the whiskey in it. "Mmm, boy," he said, and coughed.

"You usually do your drinking here?" Kapek asked.

"Hm?" Lennie asked. His eyes were watering. He took a handkerchief from his back pocket and dabbed at them. He coughed again.

"In this place?"

"Oh, I drift around, drift around," Lennie said, and made a fluttering motion with the fingers of one hand.

"Reason I ask," Kapek said, "is that I was here last night, and I didn't happen to see you."

"Oh, I was here all right," Lennie said, which Kapek already knew because this was what he had overheard in the conversation between Lennie and the bartender, a passing reference to a minor event that had taken place in Bar Seventeen the night before, the bartender having had to throw out a twenty-year-old who was noisily expressing his views on lowering the age to vote.

"Were you here when they threw out that young kid?" Kapek asked.

"Oh, indeed," Lennie said.

"Didn't see you," Kapek said.

"Oh, yes, here indeed," Lennie said.

"There was a marine . . ." Kapek said tentatively.

"Hm?" Lennie asked with a polite smile, and then lifted his glass and threw down the rest of the whiskey. He said, "Mmm, boy," coughed again, dabbed at his watering eyes, and then said, "Yes, yes, but he came in later."

"After they threw that kid out, you mean?"

"Oh yes, much later. Were you here when the marine came in?"

"Oh, sure," Kapek said.

"Funny we didn't notice each other," Lennie said, and shrugged and signaled to the bartender. The bartender slouched toward them, shooting Kapek his own warning glance: *This guy's a good steady customer. If I lose him 'cause you're pumping him for information here, I'm gonna get sore as hell.*

"Yeah, Lennie?" the bartender said.

"I'll have another double, please," Lennie answered. "And please see what my friend here is having, won't you?"

The bartender shot the warning glance at Kapek again. Kapek stared back at him implacably and said, "I'll just have another beer." The bartender nodded and walked off.

"There was this girl in here about then," Kapek said to Lennie. "You remember her?"

"Which girl?"

"Colored girl in a red dress," Kapek repeated.

"Oh, yes, Belinda," Lennie answered.

"Belinda what?"

"Don't know," Lennie said.

His eyes brightened as the bartender came back with his whiskey and Kapek's beer. Lennie lifted the tumbler immediately and drank. "Mmm, boy," he said, and coughed. The bartender hovered near them. Kapek met his eyes, decided if he wanted so badly to get in on the act, he'd let him.

"Would *you* happen to know?" Kapek said.

"Know what?"

"There was a girl named Belinda in here last night. Wearing a red dress. Would you know her last name?"

"Me," the bartender said, "I'm deaf, dumb, and blind." He paused. "This guy's a cop, Lennie, did you know that?"

"Oh, yes, certainly," Lennie said, and fell off his stool and passed out cold.

Kapek got up, bent, seized Lennie under the arms and dragged him over to one of the booths. He loosened his tie and then looked up at the bartender, who had come over and was standing with his hands on his hips.

"You always serve booze to guys who've had too much?" he asked.

"You always ask them questions?" the bartender said.

"Let's ask *you* a couple instead, okay?" Kapek said. "Who's Belinda?"

"Never heard of her."

"Okay. Just make sure *she* never hears of *me*."

"Huh?"

"You were pretty anxious just now to let our friend here know I was a cop. I'm telling you something straight, pal. I'm looking for Belinda, who*ever* the hell she is. If she finds out about it, from whatever source, I'm going to assume you're the one who tipped her. And that might just make you an accessory, pal."

"Who you trying to snow?" the bartender said. "I run a clean joint here. I don't know nobody named Belinda, and whatever she done or didn't do, I'm out of it completely. So what's this 'accessory' crap?"

"Try to forget I was in here looking for her," Kapek said. "Otherwise you're liable to find out *just* what this 'accessory' crap is. Okay?"

"You scare me to death," the bartender said.

"You know where Lennie lives?" Kapek asked.

"Yeah."

"He married?"

"Yeah."

"Call his wife. Tell her to come down here and get him."

"She'll kill him," the bartender said. He looked down at Lennie and shook his head. "I'll sober him up and get him home, don't worry about it."

He was already talking gently and kindly to the unconscious Lennie as Kapek went out of the bar.

Ramon Castañeda was in his undershirt when he opened the door for Delgado.

"*Sí, qué quiere usted?*" he asked.

"I'm Detective Delgado, Eighty-seventh Squad," Delgado said, and flipped his wallet open to show his shield. Castañeda looked at it closely.

"What's the trouble?" he asked.

"May I come in, please?" Delgado said.

"Who is it, Ray?" a woman called from somewhere in the apartment.

"Policeman," Castañeda said over his shoulder. "Come in," he said to Delgado.

Delgado went into the apartment. There was a kitchen on his right, a living room dead ahead, two bedrooms beyond that. The woman who came out of the closest bedroom was wearing a brightly flowered nylon robe and carrying a hairbrush in her right hand. She was quite beautiful, with long black hair and a pale complexion, gray-green eyes, a full bosom, ripely curved hips. She was barefoot, and she moved soundlessly into the living room, and stood with her legs slightly apart, the hairbrush held just above her hip, somewhat like a hatchet she had just unsheathed.

"Sorry to bother you this way," Delgado said.

"What is it?" the woman said.

"This is my wife," Castañeda said. "Rita, this is Detective ... what's your name again?"

"Delgado."

"You Spanish?"

"Yes."

"Good," Castañeda said.

"What is it?" Rita said again.

"Your partner José Huerta ..."

"What's the matter with him?" Castañeda asked immediately. "Is something the matter with him?"

"Yes. He was attacked by four men this morning..."

"Oh, my God!" Rita said, and brought the hand holding the hairbrush to her mouth, pressing the back of it to her lips as though stifling a scream.

"Who?" Castañeda said. "Who did it?"

"We don't know. He's at Buenavista Hospital now." Delgado paused. "Both his legs broken."

"Oh, my God!" Rita said again.

"We'll go to him at once," Castañeda said, and turned away, ready to leave the room, seemingly anxious to dress and leave for the hospital immediately.

"If I may ..." Delgado said, and Castañeda remembered he was there, and paused, still on the verge of departure, and impatiently said to his wife, "Get dressed, Rita," and then said to Delgado, "Yes, what is it? We want to see Joe as soon as possible."

"I'd like to ask some questions before you go," Delgado said.

"Yes, certainly."

"How long have you and Mr. Huerta been partners?"

The woman had not left the room. She stood standing slightly apart from the two men, the hairbrush bristles cradled on the palm of one hand, the other hand clutched tightly around the handle, her eyes wide as she listened.

"I told you to get dressed," Castañeda said to her.

She seemed about to answer him. Then she gave a brief complying nod, wheeled, and went into the bedroom, closing the door only partially behind her.

"We have been partners for two years," Castañeda said.

"Get along with each other?"

"Of course. Why?" Castañeda put his hands on his hips. He was a small man, perhaps five feet seven inches tall, and not particularly good-looking, with a pockmarked face and a longish nose and a mustache that sat just beneath it and somehow emphasized its length. He leaned toward Delgado beligerently now, defying him to explain that last question, his brown eyes burning as fiercely as had his partner's through the hospital bandages.

"A man has been assaulted, Mr. Castañeda. It's routine to question his relatives and associates. I meant no..."

"It sounded like you meant plenty," Castañeda said. His hands were still on his hips. He looked like a fighting rooster Delgado had once seen in a cock fight in the town of Vega Baja, when he had gone back to the island to visit his dying grandmother.

"Let's not get excited," Delgado said. There was a note of warning in his voice. The note informed Castañeda that whereas both men were Puerto Ricans, one of them was a cop entitled to ask questions about a third Puerto Rican who had been badly beaten up. The note further informed Castañeda that however mild Delgado's manner might appear, he wasn't about to take any crap, and Castañeda had better understand that right from go. Castañeda took his hands from his hips. Delgado stared at him a moment longer.

"Would you happen to know whether or not your partner had any enemies?" he asked. His voice was flat. Through the partially open door of the bedroom, he saw Rita Castañeda move toward the dresser, and then away from it, out of sight.

"No enemies that I know of," Castañeda replied.

"Would you know if he'd ever received any threatening letters or phone calls?"

"Never."

The flowered robe flashed into view again. Delgado's eyes flickered momentarily toward the open door. Castañeda frowned.

"Would you have had any business deals recently that caused any hard feeling with anyone?"

"None," Castañeda said. He moved toward the open bedroom door, took the knob in his hand, and pulled the door firmly shut. "We're real estate agents for apartment buildings. We rent apartments. It's as simple as that."

"No trouble with any of the tenants?"

"We hardly ever come into contact with them. Once in a while we have trouble collecting rents. But that's normal in this business, and nobody bears a grudge."

"Would you say your partner is well liked?"

Castañeda shrugged.

"What does that mean, Mr. Castañeda?"

"Well-liked, who knows? He's a man like any other man. He is liked by some and disliked by others."

"Who *dislikes* him?" Delgado asked immediately.

"No one dislikes him enough to have him beaten up," Castañeda said.

"I see," Delgado answered. He smiled pleasantly. "Well," he said, "thank you for your information. I won't keep you any longer."

"Fine, fine," Castañeda said. He went to the front door and opened it. "Let me know if you find the men who did it," he said.

"I will," Delgado answered, and found himself in the hallway. The door closed behind him. In the apartment, he heard Castañeda shout, "Rita, *esta lista?*"

He put his ear to the door.

He could hear Castañeda and his wife talking very quietly inside the apartment, their voices rumbling distantly, but he could not tell what they were saying. Only once, when Rita raised her voice, did Delgado catch a word.

The word was *hermano*, which in Spanish meant "brother."

It was close to 2 p.m., and things were pretty quiet in the squadroom.

Kapek was looking through the Known Muggers file, trying to get a lead on the black girl known only as Belinda. Carella had arrived in time to have lunch with Brown, and both men sat at a long table near one of the windows, one end of it burdened with fingerprinting equipment, eating tuna fish sandwiches and drinking coffee in cardboard containers. As they ate, Brown filled him in on what he had so far. Marshall Davies at the lab, true to his word, had gone to work on the Snow White mask the moment he received it, and had reported back not a half-hour later. He had been able to recover only one good print, that being a thumbprint on the inside surface, presumably left there when the wearer was adjusting the mask to his face. He had sent this immediately to the Identification

Section, where the men on Sunday duty had searched their Single-Fingerprint file, tracking through a maze of arches, loops, whorls, scars, and accidentals to come up with a positive identification for a man named Bernard Goldenthal.

His yellow sheet was now on Brown's desk, and both detectives studied it carefully:

PRISONER'S CRIMINAL RECORD	POLICE DEPARTMENT	IDENTIFICATION SECTION

NAME BERNARD GOLDENTHAL   B # 47-61042

ALIAS "Bernie Gold," "Goldie," "Goldfinger."   I.S. # G-21-3479

DATE OF BIRTH February 12, 1931   F.B.I. # 74-01-22

FINGERPRINT CLASSIFICATION   27 L 1 T r 26   89234
                                   L 1 U

This certifies that the finger impressions of the above-named person have been compared and the following is a true copy of the records of this section.

Date of Arrest	Location	Charge	Arresting Officer	Date, Disposition, Judge and Court
5-7-47	Isola	Burg. Juv. Del.	D of C	Jewish Home for Boys
2-9-48	Calm's Point	Burg. Fin. Chg. Unlaw Entry	Wexner 75 Pct.	Judge McCarthy County Court
6-5-49	Isola	Robbery	Janus 19 Sqd.	6-30-49 Dismissed Judge Evans Sup. Court
8-17-49	Isola	Robbery Gun	Cowper 19 Sqd.	11-28-49 Discharged Judge Mastro Gen. Sess.
1-21-51	Riverhead	Gr. Larc 1st Burg. 3rd	Franklin	3-11-51 5 to 10 Yrs. on Gr. Larc. 5 to 10 Yrs. on Burg. 3rd. Judge Lefkin, County Court.
12-19-59	Isola	Theft from Interstate Shipment	F.B.I.	3 yrs to serve followed by 10 yrs probation Judge O'Hare U.S. So. Dist. Court.
12-23-69	Isola	974 PL	Magruder 2 Div	1-28-70 $50 or 10 days Judge Fields Spec. Sess.
1-9-70	Isola	974 PL	Donovan 2 Div	1-28-70 $100/30 days Judge Fields Spec. Sess.
9-19-70	Isola	974a PL	Donato CIU	11-25-70 Gen. Sess. Unl. Poss. Policy Slips $150 or 60 days. Ashworth.

X represent notations unsupported by fingerprints in Identification Section files.
"This record is furnished solely for the official use of law enforcement agencies. Unauthorized use of this information is in violation of Sections 554 and 2050, Penal Law."

A man's yellow sheet (so called because the record actually *was* duplicated on a yellow sheet of paper; bar owners were not the *only* imaginative people in this city) was perhaps not as entertaining, say, as a good novel, but it did have a shorthand narrative power all its own. Goldenthal's record had the added interest of a rising dramatic line, a climax of sorts, and then a slackening of tension just before the denouement – which was presumably yet to come.

His first arrest had been at the age of sixteen, for Burglary and Juvenile Delinquency, and he had been remanded to the Jewish Home for Boys, a correctional institution. Less than a year later, apparently back on the streets again, he had been arrested again for Burglary, with the charge reduced to Unlawful Entry and (the record incomplete here) the courts had apparently shown leniency in consideration of his age – he was barely seventeen at the time – let him off scot-free. Progressing to bigger and better things during the next year, he was arrested first on a Robbery charge and then on a Robbery with Gun charge, and again the courts showed mercy and let him go. Thus emboldened and encouraged, he moved on to Grand Larceny First and Burglary Third, was again busted and this time was sent to prison. He had probably served both terms concurrently, and was released on parole sometime before 1959, when apparently he decided to knock over a truck crossing state lines, thereby inviting the Federal Bureau of Investigation to step in. Carella and Brown figured the "3 years to serve" were the three years remaining from his prior conviction; the courts were again being lenient.

And perhaps this leniency was finally paying off. The violations he'd been convicted of since his second release from prison were not too terribly serious, especially when compared to Grand Larceny or Interstate Theft. Section 974 of the Penal Law was defined as "keeping a place for or transferring money in the game of policy," and was a misdemeanor. Section 974a was a bit heavier – "Operating a policy business" – and was a felony punishable by imprisonment for a term not exceeding five years. In either case, Goldenthal seemed to have moved into a more respectable line of work, employing himself in the "policy" or "numbers game," which many hard-working citizens felt was a perfectly harmless recreation and hardly anything for the Law to get all excited about. The Law had not, in fact, got too terribly excited about Goldenthal's most recent offenses. He could have got five years on his last little adventure, when in fact all he had drawn was a fine of a hundred and fifty dollars or sixty days, on a reduced charge of Unlawful Possession of Policy Slips, Section 975 of the Penal Law.

Goldenthal had begun his criminal career at the age of sixteen. He was now almost forty years old, and had spent something better than ten years of his adult life in prison. If they found him, and busted him again, and convicted him of the grocery store holdup and murder, he would be sent away forever.

There were several other pieces of information in the packet the I.S. had sent uptown – a copy of Goldenthal's fingerprint card, with a complete description of him on the reverse side; a final report from his probation officer back in '69; a copy of the Detective Division report on his most recent arrest – but the item of chief interest to Carella and Brown was Goldenthal's last known address. He had apparently been living in uptown Isola with his mother, a Mrs. Minnie Goldenthal, until the time of her death three months ago. He had then moved to an apartment downtown, and was presumably still living there.

They decided to hit it together.

They were no fools.

Goldenthal had once been arrested on a gun charge, and either he or his partner had put three bullets into two men not seven hours before.

The show began ten minutes after Carella and Brown left the squadroom. It had a cast of four and was titled *Hookers' Parade*. It starred two young streetwalkers who billed themselves as Rebecca and Sally Good.

"Those are not your real names," Kapek insisted.

"Those are our real names," Sally answered, "and you can all go to hell."

The other two performers in the show were the patrolman who had answered the complaint and made the arrest, and a portly gentleman in a pinstriped suit who looked mortally offended though not at all embarrassed, rather like a person who had wet his pajamas in a hospital bed, where illness is expected and enjoyed but certainly nothing to be ashamed of.

"All right, what's the story, Phil?" Kapek asked the patrolman.

"Well, what happened..."

"If you don't mind," the portly gentleman said, "*I* am the injured party here."

"Who the hell injured you, would you mind telling me?" Rebecca said.

"All right, let's calm down here," Kapek said. He had finished with the Known Muggers file and was anxious to get to the Modus Operandi file, and he found all this tumult distracting. The girls, one black and one white, were both wearing tan sweaters, suede miniskirts, and brown boots. Sally, the white one, had long blond hair. Rebecca, the black one, had her hair done in an Afro cut and bleached blond. They were both in their early twenties, both quite attractive, long and leggy and busty and brazen and cheap as a bottle of ninety-cent wine. The portly gentleman sat some distance away from them on the opposite side of Kapek's desk, as though afraid of contracting some dread disease. His face was screwed into an offended frown, his eyes sparked with indignation.

"I wish these young ladies arrested," he said. "I am the man who made the complaint, the injured party, and I am willing to press charges, and I wish them arrested at once."

"Fine, Mr...." Kapek consulted his pad. "Mr. Searle," he said. "Do you want to tell me what happened?"

"I am from Independence, Missouri," Searle said. "The home of Harry S. Truman."

"Yes, sir," Kapek said.

"Big deal," Sally said.

"I am here in the city on business," Searle said. "I usually stay midtown, but I have several appointments in this area tomorrow morning, and I thought it would be more convenient to find lodgings in the neighborhood." He paused and cleared his throat. "There is a rather nice hotel overlooking the park. The Grover."

"Yes, sir," Kapek said.

"Or at least *I thought* it was a rather nice hotel."

"It's a fleabag," Rebecca said.

"How about knocking if off?" Kapek said.

"What the hell for? This hick blows the whistle for no reason at all, and we're supposed..."

"Let's hear what the man has to say, okay?" Kapek said sharply.

"Okay," Rebecca said.

"*Whatever* he has to say," Sally said, "he's full of crap."

"Listen, sister," Kapek warned.

"Okay, okay," Sally said, and tossed her long blond hair. Rebecca crossed her legs, and lighted a cigarette. She blew the stream of smoke in Searle's direction, and he waved it away with his hands.

"Mr. Searle?" Kapek prompted.

"I was sitting in my room reading the *Times*," Searle said, "when a knock sounded on the door."

"When was this, Mr. Searle?"

"An hour ago? I'm not sure."

"What time did you catch the squeal, Phil?"

"One-twenty."

"Just *about* an hour ago," Kapek said.

"Then it must have been a little earlier than that," Searle said. "They must have arrived at about one-ten or thereabouts."

"Who's that, Mr. Searle?"

"These young ladies," he answered, without looking at them.

"They knocked on your door?"

"They did."

"And then what?"

"I opened the door. They were standing there in the corridor. Both of them. They said..." Searle shook his head. "This is entirely inconceivable to me."

"What did they say?"

"They said the elevator operator told them I wanted some action, and they were there to supply it. I didn't know what they meant at first. I asked them what they meant. They told me exactly what they meant."

"What did they tell you, Mr. Searle?"

"Do we have to go into this?"

"If you're going to press charges, why, yes, I guess we do. I'm not sure yet what these girls did or said to..."

"They offered to sleep with me," Searle said, and looked away.

"Who the hell would want to sleep with *you*?" Sally muttered.

"Got to be out of your mind," Rebecca said, and blew another stream of smoke at him.

"They told me they would *both* like to sleep with me," Searle said. "Together."

"Uh-huh," Kapek said, and glanced at Rebecca. "Is that right?" he asked.

"Nope," Rebecca answered.

"So, okay, what happened next?" Kapek asked.

"I told them to come back in five minutes."

"Why'd you tell them that?"

"Because I wanted to inform the police."

"And did you?"

"I did."

"And did the girls come back?"

"In seven minutes. I clocked them."

"And then what?"

"They came into the room and said it would be fifty dollars for each of them. I told them that was very expensive. They both took off their sweaters to show me what I would be getting for the money. Neither of them was wearing a brassiere."

"Is that right?" Kapek asked.

"Nobody wears bras today," Sally said.

"Nobody," Rebecca said.

"That don't make us hookers," Sally said.

"Ask the officer here in what condition he found them when he entered the room."

"Phil?"

"Naked from the waist up," the patrolman said.

"I wish them arrested," Searle said. "For prostitution."

"You got some case, Fatty," Rebecca said.

"You know what privates are, Fatty," Sally asked.

"Must I be submitted to this kind of talk?" Searle said. "Surely..."

"Knock it off," Kapek said to the girls. "What they're trying to tell you, Mr. Searle, is that it's extremely difficult in this city to make a charge of prostitution stick unless the woman has exposed her privates, do you see what I mean? Her genitals," Kapek said. "That's been our experience. That's what it is," he concluded, and shrugged. Rebecca and Sally were smiling.

"They did expose themselves to me," Searle said.

"Yes, but not the privates, you see. They have to expose the privates. That's the yardstick, you see. For arrest. To make a conviction stick. That's been the, you see, experience of the police department in such matters. Now, of course, we can always book them for disorderly conduct..."

"Yes, do that," Searle said.

"That's Section 722," Kapek said, "Subdivision 9, but then you'd have to testify in court that the girls were soliciting, you know, were hanging around a public place for the purpose of committing a crime against nature or any other lewdness. That's the way it's worded, that subdivision. So you'd have to explain in court what happened. I mean, what they said to you and all. You know what I mean, Mr. Searle?"

"I think so, yes."

"We could also get them on Section 887, Subdivision 4 of the Code of Criminal Procedure. That's, you know, inducing, enticing or procuring another to commit lewdness, fornication..."

"Yes, yes, I quite understand," Searle said, and waved his hand as though clearing away smoke, though Rebecca had not blown any in his direction.

"...unlawful sexual intercourse or any other indecent act," Kapek concluded. "But there, too, you'd have to testify in court."

"Wouldn't the patrolman's word be enough? He saw them all exposed that way."

"Well, we got half a dozen plays running in this town where the girls are naked from the waist up, and also down, and that doesn't mean they're offering to commit prostitution." Kapek turned to the patrolman. "Phil, you hear them *say* anything about prostitution?"

"Nope," the patrolman answered, and grinned. He was obviously enjoying himself.

"*I* heard them," Searle said.

"Sure. And like I said, if you're willing to testify in court..."

"They're *obvious* prostitutes," Searle said.

"Probably got records, too, no question," Kapek said. "But ..."

"I've never been busted," Sally said.

"How about you, Rebecca?" Kapek asked.

"If you're going to start asking me questions, I want a lawyer. *That's* how about me."

"Well, what do you say, Mr. Searle? You want to go ahead with this, or not?" Kapek asked.

"When would I have to go to court?"

"Prostitution cases usually get immediate hearings. Dozens of them each day. I guess it would be tomorrow sometime."

"I have business to take care of tomorrow. That's why I'm here to begin with."

"Well," Kapek said, and shrugged.

"I hate to let them get away with this," Searle said.

"Why?" Sally asked. "Who did you any harm?"

"You offended me gravely, young lady."

"How?" Rebecca asked.

"Would you ask them to go, please?" Searle said.

"You've decided not to press charges?"

"That is my decision."

"Beat it," Kapek said to the girls. "Keep your asses out of that hotel. Next time, you may not be so lucky."

Neither of the girls said a word. Sally waited while Rebecca ground her cigarette in the ashtray. Then they both swiveled out of the squadroom. Searle looked somewhat dazed. He sat staring ahead of him. Then he shook his head and said, "When they think *that*, when they think a man needs *two* women, they're really thinking he can't even handle *one*." He shook his head again, rose, put his homburg onto his head, and walked out of the squadroom. The patrolman tilted his nightstick at Kapek, and ambled out after him.

Kapek sighed and went to the Modus Operandi file.

The last known address for Bernard Goldenthal was on the North Side, all the way downtown in a warehouse district adjacent to the River Harb. The tenement in which he reportedly lived was shouldered between two huge edifices that threatened to squash it flat. The street was deserted. This was Sunday, and there was no traffic. Even the tugboats on the river, not two blocks away, seemed motionless. Carella and Brown went into the building, checked the mailboxes – there was a name in only one of them, and it was not Goldenthal's – and then went up to the third floor, where Goldenthal was supposed to be living in Apartment 3A. They listened outside the door, and heard nothing. Carella nodded to Brown, and Brown knocked.

"Who is it?" a man's voice asked from behind the door.

"Mr. Goldenthal?" Brown asked.

"No," the man answered. "Who is it?"

Brown looked at Carella. Carella nodded.

"Police officers," Brown said. "Want to open up, please?"

There was a slight hesitation from behind the door. Carella unbuttoned his coat and put his hand on the butt of his revolver. The door opened. The man standing there was in his forties, perhaps as tall as Carella, heavier, with black hair that sprang from his scalp like weeds in a small garden, brown eyes opened wide in inquiry, thick black brows arched over them. Whoever he was, he did not by any stretch of the imagination fit the description on Goldenthal's fingerprint card.

"Yes?" he said. "What is it?"

"We're looking for Bernard Goldenthal," Brown said. "Does he live here?"

"No, I'm sorry," the man said. "He doesn't." He spoke quite softly, the way a very big man will sometimes speak to a child or an old person, as though compensating for his hugeness by lowering the volume of his voice.

"Our information says he lives here," Carella said.

"Well, I'm sorry," the man said, "but he doesn't. He may have done at one time, but he doesn't now."

"What's *your* name?" Carella asked. His coat was still open, and his hand was lightly on his hip, close to his holster.

"Herbert Gross."

"Mind if we come in, Mr. Gross?"

"Why would you want to?" Gross asked.

"To see if Mr. Goldenthal is here."

"I just told you he wasn't," Gross said.

"Mind if we check it for ourselves?" Brown said.

"I really don't see why I should let you," Gross said.

"Goldenthal's a known criminal," Carella said, "and we're looking for him in connection with a recent crime. The last address we have for him is 911 Forrester, Apartment 3A. This is 911 Forrester, Apartment 3A, and we'd like to come in and check on whether or not our information is correct."

"Your information is wrong," Gross insisted. "It must be very old information."

"No, it's recent information."

"How recent?"

"Less than three months old."

"Well, I've been living here for two months now, so he must have moved before that."

"Are you going to let us in, Mr. Gross?"

"No, I don't think so," Gross said.

"Why not?"

"I don't think I like the idea of policemen crashing in here on a Sunday afternoon, that's all."

"Anybody in there with you?"

"I don't think that's any of your business," Gross said.

"Look, Mr. Gross," Brown said, "we can come back here with a warrant, if that's what you'd like. Why not make it easier for us?"

"Why should I?"

"Why shouldn't you?" Carella said. "Have you got anything to hide?"

"Nothing at all."

"Then how about it?"

"Sorry," Gross said, and closed the door and locked it.

The two detectives stood in the hallway and silently weighed their next move. There were two possibilities open to them, and both of them presented considerable risks. The first possibility was that Goldenthal was indeed in the apartment and armed, in which event he was now warned and if they kicked in the door he would open fire immediately. The second possibility was that the I.S. information *was* dated, and that Goldenthal had indeed moved from the apartment more than two months ago, in which event Gross would have a dandy case against the city if they kicked in the door and conducted an illegal search. Brown gestured with his head, and both men moved toward the stairwell, away from the door.

"What do you think?" Brown whispered.

"There were two of them on the grocery store job," Carella said. "Gross might just be the other man."

"He fits the description I got from the old lady," Brown said. "Shall we kick it in?"

"I'd rather wait downstairs. He expects us to come back. If he's in this with Goldenthal, he's going to run, sure as hell."

"Right," Brown said. "Let's split."

They had parked Brown's sedan just outside the building. Knowing that Gross's apartment overlooked the street, and hoping that he was now watching them from his window, they got into the car and drove north toward the river. Brown turned right under the River Highway, and headed uptown. He turned right again at the next corner, and then drove back to Scovil Avenue and Forrester Street, where he pulled the car to the curb. Both men got out.

"Think he's still watching?" Brown asked.

"I doubt it, but why take chances?" Carella said. "The street's deserted. If we plant ourselves in one of the doorways on this end of the block, we can see anybody going in or out of his building."

The first doorway they found had obviously been used as a nest by any number of vagrants. Empty pint bottles of whiskey in brown paper bags littered the floor, together with empty crumpled cigarette packages, and empty half-gallon wine bottles, and empty candy bar wrappers. The stench of urine was overpowering.

"No job's worth *this*," Brown said.

"Don't care if he killed the goddamn *governor*," Carella said.

They walked swiftly into the clean brisk October air. Brown looked up the street toward Gross's building. Together, he and Carella ducked into the next doorway. It was better, but only a trifle so.

"Let's hope he makes his move fast," Brown said.

"Let's hope so," Carella agreed.

They did not have long to wait.

In five minutes flat, Gross came down the front steps of the building and began walking south, toward the building where they waited. They moved back against the wall. He walked past swiftly, without even glancing into the hallway. They gave him a good lead, and then took off after him, one on each side of the street, so that they formed an isosceles triangle with Gross at the point and Brown and Carella at either end of the base.

They lost him on Payne Avenue, when he boarded an uptown bus that left them running up behind it to choke in a cloud of carbon monoxide. They decided then to go back to the apartment and kick the door in, which is maybe what they should have done in the goddamn first place.

There is an old Spanish proverb which, when translated into city slang, goes something like this: *When nobody knows nothing, everybody knows everything.*

Nobody seemed to know nothing about the José Vicente Huerta assault. He had been attacked in broad daylight on a clear day by four men carrying sawed-off broom handles, and they had beaten him severely enough to have broken both his legs and opened a dozen or more wounds on his face, but nobody seemed to have had a good look at them, even though the beating had lasted a good five minutes or more.

Delgado was not a natural cynic, but he certainly had his doubts about this one. He went through Huerta's building talking to the tenants on each floor, and then he went to the candy store across the street, from which the front stoop of the building was clearly visible, and talked to the proprietor there, but nobody knew nothing. He decided to try another tack.

There was a junkie hooker in the *barrio*, a nineteen-year-old girl who had only one arm. Her handicap, rather than repelling any prospective customers, seemed instead to excite them wildly. From far and wide, the panting Johns came uptown seeking the One-Armed Bandit, as she was notoriously known. She was more familiarly known as Blanca Diaz to those neighborhood men who were among her regular customers, she having a habit as long as the River Harb, and they knowing a good lay when they stumbled across it, one-armed or not, especially since the habit caused her to charge bargain rates most of the time. Conversely, many of the neighborhood men were familiarly know to Blanca, and it was for this reason alone that Delgado sought her out.

Blanca was not too terribly interested in passing the time of day with a cop, Puerto Rican or otherwise. But she knew that most of the precinct detectives, unlike Vice Squad cops, were inclined to look the other way where she was concerned, perhaps because of her infirmity. Moreover, she had just had her 3 p.m. fix and was feeling no pain when Delgado approached her. She was, in fact, enjoying the October sunshine, sitting on a bench on one of the grassy ovals running up the center of The Stem. She spotted Delgado from the corner of her eye, debated moving, thought *Oh, the hell with it*, and sat where she was, basking.

"Hello, Blanca," Delgado said.

"Hullo," she answered.

"You okay?"

"I'm fine. I'm not holding, if that's what you mean."

"That's not what I mean."

"I mean, if you're looking for a cheap dope bust ..."

"I'm not."

"Okay," Blanca said, and nodded. She was not an unattractive girl. Her complexion was dark, her hair was black, her eyes a light shade of brown; her lips were perhaps a trifle too full, and there was a small unsightly scar on her jawline, where she had been stabbed by a pimp when she was just sixteen and already shooting heroin three times a day.

"You want to help me?" Delgado asked.

"Doing what?"

"I need some information."

"I'm no stoolie," Blanca said.

"If I ask you anything you don't want to answer, you don't have to."

"Thanks for nothing."

"*Querida*," Delgado said, "we're very nice to you. Be nice back, huh?"

She looked him full in the face, sighed, and said, "What do you want to know?"

"Everything you know about Joe Huerta."

"Nothing."

"He ever come to visit you?"

"Never."

"What about his partner?"

"Who's his partner?"

"Ray Castañeda."

"I don't know him," Blanca said. "Is he related to Pepe Castañeda?"

"Maybe. Tell me about Pepe."

Blanca shrugged. "A punk," she said.

"How old is he?"

"Thirty? Something like that."

"What's he do?"

"Who knows? Maybe numbers, I'm not sure. He used to be a junkie years ago, he's one of the few guys I know who kicked it. He was with this street gang, they called themselves The Spanish Nobles or some shit like that, this was when he was still a kid, you know. I was only five or six myself, you know, but he was a very big man in the neighborhood, rumbling all the time with this wop gang from the other side of the park, I forget the name of the gang, it was a very big one. Then, you know, everybody started doing dope, the guys all lost interest in gang-busting. Pepe was a very big junkie, but he kicked it. I think he went down to Lexington, I'm not sure. Or maybe he just got busted and sent away and kicked it cold turkey, I'm not sure. But he's off it now, I know that." She shrugged. "He's still a punk though."

"Have you seen him lately?"

"Yeah, he's around all the time. You always see him on the stoop someplace. Always with a bunch of kids around him, you know, listening to his crap. Big man. The reformed whore," Blanca said, and snorted.

"Have you seen him today?"

"No. I just come down a little while ago. I had a trick with me all night."

"Where can I find him, would you know?"

"Pepe or the trick?" Blanca asked and smiled.

"Pepe," Delgado said, and did not smile back.

"There's a pool hall on Ainsley," Blanca said. "He hangs around there a lot."

"Let's get back to Huerta for a minute, okay?"

"Why?" Blanca asked, and turned to look at a bus that was rumbling up the avenue.

"Because we got away from him too fast," Delgado said.

"I hardly know him," Blanca said. She was still watching the bus. Its blue-gray exhaust fumes seemed to fascinate her.

"You mind looking at me?" Delgado said.

She turned back toward him sharply. "I told you I'm not a stoolie," Blanca said. "I don't want to answer no questions about Joe Huerta."

"Why not. What's he into?"

"No comment."

"Dope?"

"No comment."

"Yes or no, Blanca? We know where you live, we can have the Vice Squad banging on your door every ten minutes. Tell me about Huerta."

"Okay, he's dealing, okay?"

"I thought he had a real estate business."

"Sure. He's got an acre of land in Mexico, and he grows pot on it."

"Is he pushing the hard stuff, too?"

"No. Only grass."

"Does his partner know this?"

"I don't know what his partner knows or don't know. I'm not his partner. Go ask his partner."

"Maybe I will," Delgado said. "After I talk to his partner's brother."

"You going to look for Pepe now?"

"Yes."

"Tell him he still owes me five bucks."

"What for?"

"What do you think for?" Blanca asked.

Genero was waiting on the sidewalk when Willis came out of the phone booth.

"What'd they say?" he asked.

"Nothing yet. They've got a lot of stuff ahead of what we sent them."

"So how we supposed to know if it's grass or oregano?" Genero said.

"I guess we wait. They told me to call back in a half-hour or so."

"Those guys at the lab give me a pain in the ass," Genero said.

"Yeah, well, what're you gonna do?" Willis said. "We all have our crosses to bear." The truth was that Genero gave *him* a pain in the ass. They had arranged for pickup and delivery to the lab of the plastic bag full of oregano/marijuana and had asked for a speedy report on it. But the lab was swamped with such requests every day of the week, the average investigating officer never being terribly certain about a suspect drug until it was checked out downtown. Willis had been willing to wait for the report; Genero had insisted that he call the lab and find out what was happening. Now, at twenty minutes to four, they knew what was happening: nothing. So now Genero was beginning to sulk, and Willis was beginning to wish he would go home and explain to his mother how tough it was to be a working detective in this city.

They were in an area of The Quarter that was not as chic as the section further south, lacking its distinctive Left Bank flair, but boasting of the same high rentals nonetheless, this presumably because of its proximity to all the shops and theaters and coffee houses. 3541 Carrier Avenue was a brownstone in a row of identical brownstones worn shoddy by the passage of time. They found a nameplate for Robert Hamling in one of the mailboxes in the entrance hallway downstairs. Willis rang the bell for apartment 22. An answering buzz on the inner door sounded almost immediately. Genero opened the door and both men moved into a dim ground-floor landing. A flight of steps was directly ahead of them. The building smelled of Lysol. They went up to the second floor, searched for Apartment 22, listened outside the door, heard nothing, and knocked.

"Bobby?" a girl's voice said.

"Police officers," Willis said.

"What do you want?" the girl asked.

"Open the door," Genero said.

There was silence inside the apartment. They kept listening. They knew that Robert Hamling wasn't in there with the girl, because the first word out of her mouth had been "Bobby?" But nobody knows better than cops that the female is the deadlier of the species, and so they waited apprehensively for her to unlock the door, their coats open, their guns within ready drawing distance. When the door finally opened, they were looking at a teenage girl wearing dungarees and a tie-dyed T-shirt. Her face was round, her eyes were blue, her brown hair was long and matted.

"Yes, what do you want?" she said. She seemed very frightened and very nervous. She kept one hand on the doorknob. The other fluttered at the throat of the T-shirt.

"We're looking for Robert Hamling," Willis said. "Does he live here?"

"Yes?" she said, tentatively.

"Is he home?"

"No."

"When do you expect him?"

"I don't know."

"What's your name, miss?" Genero asked.

"Sonia."

"Sonia what?"

"Sonia Sobolev."

"How old are you, Sonia?"

"Seventeen."

"Do you live here?"

"No."

"Where *do* you live?"

"In Riverhead."

"What are you doing here?"

"Waiting for Bobby. He's a friend of mine."

"When did he go out?"

"I don't know."

"How'd you get in here?"

"I have a key."

"Mind if we come in and wait with you?"

"I don't care," she said, and shrugged. "If you want to come in, come in." She stood aside. She was still very frightened. As they entered, she looked past them into the hallway, as if anxious for Hamling to appear and wishing it would be damn soon. Willis caught this, though Genero did not. She closed the door behind them, and together they went into a room furnished with several battered easy chairs, a foam rubber sofa, and a low, slatted coffee table. "Well, sit down," she said.

The detectives sat on the sofa. Sonia took one of the chairs opposite them.

"How well do you know Robert Hamling?" Willis asked.

"Pretty well."

"When did you see him last?"

"Oh ..." she said, and shrugged, and seemed to be thinking it over.

"Yes?"

"Well, what difference does it make?"

"It might make a difference."

"Last week sometime, I guess."

"*When* last week?"

"Well, why don't you ask Bobby when he gets here?"

"We will," Genero said. "Meantime, we're asking you. When did you see him last?"

"I don't remember," Sonia said.

"Do you know anybody named Lewis Scott?" Willis asked.

"No."

"Ever hear of a clothing store called The Monkey Wrench?"

"Yes, I think so."

"Ever buy any clothes there?"

"I don't remember."

"Ever buy a black silk bouse there?" Genero asked.

"I don't remember."

"Show her the blouse, Dick," Willis said.

Genero produced the manila envelope again. He took the blouse from it and handed it to the girl. "This yours?" he asked.

"I don't know."

"Yes or no?" Genero said.

"It could be, I can't tell for sure. I have a lot of clothes."

"Do you have a lot of black silk blouses bought at a store called The Monkey Wrench?"

"Well, no, but a person could get confused about her clothes. I mean, it's a black silk blouse, it could be *any* black silk blouse. How do I know it's mine?"

"What size blouse do you take?"

"Thirty-four."

"This is a thirty-four," Willis said.

"That still doesn't make it mine, does it?" Sonia asked.

"Were you here in Isola last night?" Willis asked.

"Well, yes."

"Where?"

"Oh, banking around."

"Where?"

"Here and there."

"Here and there *where*?"

"You don't have to answer him, Sonia," a voice from the doorway said, and both detectives turned simultaneously. The boy standing there was about eighteen, with long blond hair and a handlebar mustache. He had on blue jeans and a blue corduroy shirt, over which he wore an open coat with white fur showing on the inside.

"Mr Hamling, I presume," Willis said.

"That's me," Hamling said. He turned to close the entrance door. A bright orange, radiating sun was painted on the back of the coat.

"We've been looking for you," Willis said.

"So now you found me," Hamling said. "This is about Lew, isn't it?"

"You tell *us*," Genero said.

"Sure, it's about Lew," Hamling said. "I figured you'd get to me sooner or later."

"What about him?"

"He jumped out of the window last night."

"Were you there when he jumped?"

"We were *both* there," Hamling said, and glanced at the girl. The girl nodded.

"Want to tell us what happened?"

"He was on a bum trip," Hamling said. "He thought he could fly. I tried to hold him down, but he ran for the window and jumped out. End of story."

"Why didn't you report this to the police?"

"What for? I've got long hair."

Willis sighed. "Well," he said, "we're here now, so why don't you just tell us everything that happened, and we'll file the damn report and close out the case."

Genero looked at him. Willis was taking out his pad. "Want to tell me what time you went over there?"

"It must've been about four-thirty or so. Look?" Hamling said, "am I going to get in any trouble on this?"

"Why should you? If Scott jumped out of the window, that's suicide, plain and simple."

"Yeah, well he did."

"Okay, so help us close it out, will you? This is a headache for us, too," Willis said, and again Genero looked at him. "What happened when you got there?"

"Why do *I* have to be in it, that's all I want to know?" Hamling said.

"Well, you *were* in it, weren't you?"

"Yeah, but..."

"So what are we supposed to do? Make believe you *weren't* there? Come on, give us a break. Nobody's trying to get you into trouble. You know how many acid freaks jump out of the window every day of the week?"

"I just don't want it to get in the papers or anything," Hamling said. "That's why I didn't call you in the first place."

"We realize that," Willis said. "We'll do everything we can to protect you. Just give us the information we need to get a report typed up, that's all."

"Well, okay," Hamling said reluctantly.

"So what happened? Did all three of you go up there together, or what?" Willis said.

"No, I ran into him on the street," Hamling said. "I was alone at the time. I called Sonia up later, and she came over."

Willis was writing on the pad. Genero was still watching him. Genero had the strangest feeling that something was going on, but he didn't know quite what. He also had the feeling that he was about to learn something. He was both confused and somewhat exhilarated. He kept his mouth shut and simply watched and listened. "All right," Willis said, "you ran into this friend of yours and..."

"No, no, he wasn't a friend of mine," Hamling said.

"You didn't know him?"

"No, I just ran into him in this coffee joint, and we began talking, you know? So he asked me if I wanted to come up to his place and hear some records, you know, and ... listen, can I get in trouble if I *really* level with you guys?"

"I'd appreciate it if you would," Willis said.

"Well, he said he had some good stuff and maybe we could have a smoke. That's all I thought it was at the time. Just a smoke, you see. I mean, if I'd known the guy had acid in his apartment..."

"You didn't know that at the time?"

"No, hell, no. I usually try to stay away from these plastic hippies, anyway, they're usually a lot of trouble."

"How do you mean, trouble?"

"Oh, you know, they're trying to show off all the time, trying to be something they really aren't. Weekend hippies, plastic hippies, same damn thing. None of them are *really* making the scene, they're only *pretending* to make it."

"How about you?"

"I consider myself genuine," Hamling said with dignity.

"How about Sonia?"

"Well, she's sort of a weekend hippie," Hamling said, "but she's also a very groovy chick, so I put up with her." He smiled broadly. Sonia did not smile back. She was still frightened. Her hands were clasped in her lap, and she kept shifting her eyes from Willis to Hamling as though knowing that a dangerous game was being played, and wanting desperately to be elsewhere. Genero sensed this, and also sensed in his inexperienced, newly promoted way that the girl was Willis' real prey and that it would only be a matter of time before he sprang for her jugular. The girl knew this, too. Hamling seemed to be the only person in the room who did *not* know it. Supremely confident of himself, he plunged on.

"Anyway, we went up there and smoked a few joints and drank some wine, and it was then I suggested I give Sonia a ring and have her come over, join in the celebration."

"What were you celebrating?" Willis asked.

Hamling hesitated. He thought the question over for several moments, and then grinned and said. "Life. Living. Being alive."

"Okay," Willis said.

Genero was still watching very closely, learning as he went along. He knew, for example, that Hamling had just told a lie. Whatever they'd been celebrating, it had not been life or living or being alive. He could not have told *how* he knew it. And the girl knew it. And Genero knew that before long Willis would come back to the reason for the celebration, in an attempt to expose Hamling's lie. Genero felt great. He felt as though he were watching a cops-and-robbers movie on television. He didn't want it to end, ever. It never once occurred to him, as he watched and listened to Willis, that he himself was a detective. All he knew was that he was having a great time. He almost asked the girl how she was enjoying herself. He wished he had a bag of popcorn.

"So I went down to the street," Hamling said. "He didn't have a phone in the apartment. I went to a pay phone to call Sonia. She ..."

"Where was Sonia?"

"Here. I was supposed to meet her here at seven o'clock, and this was now maybe close to eight. She has a key, so I knew she'd let herself in."

"*Was* she here?"

"Oh, yeah. So I asked her to meet me uptown. She said she wasn't too familiar with that part of the city, so I told her what train to take, and I met her at the subway stop."

"What time was that?"

"She must've got there about eight-thirty. Wouldn't you say it was eight-thirty, Sonia?"

The girl nodded.

"Did you go back to the apartment then?"

"Yes," Hamling said. "That was the *first* mistake."

"Why?"

"He was naked when he opened the door. I thought at first ... hell, I didn't know *what* to think. Then I realized he was high. And then I realized he was on an acid trip. A bummer. I tried to find out what he'd dropped, there's all kinds of stuff, you know, good and bad. Like there's a whole lot of difference between white owsley and green flats; you get shit with strychnine and arsenic mixed into it, man, that's bad news. But he wasn't making any sense at all, didn't know what he'd dropped, didn't know where he was, kept running around the room bare-assed and screaming and yelling he could fly. Scared Sonia half out of her mind, right, honey?"

The girl nodded.

"When did he jump out the window?" Willis asked.

"I don't know, we must've been there maybe twenty minutes. I was trying to talk him down, you know, telling him to cool it, calm it, like that, when all of a sudden he jumps up and makes a break for the window. I tried to grab him, but I was too late. The window was closed, you dig? He went through it head first, man oh man. I looked down in the yard, and there he was laying there like..." Hamling shook his head.

"So what'd you do?"

"I grabbed Sonia, and we split. I didn't want to get mixed up in it. You got long hair, you're dead."

"Well, looks open and shut to me," Willis said, and closed his pad. "What do you think, Dick?"

Genero nodded. "Yeah, looks open and shut to me, too," he said. He was beginning to think he'd been mistaken about Willis. Was it possible his more experienced partner had *really* been after the details of a suicide? He felt vaguely disappointed.

"Just one more question, I guess," Willis said, "and then we can leave you alone. Can't thank you enough for your co-operation. People just don't realize how much trouble they cause when they decide to kill themselves."

"Oh, I can imagine," Hamling said.

"We have to treat suicides just like homicides, you know. Same people to notify, same reports to fill out, it's a big job."

"Oh, sure," Hamling said.

"Well, thanks again," Willis said, and started for the door. "Coming, Dick?"

"Yep," Genero said, and nodded. "Thanks a lot," he said to Hamling.

"Glad to be of help," Hamling said. "If I'd known you guys were going to be so decent, I wouldn't have split, I mean it."

"Oh, that last question," Willis said, as though remembering something that had momentarily slipped his mind. "Miss Sobolev..."

Hamling's eyes darted to the girl.

"Miss Sobolev, did you take off your blouse before or after Scott jumped out the window?"

"I don't remember," she said.

"I guess it was before," Willis said. "Because you both left immediately after he jumped."

"Yes, I suppose it was before," Sonia said.

"Miss Sobolev... *why* did you take off your blouse?"

"Well... I don't know why, really. I mean, I guess I just felt like taking it off."

"I guess she took it off because..."

"Well, let's let *her* answer it, okay? So we can clear this up, and leave you alone, okay? Why'd you take it off, Miss Sobolev?"

"I guess it was... I guess it was warm in the apartment."

"So you took off your blouse?"

"Yes."

"You'd never met Scott before, but you took off your blouse..."

"Well, it was warm."

"He was on a bum trip, running around the place and screaming, and you decided to take off your blouse."

"Yes."

"Mmm," Willis said. "Do you want to know how *I* read this, Mr. Hamling?"

"How?" Hamling said, and looked at the girl. Genero looked at both of them, and then looked at Willis. He didn't know *what* was going on. He was so excited, he almost wet his pants.

"I think you're protecting the girl," Willis said.

"Yeah?" Hamling said, puzzled.

"Yeah. It's my guess they were balling in that apartment, and something happened, and the girl here shoved Scott out of the window, that's my guess." The girl's mouth had fallen open. Willis turned to her and nodded. "We're going to have to take you with us, Miss Sobolev."

"What do you ... *mean*?" she said.

"Uptown," Willis answered. "Mr. Hamling, we won't be needing you for now, but the District Attorney may want to ask some more questions after we've booked Miss Sobolev. Please don't leave the city without informing us of your ..."

"Hey, *wait* a minute," the girl said.

"You want to get your coat, please?" Willis said.

"Listen, *I* didn't push anybody out that damn window!" she said, standing suddenly and putting her hands on her hips.

"Scott was naked, you had your blouse off, what do you expect ...?"

"That was *his* idea!" Sonia shouted, hurling the words at Hamling.

"Cool it, Sonia," Hamling warned.

"It was *his* idea to get undressed, he wanted to find the damn ..."

"The damn *what*?" Willis snapped.

"The damn money belt!"

Hamling was breaking for the front door. Genero watched in fascinated immobility. Willis was directly in Hamling's path, between him and the door. Hamling was a head taller than Willis and a foot wider, and Genero was certain the boy would now knock his partner flat on his ass. He almost wished he would, because then it would be terribly exciting to see what happened next. Hamling was charging for that door like an express train, and Genero fully expected him to bowl Willis over and continue running into the corridor, down the steps, into the street, and all the way to China. If he was in Willis' place, he would have got out of the way very quickly, because a man can get hurt by a speeding locomotive. But instead of getting out of the way, Willis started running *toward* Hamling, and suddenly dropped to his right knee. Hamling's right foot was ahead of his left at that moment, with all the weight on it, and as he rushed forward, Willis grabbed his left ankle, and began pulling Hamling forward and pushing him upward at the same time. The result was somewhat similar to a football quarterback being hit high and low at the same instant from two opposite directions. Hamling flew over backward, his ankle still clutched in Willis' hand, his head banging back hard against the floor.

Genero blinked.

Willis was stooping over the fallen Hamling now, a gun in his right hand, his handcuffs open in the other hand. He slapped one onto Hamling's wrist, squeezed it closed. The sawtooth edges clicked shut into the retaining metal of the receiver. Willis pulled hard on the cuffs and yanked Hamling to his feet. He whirled him around, pulled his other arm behind his back, and snapped the second cuff shut.

Genero was out of breath.

Danny Gimp was a stool pigeon who told everybody he was a burglar. This was understandable. In a profession where access to underworld gossip was absolutely essential, it was a decided advantage to be considered one of the boys.

Actually, Danny was not a burglar, even though he had been arrested and convicted for burglary in the city of Los Angeles, California, back in the year nineteen hundred and thirty-eight. He had always been a sickly person, and had gone out West to cure himself of a persistent cold. He had met a drinking companion in a bar on La Brea, and the guy had asked Danny to stop by his house while he picked up some more money so that they could continue their all-night revel. They had driven up the Strip past La Cienega and had both entered the guy's house through the back door. They guy had gone into the bedroom and come back a little while later to where Danny was waiting for him in the kitchen. He had picked up several hundred dollars in cash, not to mention a diamond and ruby necklace valued at forty-seven thousand five hundred dollars. But it seemed that Danny was not the only person waiting for his drinking companion to come out of the bedroom. The Los Angeles police were also waiting. In fact, the way Danny found out about the value of the necklace was that the police happened to tell him. Danny tried to explain all this to the judge. He also mentioned to the judge that he had suffered polio as a child, and was a virtual cripple, and that jail would not be very good for his health or his disposition. The judge had kindly considered everything Danny had to say and then had sentenced Danny and his drinking companion to a minimum of five and a maximum of ten. Danny never spoke to his drinking companion again after that night, even though the men were in the same cell block. The guy was killed by a black homosexual prisoner a year later, stabbed in the throat with a table knife honed to razor sharpness in the sheet metal shop. The black homosexual stood trial for murder, was convicted, and was executed. Danny served his time thinking about the vagaries of justice, and left prison with the single qualification he would need to pursue a profitable career as a snitch. He was an ex-con. If you can't trust an ex-con, who *can* you trust? Such was the underworld belief, and it accounted for the regularity with which Danny Gimp received choice bits of information, which he then passed on to the police at a price. It was a living, and not a bad one.

Carl Kapek had put in a call to Danny that afternoon. The two men met in Grover Park at seven minutes before five. The afternoon was beginning to wane. They sat together on a park bench and watched governesses wheeling their charges home in baby buggies, watched touch football games beginning to break up, watched a little girl walking slowly by on the winding path, trailing a skip rope behind her and studying the ground the way only little girls can, with an intense concentration that indicated she was pondering all the female secrets of the universe.

"Belinda, huh?" Danny said.

"Yeah. Belinda."

Danny sniffed. He always seemed to have a cold lately, Kapek noticed. Maybe he was getting old.

"And you don't know Belinda *what*, huh?" Danny said.

"That's why I called you," Kapek said.

"She's a spade, huh?"

"Yeah."

"I don't read her right off," Danny said. He sniffed again. "It's getting to be winter already, you realize that?"

"It's not so bad," Kapek said.

"It stinks," Danny answered. "Why do you want this broad?"

"She mugged a marine."

"You're putting me on," Danny said, and laughed.

"She didn't do it alone."

"A guy was in it with her?"

"Yeah. She played up to the marine in a bar on Seventeenth, indicated she wanted him to follow her. When he did, she led him to her partner, and they put him out of action."

"Is the guy a spade, too?"

"No, he's white."

"Belinda," Danny said. "That's a pretty name. I knew a girl named Belinda once. Only girl I ever knew who didn't mind the leg. This was in Chicago one time. I was in Chicago one time. I got people in Chicago. Belinda Kolaczkowska. A Pole. Pretty as a picture, blond hair, blue eyes, big tits." Danny demonstrated with his hands, and then immediately put them back in his pockets. "I asked her one time how come she was going out with a guy like me. I was talking about the limp, you know? She said, 'What do you mean, a guy like you?' So I looked her in the eye, and I said, 'You know what I mean, Belinda.' And she said, 'No, I don't know what you mean, Danny.' So I said, 'Belinda, the fact is that I limp.' So she smiled and said, 'You *do*?' I'll never forget that smile. I swear to God, if I live to be a hundred and ten, I'll never forget the way Belinda smiled at me that day in Chicago. I felt I could run a mile that day. I felt I could win the goddamn Olympics." He shook his head, and then sniffed again. A flock of pigeons suddenly took wing not six feet from where the men were sitting, filling the air with the sound of their flight. They soared up against the sky, wheeled, and alighted again near a bench further on, where an old man in a threadbare brown coat was throwing bread crumbs into the air.

"Anyway, that ain't the Belinda you're looking for," Danny said. He thought a moment longer, and then seemed to supress the memory completely, pulling his head into his overcoat, thrusting his hands deeper into his pockets. "Can you give me a description of her?" he asked.

"All I know is she's black, and well built, and she was wearing a red dress."

"That could mean two thousand girls in this city," Danny said. "What about the guy?"

"Nothing."

"Great."

"What do you think?"

"I think you're very good for a chuckle on a Sunday when winter's coming, that's what I think."

"Can you help or not?"

"Let me listen a little, who knows? Will you be around?"

"I'll be around."

"I'll get back."

There are times in the city when night refuses to come.

The afternoon lingers, the light changes only slowly and imperceptibly, there is a sense of sweet suspension.

This was just such a day.

There was a briskness to the air, you could never confuse this with a spring day. And yet the afternoon possessed that same luminous quality, the sky so intensely blue that it seemed to vibrate indignantly against encroachment, flatly resisting passage through the color spectrum to darkness. When the street lights came on at five-thirty, they did so in vain. There was nothing to illuminate, the day was still bright. The sun hung stubbornly over the buildings to the west in downtown Majesta and Calm's Point, defying the earth's rotation, balking at extinction behind roof copings and chimney pots. The citizens of the city lingered in the streets bemused, reluctant to go indoors, as though witnessing some vast astronomical disorder, some realized Nostradamus prediction – it would be daytime forever, the night would never come; there would be dancing in the streets.

The sky to the west yielded at last.

In Herbert Gross's apartment, the light was beginning to fade.

Carella and Brown had been in there for close to three hours now, and whereas they had searched the place from floor to ceiling, wall to wall, timber to toilet tank, they had not found a single clue that told them where Gross had been heading when he hopped that uptown bus.

The clue was everywhere around them. They just hadn't found it yet.

The apartment was a contradiction in itself. It was small and cramped, a cubicle in a crumbling tenement surrounded by warehouses. But it was crowded with furniture that surely had been purchased in the early thirties, when solidity was a virtue and inlaid mahogany was the decorative rule. In the living room, a huge overstuffed sofa was upholstered in maroon mohair, its claw feet clutching the faded Persian rug that covered the floor. The sofa alone would have been quite enough to overwhelm the dimensions of the small room, but there were two equally overstuffed easy chairs, and a credenza that seemed to have wandered in from some ornate dining room someplace, and a standing floor lamp with a pink, fringed shade, and an ornately framed painting of snow-clad mountain peaks towering over a placid lake, and a Stromberg-Carlson floor model radio complete with push buttons and jukebox look, and mahogany end tables on either side of the sofa, each with a tiny drawer, each carrying a huge porcelain lamp with a shade covered in plastic.

The first bedroom had a huge double bed with mahogany headboard and footboard and an unmade mattress. A heavy mahogany dresser of the type that used to be called a "bureau" when Busby Berkeley was all the rage, complete with its own mahogany-framed mirror, was on the wall opposite the bed. A taller version of it – the male counterpart, so to speak – with longer hanging space for trousers and suits and a row of drawers one atop the other for the storing of handkerchiefs, cuff links, and sundries (Jimmy Walker would have called it a "chiffonier"), was on the window wall.

The second bedroom was furnished in more modern terms, with two narrow beds covered with simple throws, a Mexican rug hanging on the wall over them. A bookcase was on the wall opposite, alongside a closet without a door. With the exception of the kitchen and the bathroom, there was one other room in the apartment, and this room seemed to have escaped from Arthur Miller's play *The Price*. It was literally packed from floor to ceiling with furniture and china and glassware and marked and unmarked cartons (among those marked was one lettered with the words "WORLD'S FAIR 1939") and piles of books tied with twine, and cooking utensils, and even old articles of clothing draped over chairs or cartons, a veritable child's dream of an attic hideout, equipped with anything needed to serve whatever imaginary excursion suited the fancy.

"I don't get this place," Carella said.

"Neither do I," Brown said. He turned on the floor lamp in the living room, and they sat opposite each other, tired and dusty, Carella on the monstrous sofa, Brown in one of the big easy chairs. The room was washed with the glow of the pink, fringed lampshade. Carella almost felt as if he were sitting down to do his homework to the accompaniment of "Omar the Mystic" flooding from the old Stromberg-Carlson.

"Everything's wrong but that one bedroom," he said. "The rest of it doesn't fit."

"Or maybe vice versa," Brown said.

"I mean, who the hell has furniture like that nowadays?"

"My mother has furniture like that," Brown said.

Both men were silent. It was Carella who broke the silence at last.

"When did Goldenthal's mother die?" he asked.

"Three months ago, I think the report said. He was living with her until then."

"You think all this crap might have been hers?"

"Maybe. Maybe he moved it all here when he left the other apartment."

"You remember her first name?"

"Minnie."

"How many Goldenthals do you suppose there are in the telephone book?"

They did not even consider looking in the directories for Bethtown, Majesta, or Calm's Point, because Gross had been heading *uptown*, and access to all those other sections of the city would have required going *downtown*. They did not consider looking in the Riverhead directory, either, because Gross had taken a bus, and bus transportation all the way to Riverhead was a hell of a slow way to go, when there were express trains running all day long. So they limited their search to the Isola directory alone. (There was one other reason they consulted just this one phone book; it happened to be the *only* one Gross had in the apartment.)

There were eight Goldenthals listed in the Isola directory.

But only one of them was Minnie Goldenthal – now deceased, poor lady, her name surviving in print only until next year's directory would be published by the telephone company.

Sic transit gloria mundi.

The building in which Minnie Goldenthal had lived was a twelve-story yellow brick structure bristling with television antennae. It was fronted by a small cement courtyard flanked by two yellow brick pillars, atop which sat two stone urns that were probably planted with flowers in the spring, but that now contained only withered stalks. Enclosing this courtyard were the two wings of the building, and a row of apartments connecting both wings, so that the result was an architectural upside-down U facing the low flat entrance steps to the courtyard. The mailboxes for each wing were in the entryway to the right and left. Carella checked one entry, Brown the other. There was no listing for Goldenthal, Minnie or otherwise.

"What do you think?" Carella asked.

"Let's check the super," Brown suggested.

The superintendent lived on the ground floor, in an apartment behind the staircase. He came to the door in his undershirt. A television set was going somewhere in his apartment, but apparently the show had not completely captured his attention, because he was carrying the Sunday comics in his right hand. The detectives identified themselves. The super looked at Carella's shield. He looked at Carella's I.D. card. Then he said, "Yes?"

"Was there a Minnie Goldenthal living here recently?" Carella asked.

The super listened attentively to his every word, as though he were being asked a question which, if answered correctly, would cause him to win a hundred-thousand-dollar jackpot.

Then he said, "Yes."

"Which apartment?"

"Nine-D."

"Anyone living in that apartment now?"

"Son's still living in it."

"Bernie Goldenthal?"

"That's right. Don't know *why* he's living in it, mind you. Moved all the furniture out a little while after Minnie died. Still pays the rent though." The super shrugged. "Tell you the truth, the owners wish he'd get out. That apartment's price-fixed. Nice big old apartment. If he gets out, they can put a new tenant in and legally raise the rent."

"Anybody up there now?" Carella asked.

"Don't know," the super said. "Don't keep tabs on the comings and goings of the people who live here. Their business is their business, and mine is mine."

"Law requires you to have a key to all the apartments in the dwelling," Carella said. "Have you got one for Nine-D?"

"Yep."

"All right if we use it?"

"What for?"

"To enter the apartment."

"That's illegal, ain't it?"

"We won't tell anybody if you won't" Brown said.

"Well," the super said, and shrugged. "Okay," he said, and shrugged again. "I guess."

Carella and Brown took the elevator up to the ninth floor and stepped into the corridor. Neither man said a word to the other, but both simultaneously drew their revolvers. 9D was at the far end of the hall. They listened outside the door and heard nothing. Cautiously, Carella inserted the passkey into the lock. He nodded to Brown, and twisted the key. There was only a small click as the lock turned, but it must have sounded like a warning shot inside that apartment. Carella and Brown burst into a long narrow entrance foyer. At the far end of the foyer, they saw Herbert Gross and a blond man they assumed to be Bernard Goldenthal, both of them armed.

"Hold it right there!" Carella shouted, but neither of the two men were holding anything right there or right anywhere. They opened fire just as Carella and Brown threw themselves flat on the linoleum-covered floor. Goldenthal made a break for a doorway to the right of the long foyer. Brown shouted a warning and fired almost before the words left his lips. The slug caught Goldenthal in the leg, knocking him off his feet and sent him flailing against the corridor wall, where he slid to the floor. Gross held his ground, firing down the length of the foyer, pulling off shot after shot until his pistol clicked empty. He was reaching into his jacket pocket, presumably for fresh cartridges, when Carella shouted, "Move and you're dead!"

Gross's hand stopped in mid-motion. He squinted down the corridor, silhouetted in the light that spilled from the room Goldenthal had tried to reach.

"Drop the gun," Carella said.

Gross did not move.

"*Drop* it!" Carella shouted. "Now!"

"You, too, Goldie!" Brown shouted.

Goldenthal and Gross – one crouched against the wall clutching his bleeding leg, the other with his hand still hanging motionless over his jacket pocket – exchanged quick glances. Without saying a word to each other, they dropped their guns to the floor. Gross kicked them away as if they were contaminated. The guns came spinning down the length of the corridor one after the other, sliding along the waxed linoleum.

Carella got to his feet, and started toward the two men. Behind him, Brown was crouched on one knee, his gun resting on his forearm and pointing directly at the far end of the foyer. Carella threw Gross against the wall, quickly frisked him, and then bent over Goldenthal.

"Okay," he called to Brown, and then glanced into the room on the right of the foyer. It, too, was loaded with household goods. But unlike the stuff in the apartment downtown, this had not come from a dead woman's home, this was not the accumulation of a lifetime. This was, instead, the result of God knew how many recent burglaries and robberies, a veritable storehouse of television sets, radios, typewriters, tape recorders, broilers, mixers, luggage, you name it, right down to a complete set of the Encyclopaedia Brittanica – a criminal bargain basement, awaiting only the services of a good fence.

"Nice little place you've got here," Carella said, and then handcuffed Gross to Goldenthal and Goldenthal to the radiator. From a telephone on the kitchen wall, the late Minnie's last shopping list still tacked up beside it, he called the station house and asked for a meat wagon. It arrived at exactly 6 p.m., not seven minutes after Carella requested it. By that time, Goldenthal had spilled a goodly amount of blood all over his mother's linoleum.

"I'm bleeding to death here," he complained to one of the hospital orderlies who was lifting him onto the stretcher.

"That's the least of your worries," the orderly answered.

Delgado had not found Pepe Castañeda in the pool hall, nor had be found him in any one of a dozen bars he tried in the neighborhood. It was now a quarter past six, and he was about ready to give up the search. On the dubious assumption, however, that a pool shooter might also be a bowler, he decided to hit the Ponce Bowling Lanes on Culver Avenue before heading back to the squadroom.

The place was on the second floor of an old brick building. Delgado went up the narrow flight of steps and came into a fluorescent-lighted room with a counter just opposite the entrance doorway. A bald-headed man was sitting on a stool behind the counter, reading a newspaper. He looked up as Delgado came in, went back to the newspaper, finished the story he was reading, and then put both hands flat on the countertop. "All the alleys are full," he said. "You got maybe a half-hour wait."

"I don't want an alley," Delgado said.

The man behind the counter looked at him more carefully, decided he was a cop, gave a brief knowledgeable nod, but said nothing.

"I'm looking for a man named Pepe Castañeda. Is he here?"

"What do you want him for?" the man said.

"I'm a police officer," Delgado said, and flashed the tin. "I want to ask him some questions."

"I don't want no trouble here," the man said.

"Why should there be trouble? Is Castañeda trouble?"

"*He's* not the trouble," the man said, and looked at Delgado meaningfully.

"Neither am I," Delgado said. "Where is he?"

"Lane number five," the man said.

"Thanks."

Delgado went through the doorway adjacent to the counter and found himself in a larger room than the small reception area had promised. There were twelve alleys in all, each of them occupied with bowlers. A bar was at the far end of the place, with tables and chairs set up around it. A jukebox was playing a rock-and-roll song. The record ended as Delgado moved past the racks of bowling balls against the low wall that separated the lanes from the area behind them. A Spanish-language song erupted from the loudspeakers. Everywhere, there was the reverberating clamor of falling pins, multiplied and echoing in the high-ceilinged room, joined by voices raised in jubilant exclamation or disgruntled invective.

There were four men bowling in lane number five. Three of them were seated on the leatherette banquette that formed a semicircle around the score pad. The fourth man stood waiting for his ball to return. It came rolling down the tracks from the far end of the alley, hit the stop mechanism, eased its way toward his waiting hand. He picked up the ball, stepped back some five feet from the foul line, crouched, started his forward run, right arm coming back, left arm out for balance, stopped dead, and released the ball. It curved down the alley and arced in true between the one and three pins. The bowler hung frozen in motion, his right arm still extended, left arm back, crouched and waiting for the explosion of pins. They flew into the air like gleeful cheerleaders, there was the sound of their leap as the ball sent them helter-skelter, the additional sound of their pell-mell return to the polished alley floor. The bowler shouted, "Made it!" and turned to the three men on the banquette.

"Which one of you is Pepe Castañeda?" Delgado asked.

The bowler, who was walking back toward the score pad to supervise the correct marking of the strike, stopped in his tracks and looked up at Delgado. He was a short man with straight black hair and a pockmarked face, thin, with the light step of a dancer, a step that seemed even airier in the red, rubber-soled bowling shoes.

"I'm Castañeda," he said. "Who're you?"

"Detective Delgado, Eighty-seventh Squad," Delgado said. "Mind if I ask you a few questions?"

"What about?"

"Is Ramon Castañeda your brother?"

"That's right."

"Why don't we walk over there and talk a little?"

"Over where?"

"The tables there."

"I'm in the middle of a game."

"The game can wait."

Castañeda shrugged. One of the men on the banquette said, "Go ahead, Pepe. We'll order a round of beer meanwhile."

"How many frames we got to go?"

"Just three," the other man said.

"This gonna take long?" Castañeda asked.

"I don't think so," Delgado said.

"Well, okay. We're ahead here, I don't want to cool off."

They walked together to the bar at the far end of the room. Two young girls in tight slacks were standing near the jukebox, pondering their next selection. Castañeda looked them over, and then pulled out a chair at one of the tables. The men sat opposite each other. The jukebox erupted again with sound. The intermittent rumble of exploding pins was a steady counterpoint.

"What do you want to know?" Castañeda asked.

"Your brother's got a partner named José Huerta," Delgado said.

"That's right."

"Do you know him?"

"Yeah, I know Joe."

"Do you know he was beaten up this morning?"

"He was? No, I didn't know that. You got a cigarette? I left mine on the table back there."

"I don't smoke," Delgado said.

"I didn't used to smoke, either," Castañeda said. "But, you know..." he shrugged. "You break one habit, you pick up another, huh?" He grinned. The grin was wide and infectious. He was perhaps three or four years younger than Delgado, but he suddenly looked like a teenager. "I used to be a junkie, you know. Did you know that?"

"Yes, I've heard it."

"I kicked it."

"I've heard that, too."

"Ain't you impressed?"

"I'm impressed," Delgado said.

"So am I," Castañeda said, and grinned again. Delgado grinned with him. "So, I still don't know what you want from me," Castañeda said.

"He got beat up pretty badly," Delgado said. "Broke both his legs, chopped his face up like hamburger."

"Gee, that's too bad," Castañeda said. "Who done it?"

"Four men."

"Boy," Castañeda said, and shook his head.

"They got him on the front stoop of his building. He was on his way to church."

"Yeah? Where does he live?"

"On South Sixth."

"Oh, yeah, that's right," Castañeda said. "Across the street from the candy store, right?"

"Yes. The reason I wanted to talk to you" Delgado said, "is that your brother seemed to think the four men who beat up Huerta were *asked* to beat him up."

"I don't follow you," Castañeda said.

"When I asked your brother who disliked Huerta, he said, 'No one dislikes him enough to have him beaten up.'"

"So? What does that mean?"

"It means..."

"It don't mean nothing," Castañeda said, and shrugged.

"It means your brother thinks the men who beat up Huerta were doing it for somebody else, not themselves."

"I don't see where you get that," Castañeda said. "That was just a way of speaking, that's all. My brother didn't mean nothing by it."

"Let's say he did. Let's say for the moment that somebody *wanted* Huerta beaten up. And let's say he asked four men to do the favor for him."

"Okay, let's say that."

"Would you happen to know who those four men might be?"

"Nope," Castañeda said. "I really could use a cigarette, you know? You mind if I go back to the table for them?"

"The cigarette can wait, Pepe. There's a man in the hospital with two broken legs and a busted face."

"Gee, that's too bad," Castañeda said, "but maybe the man should've been more careful, you know? Then maybe nobody would've *wanted* him beaten up, and nobody would've talked to anybody *about* beating him up."

"Who wanted him hurt, Pepe?"

"You interested in some guesses?"

"I'm interested."

"Joe's a pusher, did you know that?"

"I know that."

"Grass. For now. But I never met a guy selling grass who didn't later figure there was more profit in the hard stuff. It's just a matter of time, that's all."

"So?"

"So maybe somebody didn't like the idea of him poisoning the neighborhood, you dig? I'm only saying. But it's something to consider right?"

"Yes, it's something to consider."

"And maybe Joe was chasing after somebody's wife too. Maybe somebody's got a real pretty wife, and maybe Joe's been making it with her, you dig? That's another thing to consider. So maybe somebody decided to break both his legs so he couldn't run around no more balling somebody else's wife and selling poison to the kids in the *barrio*. And maybe they decided to mess up his face for good measure, you dig? So he wouldn't look so pretty to other guys' wives, and so maybe when he come up to a kid in the neighborhood and tried to get him hooked, the kid might not want to deal with somebody who had a face looked like it hit a meat grinder." Castañeda paused. "Those are all things to consider, right?"

"Yes, they're all things to consider," Delgado said.

"I don't think you're ever gonna find those guys who beat him up," Castañeda said. "But what difference does it make?"

"What do you mean?"

"He got what he deserved. That's justice, ain't it? That's what you guys are interested in, ain't it? Justice?"

"Yes, we're interested in justice."

"So this was justice," Castañeda said.

Delgado looked at him.

"Wasn't it?" Castañeda asked.

"Yes, I think it was," Delgado said. He nodded, rose from the table suddenly, pushed his chair back under it, and said, "Nice talking to you. See you around."

"Buy you a drink or something?" Castañeda asked.

"Thanks, I've still got an hour before I'm off duty," Delgado answered, and walked away from the table.

Behind him, Castañeda raised his hand in farewell.

It was 7 p.m. by the time Brown finally got around to Mary Ellingham, the lady who had called in twelve hours before to report that her husband was missing. Full darkness was upon the city now, but it was not yet nighttime; it was still the time of day called "evening," a poetic word that always stirred something deep inside Brown, perhaps because he had never heard the word as a child and only admitted it to his vocabulary after he met Connie, his wife-to-be, when things stopped being merely night and day, or black and white; Connie had brought shadings to his life, and for that he would love her forever.

North Trinity was a two-block-long street off Silvermine Oval, adjacent to fancy Silvermine Road, which bordered on the River Harb and formed the northern frontier of the precinct. From where Brown had parked the car, he could see the waters of the river, and uptown the scattered lights of the estates in Smoke Rise, the brighter illumination on the Hamilton Bridge. The lights were on along Trinity, too, beckoning warmly from windows in the rows of brownstones that faced the secluded street. Brown knew that behind most of those windows, the occupants were enjoying their cocktail hour. One could always determine the socio-economic standing of anybody in this city by asking him what time he ate his dinner. In a slum like Diamondback, the dinner hour had already come and gone. On Trinity Street, the residents were having their before-dinner drinks. Further uptown in Smoke Rise, the dinner hour would not start until nine or nine-thirty – although the cocktail hour may have started at noon.

Brown was hungry.

There were no lights burning at 742 North Trinity. Brown looked at his watch, shrugged, and rang the front doorbell. He waited, rang the doorbell a second time, and then stepped down off the front stoop to look up at the second story of the building, where a light had suddenly come on. He went back to the steps and waited. He heard someone approaching the door. A peephole flap was thrown back.

"Yes?" a woman's voiced asked.

"Mrs. Ellingham?"

"Yes?"

"Detective Brown, Eighty-seventh Squad."

"Oh," Mrs. Ellingham said. "Oh, just a minute please." The peephole flap fell back into place. He heard the door being unlocked.

Mary Ellingham was about forty years old. She was wearing a man's flannel robe. Her hair was disarrayed. Her face was flushed.

"I'm sorry I got here so late," Brown said. "We had a sort of busy day."

"Oh," Mrs. Ellingham said. "Yes."

"I won't keep you long," Brown said, reaching into his pocket for his pad and pen. "If you'll just give me a description of your husband..."

"Oh," Mrs. Ellingham said.

"His name is Donald Ellingham, is that correct?"

"Yes, but..."

"How old is he?"

"Well, you see..."

Brown looked up from his pad. Mrs. Ellingham seemed terribly embarrassed all at once. Before she uttered another word, Brown realized what he had walked in on, and he too was suddenly embarrassed.

"You see," Mrs. Ellingham said, "he's back. My husband. He got back just a little while ago."

"Oh," Brown said.

"Yes," she said.

"Oh."

"Yes. I'm sorry. I suppose I should have called..."

"No, no, that's all right," Brown said. He put his pad and his pen back into his pocket, and reached behind him for the doorknob. "Glad he's back, glad everything worked out all right."

"Yes," Mrs. Ellingham said.

"Good night," Brown said.

"Good night," she said.

She closed the door gently behind him as he went down the steps. Just before he got back into his automobile, he glanced back at the building. The upstairs light had already gone out again.

Back at the squadroom, the three detectives who had been called in off vacation were bitching about the speed with which Carella and Brown had cracked the grocery store case. It was one thing to interrupt a man's vacation if there was a goddamn *need* for it; it was another to call him in and trot him around all day asking questions and gathering data while two other guys were out following a hot lead that resulted in an arrest.

"You know what I coulda been doing today?" Di Maeo asked.

"What?" Levine said.

"I coulda been watching the ball game on television, and I coulda had a big dinner with the family. My sister is in from Scranton, she come all the way in from Scranton 'cause she knows I'm on vacation. So instead I'm talking to a bunch of people who couldn't care less whether a grocer got shot, and who couldn't care at *all* whether a cop caught one."

Meriwether the hairbag said, "Now, now, fellows, it's all part of the game, all part of the game."

In two separate locked rooms down the corridor, Willis was interrogating Sonia Sobolev, and Genero was interrogating Robert Hamling. Neither of the suspects had exercised their right to an attorney. Hamling, who claimed he had nothing to hide, seemed pleased in fact that he could get his story on the record. He repeated essentially what he had told them in the apartment: Lewis Scott had been on a bum acid trip and had thrown himself out the window while Hamling had done all he could to prevent the suicide. The stenographer listened to every word, his fingers moving silently over his machine.

Sonia Sobolev apparently felt no need for an attorney because she did not consider herself mixed up in the death of Lewis Scott. Her version of the story differed greatly from Hamling's. According to Sonia, Hamling had met the bearded Scott that afternoon and the two had banked around the city for a while, enjoying each other's company. Scott was indeed celebrating something – the arrival from home of a two-hundred-dollar money order, which he had cashed and which, in the form of ten-dollar bills, was now nestling in a money belt under his shirt. Hamling had gone back to Scott's apartment with him, and tried to get him drunk. When that failed, he asked Scott if he didn't think they needed a little female company, and when Scott agreed that might not be a bad idea, Hamling had gone downstairs to call Sonia.

"What did he tell you when he met you later?" Willis asked.

"Well, I got off the train," Sonia said, "and Bobby was waiting there for me. He said he had this dumb plastic hippie in an apartment nearby, and the guy had a money belt with two hundred dollars in it, and Bobby *wanted* that money. He said the only way to get it was to convince the guy to take off his clothes. And the only way to do that was for me to do it first." Sonia shrugged. "So we went up there."

"Yes, what happened then?"

"Well, I went in the john and combed my hair and then I took off my blouse. And I went out to the other room without any blouse on. To see if I could, well, get him excited, you know. So he would take off his clothes. We were all drinking a lot of wine."

"Were you smoking?"

"Pot, you mean? No."

"So what happened?"

"Well, he finally went in the john, too, and got undressed. He was wearing blue jeans and a Charlie Brown sweat shirt. And he *did* have a money belt. He was wearing a money belt."

"Did he take that off, too?"

"Yes."

"And then what?"

"Well, he came back to the mattress, and we started fooling around a little, you know, just touching each other. Actually, I was sort of keeping him busy while Bobby went through the belt. Trouble is, he *saw* Bobby. And he jumped up and ran to where Bobby was standing with the money belt in his hands, and they started fighting, and that ... that was when Bobby pushed him out the window. We split right away. I just threw on my jacket, and Bobby put on his coat, and we split. I didn't even remember the blouse until much later."

"Where's the money belt now?" Willis asked.

"In Bobby's apartment. Under his mattress."

In the other room, Hamling kept insisting that Lewis Scott was an acid freak who had thrown himself out the window to the pavement below. Di Maeo knocked on the door, poked his head inside, and said, "Dick, you send some suspect dope to the lab?"

"Yeah," Genero said.

"They just phoned. Said it was oregano."

"Thanks," Genero said. He turned again to Hamling. "The stuff in Lewis Scott's refrigerator was oregano," he said.

"So what?" Hamling said.

"So tell me one more time about this big acid freak you got involved with."

In the squadroom outside, Carella sat at his desk typing a report on Goldenthal and Gross. Goldenthal had been taken to Buenavista, the same hospital that was caring for Andy Parker, whom he had shot. Gross had refused to say a word to anyone. He had been booked for Armed Robbery and Murder One, and was being held in one of the detention cells downstairs. Carella looked extremely tired. When the telephone on his desk rang, he stared at it for several moments before answering it.

"Eighty-seventh Squad," he said, "Carella."

"Steve, this is Artie Brown."

"Hello, Artie," Carella said.

"I just wrapped up this squeal on North Trinity. Guy came home, and they're happily in the sack."

"Good for them," Carella said. "I wish *I* was happily in the sack."

"You want me to come back there, or what?"

"What time is it?"

"Seven-thirty."

"Go home, Artie."

"You sure? What about the report?"

"I'm typing it now."

"Okay then, I'll see you," Brown said.

"Right," Carella said, and put the receiver back onto its cradle, and looked up at the wall clock, and sighed. The telephone on Carl Kapek's desk was ringing.

"Eighty-seventh," he said, "Kapek speaking."

"This is Danny Gimp," the voice on the other end said.

"Hello, Danny, what've you got for me?"

"Nothing," Danny said.

Di Maeo, Meriwether, and Levine were packing it in, hoping to resume their vacations without further interruption. Levine seemed certain that Brown and Carella would get promotions out of this one; there were always promotions when you cracked a case involving somebody doing something to a cop. Di Maeo agreed with him, and commented that some guys had all the luck. They went down the iron-runged steps and past the muster desk, and through the old building's entrance doors. Meriwether stopped on the front steps to tie his shoelace. Alex Delgado was just getting back to the station house. He chatted for only a moment, said good night to all of them, and went inside. It was almost seven thirty-five, and some of the relieving shift was already in the squadroom.

In a little while, the daywatch could go home.

Kapek had been cruising from bar to bar along The Stem since 8 p.m. It was now twenty minutes past eleven, and his heart skipped a beat when the black girl in the red dress came through the doors of Romeo's on Twelfth Street. The girl sashayed past the men sitting on stools along the length of the bar, took a seat at the far end near the telephones, and crossed her legs. Kapek gave her ten minutes to eye every guy in the joint, and then walked past her to the telephones. He dialed the squadroom, and got Finch, the catcher on the relieving team.

"What are you doing?" Finch wanted to know.

"Oh, cruising around," Kapek said.

"I thought you went home hours ago."

"No rest for the weary," Kapek said. "I'm about to make a bust. If I'm lucky."

"Need some help?"

"Nope," Kapek said.

"They why the hell did you call?"

"Just to make some small talk," Kapek said.

"I've got a knifing on Ainsley," Finch answered. "Go make small talk someplace else."

Kapek took his advice. He hung up, felt in the coin return chute for his dime, shrugged, and went out to sit next to the girl at the bar.

"I'll bet your name is Suzie," he said.

"Wrong," the girl said, and grinned. "It's Belinda."

"Belinda, you are one beautiful piece," Kapek said.

"You think so, huh?"

"I do most sincerely think so," Kapek said. "May I offer to buy you a drink?"

"I'd be flattered," Belinda said.

They chatted for close to twenty minutes. Belinda indicated that she found Kapek highly attractive; it was rare that a girl could just wander into a neighborhood bar and find someone of Kapek's intelligence and sensitivity, she told him. She indicated, too, that she would like to spend some time with Kapek a little later on, but that her husband was a very jealous man and that she couldn't risk leaving the bar with Kapek because word might get back to her husband and then there would be all kinds of hell to pay. Kapek told her that he certainly understood her position. Still, Belinda said, I sure would love to spend some time with you honey. Kapek nodded.

"What do you suppose we can do?" he asked.

"You can meet me outside, can't you?"

"Sure," he said. "Where?"

"Let's drink up. Then I'll leave, and you can follow me out in a few minutes. How does that sound?"

Kapek looked up at the clock behind the bar. It was ten minutes to twelve. "That sounds fine to me," he said.

Belinda lifted her whiskey sour and drained it. She winked at him and swiveled away from the bar. At the door, she turned, winked again, and then went out. Kapek gave her five minutes. He finished his scotch and soda, paid for the drinks, and went out after her. Belinda was waiting on the next corner. She signaled to him, and began walking rapidly up The Stem. Kapek nodded and followed her. She walked two blocks east, looked back at him once again, and turned abruptly left on Fifteenth Street. Kapek reached the corner and drew his pistol. He hesitated, cleared his throat to let them know he was coming, and then rounded the corner.

A white man was standing there with his fist cocked. Kapek thrust the gun into his face and said, "Everybody stand still." Belinda started to break. He grabbed her wrist, flung her against the brick wall of the building, said, "You too, honey," and took his handcuffs from his belt.

He looked at his watch.

It was a minute to midnight.

Another day was about to start.